Confessions of a

Beauty Addict

By Nadine Haobsh

Fiction

CONFESSIONS OF A BEAUTY ADDICT

Nonfiction

BEAUTY CONFIDENTIAL:
*The No Preaching, No Lies, Advice-You'll-Actually-Use
Guide to Looking Your Best*

Confessions of a
Beauty Addict

Nadine Haobsh

AVON

An Imprint of HarperCollinsPublishers

CONFESSIONS OF A BEAUTY ADDICT. Copyright © 2009 by Nadine Haobsh, Inc. All rights reserved. Printed in the United States of America. No part of this book may be used or reproduced in any manner whatsoever without written permission except in the case of brief quotations embodied in critical articles and reviews. For information address HarperCollins Publishers, 10 East 53rd Street, New York, NY 10022.

HarperCollins books may be purchased for educational, business, or sales promotional use. For information please write: Special Markets Department, HarperCollins Publishers, 10 East 53rd Street, New York, NY 10022.

FIRST AVON PAPERBACK EDITION PUBLISHED 2009.

Designed by Elizabeth M. Glover

Library of Congress Cataloging-in-Publication Data
Haobsh, Nadine.
  Confessions of a beauty addict / Nadine Haobsh.
    p. cm.
  ISBN 978-0-06-112862-2
  1. Women journalists—Fiction. 2. Beauty, Personal—Fiction. 3. Manhattan (New York, N.Y.)—Fiction. 4. Chick lit. I. Title.
  PS3608.A7238C66 2009
  813'.6—dc22   2008028549

09 10 11 12   OV/RRD   10 9 8 7 6 5 4 3 2 1

For my mother, Nancy. I love you.

Chapter 1

Oh my God.

Oh my *God*.

My hair is orange.

How could this happen?

I applied the dye carefully in sections, ran it all the way through to the ends, and left it on for exactly fifteen minutes. I wore the stupid plastic gloves and used the timer on my kitchen stove to make sure it didn't overprocess.

And it turns *orange*?

Damn it!

Calm down. Breathe. It's not so bad. It's not orange, per se. It's . . . auburn. Slightly amber. Burnt sienna, really.

Stop fooling yourself, Bella. It's orange, you idiot.

"Crap!" My voice echoes around the small, product-laden bathroom, every available inch of counter space smothered with bottles of mousse, antiaging serum, eye cream, and mascara, and I wonder if my roommate Emily Tyler can hear me. Her bedroom is down the hallway, but our walls are paper thin. Sure enough, her scratchy voice calls accusingly, "Bella? What did you do?"

"Nothing! It's nothing! I just . . . *uh,* tripped!" I yell back, my heart skipping beats as I envision the ribbing I'll have to endure if my best friend walks in and sees the catastrophe my beauty "skills" have caused. She'd never let me live it down.

I need to fix this *immediately*. I am a *beauty writer*. I am supposed to be able to handle something as elementary as dyeing my hair without ending up with a pumpkin on my head. This is much worse than the unfortunate time I burned off my eyebrows trying to dye them blonde. If I show up tonight at my profile interview for the *New York Post* looking like this, I will become a laughingstock of the beauty industry, and my editor, Larissa Lincoln, will inevitably decide I have no business writing my monthly The Beauty Expert column for *Enchanté*, and she will fire me for being incompetent and useless, and then I will have no income and will not be able to afford living in New York. I'll be homeless. Worse, I'll have to go back to Ohio. My life will be ruined!

And all because of a stupid dye job! Damn it.

I silently berate myself for freaking out. Get it together, Bella. It's just hair.

What to do? Dye it back to blonde? Half my hair might fall out. Besides, the whole point of my assignment is to see what it's like being brunette.

Why? Why did I decide to do this two hours before my interview? I went to Northwestern. I have a degree in journalism. I am, at least, *theoretically,* intelligent, although lately it seems like nothing I do reflects this. So how do I end up in situations like this time and time again? My father's voice floats through my head, clear as crystal, pulling me back fifteen years to a dinner with his Lieutenant Colonel: "Bella's book smart, but doesn't have much common sense. Now, Susan, on the other hand. She *is* the elder child, after all . . ." My mother squeezed my hand under the table as she interjected, "Chuck, please don't compare the girls! They each have their own gifts." Yes, indeed. Where shall I collect my first-class prize for being a total spaz?

I have an hour to fix this before I have to hop in a cab and rush down to Pamplona, the magazine industry hot spot

I'm meeting the *Post* reporter at. Even if I wanted to dye it back and then fix it tomorrow, I wouldn't have time to blow it out. And in any case, I'm going to be photographed, so I'm *definitely* not going to make the mistake of trusting my own dyeing skills again. I'm getting my first big profile piece, in one of the most widely read, influential papers in the country . . . and I'm going to look like I stuck my head in a vat of carrot juice.

Can I wear a hat? I don't own any hats. I hate hats. Showing up in a hat is even more embarrassing than showing up with orange hair. What about a head scarf? Jackie O wore head scarfs. Princess Grace wore head scarfs. It's very Monaco circa 1971 and is so ridiculously out there that I think it might work. The photographer will probably think I'm just another diva, self-absorbed, magazine head case.

I run into my bedroom and yank open the top drawers of my wooden dresser, rummaging frantically through them. Through the years, I've accumulated countless fancy scarves that I've never once worn, all sent by beauty publicists as thank-yous for stories written about their products. Finally, they'll come in handy.

I dump the scarves onto my bed and spread them out, surveying the stock before picking out two possibilities. Tan and cream silk Hermès dotted with chain links? Or psychedelic blue cotton Pucci with a green and white geometric print?

The Pucci projects more of an image—a style *moment*. This, I can work with—all I need to complete the look is an A-line coat, shift dress, knee-high boots, and sunglasses. It's more than a little costumey, but after years of holding court at photo shoots, I know that the getup will at least photograph well. Very retro.

Wrapping the scarf around my head is more complex than I'd anticipated, however. How do celebrities do it so effortlessly? I try tying the ends around my chin, but I look like

Queen Elizabeth with her dogs. Tying the ends behind my head near the nape of my neck simply makes me look like a Von Trapp.

Fifteen minutes of playing with the scarf yields nothing. I've mastered the Erykah Badu–thing, but not the St. Tropez-with-Roger-Vadim-at-my-side thing.

I only have half an hour left. The restaurant will inevitably be crawling with other editors and it's too late to change the location. I have to fix this now.

The answer—so obvious that I can't believe I didn't think of it immediately—pops in my head: Nick.

Nick Darling is one of my closest friends, and a professional makeup artist and hair stylist who just happens to have done practically *everybody*. Julia Roberts, Jessica Simpson, Kate Hudson, Beyoncé, JLo, Reese Witherspoon; you name it, he's glammified them After months ringing him up on deadline looking for a quote about girl-of-the-moment's makeup, we became "real world" friends, and Nick has slowly wormed his way into the tight-knit group Emily and I share with our friend Jocelyn Reeves, a beauty publicist. Before meeting Nick in person, I incorrectly assumed he was gay, just by sheer virtue of his industry position. It took only five minutes of watching Nick at one of our photo shoots, trying to coax three of the Amazonian models to come back to his pad later for "a small party," for me to realize that my assumption was sorely mistaken.

It rings four times before he answers. "Yeah, it's Nick," he says in a deep, lazy voice that would be rather sexy if I didn't know what a dirty tramp he is—a fact Joss, Em, and I harass him about to no end. (This, of course, only makes him prouder.)

"Hey, babe! It's Bella!"

Short pause.

"Bella? What's wrong?"

"What?" I ask innocently. "Nothing! Why do you automatically assume—"

"Cut the crap," he interrupts, laughing. "I can hear the panic in your voice. What did you do this time?"

"It wasn't my fault!" I huff. "I was supposed to dye my hair brown for the July column—a 'Blondes don't always have more fun' angle—and somehow I messed up."

"What do you mean 'messed up'?"

I hesitate to give Nick ammunition to use against me later, but fixing my hair in the next half hour is, for now at least, more important than my pride. "It's . . . orange."

He snorts. "Only you."

"You jerk. I'm The Beauty Expert!"

"Beauty expert . . . beauty disaster . . ."

"I didn't call so you could make fun of me," I say indignantly. "The *Post* is interviewing me for the Pulse section and I'm supposed to be crosstown for the interview and photos in forty-five minutes."

"Hey, why didn't you tell me? That's a big deal."

"I *know* it's a big deal, Captain Obvious. That's why I'm calling you."

"Don't snip at me because you butchered your hair *yet again*. Your problem, not mine. If you're not nice, I'll call the *Post* and give an anonymous tip about how the golden girl of the beauty industry is a secret disaster."

"You wouldn't dare!" I gasp, horrified.

He erupts into hearty laughter. "No, I wouldn't. But the threat was worth it just to hear you go all *Dynasty* on me. I have a date in fifteen minutes, so hurry up—how can I help?"

"You have to leave in fifteen minutes?" I ask, my heart still pounding at the thought of Nick exposing my complete and utter ineptitude when it comes to, well, basically everything.

"No, no, the date is in fifteen minutes. So I need to leave in twenty, which will make me about fifteen minutes late. It's just round the corner."

Nick's guerrilla dating tactics never cease to amaze. "Let me get this straight. You're *planning* to be late? Do you hate the girl? Are you trying to get her to break up with you? Which girl is it, anyway?"

"Annika. The Swede? The one I met at the gym and have been trying to sleep with for two months? She's way too hot. I need to take her down a few pegs, *then* she'll sleep with me."

Despite myself, I smile. "You have serious problems, my friend."

"Yup. Okay, so, your hair. Tell me again why you decided to dye it an hour before a photo shoot for a major newspaper?"

"I wasn't thinking." My voice trails off as I mumble something about glamour and reinvention.

He snickers.

"Nick, come on! I thought I might wear a scarf, but I've been playing with one for almost half an hour now, and depending on how I tie it, I either look like a chambermaid, a snake charmer, or Queen Elizabeth."

"And you're hoping for Bardot, right?"

"Exactly!"

"How long is the scarf?"

"What do you mean?"

"Is it square? Or is it long and skinny, like a chubby tie?"

"Well, neither. It's long, but it's rectangular, like the kind that old French ladies wear. I want to *completely* cover my hair so that no orange peeks out, otherwise I'd just go for the long, skinny headband."

"Get some bobby pins," he commands. "Here's what you need to do . . ."

Nick spends the next ten minutes talking me through it. Once he's done instructing, I'm giddy—it's perfect! (Well, I suppose "perfection" wouldn't *technically* be orange hair with a scarf covering it—but that's a minor detail.)

We make plans for drinks over the weekend with Emily and Joss and hang up, Nick promising to bring along Annika, who will be "putty in my hands" by Saturday, he claims. I'm already ten minutes late and I'm still in my "hair-dye outfit": black bleach-stained Pearl Jam concert T-shirt and red-and-black-tartan flannel boxers. Combined with my chic headgear, it makes for quite a picture.

Back up a step. I'm Bella Hunter, beauty writer for *Enchanté* magazine, the fastest growing, hottest women's magazine in the country. (At least, according to last week's killer article in the *New York Times,* which actually mentioned me by name!) We just passed one million circ, which means that we're under pressure like never before to make each issue innovative, exciting, informative, and—it goes without saying—fun to read. I graduated from college nearly eight years ago and have been with the magazine ever since, from conception to its current status as the industry darling.

Now, most people know all about the fashion industry (or at least *think* they do), but really have no idea what goes on in beauty. Beauty is one of those jobs that you can't quite believe you actually get paid to do. In a nutshell, I research beauty trends—hair, makeup, skincare, spas, celebrity looks . . . you name it—and then write about them. Each day I meet with public relations people, makeup artists, and beauty executives, and they explain to me why their client is the best, their skills the hottest, their company the most innovative. Of course, I get inundated with all the newest makeup and face creams and perfumes before they're released to the public, because I have to test them before creating a nice little write-up to ensure that the masses go out and buy them. That's the normal part of the job—goes with the territory. But then there are the perks. That's where the real action is.

Let's say I need a haircut, or my roots are threatening to expose my natural hair color (drab brown) to the world. A quick call to a public relations person gets me in—gratis—to see Roberto, or Jean-Pierre, or Lalo, who all own the hottest salons in the city and charge the price of a Louis Vuitton bag for an appointment. Or what if my neck is aching? A normal person with a real job would have to call up a spa and fork over one hundred dollars for a massage. But if I call one of my favorite people (PR execs are miracle workers), I can get in *that very day* to Lei or Relief or one of the other countless chichi spas in New York for a ninety-minute hot-stone massage . . . during work hours . . . as "research" . . . for free. And that miracle antiaging cream that's featured in every magazine and costs $575? If I call it in, it'll arrive at my desk via messenger within the hour.

And this doesn't even take into account that I've somehow become a bold-faced beau-lebrity who breezes past velvet ropes at clubs and has lunch and dinner at Nobu or Waverly Inn or Pastis every other day with PR people who insist on picking up the tab because a mention in my column ensures product sales.

Honestly? It's mind-blowing. I love to write, I love beauty, I *love* getting free things. And whenever I see myself on Page Six or in Gawker, I think, *I'm a nobody. How the hell did I get here?* Luckiest girl ever, right?

Definitely.

Except . . .

Well . . .

Okay, here's the deal.

I adore beauty, and I'm thrilled to have such a creative, recognized position. (It's a public-service job, really. Any girl who's ever felt depressed after being dumped can attest to the power of a sexy haircut or great eyeliner.) But while on the surface it seems as though everything's perfect and I'm a whiz at beauty and understanding the market . . . it's all a total fluke. I feel like the biggest fraud this side of James Frey. Let's put aside the fact that I'm a former army brat from small-town Ohio—not Darien or Chatham or Oyster Bay like all the other editors—and have had to spend the better part of the last decade secretly and frantically learning the ins and outs of the charmed life to appear as though I, too, belong. For argument's sake, we'll ignore my pathological need for acceptance and approval—apparently caused by my militaristic father, identified after months of twice-weekly sessions with a very patient therapist down in the Village—which leads me to agree to the most insane requests from my even more insane boss, Larissa. And my appearance? Well, let's just say that while I might appear well groomed and, I suppose, attractive *now*, it's taken me years of beauty-hamstering (you know, running endlessly toward an unattainable physical goal) to get this way: highlighting, hitting the gym, waxing, lasering, blowouts, and manicures ad infinitum. Middle school was a nightmare, and though I "blossomed" toward the very end of high school into something socially and physically acceptable, I've never been able to shake that awkward, outsider, oh-shit-is-everybody-staring-at-me? feeling of panicky otherness. I'm kind of obsessed with my appearance, actually, which is humiliating to admit—who wants to own up to being a narcissist?—but . . . it's the truth. Sometimes I feel as though it's the only thing I *can* control—and even then, I muck it up regularly.

Right, my appearance. I believe in focusing on your positive attributes (otherwise you'll lose sleep over the negative ones!). So, I thank the genetic gods daily for long, thick, wavy hair that could give Elle Macpherson a run for her money. It's still fairly shiny and smooth, considering the hell I've put it through over the years (current color: orange; twenty minutes ago: blonde; last month: brunette), although one day I'm expecting it all to just fall off. I like my green eyes, too, but they aren't a gorgeous emerald green or even a complex hazel. They're so dark most people think they're brown, which kind of defeats the entire purpose, in my opinion. As for the rest of me, well: I'm five-nine, snub-nosed, slim (but only because I live at the gym, believe me), and have no butt and no breasts, which makes me feel incredibly self-conscious around guys or in a bikini, but *is* pretty useful for wearing clothes. I've been told now and again that I look like a cross between Jennifer Garner and Mandy Moore (I can see the Mandy thing, but I look *nothing* like Jennifer Garner—people automatically make the connection because of my dimples, another plus I try to focus on when the rest of my face is completely broken out or my bottom teeth look like they've become even more crooked), although I wish with all my heart and soul that I looked tough and sexy like Angelina Jolie or Scarlett Johansson, who's a dead ringer for Emily. Instead, I get "cute," like a koala or some diaper advertisement.

To be perfectly honest, since high school, the years have been kind to me. I felt incredibly ugly then, and I'm still coming to terms with the fact that something, somewhere, eventually went right, and I now look okay—better than okay, maybe—to people. What they see doesn't reflect what I see in the mirror, though. You never shed your gawky preteen skin, and the bigger the trauma, the deeper the scar.

This wouldn't be such a problem—everybody has the occasional twinge of feeling as though they don't belong, don't they?—if I weren't (1) working for the universally acknowledged chicest, snobbiest, most exclusive magazine in the history of the world, and (2) suddenly in possession of a beauty page that was dubbed by the *New York Times* as "the most influential page in beauty." Translation? I'm not just some girl who's worked her way up the masthead and writes about lip gloss. I'm "The Beauty Expert." That's what my page is called, at least, and the sudden zoom to the top of the pack has left me with a distinct and all-too-queasy feeling of vertigo.

Millions of people look to me—me!—for beauty advice every month, and I feel as though I have no idea what the hell I'm doing. So when is the other shoe going to drop?

I've been at a crossroads recently, which has led me to countless hours spent listening to the Shins and the Arcade Fire, staring moodily out of my bedroom window onto Fourteenth Street and wondering about my future, like I'm a ridiculous character in some bad Zach Braff movie. Grace Donovan, the beauty director at *Catwalk* magazine, called me last week on the DL to offer a position as her new beauty editor. While, yeah, *Enchanté*'s hot *now*, *Catwalk* has been the industry standard for decades. A job with them would firmly ensconce me on the A-list . . . but there's no way I could hack it at *Catwalk*—surely Grace, an ice queen to the manor born, would see right through me. I live in fear of somebody discovering that I'm a certified beauty disaster. I'm supposed to be the guinea pig, helping women achieve better, lip-glossier, frizz-free lives through beauty, and instead I'm barreling around salons like a train wreck, getting green-enhancement contacts stuck in the back of my eye socket and turning my hair orange.

Really. It's just embarrassing.

But no time to think about that now. I'm supposed to be out the door for this interview in the next five minutes, and I have to at least *attempt* not to look like an utter disaster.

Twenty minutes later, I'm standing outside the door of Pamplona, gathering my courage before walking inside. I catch my reflection in a window and my cheeks begin burning as I survey my outfit. To offset the scarf, I decided to go for a retro '60s vibe, with a multicolored Pucci mini-shift and knee-high brown leather stiletto boots. It's either going to flop spectacularly . . . or set a trend. My fingers are crossed.

As I walk in, my eyes dart around the room like heat-seeking missiles, scoping out who's here and where everybody's standing. The media crowd tend to gravitate toward the same two or three venues—whatever's hottest that season—so if you're out and about in the city, you're guaranteed to run into the same few socialites, alcoholics, and writers (all the same, really) over and over. After years of going to beauty events three or four times a week (sometimes more during Fashion Week and the product launch seasons in May and December—in time for the huge September and March fall and spring issues), I've perfected the vital skill of instantaneous room scoping, which helps me walk through a door and immediately head in the appropriate direction. (Friendly editors to the right. Hostile fashionistas to the left: Abort! Abort!)

Beauty and fashion editors clutter the room, scattered between the "civilians", clustered in groups of threes and fours and clutching cosmos and glasses of red wine (for the poly-phenols, of course). I spy Adrienne Loman, beauty director of *Silk;* Danielle Rousseau, director of *Amour;* Heidi Svenson, beauty director of *Flash;* Mandy Milano from *Velvet;* Kelly (or is it Katie?) from *Glamour;* Jill from *Woman;* Courtney from *Plenty;* Sabrina from *Better Ladies,* the new girl from *Cosmo*—check, check, and check. The gang's all here.

Adrienne and I make eye contact across the room, where she's at the expansive glass-covered bar holding court with several attractive but vaguely sleazy-looking men with plentiful stubble and messy hair—probably writers at one of the lad mags. Her face brightens and she smiles, waggling her fingers at me before returning her attention to the group of wannabe lotharios.

"Hi, Bella!" calls Mandy, who's standing at the bar next to Heidi. The two of them are like Siamese twins; always joined at the hip. Whereas Mandy is a tiny sprite of a girl, with pixie-ish Winona Ryder hair, chocolate brown eyes, and the skinniest frame this side of Hollywood, Heidi is a cool, statuesque brunette, with striking hazel eyes and a killer fashion sense. Heidi and I don't know each other very well, although we've of course chatted countless times at events. Mandy and I worked briefly together a few years ago, before she moved over to *Velvet,* and while we were never best friends, our exchanges at work and at beauty events have always been pleasant and cheery.

Heidi sees me and lights up. "How are you?" She leans in to give me a kiss on each cheek, European-style, then gestures broadly to my outfit. "What's with all this? I *love* it. Very chic."

"Very retro," agrees Mandy. "I read your February column yesterday in Dr. Brandt's waiting room. Killer! So fabulous."

"Thanks." I thought this column—on the latest breakthroughs in lunchtime cosmetic surgery and dermatology, peppered with quotes from the top docs and a few off-the-record celebs and socialites—was insanely dull, but Katharine Whitefield, the steely, Eva Perón–chignoned editor in chief of *Enchanté,* steadfastly rejected all my attempts to liven it up. She perpetually seems less than thrilled by my presence at her magazine; Emily reassures me constantly that I'm simply being paranoid.

"Did you get your invite for the Face Group Paris trip yet?" Mandy asks. "I am *so* excited!"

The Face Group, one of the biggest companies in beauty, is flying a group of ten editors to Paris in late July, five months from now, for five days, and it promises to be one of the most lavish press trips ever. For the uninitiated, a press trip is the *Can-You-Believe-This-Is-Actually-Considered-Work?* practice of a beauty company taking editors to some far-flung locale for several days and nights of breakfasts, lunches, dinners, cocktail parties, sightseeing, and events, all designated to make you think that their new product is the most amazing thing to ever hit the market in the history of the world. Usually it's just three or four days celebrating a new eye cream or a hairbrush or something similarly unexciting. Those are the smaller scale trips: San Francisco, Miami, Phoenix, Southampton, Las Vegas. Small potatoes. But every once in a while the big companies—the ones that own practically every single beauty item you've ever heard of—throw a press trip. Those trips feature voyages that the average person will experience once in a lifetime, if they're lucky: South Africa, Peru, New Zealand, Egypt, the Maldives, or Fiji. There's a rumor that Ice Skincare is organizing an expedition in Antarctica next year to promote their new Wrinkle-Freezing range. (I'm surprised some PR company hasn't flown all the editors into outer space for a weekend.) *Those* trips are mind-blowing. Private jets, five-star hotels, dinners personally created by Alain Ducasse or Nobu Matsuhisa or Thomas Keller, seventy-five-year-old bottles of wine, four-hour massage "journeys" and helicopter trips to the Pyramids or the ancient Greek ruins or the Great Barrier Reef. Of course, the president or CEO of the company will come with all the chief marketing and advertising executives, and they'll wine you and dine you while extolling the virtues of their face cream or makeup line. And when you leave the cozy fantasy world they've created to return to your life, they give you a parting gift—invariably Gucci, Chanel, Louis Vuitton, or Hermès. (The sunglasses, purses, and wallets are nice, but the thing that *really* gets everybody excited is store credit.)

I studied in Paris my junior year of college—it's where Emily and I met, and we kept in touch until we both moved to New York after graduation—so I'm pretty familiar with the city, though I haven't been back since I was twenty. Now that I'm older and have a different life perspective, I think the experience will be richer. The City of Lights! The Eiffel Tower! River cruises on the Seine! Eight-hundred-thread-count Egyptian cotton sheets at the Ritz! And, of course, *l'amour*. I can practically hear Édith Piaf warbling "La Vie en Rose" right now.

I snap back to reality. "I got my invite a couple of days ago—I can't wait!" I say.

A sweet-looking blond girl with a wide, round face, saucer blue eyes and a sprinkling of freckles across her rosy cheeks and pinkish nose walks by. "Hi, Bella. Hi, Heidi . . . Mandy."

"Hi, there!" Mandy says, turning to the bar to order another Porn-Star Martini—*the* cocktail *du jour*.

Heidi smiles and nods her head regally. "Sarah. How are you? Enjoying yourself?"

"Yes, thanks," she says, smiling shyly. "Just on my way to the bathroom."

"It's over there," Heidi says, pointing to the back of the restaurant. "Steer clear of Justin Utney, or he'll demand that you dance with him," she laughs. Justin is one of the few male editors in the business—gay, of course.

Sarah scuttles away. "Who was that?" I ask.

"Sarah Jeckles. Assistant at *Beauty* magazine. Really sweet girl, but so shy. Having a conversation with her is painful, poor thing. Why is she even here? Don't the assistants all hang out in the Meatpacking, or somewhere tragic like that?"

"Oh my God, I *love* this song!" Mandy squeals, shimmying by the bar and grabbing my hand. "Come on, Bella, dance with me!"

"Thanks, but I'm here for an interview and quick photo shoot with the *Post* and I'm insanely late." I politely extricate myself from Mandy's grip as I gesture toward a table where a petite redhead is waving at me. "I think that's the reporter. Have fun, girls!" I say, excusing myself.

Maddie Daniels, one of Page Six's new additions, kisses me on both cheeks as I walk over and introduce myself, removing my coat. A slip of a girl with wavy red hair and Lisa Loeb–style glasses, Maddie waves her hand up and down at my outfit. A tape recorder rests on the table in plain sight.

"You Bonneau-Martray girls are so chic! What's the look, Brigitte Bardot?" she asks, pointing at my scarf, which covers every last inch of orange hair thanks to Nick's tutorial.

"Right, I was going for Bardot—or maybe Grace Kelly," I say in my best media voice, trying to shake off the sudden feeling of nervousness that has washed over me. *Sit up straight, Bella! Project your voice! Feign confidence! Just . . . don't make an ass of yourself by being* too *confident. Nobody likes a stuck-up snob.*

"*So* fashion forward. Love it. Tell me, have you ever been interviewed before?"

"No," I say, silently pondering the countless ways I could possible screw up this interview. As long as I say as little as possible, throwing in the occasional winning smile—a tactic that has guided me through the better part of a decade—I should be fine. Maddie might simply peg me as aloof, like all the other Bonneau girls.

Maddie opens her mouth and a torrent of high-pitched words speeds out. "Don't worry about it! Relax! I'm interested in your background, where you're from, how you got this job so young, what it's like being the biggest columnist at the most popular magazine in the country, how much fun it is being a beauty editor. You know. The usual! If you don't want to talk about anything, let me know and we won't even go there. Promise! I'm keeping this recorder here so I don't have to write anything down. Just chat naturally and I'll transcribe everything later. If I ask you anything you don't want to answer, feel free to let me know. Okay? Then we'll have the photographer take a few pictures of you afterward, you know, sipping your wine and stuff. Sounds good?"

"Sounds good."

We study the menu and a minute later a waiter appears. Maddie orders a bottle of red wine before rubbing her hands together excitedly. "Okay! So, where are you from?"

"I was an army brat for most of my childhood, but we eventually settled in Ohio. Sweet Falls."

"Right, right," she says, nodding. "And where did you go to college?"

"I went to Northwestern. Journalism major."

"*Whoo,* fancy!" she teases. "How was that? Did you just love it?"

"It was phenomenal. Northwestern is fifteen minutes outside Chicago, and it was my first time near a big city, so we went out frequently. You can imagine what *that* was like— college kids on the loose! And the program, of course, is fantastic. It was there I first entertained the idea of becoming a magazine editor." God, I sound so formal. Loosen up, Bella.

The wine arrives and Maddie waves off the waiter, indicating that we don't need to 'test' it before he pours. "So how did you land a job at *Enchanté*? Bonneau-Martray is one of the hardest companies to break into, but you were hired right out of college, right?"

"Yes," I admit, "but I spent years working at internships during the summer. I lucked into an internship at *Plenty* following my freshman year, and after I had that on my résumé, I was able to get internships at *Bazaar, Cosmo, Velvet,* and *Beauty.* I essentially harassed the human resources woman at Bonneau until she agreed to meet with me!" I say, chuckling politely, hoping I don't sound too braggy while listing my credentials.

"And fast-forward to now, when you're one of the most celebrated writers in New York City," she says admiringly. "How does that make you feel?"

My heartbeat speeds up. How do I answer this question? Should I be modest? Aggressively confident? Do I admit my rampant insecurities? I decide to respond cautiously. "Well, I'm only a beauty writer, and there are so many writers in this city who are better than I am, I couldn't even begin to count them! But I do feel very lucky to be where I am right now, and all I can hope is that readers are enjoying the column," I conclude diplomatically. Miss America, eat your heart out.

"Did you always know you wanted to work in beauty?"

"Not at all! I was the original tomboy growing up—climbing trees, camping in the backyard, playing baseball every night with the neighborhood boys. When I was in college, I wanted to be a journalist, but a friend of mine landed an internship at *Plenty*, which is how I got in the door. After that, I interned in fashion, and my next two internships were in beauty. It's addictive. Once you've sampled the beauty goods, it's hard to go back! I think I'd probably be a terrible journalist, anyway."

"But, in a way, you are a journalist," she points out, sipping her wine. Behind Maddie, I notice Heidi dancing seductively by the bar, the gaggle of men smiling drunkenly as they encircle her. "As far as beauty goes, you're referring, of course, to the swag and all the free products you get."

"The swag is insane, but it's the orgy of products that blows your mind. And haircuts, highlights, massages, et cetera, are all on the house. Don't get me wrong, it's not a free-for-all—it's our job to sample the new products and services on the market so we can write about them. If they weren't free, there's no way we editors would be able to afford it all!"

"Of course. By the way, let's talk more about your outfit. Totally stylish!"

I feel my cheeks reddening. "You know," I say vaguely. "Just wanted to mix it up a little." Or hide the fact that my hair looks like a school crossing guard vest. Toss up.

"The scarf is to die for! Was it a gift?"

"From one of the PR companies. Q Communications, I think. It's hard to keep track."

"I'm not surprised. Back to the swag—you guys get so much stuff, don't you?"

"You have *no* idea," I snort, sipping my glass of red wine. So delicious! Maddie ordered a bottle of Stag's Leap, one of my favorites I'd noticed while perusing the menu. "My bedroom looks like I robbed Barneys."

She laughs. "What kind of things do you get?"

"Oh, you name it. Purses, plane ticket vouchers, gift cards to the Apple store and Saks, *tons* of designer stuff. Christmas is when the real action is." I suddenly realize that I probably shouldn't be discussing this. Everybody knows about the swag—it's been publicized to high heaven, and some magazines have even banned employees from receiving gifts—but talking about it is frowned upon. Shit. I've probably already been too loose lipped.

"Okay, but do you think it's ethical that you get all of this free stuff?"

I frown, trying to toe the line and produce an acceptable, top-level sanctioned response. "I suppose it's technically not very ethical to send somebody free purses while you're sending them products to write about, but no editor worth her salt would cover a bad product just because a publicist had sent her a nice present. Gifts have *no* bearing upon what gets written."

"Are you sure?"

"Yes," I say firmly. "Why?"

"I don't know," she shrugs. "It seems weird. If I were a reader who knew all the behind-the-scenes dirt, I wouldn't trust the magazines as much." She pauses. "Do you think readers know about the relationships between the publicists and the editors?"

"We recommend great products that actually work, so what's not to trust? If there's a little odd action behind the scenes, I don't think readers really care."

"What's the daily schedule of a beauty editor like? Is it all glitz and glam?"

"It *is* glamorous," I admit. "At least compared to most professions. But, no, it's not all fun. A typical day . . . let's see. A few deskside interviews with various beauty companies and publicists—that's where they present their latest beauty products and try to get you to write about them—maybe a lunch or dinner event, and then a lot of writing and researching."

"No press trips?"

"Not every day!" I laugh. "Can you imagine? Press trips are a once-every-three-or-four-months kind of thing."

"So how do you decide what to write about? When you're not getting bribed by publicists, that is," she says, winking. Maddie's pushy, but down-to-earth, I think, deciding that I like her.

"Every time we—that is to say me, the beauty director, the associate beauty editor, or the assistant—meet with a publicist or go to an event, we bring the products back to the office and put them in our beauty closet—"

"Oh! I've heard about the beauty closet!" she squeals. "That's the magic room with Chanel and La Mer products for you to do whatever you want with!"

"In a nutshell," I smile. "So, once a month, we go through all the new products, and we spot trends or breakthroughs and then write about it. For my column, the beauty director, Larissa, either assigns me a story or lets me pitch ideas to Katharine, our editor in chief."

My cell phone rings—it's Larissa. I look at Maddie apologetically. "Speak of the devil. I'm so sorry, but it's my boss. It could be an emergency."

"Please, go ahead!"

"Riss?" I answer quietly, putting my hand over the phone and speaking into my lap.

"Doll face! What's the scoop? What are you doing? Are you with the reporter? Remember, don't say anything that makes me look bad, but don't forget to mention what a *wonderful* boss I am. And beautiful. Wonderful and beautiful," says Larissa, her voice perpetually low and smoky after decades of late night partying.

"Yes, we're here at Pamplona. I was indeed just saying how wonderful you are."

"Good girl. Pamplona? Is it *maddeningly* packed?" Larissa is dating an Englishman, Daniel, and has taken to speaking in a faux-Brit accent. Half the time, she sounds like a bad Madonna impersonator, but despite my pleas to speak normally, she insists on making up her own bizarre mid-Atlantic accent.

"It's pretty crowded. Heidi and Mandy, Adrienne, Courtney—"

"That *bitch*," she says savagely. Who knows what that's about? Larissa is notoriously mercurial.

"Yeah . . . *er.* Tons of industry people here, anyway."

"Send them all kisses for me. Listen, a quick question. For the life of me I *cannot*"—(cah-naww-t)—"remember the name of the bloody celebrity spokesperson for Fabergé Cosmetics."

"It's Jessica Biel." I look at Maddie apologetically and mime that I'll be off the phone in two seconds.

"Jessica Biel? I could have sworn it was either Keira or Scarlett."

"No, they offered it to Scarlett, but she passed, and they

were trying to sign Keira, but something came up. So now it's Jessica—the contract is for two years and she's getting four million. Not too shabby, huh?"

"Doll, you're the best. What *would* I do without you?"

"See you Monday," I say, laughing, then I hang up and apologize to Maddie.

"That was your boss? How is she? Do all the editors get along? Are they a catty bunch?"

"No! I mean, there *are* a few . . . but . . . well, no, not really." Shut up, Bella. "Definitely not."

"This isn't part of the article," she says quickly. "Just background for my own benefit."

I hesitate. The more she understands my world, the more she can write, but I don't want to fall into the trap of selective quoting. "We're people. Some editors don't get along, but most do," I say firmly. As if on cue, the door of Pamplona is flung open and in steps Delilah Windsor, the one person in this world I despise.

My former protégée, Delilah was beauty assistant at *Enchanté* years ago, back when I was associate beauty editor. Larissa loathed her on sight—too sugary, too much competition—but I was seduced by Delilah's long flaming-red hair, photo-shoot-ready makeup (beauty editors habitually look put-together, but Delilah is the only one who *always* wears foundation), rosy lips; hypnotic blue eyes; and charming southern accent. What can I say? I'm a beauty girl—a sucker for a pretty face. We'd instantly bonded, Delilah being only two years younger than I and seemingly on the same wavelength with me about everything from our love of the same rock music to a shared despair over the increasing lack of manners in society to a twisted, but normally hidden, sense of humor. I begged Larissa to hire her and quickly took her under my wing as my own. To this day, I can't fathom how she could greet me chirpily every morning, eagerly bring me coffee, text me nonstop and—the killer—throw my twenty-fourth birthday party, all the meanwhile secretly spreading rumors around the office behind my back. They got back to me, of course, but who was I going to believe: the catty girls in the fashion closet or my darling best work friend? At my party, I caught her straddling Olivier, my college sweetheart of three years, in a dingy, half-hidden stairwell at the back of the bar, her hand down the back of his pants, his hands creeping up the front of her shirt, as they made out. I don't play the "blame the girl, forgive the guy" game—it takes two to tango, and I cut them both out of my life instantly. But what I couldn't forgive Delilah for was the fact that she *wanted* me to see them. She'd sent me a text ("Where R U? Come find me!"), and when I stumbled upon them, she locked her eyes onto mine, leaned her neck to the side for Olivier to kiss, and smiled languidly. Larissa froze her out against Katharine's wishes, refusing to speak to her until at last Delilah found another job two months later at *Velvet*. Delilah plays the victim, feigning innocence when other editors ask why we're not friends anymore, but the story inevitably "leaked out." (Larissa practically bought ads spreading the word.)

Maddie takes one look at my face, which must look as though I've just smelled something revolting, and swivels around in her chair to face the doorway. I take a huge swig of wine, finishing my glass and then pouring myself another.

"Do you know that girl?" she asks.

"Yes. She's another beauty editor."

"Friend of yours?"

I'm silent. I don't want to break down and give Maddie the whole story, but even though it's been nearly five years, I'm incapable of hiding my distaste for Delilah.

"Not really." I gulp more wine, hoping to calm my nerves. Delilah wears a strapless white minidress, her ample breasts smushed up against her collarbone, and walks into the fray, immediately eclipsing Heidi's position as the center of attention with the lad maggers. She spots me and grins cruelly, blowing me a kiss, which causes Heidi and Mandy to look at each other in alarm, as if worried I'm going to charge over and throw down with Delilah in the middle of the bar.

Maddie looks at me carefully. "We can talk about it later. Next question. What's the best part of being a beauty editor?"

For the next two hours, we talk about the industry and drink, eventually polishing off two bottles. By the time the photographer has finished taking my picture, I'm completely drunk.

"*So* cute!" Maddie squeals, peering at the camera screen to look at one of the images. "The outfit photographs perfectly. You're going to look gorgeous—not that you need any help."

"Thanks," I say, surreptitiously peeking down at my chest to see if it's red and splotchy from all the wine. The edges of my vision are slightly fuzzy, like in those old films where the director smeared Vaseline on the lens. I think back over my conversation with Maddie. I didn't say anything inappropriate, did I? I've already forgotten half of what we talked about. I've purposely been ignoring the bar area during our conversation, but I allow myself a quick peek. Delilah, mercifully, has left.

"We're done. I think I've got the shot," the photographer says.

"Fab!" Maddie turns to me. "Do you have any plans tonight? A boyfriend?"

"Who has time? My friend Nick keeps trying to set me up with his friends, but they're all sluts," I say, wondering if I'm slurring. "He's straight, though. Cute, too. But a total player. He's a makeup artist."

"*Ooh,* he sounds fun."

"Who does?"

"Your friend Nick. He sounds fun!"

"Oh, he's a total blast! We kissed a million years ago, but there's no real chemistry. He's my friend, you know?" I say, suppressing a hiccup. "I call him whenever I have a crisis. He's like my gay best friend . . . except he's straight. He's a makeup artist. I had to call him tonight, to help with my orange hair!" I'm putting my phone in my purse and clumsily pawing through my bag, looking for a tube of Kiehl's # 1 lip balm when I realize what I've said.

Maddie looks stunned. "Your what?"

"Nothing."

She peers at my head. "Is that why you're wearing a scarf?"

"No."

"No, seriously!" she laughs. "Show me your hair!"

"I was . . . it's nothing . . ."

"You know," she says thoughtfully, "I saw an orange wisp peek out earlier, but I assumed it was my imagination. Were you doing a story?"

"Um . . ." I'm panicking. I'm completely drunk and this writer has just caught onto the fact that I've accidentally dyed my hair crimson, and as I see it, my options are either to flee—which is childish and unprofessional and, more importantly, would ruin the article—or swallow my pride and explain the situation. As much as I want to bolt out of the room, I've got to choose door number two.

"I was dyeing my hair brunette for an article, and somehow it ended up orange," I confess, looking around to make sure no beauty girls are in sight before quickly pulling my scarf up a few inches to show Maddie the color.

"Oh *no*. How traumatizing! And right before the photo shoot, too!"

"I was kind of freaking out," I confess. "I seem to find myself in these ridiculous scenarios a lot."

"Everybody has bad luck once in a while. Don't worry about it!" she says, and smiles, looking at me fondly like an indulgent child. "It doesn't mean anything. And you couldn't see the orange in the pictures, I promise. It looked mysterious. Very chic. And you're *Bella Hunter,* so everybody will assume you're starting a new trend, or something."

"I hope so," I say weakly, my head spinning.

Maddie dips her finger in her glass of wine and brings it to her lips, licking the tip thoughtfully. "This article is going to be killer, I can already tell."

"Please don't say anything about the orange hair," I beg.

"Your secret is safe with me," she says, winking. "The piece runs Monday—you're going to love it."

Chapter 2

I drag myself out of bed at 8:15 Saturday morning—why-oh-why did I drink so much wine last night?—wrapping my head in a scarf again before catching a cab to the Carlyle. American Beauty Women, a charity I've become heavily involved with these past few years, is discussing a June polo match in the Hamptons that *Enchanté* is sponsoring. I yawn my way through the meeting, tuning out the conversation, which has nothing to do with polo but instead focuses on which items we're planning to contribute to the gift bags and whether we can get Reese Witherspoon to come on our behalf. Finally, after two hours of debate (consensus: if Reese says no, we're going to go after Katherine Heigl, followed by Hayden Panettiere, and then Kristen Bell), I'm free to go, rushing to my stylist, George, who fixes the color with a lot of head-shaking and sighing. My hair's now a cross between dirty blonde and dishwater brown—not the sexiest color, but easily fixable with the strategically placed at-home highlights I plan on adding later for my story.

Monday morning, I sleep in, skipping the gym to head downtown for a cover shoot. Magazines typically work three months in advance, which means that, even though it's only February, we're already putting the May issue to bed. Larissa isn't going to be in the office until late—she informed me last week that she has a beauty breakfast, but

I think she probably just doesn't want to be bothered with waking up early for the shoot—so she's allowed Julie Pomelini, the beauty assistant, to come meet me at the studio. Julie's still new enough that she thinks these things are glamorous.

Most beauty editors seem to be late sleepers by nature. I'm firmly in the snooze-button camp, too, but have forced myself to wake up at 6:15 for the past several years in order to be at Equinox by 6:45. My routine is a punishing hour on the elliptical two days a week, an hour on the treadmill two days a week, and either workout followed by half an hour of weights and abs. I read articles in *US Weekly* and *InStyle,* celebrities bouncily proclaiming that they just *love* exercising and the endorphins it releases and the rewarding feeling they get after a workout, and I want to track them down and strangle them in their beds. Who *loves* exercising? I grit my teeth as the alarm blares, drag myself from under my warm duvet, and show up at the gym dutifully so that I can fit into my sample-sized designer clothes—I earn a decent salary, but unlike Emily, Larissa, or most of the girls I work with, I can't afford to spend five thousand dollars on a shirt, so I've made a career of borrowing clothes from designers, hitting the sample sales, or scouring Emily's massive closet.

When I arrive at Jack Studios in Chelsea, Julie is already there with a steaming latte, her hair and makeup beauty-editor-flawless. Julie's one of those lucky girls who don't need makeup, her perfectly even olive complexion set off by naturally-defined black eyes. The thick jet-black mane cascading down her back—long, always long; no beauty editor would be caught dead with hair above her shoulders, unless in a cropped Mia Farrow–style pixie—are a legacy she claims from her Sicilian grandmother and could be bushy on another girl, but even in the lowly beauty assistant position, Julie knows the vital tricks to keep her hair silky and smooth.

"Going curly today?" she asks.

I self-consciously pat my hair. The extra minutes of sleep meant I couldn't give myself a proper blowout, so I dried it halfway, threw in some Kérastase cream, and then plaited my damp hair, releasing it from the braid just before I got out of the cab. It's in loose, hippie-ish waves now—pretty, but a departure from my standard glass-smooth style.

"Yeah, it's going to be all about wavy hair this fall," I fib. "I'm totally over the blowout."

Julie looks panicked. "Straight is over?"

"Well, I'm projecting. Not *yet*, of course, but, hey, we sort of set the trends, don't we?"

She nods eagerly and I feel guilty. I'd bet money that she'll come in tomorrow with wavy air-dried hair, too.

I look around, surveying the surreal scene that's become a normal part of my life. Every inch of the enormous cube-shaped studio is blindingly white, with floor-to-ceiling windows overlooking the Hudson River, Chelsea Piers, and downtown Manhattan, and countless racks of not-yet-released designer duds. Photography and wardrobe assistants scuttle around, cell phones glued to their ears as they remove clothing from black bags and place it on the racks. A quick glance at the clothing, accessories, and jewelry suggests that there's easily a million dollars worth of merchandise in the room. Most of the New York City magazine shoots happen here, and the studio is beloved not only for its light and airy feel, but also for its ability to morph into any sort of background. Numerous "wilderness-style layout" shoots have taken place here over the years with penguins, llamas, and even Siberian tigers. The hair and makeup tables are lined in a row by the bank of corner mirrors along one wall. One of our regular makeup artists, the celebrated Mindy Gunnerman, is already there.

I nod at Julie and jerk my thumb in Mindy's direction,

and the two of us walk over. Mindy has her makeup kit set up and is pawing through her Make Up For Ever, Armani, and Smashbox, setting aside key pieces to use on the model.

"Hey, Mindy," I say warily. The laws of the industry dictate that I shouldn't be intimidated by her. After all, I'm a good three inches taller, at least twenty pounds skinnier, and objectively prettier by any standard. While some industries measure success by other yardsticks, like money, talent, or fame, beauty—like the majority of the magazine industry—bends over backward to accommodate a pretty face or a superior physique. After spending so much of our lives devoted to the pursuit of looking our best—and helping our readers look their best, too—we're both suspicious of and adulatory toward those who've reached the promised land of physical perfection. Unsurprisingly, it's one giant twenty-first-century beauty pageant, with each girl subconsciously—or consciously—striving to outshine the others . . . while effortlessly appearing dainty and charming, of course. Mindy doesn't fit into the scheme. She's not exactly a model herself, with too-close-set muddy brown eyes, platinum blonde hair, and pasty skin that could benefit from a tan—or a layer of St. Tropez. Amazingly, she doesn't seem impressed by the looks of the models, the self-confidence of the editors, or deterred by her own physical shortcomings, maybe because she's famous in her own right. It seems like she's immune to appearance—ironic for a makeup artist, no?—which makes me insanely uncomfortable. I always feel like she's in on some secret I'm not privy to.

She looks at me strangely. "Hey . . . Bella. What's going on?"

"Same old. How are you?" I ask dutifully, adding, "Have you met Julie, our beauty assistant?" before she can respond.

They shake hands limply, then Mindy asks, "Is the model here yet?"

"I spied her on the way in. I think she's in the bathroom. Let's get her in hair and makeup when she gets out. Do you want her first or should Javier do it?"

"I don't know. He usually likes taking the girls first. Javier?" she bellows into the air.

"What?" a voice calls back from across the studio. Javier's curly black head pops up from behind the clothing rack. He's compact, built like a wrestler, and so short that his eyes are barely visible over the tops of the clothes.

"C'mere!" she calls.

Javier dutifully lopes across the studio, pausing to give me a quick kiss on the cheek. "How are you, baby? Crazy stuff! Let those bitches have it!"

What is he talking about? I think, shrugging it off. "You look great, Javy!"

"As always," he grins, batting his eyelashes at me. Javier used to be George's number two but left last year in a high-profile split to start his own salon. The break with George was drenched in animosity, and he still refuses to utter Javier's name. I'm thankful that Javy is here to break the tension in the room between Mindy and me—or is it just my imagination? I'm becoming such a paranoid pill lately. I think it's the stress. I need a vacation.

"Do you want to do Tania first, or should I?" Mindy asks.

"Are you stupid, woman? Of course I need to do her first. The hair magic—it takes *time*."

"Whatever," Mindy says, rolling her eyes and turning back to her makeup.

"Have you met Julie, Javy?" I ask.

"We met a few minutes ago," Julie grins, batting her long lashes at him. "Javier was showing me all of his tools."

"I'll bet he was."

"Excuse me!" Javier says, swatting me on the arm. "Somebody left this poor girl all alone while they dragged their late ass here, so I had to keep her entertained." He winks at Julie.

"Okay, you two," I say, smiling at Javier and waggling my finger. "Mommy's here and playtime's over. What are you planning on doing with Tania's hair?"

Tania the one-name Russian model walks into the room clutching a venti Starbucks, followed by two stick-thin brunette women in their midthirties dressed in head-to-toe black. Tania's the current magazine world favorite, with every book falling over itself to land her on the cover. A few months ago, she was on nine different top magazine covers at the same time, an unprescedented coup, and in the past four weeks has been announced as the new face of Victoria's Secret, Louis Vuitton, *and* Calvin Klein. Tania's last name is Valenskya, but nobody ever refers to her by both of her names: she's just Tania. (Best said with a breathless whisper: *Tania*.) According to *US Weekly* she's secretly seeing Leonardo DiCaprio, so I'm curious to see if he calls her or shows up at this shoot.

"Come here," Javier commands. She walks over wordlessly, ignoring the rest of us. Even though I've met her on at least three different occasions, I decide to let it go. I'm obviously not important enough to acknowledge.

Tania sips her coffee while Javier runs his fingers through her hair, flipping her part this way and that, pulling it up in back, holding it to one side with his left hand as he strokes her strands with his right. "Do you see her texture?" he demands.

"Yes?"

"This is *amazing* texture. You don't see texture like this anymore. All of the skinny little anorexic models have skinny little anorexic hair, but not Tania." She smiles wanly at the compliment, then yawns, her eyes fixed on some random point on the opposite wall. "It's thick," he continues, fondling her hair as he talks. "We have to do something with this. It's for June, no? I don't want some stupid summer thing, no slicked back, no wavy limp noodle. Sexy! She is so sexy! She needs Tom Ford hair, she needs Serge Normant hair. Julia Roberts on the cover of *Metamorphosis*? That's what she needs."

"You're keeping her hair down, right?" one of the women says worriedly, putting her hands on her hips. "Because she looks better with it around her shoulders. It doesn't look good up. Her face is too long."

"And no bangs," the other woman adds, shaking her head for emphasis. "Under no circumstances. We don't do bangs anymore."

Javier raises an eyebrow disdainfully. "And *you* are . . . ?"

"Gail Cash. Manager."

"Trudy Stein. Publicist."

"Well, *I* am Javier. Hairstylist. And Tania is shooting for *Enchanté*. And we will do her hair however we please. And Bartolomo is shooting, and he is a genius so it will look fabulous, and you *will* love it. So please go away while I work," he barks.

"What—?"

"Do you know who—?"

"I know exactly who sits in my chair," Javy says, interrupting both seething women. "Now go over there. *Please*."

Tania floats her right hand up in the air, as if waving away a butterfly, and Gail and Trudy reluctantly walk over to the craft services table, muttering darkly to each other as they pour cups of coffee.

"Now," Javy says, turning back to me and continuing brightly. "Serge hair! What do you think, baby? Yay or nay?"

"Yay, of course. You're the hair expert—I'm sure it'll look phenomenal."

"This is why I love Bella!" he shrieks, dropping Tania's hair and stepping past her to engulf me in a hug. Julie stifles a giggle as I look helplessly over Javier's shoulder, my arms pinned to my sides. "You have vision! You're not afraid to take risks! You say what must be said!"

"Do you need me?" Tania interrupts in a bored voice.

Javier turns back to look at her and shoos her over to his chair. "Yes. Go sit down. Now."

As Tania glides over to the chair, Javier turns to me and shakes his head ruefully. "Models. They're such divas."

Javier spends the next hour working on Tania's hair, teasing pieces, straightening others and curling the rest until she has a virtual Medusa's nest on her head. Gail and Trudy wordlessly circle him, staring worriedly at Tania and sending e-mails on their BlackBerrys every five minutes, but Javy's temper tantrum seems to have scared them off and they keep their distance. Javier finishes it all off with several generous sprays of Elnett, then sends her to Mindy's chair.

"What advertiser are you going with?" Mindy asks absentmindedly as she starts painting Armani foundation onto Tania's face with a brush.

Julie and I sit on chairs on either side of Mindy, watching as she works. Even after all these years, I still get a palpable thrill out of watching a professional makeup artist at work. "I think it's M·A·C this month." Mindy's referring to the process of crediting a makeup company on the inside cover of the magazine. Every issue, a tiny inset of the cover photograph is displayed with notes explaining what kind of eyeshadow, foundation, and lip gloss the cover model is wearing. The real makeup used on these shoots never matches the products described—not at any magazine in the industry. In actuality, the publishing side of the magazine cuts a deal with the beauty company and then informs editorial—i.e., me—which brand we'll be pretending to credit. When I first found out about the scam years ago, I was horrified, since I'd always accepted those credits as gospel in high school and college. Now, I barely bat an eyelash. It's just how the industry works.

We examine Tania. She looks fantastic, albeit fantasticlly bored. She flips through an issue of the *Post*. Today's the day my article is supposed to come out, I realize.

"Hey," she says suddenly. "Is this you?"

She holds the paper toward me and I put down my coffee as I step closer to get a better look. The headline reads: TOP BEAUTY EDITOR EXPOSES INDUSTRY—EXCLUSIVE! by Maddie Daniels. My eyes widen and I snatch the paper from her.

"What?!"

"Yeah," she says languidly. "I just read the article, but I didn't realize it was you until a second ago. What's with the outfit? That's a really bad picture."

"Horrible," agrees Gail, who's appeared behind Tania out of thin air.

"Thanks," I snap, my eyes running over the page. Words like "divas," "greedy," "obscene," and "nasty" flash out at me. I feel myself getting dizzy and I sink into a chair as I read the piece.

BELLA HUNTER is the marquee beauty writer at *Enchanté* magazine, the chicest, most exclusive glossy in the world, and is considered by many to be the most influential woman in beauty. "One word in Bella's column, and a product will instantly sell out, or a trend will immediately take root," says a source, adding, "Celebrities, socialites, makeup artists, and designers all flip to her page first—she sets the trends that the trendsetters themselves follow." Unlike her coworkers or most of her readers, however, Bella wasn't born with a silver spoon in her mouth and reveals in an exclusive interview with *the Post* that she is often baffled by the widespread snobbery. "The girls (at *Enchanté*) are selfish divas," says Bella. "It's a sorority mentality."

Few realize that Bella had a poor upbringing in the Midwest, as the daughter of an army major who bounced from town to town, including a three-year stint at a base in Germany, and suffered feelings of insecurity—a self-described "ugly duckling." Those who turn to her as the expert on all things chic will be surprised to learn that Bella is one of the few in her world who doesn't summer in St. Barth's or take winter trips to the family home in Palm Beach. Bella's compatriots—both at *Enchanté* and in the rareified world of beauty editors, where swag flows like wine and press trips on private jets are the norm—inhabit a fairy-tale land of privilege and pedigree, something Bella seems to scorn, despite her own exalted position.

As a beauty editor, Bella writes about hair, makeup, skin care, celebrities, and other frivolous but fun topics. The world of beauty is anything but low-key, however, awash in advertising dollars that beauty companies lavish on editors in return for product placement. "The swag is obscene! Free beauty products, haircuts, highlights, press trips, massages. It's not very ethical. But most readers don't care. They don't spend two seconds thinking about how the magazine is actually put together. If we recommend products that sound fantastic, that works for them. They learn to trust us," Bella says.

On the other editors at *Enchanté*, Bella is only too happy to dish about their nasty sides. "There are always editors who get off on making your life a living hell," she says, refusing to give details out of respect for her colleagues. She lets slip on the problem of stealing from the fashion closet, however, revealing, "There's a real problem in fashion with the *borrowing* of the merchandise," says Bella, using air quotes. "The fashion department is all drama."

Lest you think it's just the editors who engage in such bad behavior, think again. "Freelance writers are a big problem, too. They get really greedy in the fashion closet. They think nobody will miss another pair of Jimmy Choos or a Prada belt and they get sticky-fingered with it. It's always the poor fashion assistants who take the heat." Bella reveals that interns are often blamed for the crimes of their superiors, such as one widely whispered about incident when a well-known fashion designer's daughter set fire to the Looking Glass fashion closet during a smoke break, only to have her intern fired in response.

Regarding publicists, Bella hints about their bitchiness, mentioning Morrison public relations, but refusing to divulge their inner secrets. "My best friend in the world is a beauty publicist." Bella won't name names, but her MySpace page includes a Jocelyn Reeves in her Top 8. A look at the Morrison Web site also shows an account director named Jocelyn Reeves. "Publicists can be nasty," says Bella, "but so can the editors. They're all on edge. But, really, how often can you write about toothpaste or maxi pads? Things come to a head." Bella admits that publicists work like dogs, however, and often have to put up with editors calling in expensive products for made-up stories, secretly planning to take them home.

I sit back in the chair, stunned, as I read the rest of the article, which recounts catfights between nameless editors, pries into my personal life, questions how long I can remain at the top of the industry, quotes an anonymous editor who calls me "incredibly stuck-up and pretentious," and intimates that I have a drinking problem. Javier and Mindy crowd around me worriedly as Tania yawns and checks e-mails on her BlackBerry. She looks up and shrugs her shoulders. "Man. That sucks. You think your bosses will be pissed?"

Behind me, Julie's stiff, her hand covering her mouth. As I look at her, she slowly backs away, shaking her head. Whatever I have, she doesn't want to catch it. I flee the shoot, racing back to the office in a cab, my heart pounding. How could I have been so *stupid*? I don't remember saying half of that, but, as all my friends know, I do tend to drink when I get stressed . . . and get chatty when I drink, which isn't even that often. (Alcoholic, my ass. Bastards!) The article triggers my memory—I vaguely remember talking about publicists and telling the Looking Glass–fire story, but would I really have been idiotic enough to verbally tar and feather the entire industry under the influence of a few glasses of wine? Apparently so. Goddamn it. I blame it on Delilah—seeing her completely unnerved me. As I speed through the huge Bonneau-Martray glass doors on Forty-fourth Street, I feel as if everybody in the lobby is staring at me. The guard behind the visitor's desk raises an eyebrow as I rush past.

"Bad day?" he asks.

"Yehmphmygod," I mumble, stepping into the elevator. The door is about to close when a tall, wire-thin blonde stomps through the doors. My back stiffens—it's Grace Donovan, the director who secretly called me about a job just last week. A ringer for the late Carolyn Bessette Kennedy, Grace is a major beauty industry queen bee. It's a running debate as to who's more influential—Grace or Larissa. I think she's secretly a robot. (I mean this literally.) She's surely read the paper by now. Please let her be nice to me!

"Hi, Grace," I say timidly. "How are you?"

Grace stares straight ahead at the news ticker.

"*Uh* . . . about what we discussed a few days ago. I'm going to e-mail you my résumé this afternoo—"

"Don't bother."

I'm through. Where Grace leads, others follow. If she's decided that I'm out, my reputation is dust.

"'Bye," I say softly as the elevator doors open at her floor. No response.

As I ride up in the elevator, eyes fixed unblinkingly on the TV panels displaying the news ticker, I mentally prepare myself for what's to come. I exit at the *Enchanté* floor and walk quietly down the blue-and-purple-hued neon-lit hallway. Maybe if I tread as gently as possible, nobody will notice me and I'll be able to slip back to my desk unnoticed. Tasha Miller, the associate editor, is at her desk with the *Post* spread out in front of her, talking a mile a minute on the phone, her long blond bangs artfully covering *just* enough of her left eye to look sexy yet edgy. A big, bawdy pre-weight-loss Sophie Dahl of a girl with chalky white skin, azure eyes, and wheat-colored hair that tumbles past her shoulders in messy waves, Tasha prides herself on her "realness" and her "'tude" but often neglects to mention that her father owns one of the biggest hedge funds in the city. The irony of our positions—billionairess Tasha sporting tatty thrift-store dresses to look poor as I raid my roommate's closet and blow my wad at sample sales to look "*Enchanté* appropriate"—has not been lost on me.

"And then it calls us all a bunch of spoiled divas! Can you believe the nerve? It's unbeli—" Tasha sees me and clams up.

I nod at her, my cheeks burning, and then sit down at my desk, staring at my computer. Behind me, Tasha whispers, "Yeah." Pause. "Yeah, she just walked in." Pause. "I don't know yet. Larissa's not back. There's no way they'll keep her after this, though." Pause. "You know how Katharine feels about her." Pause. "Okay, yeah, call Callie and let me know what she says. As soon as I find out, I'll tell you. Bye."

I'm numb. I sit at my desk staring into space for I don't know how long, until I realize that Julie is back from the shoot and standing next to me, her hand on my shoulder.

"Are you okay?" she asks softly.

I shake my head, fighting back tears.

"Why did you say all that stuff, Bella?"

"I don't know," I whisper. "I don't remember saying most of it . . . but we had a lot of wine. I feel like such an idiot. I can't believe I would have—"

"You didn't say that the beauty industry is like a catty sorority?" Tasha asks archly, appearing from nowhere. Two associate fashion editors walk by, pointedly not looking at me. "Disgusting," mutters one to the other.

"No!" I pause, some of my words floating up at me through the wine-soaked haze of that evening. "I mean . . . not exactly. Not in those words. That's not what I meant!"

Tasha nods and then turns her back, walking to her desk.

"Bella," Julie whispers, "this is bad. I mean, *really* bad. You say that—" Julie picks the paper up and peers at it, "—'Nobody at *Enchanté* knows the meaning of the word 'work.' How can you, when you've grown up summering in St. Tropez and skiing in Val d'Isere? It's not reality over there.'"

Somehow it didn't seem that bad when Maddie and I were giggling about everything over a bottle of Stag's Leap.

"I mean, holy crap," Julie continues. "Katharine is going to kill you, Bella. *Kill you.* You should talk to Larissa about this."

"Have you seen her? Does she know?"

"She's been out all morning. Maybe she went shopping . . . ?" Julie offers lamely.

I sit down at my desk, my heart pounding. This is not happening. I have ruined my life.

Maybe it will all blow over! Maybe nobody else read today's issue of the *Post*! You always hear stories about people buying up all the copies of papers and dumping them. Can I do that? Is there enough time for me to stop at every newsstand in the area and buy up every issue? They're a quarter each. It would only cost a few hundred bucks, right? I sit at my desk and fret.

My phone rings and I don't recognize the number, so I let it go to voice mail, listening to the message as soon as the red light starts blinking.

"Bella? This is Maddie Daniels. Listen to me, I am so sorry about today's article. You have to believe me—I didn't write half of it. I wrote something fun and gossipy, but not *that*. The draft I submitted to my editor is completely different from what ended up being printed. I have no idea what happened. I submitted the transcript of the interview, too, and I guess that's where all the quotes came from, but my editors must have changed it later . . . listen. Please call me and let me know you're okay and . . . *uh* . . . that you're not in trouble at work or anything. Okay? My number is 212-555-0823. Thanks. This is Maddie Daniels from the *Post*. Bye."

What a snake! My hands start shaking and I feel the pressure building behind my temples. I'm considering calling her back to yell, or cry, or maybe just have a nervous breakdown, when I hear Larissa's voice behind me.

"Bella," she says quietly. "Can you come into my office, please?"

She has a tone. I don't know this tone. I don't like this tone.

I tiptoe into her office and take a seat in the chair facing Larissa's desk. She doesn't sit down.

"Babes . . ." Larissa's voice falters as she stands stiffly in the doorway. "This is . . . I assume you know why we're in here."

"Yes," I say in a small voice. "The *Post* article."

Larissa paces, picking up and squeezing a L'Artisan Parfumeur sachet that she keeps on her desk. As she flicks her long black hair behind her shoulders, I stare at her outfit, a slinky silver minidress covered by a shrunken white Jil Sander oxford shirt and black Comme des Garçons duster, plus four-inch Christian Louboutin stilettos, feeling as though I'm in a time warp. When I came to Larissa eight years ago as her assistant, I was terrified of her—you never knew whether she'd hug you and bring you little presents from Hermès or Fauchon just because it was Tuesday, or scream for you to remove your useless, incompetent ass from her office before she had you fired. Her divaness is as legendary as the fact that, like her doppelgänger Demi Moore, she actually appears to get *younger* with every passing year—and has such a bad memory that if information doesn't pertain to beauty, fashion, restaurants, or men, she'll only retain it for five minutes. Julie tiptoes around the office on eggshells, bearing the brunt of her moods. Over the years, I've come to regard Larissa as my family—like a slightly unbalanced older sister who gives killer advice and will gladly set you up with all her hot male friends, but who'll also ruin Thanksgiving dinner by throwing the turkey against the wall and making out with your boyfriend if she doesn't take her lithium. I feel our history collapsing upon itself—right now, I'm not her trusted right-hand woman, but an idiotic neophyte who must be put in place. It's like I'm twenty-one all over again.

I feel a stabbing pain in my chest. "Riss, be straight with me. How bad is it?"

She looks directly at me. "It's fatal. I had to stop Katharine from storming over and firing you herself." She screws her face into an ugly pout, then throws the sachet back on the desk. "Goddamn it, Bella. Why?"

"I don't know! It just came out! I didn't mean anything negative, I swear. We were chatting and everything was fine, but then Delilah came in and I started downing the wine— you know how she upsets me!—and I guess I just . . . spilled everything. Larissa, I honestly don't remember saying half of it."

"Delilah?" she spits. "Because you got *drunk*? No excuse. *No* excuse."

"I'm sorry," I say shakily, taking a deep breath and trying to steady my voice to sound professional. "I don't feel like that. You *know* I don't feel like that. I love *Enchanté*. I'm honored to work here."

"Do you? Are you? I know Grace called you about the *Catwalk* job. And these past couple of months . . . I love you like my family, but this poison . . . Jesus—talk about biting the hand that feeds you. You could have at least let me *know*."

"But I don't feel like that! Larissa, I think the world of you! There's no better magazine than *Enchanté*. Why wouldn't I love it here?"

She shrugs angrily. "I know how it goes—*Enchanté*'s tough. Sometimes it downright sucks. The editors are spoiled. We get too much free stuff. Most of these girls have never worked a real day in their lives. But to trash our industry like that in the *New York Post,* of all places? Un-bloody-believable. I expected so much more from you. From *you*."

"Larissa," I plead, my heart racing, "There is no excuse, but I am sorry from the bottom of my heart. I shouldn't have said anything, I realize that. I swear to God, next time I will keep my lips utterly zipped and won't say anything that's even remotely along the lines of a complaint to a reporter, ever. At all. Please."

"Babes, my hands are tied. Katharine wants you gone by the end of the day. She doesn't want to see your face before you leave."

I can't speak. I sit dumbly, staring at Larissa as if I can force her to change her mind with my eyes.

"I'm sorry, doll, I really am," she says, her tone softening. "Katharine is livid. She won't budge. I tried."

"Okay," I whisper, repeating stupidly. "I'm sorry."

"So am I."

Chapter 3

"Bella, open the door," Emily commands, standing in the hallway separating our rooms.

"It's open," I call dully, lying face-up on my bed as I scan the corners of my ceiling, noticing for the first time what a shoddy paint job I'd done months prior. Thin slits of white are still visible a full half inch below the ceiling, where the wall should be a solid shade of sky blue.

Emily enters, leaning in the doorway and crossing her arms. She slowly surveys the mess in my room and I can only imagine what a catastrophe it must appear: empty Ben & Jerry's New York Super Fudge Chunk ice-cream carton on my chestnut-colored antique nightstand, next to an open bottle of shiraz and Emily's own half-used bottle of Xanax that she'd "passed on" to me last week when she realized that I wasn't sleeping; sample-sale-and-eBay-acquired Jimmy Choos and Christian Louboutins sprinkled across the floor at random, next to piles of Theory and Tocca dresses and Nanette Lepore blazers—the result of an impromptu fashion show at 3:00 this morning while listening to the Killers on my iPod; six Harry Potter books at the foot of my bed, with *Goblet of Fire* resting unopened on my lap; a stack of *Enchanté*s in the middle of the room, alternately read and torn up.

"Are you trying to make some sort of statement?" she asks

dryly. "Or have you just been reading *Nervous Breakdowns for Dummies?*"

"See that corner?" I ignore her, pointing at the ceiling above my closet. "Have you ever noticed the big patch of white there? I don't know why, but I've never noticed it before."

"Bella, who fucking cares about your ceiling? You have to leave your room at some point. This is not okay. You officially passed 'wallowing' about ten days ago. I think we've entered the realm of 'cliché.'"

When I met Emily in Paris during our junior year abroad, we'd both broken up with college boyfriends in order to be single in the city of love. Ten minutes after meeting her while simultaneously trying to catch the bartender's attention at the expat haunt The Frog and Princess, I knew we'd be friends for life. Emily's mom, Josie Tyler, is a famous fashion designer (she practically invented luxe, over-the-top logo worshipping in the early '80s) who took over the reins at Avignon about ten years ago and turned it from a luggage and leather outfit into the hottest label this side of Louis Vuitton. I was hypnotized by Emily's no bullshit, tell-it-like-it-is demeanor, effortless sense of style and impossible-to-get handbag with a six-month waiting list (an Avignon bag, natch); she claims she was mesmerized by my shiny hair, perfect-but-not-too-heavy makeup, and the Midwestern-milkmaid look of terror on my face. We instantly became best friends, and Emily's acted as my secret guidebook to side-stepping social landmines ever since, having learned a thing or two through her younger sister Gabrielle, who's always in the papers as a girl-about-town and seems to be majoring at the Paris Hilton School of Seducing the Paparazzi. Needless to say, Emily's family is ridiculously wealthy. She's a New York City girl through and through, but after her parents' divorce, her polo-playing English father moved back to the

Sussex countryside, and Josie acquired apartments in New York and London, plus a house in Montecito down the hill from Oprah. Emily is remarkably down-to-earth and shuns her family's wealth and high-profile status—except on the rare occasions when it suits her, since the patina of fame cocooning her family has turned her into a minor celebrity herself. She's been known to trot out the C-list wattage to get into restaurants on dates, and goes skiing with Josie and Gabrielle every winter in Verbier on the slopes of Mont Fort . . . although she *claims* it's all a huge drag. I think Emily sometimes goes a little overboard in her attempts to piss off her mom, though, like the phase when she only wore clothing from Target (of course, that backfired after Josie suggested to the CEO that Tar-jay start partnering with famous designers; Josie's Target collection is still their best-selling one, to Emily's dismay) and the fact that she's getting her masters in psychology at Columbia, refusing to embrace her fashion talent, despite increasingly styling Gabrielle for almost every event she attends. Lucky for me, Emily's mom sends her boxes of samples at the beginning and end of every season—which Emily usually refuses to wear—and so the pieces make their way into my closet, beefing up my sample-sale-purchased DVF and Nanette Lepore staples. If only clothes were happiness.

I glare at her. "I don't feel like talking right now."

She moves into the room and sits on the edge of my bed, crossing her thin legs. "I know you don't want to talk about it. *I* don't want to talk about it. Josie is harassing me nonstop and Gabrielle went on a bender last night and punched some idiot photographer in the face and now he's suing her. It's all over Perez Hilton and TMZ. But that's what happens. Shit. And we deal. And you're my best friend, not to mention, much more importantly, my roommate, so if you spend one more day moping around your room to only come out after midnight and raid the fridge for ice cream like some pathetic lovelorn fifteen-year-old whose boyfriend has just dumped her, *I'm* going to have a nervous breakdown. So we're going to talk about this right now, damn it. My nerves can't fucking take it."

I sit up, cracking a smile. "Have you been practicing that speech in your mirror?"

"For the past twenty minutes," she deadpans.

"And I'm supposed to make you feel better now?"

"Might be nice! For once! Can we have one day where I'm the one with the life-altering crisis? Please?"

I sigh. "How can I help you? Talk to me."

"You can help by dealing with everything, for starters. What are you doing for money? Have you sent your résumé anywhere? Are you going to start freelancing? What's your plan?"

"You sound like my mother." She's left at least ten messages on my phone in the past two weeks.

"Don't be like that. I'm trying to help." She picks up *Goblet of Fire* and turns it over in her hands, giving me an incredulous look. "Harry Potter?"

"They're classics!" I say defensively. "You don't know what you're missing."

She wrinkles her nose doubtfully. "Maybe." Emily was an English major at Brown.

"Don't be like that. I've read just as much literature as you, you snob. Harry is epic. He's timeless. The narrative arc is astounding—just last night I finished rereading *Order of the Phoenix* and I realized that J. K. Rowling was referencing things that happened in book—"

"You win," Emily says forcefully, holding her hands up in surrender. "Rowling is the Dickens of our time, I get it. I don't get what you're accomplishing by holing up in your room, though. Let me take you out and buy you a drink. I'll

buy you an entire magnum of champagne, if it'll motivate you
to rejoin the real world."

"You just want an excuse to drink Veuve, you lush," I tease,
hoping some forced levity will wrench me out of my mood. It
doesn't work. I lay back down, hugging my knees to my chest.
"I don't feel up to it. After what happened, I have no excuse
to drink as long as I live."

"God, could you be a bigger drama queen? It's not like you
downed a bottle of tequila and slept with an entire football
team."

I look at her suspiciously. "You were awfully quick with
that example . . ."

"Don't even go there."

I love Emily. I know she hates discussing her emotions, so
this conversation must have required tremendous effort on
her part. "I know you're trying to help, and I really appreciate
it. I do. But I've *ruined my life*. Don't you get it? I've black-
balled myself from an entire industry, and I'm only twenty-
eight."

"Well, yeah. Okay. So when you screw up, you do it big-
time. Look on the bright side. It's quite impressive. You are
the *champion* of personal disasters! Nobody can take that
away from you." She grins and crosses her eyes at me, then
starts bouncing on her knees on the bed, her choppy dark
blonde hair flopping around her narrow shoulders. "Enough!
You're making me crazy and I'm not willing to let you linger
in this funk for one minute longer! I won't take no for an
answer. We don't even have to discuss the job thing. I'll wait
until tomorrow to harass you about it." Without waiting for
a response, she walks to my closet and opens the door, picking out a black Avignon dress. "Put this on. It's sexy and it'll
make you feel better."

I open my mouth to protest and she puts her hand up
again. "Let me repeat myself: *I won't take no for an answer.*

Now, let's go out and get hammered. It's for your own good."

My mom calls about seventy-five times over the course of the next week, but doesn't leave any messages. I know she's worrying because I haven't called since being fired and is hoping to offer me reassurance. A more supportive mother doesn't exist in the world, but I simply can't face up to talking with her, mostly because I'm too scared to hear my not-quite-as-supportive father's opinion. Instead my older sister Susan, an accountant in Cleveland, leaves three messages on my cell phone, each with increasing urgency.

"Hi. It's Suze. Mom told me what happened. I'm so sorry, Izzie-bear. Don't beat yourself up about it, but take it as a lesson. Next time you feel the urge to spill secrets about your industry, remember you can't bite the hand that—" *Delete.*

"Bel, it's Suze. None of us have heard from you in weeks. Mom is practically hysterical. What are you going to do? Are you coming home to Ohio? If you need a place to stay, you can move in with me. Harold won't mind, I'm sure. It'll be fun—you can help me plan the wedding, and I'd be delighted to have you here. The most important thing is that you're with family and we're all behind you. Dad and I were talking, and he brought up that he *did* tell you that New York is not the best—" *Delete.*

"I know what you're doing. You're sitting on the couch, crying into a pint of ice cream and watching bad movies on TV. Now is not the time for self-pity. You need to be putting your résumé out there, going on interviews, getting out of the house and starting your life again. Have you given any thought to moving back home to Clevel—" *Delete.*

After four and a half weeks of self-imposed exile and literally hundreds of missed calls—though the only industry person who calls is Joss, I note bitterly—I get a message on my cell phone from Larissa.

"Hi, Bella . . . it's Larissa. I've been thinking about you, darling. You don't hate me, do you? If you're planning to do something stupid like downing a bottle of painkillers, I'll *murder* you. Listen, babes, we can't let a decade of friendship, give or take, go down the tubes because of your temporary insanity. Call me, doll. I might have another beauty job for you."

I delete the message and stare at the phone in my hand as if it's a bomb. Larissa has a job for me? Is this a joke? I'm not surprised that she called—she can't hold a grudge for long, and I *was* her faithful right-hand woman for eight years—but I can't possibly imagine which magazine would be desperate enough to touch me now. Page Six ran an item the day after I was fired, describing how I'd broken down in tears and had been given an hour to pack up my desk before security guards came to escort me from the Bonneau-Martray building. An anonymous editor was quoted as saying I'd never be hired in beauty again. Sure, people in this industry have a short attention span, but it's been less than a month! I weigh the pros (I'll have a salary again, not to mention something to do with my days other than watch E! and MTV) and cons (facing my former colleagues at beauty events after being publicly humiliated, and being forced to do something with my days other than watch E! and MTV), and my curiosity gets the better of me. There's an open position at *Velvet*, but *Velvet* is such a wasteland—sure, it's the number four women's magazine, but it's so literal and boring. Plus, I'd be forced to work alongside Delilah. I'd rather get a job as a garbagewoman.

I dial Larissa's number. "Riss?"

"Babes! I'm *so* happy you called. How *are* you? Nobody's seen you for weeks—I thought you might go to Pamplona or Harajuku this weekend, to make an appearance, at least."

"I couldn't face the idea of seeing anybody," I admit.

"Emily dragged me to some dive in the East Village a couple of nights ago. I figured I'd be safe there."

"How *ghastly*. Why *does* Emily insist on going to those disgusting rat holes? She should be at Beatrice Inn. It's her birthright."

"Yes, well . . ."

"Surviving all right?" she interrupts. "You have food and water? Do you need money? Should I messenger over something from Barneys to cheer you up?"

"I'm not living on the streets, Riss—at least not yet," I say wryly. "Although if you want to send over a beauty care package, I won't complain. I'm feeling completely out of touch."

"That's why I called. I've pleaded with Katharine to take you back, but she's still very upset, as you can imagine." Katharine never seemed to like me much. Then again, Delilah was one of the few girls in the office she ever *did* like—so much for superiors not taking sides.

"Yes," I say quietly. "I can imagine."

"You know how this industry is. Of course you do, that's what got you into trouble in the first place!" she chuckles before continuing. "Anyhow, you'll understand that some of the magazines of *Enchanté*'s caliber are slightly . . . reluctant . . . to touch you right now."

"Of course," I say, frowning.

"I talked to my friend Rania Hassani over at *Womanly World*. We worked together a billion years ago and she's one of the brightest, most talented women in the industry."

"*Mmm.*" Why is she talking about *Womanly World*? My mother reads *Womanly World*. My *grandmother* reads *Womanly World*.

"They need a new beauty editor. Their old one just left and Frances McCabe, who's their current beauty director, is more of a fashion chick. She was one of the most important fashion directors in the industry thirty years ago. She's quite hip, actually . . . you know, in a more . . . *mature* fashion . . ."

"*Womanly World*? It's for suburbanites. They don't even go to the shows." I try, very unsuccessfully, to keep the displeasure from seeping into my voice.

I hear Larissa stifling a sigh on the other end of the phone. "I know it's not exactly *Vogue*, doll, but you need to take what you can get. You don't want to have to go work in . . . I don't know . . . advertising or public relations, do you? You couldn't even *get* a job in PR—no magazine would deal with you!"

Right though she is, the truth still hurts. I remember just weeks ago, when I was secretly bemoaning my good fortune at *Enchanté*, and I think about how I'd now do anything to go back. Funny how making an ass of yourself and getting brutally fired makes you appreciate your old job. "But what would I do at *Womanly World*? I don't know anything about that market. I've spent the last eight years at a fashion magazine. *The* fashion magazine."

"Didn't you grow up in the Midwest? I'm sure it'll come back to you in a flash! Frances wants to focus more on fashion than beauty, so you'll have some autonomy, and it'd be a good way for you to lay low for six or nine months, let this scandal blow over, and then apply for a better job in the winter. Think about it, Bella. No way in hell could you get any freelance work. It's the right move. I wouldn't steer you wrong." I've never heard Larissa sound so straightforward.

If I don't want to starve and be forced to waitress in Ohio for a year until everybody forgets about this, I'm going to have to take a low-profile job. But *Womanly World*? My scorn makes me feel guilty—I should be thrilled. Dear God, I've become the very snob I used to make fun of.

"Well," I ask doubtfully, "why is *Womanly World* willing to hire me? Did they hear about what happened?"

"To be sure, but like I said, Rania's an old friend of mine. We talked on the phone yesterday, and I mentioned your sitch. She's familiar with your column and is trying to bring the magazine a younger readership. She thinks your voice is exactly the shot of adrenaline it needs."

"Be honest. Is this my best bet?"

"Babes, you're a star, but the way you stepped on everyone's toes . . . this is the best offer you'll get, bar none. I'd take it."

Larissa arranges an interview for me the following week with Rania. I have no idea what to expect. On the one hand, Rania came to *Womanly World* from *Chic,* which leads the pack of cool, young magazines. On the other hand, Rania's been at *Womanly World* for almost two years now. Any snobbery over *Womanly World*'s position in the magazine hierarchy aside, I can't help feeling suspicious about a magazine that would voluntarily want to hire me. Aren't I damaged goods? So isn't this proof that *Womanly World* must be *really desperate*? When I'm using my own status as a social pariah against them, you know it's bad.

On the subway heading to the *Womanly World* offices, I surreptitiously pull their latest issue out of my bag; Diane Sawyer graces the cover. I feel ashamed to realize I hope nobody sees me reading it. But who cares, right? Not me. A job is a job. *Womanly World* has about fifteen times the readers that *Enchanté* does. Surely that should count for something. *Yes, but it's all the* wrong *readers*, a tiny voice whispers in my head. *Shut up! Stop being such a snob! You practically ruined your career, you moron—now you have to take what you can get.*

I open the magazine, sheepishly folding the cover back as I glance around the crowded subway car. Of course, everybody is too focused on themselves and their own problems to pay me the slightest bit of attention. Mental note: people are *not* always staring at you, Bella. I flip to the editor's page and study Rania's photo. She looks Arab, or maybe Indian, with light caramel-colored skin, glossy dark hair cascading down her back, accented by toffee-colored highlights, and almond-shaped green eyes. She's gorgeous, and not what I pictured the editor of the most mainstream, all-American, boring magazine in the nation to look like. I wonder if my mother knows anything about her. She subscribed to *Womanly World* years ago and used to read it fanatically, like all the women in our neighborhood, but since moving to New York, I've lost track of her magazine tastes.

I get off the J train and wander around midtown for a few minutes, walking back and forth up Third Avenue searching for the address. Finally, I realize that the entrance is located on a side street and I enter the Beckwith Media building, a nondescript dark-glass tower that's exactly the same height as all the buildings surrounding it. It's a far cry from the "Look at me!" facade of the flashy chrome, glass, and neon Bonneau-Martray tower in Times Square.

I sign in at reception and head up to the fifteenth floor, checking in with the receptionist and then settling on a couch to calm my nerves. I wonder what Rania is like. She won't be mean to me, will she? She agreed to this interview, so surely she wants to meet with me. But what if she doesn't? What if it's all a horrible mistake and she's sitting at her desk right now preparing to tell me off for daring to sully her office with my horrible, magazine-exposing ways? Oh God, I don't think my nerves can take more stress.

"Bella Hunter?"

I snap to attention. A cute young girl is standing in front of me, her curly brown hair pulled back in a ponytail. On the whole, her outfit is pretty boring—black pants, nondescript blue button-down shirt—but her shoes are adorable: Marc by

Marc, from two seasons ago. Emily has them in four colors—
thanks to a shipment from her mother—although she never
wears them, preferring her Converse sneakers and beat-up
ballet flats for classes. I *love* those shoes.

"That's me," I say, standing up and shaking her hand.

"I'm Lauren, Rania's assistant. I hope you weren't waiting
for long."

"Oh no, not at all." Well, at least it's a relief to know that
Rania's expecting me. So, there will *probably* be no public humiliation at her hands today. Then again, the meeting hasn't
started yet. I don't want to jinx myself—with my track record,
so much could go wrong.

We walk down the narrow hallway. The walls are painted
a cheerful yellow color, plants are draped off cubicles and
nestled in corners, and desks look cozily lived in. Joaquin
Mouret, the editorial director of Bonneau-Martray, had a
cleanliness fetish, so weekly inspections were carried out on
every floor to make sure that each magazine adhered to his
minimalist aspect. There, the dark blue, green, and purple
walls had no hangings on them, only a neon strip of bright
white panel lighting along the edge of the ceiling, giving the
walls an eerie, futuristic glow. You got used to it eventually,
but when I'd first started, I felt like I was working on a space-
ship. Beckwith has a simple, homey feeling, on the other
hand, as though you might stumble upon a bake sale if you
took a wrong turn.

"Here we go," she says, gesturing to an open door. I enter
a huge office and see Rania Hassani sitting at the end of the
room, dwarfed by a massive oak desk.

"Hello, there!" she says warmly, standing up and walking toward me, hand outstretched. "You must be Bella. I'm
Rania." As we shake hands, I size her up. She can't be taller
than five three—I tower over her by at least six inches! Her
skin is creamy, either the product of excellent genes or a me-

ticulous beauty regimen, and I peg her as late-thirties—much younger than the average editor in chief.

"Hello, Rania, it's wonderful to meet you," I say, putting on the "professional" voice.

"Likewise! How have you been holding up? I understand you've had a rough couple of weeks."

"That's true," I say cautiously. "Larissa told me you know . . . what happened?"

"I read the article, if that's what you mean. I must say— you made quite a splash. Not politically correct, but honest. Women's magazine editors don't like having the cover blown on the industry. It makes them nervous that all the perks will dry up."

She laughs at the shocked expression on my face. "*Shh*. Let's keep it between us. No need for me to end up in the *Post,* too."

I smile tentatively and clear my throat. "My lips are sealed."

She sits up straight and shuffles some papers on her desk. "I've known Larissa for years and she's always spoken highly of you."

"Oh! That's nice. We had a great relationship."

"It says a lot about you that she called me recommending you for this position, even after 'the article,'" she says dramatically, smiling as she curls her fingers in air quotes. "I've read your column. It's very good."

"Thank you," I say sincerely. "I appreciate it. I love writing it . . . or, *er, loved* writing it, I guess."

"How long were you at *Enchanté*?"

"About eight years."

She looks at a piece of paper on her desk. I follow her gaze and realize that it's my résumé, which I e-mailed to her assistant at Larissa's request. I'd had to update it first, something I hadn't done since college.

"Have you met Frances, our beauty director?"

"Technically, no, although I've seen her before at beauty events. She seems very nice." This is code for: she seems boring and uptight.

"She's great. She might initially come across as prickly, but, between us, she's one of my favorite people in the office. It's important to find somebody that can provide Frances with the support she needs for the beauty pages—they've been lacking over the past year. Are you familiar with the magazine?"

I'm tempted to fib that I absolutely *adore Womanly World*, but Rania doesn't seem the type to be fooled by empty flattery. "To be honest, not really. It was always in my house when I was growing up. My mother had a subscription, my friends' moms all read it, that sort of thing, but I generally read magazines that are more . . ." I struggle for an inoffensive word, " . . . *appropriate* for my age. I like *Catwalk, Chic, Lucky, Vogue, Glamour, Flash* . . . magazines like that." I look at Rania carefully, half expecting her to pound her fists on the table in fury and banish me from her office. Instead, she laughs.

"No, I wouldn't peg you as one of our readers! You're a twentysomething girl in New York City, trendy, no kids, no husband, probably ordering takeout every night of the week. *Womanly World* doesn't appeal to you. Right?"

"Right," I say hesitantly.

"That's why you're here now. You probably know, I used to be the editor in chief of *Chic*. I'm not daft—*Womanly World* isn't as cool as *Chic,* or, even, hell, *Redbook* or *O*. It's still one of the most popular magazines in the country, though, not to mention among the oldest, and it *is* a national icon. Right now it's about youth; the advertisers are wetting themselves over the eighteen to thirty-fours, which isn't in sync with us. So, rather than hiring a beauty editor to keep cranking out pages like what we've got now, I want somebody to shake up our beauty pages, make them younger. I want to make our advertisers take notice." She shrugs. "We need more beauty money, to put it simply."

"I see," I nod. "That makes me feel better about being here!" I realize that this might sound rude and I hurry to explain, ". . . because I was worried that I had nothing to offer the magazine. I don't really know very much about the older market, unless we're talking plastic surgery procedures and expensive dermatological lines."

"Our readers won't be getting face lifts or spending two hundred dollars on antiwrinkle creams, but they *are* curious about Botox, and they'll be interested in the latest antiaging technology and lingo. They're smart, and I don't want to talk down to them just because they can't necessarily afford a week at a spa or the full line of La Mer products. I know you have a serious background because of your scientific articles at *Enchanté,* and I know that you're used to writing for a much younger reader. I think these are both strengths, and could be hugely valuable assets for our beauty pages."

"What does the position entail, exactly?" As if it matters. If they hire me, I'm taking it.

"It'll be similar to your work at *Enchanté,* but for a different audience. I loved your beauty column, so I'd like to introduce that format here, in your voice, tailored to the *Womanly World* reader. They won't relate to the five-hundred-dollar haircuts, et cetera, but experiments like dyeing your hair at home, seeking the perfect shade of foundation, going undercover at department stores, interviews with *Womanly World*-relevant celebrities—they'd all fit in perfectly with our coverage and our reader."

"I'd still be able to write the column?"

"Absolutely. In a modified format."

"Great," I say, nodding. It's not as good as if I was still at *Enchanté,* but at least I can keep writing something with my name on it. *It'll just have the* Womanly World *name attached,* I think, cringing.

Maybe, if I'm really lucky, it'll almost be like I never even got fired. Then I'll wow everybody with my new column at *Womanly World,* and it'll be so popular that the circulation will go through the roof. *Would it be possible to single-handedly reinvigorate the magazine?* I muse. Why not? My column was the most widely read page at *Enchanté.* No reason it can't be the same here! Larissa will be so impressed with what I've done at *Womanly World* that she'll convince Katharine to hire me back in my old job—with a raise! No—with a title change. With both! Or maybe Katharine will call me back herself. With all the great publicity *Womanly World* will get from having the former top writer from *Enchanté,* surely Katharine will feel remorse at letting me go.

Dream on, idiot. You're stuck here.

Chapter 4

At 8:30 the following Monday morning, I'm on the J train, headed to my new job as beauty editor of *Womanly World* magazine. When I called my mother over the weekend to tell her the news, she was both excited ("Congratulations, honey! I love *Womanly World*! It's my favorite magazine! The baking tips are super-duper") and dejected ("So, I guess this means you're not coming home until Suze and Harold's wedding in June?").

I walk up to the reception desk and show my ID, then receive a guest pass. "Twelfth floor," the guard says, pointing at the elevator bank.

A woman in khaki pants and a stiff button-down shirt walks into the elevator, Starbucks in hand. She's carrying a bag that says Beckwith Media and smiles at me, probably seeing my guest pass and nervous, deer-in-the-headlights look. I'll admit that I was happy when Rania called the following day and officially offered me the job, but was quickly dismayed to learn it was for less salary, and with only the title of "beauty editor," not even "senior beauty editor" or "deputy beauty director." Beggars can't be choosers, of course, and a job is a job, but I'm acutely aware of what a huge step down on the totem pole of Magazine Cool I've taken. I have no choice but to remain positive. Otherwise, I'll kill myself.

"First day?"

"Yes."

"What magazine will you be working at?"

"At *Womanly World*."

"Oh, splendid! I'm Lorelai, by the way."

"Bella," I say, shaking her hand.

I feel self-conscious about my outfit and can't stop compulsively smoothing my skirt, which is a half size too small and keeps riding up—a month straight of eating ice cream and shunning the gym has caught up with me in a big way. I've chosen a "look how chic and sophisticated our new girl is" ensemble, remembering how important it had been to look the part right off the bat at *Enchanté*: cream knee-length Burberry spring jacket, kelly green round-toe three-inch Marc Jacobs platforms, a tight black knee-length Jil Sander skirt and a cream lace-and-satin Peter Pan–collar Stella McCartney shirt with a Cosabella camisole underneath. I'm carrying Emily's tan Birkin. Out of the corner of my eye, I see the woman openly staring at my outfit.

"Let me guess . . . Bonneau-Martray?"

"How did you know?"

She smiles gently. "You look like a runway model. People at Beckwith tend to dress a little more comfortably." She wiggles her tan loafers. "I wish I could wear heels, but I'd never last more than three minutes in them!"

"My shoes are *very* comfortable," I lie, ignoring the pinching in my toes and the prickling under the ball of my foot. "I could probably run a mile in these! Marc Jacobs, very well made."

"If you say so, dear," she says doubtfully as the elevator stops on twelve. "Take a left and then follow the corridor to the end of the hallway. You'll see the door for HR there. Good luck, Bella! I know you'll have a wonderful first day!"

I step out of the elevator and walk down the hallway, which is decorated with pictures of a square, flat building in a tree-less area. I peer at one of the captions. It reads "Beckwith Media Home Offices, Kansas City, Kansas, 2003." Oh God, the home offices of Beckwith are in *Kansas*? Toto, we're home.

I tell the receptionist that today is my first day and she kindly asks me to take a seat, pointing to a love seat in front of a wooden coffee table. Magazines are spread out across the table, all published by Beckwith, no doubt. This is customary when you walk into magazine HR offices. It's a chance for them to say, "Look at all of the wonderful magazines we publish! Aren't we just great? Yay for us!" But unlike at Bonneau-Martray, where the featured magazines are *Enchanté, Chic, Beauty, Catwalk, Physically Fit, Flash, L'Homme, Looking Glass,* and *The Apple*—basically any and all of the most popular magazines in the country—the Beckwith "showcase" consists of a bunch of titles I've never heard of, let alone seen on a magazine rack: *Comfortable Living, Toddler, MidWest, Gardener's World, Dig!, American Pottery Life, Sewing Circle* and, of course, *Womanly World.*

I pick the magazine that looks the least boring—*Comfortable Living*—and flip through it. It features page after page of furniture ads, tips on how to go antiquing, ideas for sprucing up your new garden, and suggestions on how to pick out the best duvet. The content is mind-numbingly boring, but I have to admit that the photos are pretty. One of the spreads, entitled "Back to the Estate," features a bedroom painted in the exact same shade of creamy, faded yellow that I've been thinking about using to redo my own room. I make a mental note to rip this page out later and take it with me to Home Depot.

"Hello, are you Bella?" A short, bowlegged woman wearing a shapeless maroon skirt suit and black stockings stands in front of me, holding a file. Her haircut is atrocious—a dishwater blond bob with severe bangs that looks straight out of 1985. Would that I could take her by the hand, put her in a cab, and send her to see Ted Gibson at his salon, pronto.

I stand up and extend my hand. "Hi, yes, that's me. Bella Hunter."

"Great to meet you. Margie Sullivan, head of Human Resources here at Beckwith. Welcome!"

"Thanks, Margie," I say awkwardly. "It's a pleasure to be here." This is partially true. It's a pleasure to have a job again.

Margie turns and starts walking down the hallway, motioning for me to follow her. "We have a few papers that we need you to sign before we get started. Standard stuff: tax forms, insurance forms, notification in event of emergency forms. You'll be all formed-out by the time you head upstairs!" she chuckles, rifling through the papers in her hands. "So, you were at *Enchanté* for, let's see, eight years? My, that's certainly a long time nowadays!"

"*Er* . . . yes, well . . . I had a wonderful time there," I say quickly, not wanting to go into the details of why I left. Margie won't know the backstory, will she? She doesn't seem like the type who even knows what Page Six is. "But all good things must come to an end, right?"

"Exactly! Bonneau-Martray's loss is our gain, *mmm?*"

We spend thirty minutes going through forms and signing papers until Margie is finally satisfied that I have completed all of the necessary information. She gives me directions to the fifteenth floor, as well as a thick folder that says "Welcome to Beckwith! It's a pleasure to have you as a new employee!" on the front. I walk upstairs, unsure of what to expect from my new colleagues. Rania's chic, so surely they're not *all* going to be as dowdy as Margie. It definitely can't be as scary as my first day at *Enchanté*—Amazonian wannabe-supermodel editors stomping around everywhere in conceptual outfits with their cheekbones protruding—but I still worry about sticking out. What will I possibly have in common with any of these people? I'm torn between a desire to run from the building, get under the covers, and watch endless reruns of *The O.C.*—Adam Brody . . . *yum*—and the knowledge that if I screw this up, it's back home for me. No way will I be able to get another magazine job in New York if I fail here. Everything hinges upon my success at *Womanly World. Just a few months and then—God willing—you can go back to a real magazine*, I tell myself.

An hour later, I've been escorted around by Tammy, the office manager, and introduced to so many smiling faces that I think my lips might fall off from mimicking them. Within five minutes, I realize that I am the only person wearing high heels. Even the younger girls who are wearing fashionable but lower-priced labels, like Rania's assistant, are in flats or sandals.

Tammy finally shows me to my desk and wishes me good luck, telling me to stop by at any time if I have questions. I thank her and then breathe a sigh of relief—finally alone. I need some time to gather myself. I haven't officially met my new boss, Frances, although I have seen her out and about at events on occasion. She always seems so . . . boring. Maybe she's one of those types that *looks* dull, but is actually the life of the party once you get to know them.

I start decorating my desk with the few things I've thrown in my bag: a photo of me, Emily, Joss, and Nick; my desk calendar; pens; and a small Diptyque candle in the Baies flavor. When I left *Enchanté*, I messengered a box of my things home—on the magazine's dime, of course—then re-sent the box here on Friday afternoon, so everything would be waiting for me. The box must be in the beauty closet. Where could it be?

I wander around the area surrounding my cubicle, marveling at the difference between this building and Bonneau-Martray. The walls are painted a soft yellow color with trim at the top, and black-and-white framed photos are placed at intervals throughout the hallways. I peer at one that's across the hall from my desk: it's a photo of a petite woman in her sixties or seventies carrying a notebook and pen and it reads, "Essie Michaels: The Mother of Womanly World." *Who?* I think. Several of the cubicles in my vicinity boast potted plants on top of their partitions, and as I walk down the hallway away from my desk, I spy one of those "Success and Determination" posters that I used to see at the mall in Cleveland. Who *are* these people? Is this a magazine or an insurance office?

There's a woman in one of the cubicles that I didn't meet during Tammy's office tour, so I decide to kill two birds with one stone: I'll introduce myself and also ask her if she knows where the beauty closet is. I pick up a key clearly labeled "Beauty Closet" sitting next to my computer and walk over.

"Excuse me?" I say. "We haven't met yet. I'm Bella Hunter, the new beauty editor."

"Hi, Bella! I'm Vivian Lewis, the relationship columnist. It's nice to meet you!"

"Likewise," I say politely, giving her a quick once-over. She's pretty, with shoulder-length dark-blond hair, light blue eyes, and a rosy complexion. Vivian has a pleasant look, but it's marred by frown lines and deep nasolabial folds, making me think that she could be about forty-five years old. Dr. Gross could do *wonders* on her with a little Botox and Restylane! When she was my age, Vivian must have been a knockout. Unfortunately, she also seems to have fallen prey to the *Womanly World* dressing curse: her outfit is something I wouldn't let my grandmother out of the house wearing.

"So, where did you come from?"

"I'm sorry? Do you mean which magazine, or originally . . . ?"

"Which magazine? You're obviously a New Yorker in an expensive getup like that!" Vivian has a thick accent—one of the islands. Staten? Long?

I look down, feeling self-conscious about my outfit again. "What do you mean?"

"I'm not saying anything negative about your outfit! But you look like you stepped off the pages of a fashion magazine. People around here don't put that much care and thought— or money—into their outfits." She gestures at herself. "As you can see."

"That's the second time in two hours somebody's told me I look like I came from a fashion magazine. That's sort of ironic, being *at* a fashion magazine!"

"Well, *Womanly World* is hardly a fashion magazine, dearie. Maybe way back when, but now . . ." Vivian's voice trails off as she throws her hands up in the air. "You have to embrace what you are! No use in pretending to be something you're not!" She takes a sip from a mug on her desk. "Have you met Rania yet?"

"I met her recently, when I interviewed, but I haven't seen her today."

"Did she explain 'the mission' to you?"

"The mission?"

"She's trying to remake *Womanly World*. She wants to make it more like *Chic,* but for older women. We'll never be one of those Bonneau-Martray magazines, but *Womanly World* hasn't been so profitable in the past few years, and with so many magazines closing up shop . . ." She shakes her head. "We need a revamp desperately."

"Or . . . what?" I ask.

"Or else we're all gonna have to look for new jobs! Or else you'd better have a rich daddy to support you!" she laughs.

She scrutinizes my outfit again, smiling at me warmly. "You must get told about seven times a day how beautiful you are."

I blush. "Please. Hardly."

"Modest," she says, shaking her head. "With that hair, that figure, those eyes? You have a unique look. Let me guess. . . You came from *Beauty*?"

"*Enchanté.*"

"Wow. *Enchanté*? Excuuuse me! Now, that's one high-falutin' magazine!" She leans in closer, her eyes full of mischief. "Tell me the truth. I bet it's full of bitches. Are they all terrible?"

I burst out laughing at her disarming candor. "Not really . . . a lot of them are surprisingly nice . . ."

"Oh, come on, chickadee. You're not in their clutches anymore! You can be honest!"

Despite myself, I feel a grin playing at my lips. "You have no idea."

"I knew it!"

"It's mostly trust fund babies and girls working two and a half days a week to support their Manolo habit."

"Total cliché!" she shrieks.

"I loved being at *Enchanté*. But it was nothing *but* one big cliché."

"So, why did you leave?"

The dreaded question. "Well . . . I had an . . . incident." I explain the story to her.

"Oh no! You got fired?"

"Wait," I say. "You mean you really didn't hear about it?"

"Nope," she says, and shrugs. "We're not much for industry gossip over here, unless it concerns ad revenues or things like that. Everybody is much more concerned with what happened last night on *American Idol* or *Dancing with the Stars*."

"That's . . . *huh*. Well."

She leans in and pats me on the shoulder. "You're in for a shock, honey. This place is *nothing* like Bonneau-Martray."

"So I'm learning." Suddenly I remember why I came over here in the first place. "By the way—I'm looking for the beauty closet. Would you happen to know where it is?"

"Sure, let me show you."

She leads me down the hallway and to a closed door at the end of the corridor, next to a window. "Voilà! I'm jealous you girls have the run of this stash of beauty products. You're so lucky."

"It's one of the perks." I grin, turning the key in the lock. I open the door and—

Wait. Where's the rest of it?

This really *is* a closet.

I turn to her, confused. "This is just a cabinet. I was looking for the actual closet. I had some boxes shipped and I assumed they would be in there."

She looks back at me quizzically. "This is it, hon. You had more than this at *Enchanté*?"

"We had a whole room at *Enchanté*!" I exclaim. "It was as big as my bedroom! This is . . . this is the size of the *Enchanté hair accessories* cabinet!"

The cabinet is about six feet tall and five feet wide, with six shelves separated into hair, skin, makeup, and spa products. I do a quick once-over of the inventory and estimate that there can't be more than a few hundred beauty products crammed in. I examine the labels more closely. With the exception of a few designer goods here and there, everything says L'Oreal, Cover Girl, Max Factor, Garnier, Maybelline, Revlon, John Frieda, Dove, or Jergens. It's all *drugstore* stuff! Where is the Chanel? Where is the La Mer? Shiseido? MD Skincare? SK-II? Shu Uemura? Jo Malone? Diptyque? La Prairie? How will I survive without my beloved designer products? I can't use this stuff! I think back to all the times I'd assured my friends and readers, "You don't always get what you pay for. Drugstore products are just as effective and technologically advanced as some brands five or six times the price." That was all *bullshit*! Everybody knows the expensive stuff is better! I suddenly feel panicked, wishing I'd raided the *Enchanté* beauty closet before leaving.

"Are you all right?" she asks. "You're sweating."

"I . . . I . . . it's just . . . I mean. . . ." I'm speechless.

Vivian is quiet for a moment and then says. "This is nothing like the *Enchanté* beauty closet, right?"

"Not . . . at . . . all," I whisper, my voice faltering. I feel like my puppy has just died.

She pats me on the shoulder. "There, there. I know. It must be a shock. You were at the fanciest magazine in the world, and now you've downgraded to boring old *Womanly World*." She nods sympathetically. "It's not all bad. You'll get used to it, I promise."

I finally find my box in Frances's office, although Frances herself is nowhere to be found. I'm staring at the huge box, wondering how to transport it back to my desk when a girl with a short brown bob walks in, jumping in fright as she sees me.

"Oh, sorry! I didn't know there was anybody in here."

"No, it's my fault." I stand there awkwardly, expecting the girl to suddenly growl, "What the hell are you doing in here?" Instead, she stares at me, a look of recognition dawning on her face.

"You're Bella Hunter!"

"*Uh* . . . Guilty as charged." I walk forward, extending my hand. "You are . . . ?"

"Oh, sorry! I'm Megan Murphy. Your beauty assistant!" Megan's tone makes plain that she is thrilled to see me.

"Great," I say, nodding in a manner that I hope is enthusiastic. "It's really nice to meet you."

"Me, too! I'm so excited you're here! Frances called just this morning and told me you were hired here. It's so great! I was such a huge fan of your page at *Enchanté*."

"Oh, good. Thank you! I'm glad to hear it."

"So, you just got here? How's everything? Did you meet everybody? I can give you a tour!"

"Thank you, but Tammy just showed me around the office," I say politely. "It'll probably take some getting used to, but . . . I'm up to the challenge."

Megan nods enthusiastically, hands clasped together as she beams at me. "Do you need help carrying your box back to your desk?"

"Yes, please! If you don't mind?"

"Not at all!" She darts forward, picking up one side. "If you grab the other side, we should be able to do it just us girls. Wow, it's heavy!" she exclaims as we hoist the box up to our chests and begin walking back to my cubicle. With a soft grunt, Megan deposits it next to my desk and then stands back up, looking at me expectantly. "Do you need any help unpacking? Or maybe you want some coffee?"

"No, thank you, Megan. I appreciate it."

"Okay, well, if you need anything my extension is five-four-eight-two. Or just holler! I'm right over there." She points to her cubicle across from Frances's office and then starts giggling nervously. "Oh, but of course you know that, you just saw my desk! Well, okay, then."

"Thanks, Megan."

"Okay, see you in a little bit! Frances will be here in an hour. She's at an event."

"Great," I say, not wanting to be rude, but desperately wanting Megan to leave so I can unpack in peace. Finally, with a sort of jerking motion that resembles a curtsy, she hurries back to her cubicle.

I'm so absorbed in setting up my e-mail account that I don't notice when the light on my phone starts blinking. I check my messages—it's from Frances saying simply, "Bella, this is Frances McCabe, the beauty director. It's 11:03. Please come to my office. Thank you." I look at my computer clock. It reads 11:06.

I walk into her office, hand outstretched. Should you shake hands with somebody you've sort of but not quite met? I'm not sure. "Hi, Frances. Good to see you." The standard greeting when you don't want to say "Nice to meet you" and risk having them frostily reply, "We've already met."

"Hello, Bella. I see you picked up your box," she says, gripping my hand firmly.

"Megan helped me. Very sweet of her."

"Please have a seat," she says.

I sit down and marvel at how Frances looks nothing like a beauty editor. Most editors, even at the lesser magazines, are all glitz and glam, with expensive haircuts by Oribe or Sally Hershberger, highlights by Louis Licari or Ritz Hazan, and perfectly tended skin courtesy of Dr. Wexler, Dr. Brandt, or Dr. Gross. Frances, on the other hand, does everything that beauty editors *aren't* supposed to: she wears makeup, but it's all wrong for her complexion and looks like she's chosen colors from 1983; she has a short, grandmotherly style, and she's let her hair grow out gray without any highlights. She is a mass of crimes against beauty.

Larissa gave me some background on Frances. Apparently, she was one of the biggest fashion editors in the industry in the

1970s, making her mark at *Vogue* and *Harper's Bazaar,* before moving over to *Womanly World* in 1978. Under her direction, the fashion pages of *Womanly World* were full of the hottest and newest models, balancing the magazine's award-winning lifestyle coverage. But in the late '80s, the magazine began to fall apart, and by the end of the '90s, it was one of those marginalized magazines that held no cultural relevancy, took itself way too seriously, and, worse, had lost all its advertisers. Readers had held on, loyal to the name that their mothers and grandmothers had grown up with, but now, even they were leaving in droves. Frances is one of the last relics of a bygone era, and, according to Larissa, she resents the importance that beauty advertising revenue lends to the magazine. In order to do the fashion shoots she wants, she's had to busy herself with beauty, too. Unfortunately, at this point—so Larissa told me—she was doing neither well, as good fashion went hand in hand with successful beauty. Hence . . . me.

"So, Bella," she says sternly. "I trust that Rania has told you about our mission here."

That word again: *mission.* I feel like I'm on a space quest.

"Yes," I say, putting on my most professional cut-glass impress-the-boss voice. "She said she's hoping to revamp the beauty pages with an aim toward bringing in more advertisers and freshening up the magazine. She seeks to make it newer and more relevant. A shot of fresh air, if you will."

"*Uh-huh,*" she says doubtfully. "I'm going to be up front with you. I don't believe you're right for the magazine. I don't think you have the right sensibility and I'm upset that Rania rushed your hiring through despite my protestations. I've followed your work, and you were fine for *Enchanté,* but you're simply too young to bring the type of world experience, not to mention beauty knowledge, that our readers require. These aren't socialites with unlimited financial resources. They're wives and mothers. They have values. They're *real* people—*real* Americans. Our magazine is a safe haven for them. It's a place they go for advice, for a friend, for comfort. We will not be 'jazzing things up' with stories about Britney Spears and glittery eye shadow and spa vacations in Sedona, do you understand? I will not turn these pages into a teeny-bopper paradise just to whore ourselves out to the beauty conglomerates. This magazine still has a shred of dignity and I will not see it strangled and stomped out."

I am stunned. Frances has just informed me that I am a valueless, frivolous, un-American commie. Worse—one who likes glittery makeup.

"Now," she continues, "I am primarily involved with the fashion pages, since our shoots take several days a month, but I will expect to review all of your beauty ideas, memos, and copy before you send them to Rania. When I am out of the office on a shoot, you will fax me the memos. I do not use e-mail. Please do not send them to me online—they will be unread and unanswered. When Rania sends you a memo, please make me a copy and then put it on my desk or Megan's desk, or interoffice it to me." Interoffice? She works ten feet away from me! And how am I supposed to work with no e-mail? Madness!

"Clear?" she asks.

"Crystal," I say, sitting up straight as if my posture will make her suddenly decide to take me seriously. I haven't yet had to deal with scorn from editors after my *Post* fiasco—it begins now.

She regards me silently, her eyes narrowing. "Bella, I know that things were done—" she pauses, pursing her lips, "a *certain way* at *Enchanté* and Bonneau-Martray, but you will find that this organization is very different. We pride ourselves on hard work here."

"Yes! Of course!" I exclaim, my face hot. "I wouldn't dream of—yes. No problem." I've been accused numerous times by Emily and Nick of being a kiss-ass. I can't help it, and I never mean to be insincere, but I'm so determined to make people like me that I'll bend over backward, even if it means suppressing my true feelings.

"Good," she says firmly. "As long as we understand each other, we will have a positive working relationship."

"Wonderful," I say weakly, feeling my chest tighten.

Frances and I meet for an hour, going over all the logistics I'll need to know at *Womanly World*. We also have our first invite meeting, and she informs me that, now that I'm her second in command, I will go to Paris in her place on the upcoming Face Group press trip. This is the only good piece of news I hear today.

On Wednesday, Larissa calls. I expect that she's checking in, wanting to know how my first week is going and hoping I'm holding up okay. But no.

"What the hell is going on with this weather?" she demands by way of greeting.

"Hi, Larissa."

"It's nearly April. Surely we deserve a bit of sunshine? Some spring cheer? Who can *live* like this? It's practically snowing out there!" It is, in fact, about fifty-eight degrees today. "I am *not* in the mood to be formulating 'Recover from the Summer Sun' stories for September when I haven't even thrown my winter coat into storage," she moans. Larissa's winter coat is an insanely expensive J. Mendel fur that costs more than my yearly rent. I doubt she'll be throwing it anywhere.

"You're working on September *already*?"

"Allegedly. If Katharine has her way. That woman, I swear to God. She lives to torture me."

"Why? What's she doing now?"

"Oh, nothing, nothing." She sighs heavily. "It's just the whole hiring fiasco. Replacing *you* is turning into a monstrous to-do. Everybody has an opinion, this one's not good enough, that one's too controversial, *nobody* has enough writing talent. I don't think HR's bothering to read résumés anymore. They're simply sending me people who wander in off the streets!"

"Do you have any real candidates yet?"

"Yes, we received about a billion résumés—and I'm not exaggerating, Bella, it really was that many—but we've whittled it down to three. I'm fighting for one, Katharine wants the other. But I'll be *damned* if we hire her."

"And the third?" I ask casually, dying to know which girls are vying to replace me. Nothing like a little schadenfreude to brighten the mood.

"Oh, complete disaster. Utterly tragic. But she's Joaquin Mouret's niece, so we have to pretend to consider her. I'm not allowed to talk about the process though, as you know, so my lips must be zipped." She pauses. "I'll just say that I'm not too happy with the way the hiring is going, and then be done with it." She sighs, continuing, "I mean, these girls! Where do they find these people? You should have seen this tragedy HR sent to me; she thought Mally Roncal was one of the contestants on *America's Next Top Model*."

"No."

"Yes! And another—her résumé was fine, I suppose, but she looked like some sort of *goth*!" she sputters, her disgusted tone more suited to a discussion of venereal diseases. "We have an image to maintain! Would Human Resources have sent Marilyn Manson's illegitimate love child down to interview with *Grace Donovan*?" she asks indignantly.

"Not in a million years."

"Not in a million years is exactly right. It's going to be awful. Tasha wants me to promote her." She laughs. "Never going to happen! No, we're going to have to make a lateral move, and I'll just tell you that I'm not happy about it at all," she says darkly.

"Riss, I'm sure whoever you hire will be great. Not as great as I was," I tease, happy that my friendship with Larissa seems to have endured, "but good, nonetheless."

"Yes . . . ," she says, sounding as if she wants to add something. "Anyway. We need to schedule drinks, my disgraced little pistachio. I want you to meet Daniel—he's *to die* for. So sexy. I think he's the one."

"This is the British guy? The reason you perpetually sound like you're auditioning for a Jane Austen movie?"

"Nothing of the sort! Are you mad? I've always—" auhl-waaays "—spoken like this."

"Mmm-hmm."

She gasps. "I have!"

"Whatever you say, Larissa."

"I'm hanging up now! I'm swamped. You should be working, too. It's your first week! Making phone calls all over town to chatter away will not impress your new boss. Frances is a tough old bird."

"You called me!"

"I suppose," she says doubtfully. "Do be in touch."

"Perhaps you could be so kind as to pop by my flat for a cup of tea? Or ring me on my mobile?"

"Lovely!" she says, my sarcasm completely flying over her head. "Cheers, darling."

"Bye, Riss."

Finally, it's Friday. My first week at *Womanly World* speeds by in a blur of meetings, interoffice memos, and the standard getting up to speed that's necessary whenever you begin a new job. I have my new e-mail address, phone number, and mailing address taped to my phone in huge letters. After eight years at *Enchanté,* I keep accidentally giving publicists the wrong details and responding, "It's Bella from *Enchant—er . . . Womanly World,*" when making phone calls.

At *Enchanté,* I received about forty packages a day. Here, it's closer to ten. When I was promoted to beauty writer from associate beauty editor four years ago, a slew of companies sent me a barrage of gifts, ranging from silver Tiffany picture frames to Chanel key rings to flower arrangements to Magnolia Bakery cupcakes. Here, I receive two things: a card from the girls at Tunnel Communications saying, "Hope your first week at *Womanly World* is wonderful!" and an embarrassingly small desk plant from Simpson Beauty. They're a drugstore company, so it makes sense that they'd try buttering me up. But nobody else even bothers! They've all written me off.

My phone rings, and the caller ID displays Joss's number at Morrison Communications, one of the top beauty publicity firms.

"Joss?"

"Hey, sexy. How'd the first week go? Slit your wrists yet?"

"Please don't tempt me. I'm trying to make the best of it."

"Hang in there, Bel. If I got fired from Morrison and re-hired at some piece of crap firm, I think I'd kidnap Gary, force him to marry me, get knocked up instantly, and then never work again." Joss envisions this scenario at least once a week, something she used to blame on pressure from her Jewish mother, until she finally realized the dream had become her own. "Speaking of, can I tell you what he said to me yesterday? We're in Hewlitt, about to get on the train after having dinner at his parents' house, and he says he's thinking about quitting his job and getting his MBA. His MBA!"

"That's great!" I say, cradling the phone on my shoulder as I multitask by shuffling through magazine tear sheets, separating them into different piles to work with later. Once Joss starts talking about her issues with Gary, the conversation could last for hours. Half of the tears are beauty stories I want to read; the other half are ads and photo shoots that might give me inspiration for ideas. Frances is going to be a tough nut to crack; I want to produce an inspired ideas memo to prove to Frances that I'm not some dizzy blonde with half a brain and even less writing talent. Of course, getting into the *Womanly World* mindset is *not* going to be easy.

"Great? Are you nuts? If he quits his job, not only is you-know-who going to have to support his ass—that'd be me—but then he'll burn through his savings, and that means no wedding until after he finishes school. And do you know how long MBA programs take? Two years! Two years wasted. I should have dumped him eons ago. Now I'm stuck."

"At least if he gets his MBA he'll make more money in the long run," I point out. "And then you can quit your job and stay at home watching *Oprah* and baking cookies for the rest of your life." The idea of giving up my career for some unworthy man who will probably end up saddling me with children, cheating on me, and then forcing me to divorce him is less appealing than a lobotomy. For Joss, however, it's the dream that sustains her through the long hours and bitchy clients.

"That's what my mother said," she scoffs. "Anyhow, it's all bullshit. He's trying to push my buttons, God knows why. I think he got jealous when he saw me flirting with my sister's boyfriend last weekend over dinner. But I was only doing it to *make* him jealous! I'm not going to have an affair with my sister's boyfriend. How tacky. Seriously!"

I smile as Joss talks, thinking about how I seem to collect crazy friends like it's my job, and wondering if they similarly question my sanity when I unburden my silly problems on them. Well, at least we're never boring.

"Did you ever call back that *Post* reporter?" Joss asks, switching gears.

"No. What would I even say?"

"Please, you'd say: 'You ruined my life, you bitch, and I'm going to sue you for libel.' See? It rolls off your tongue. Easy. We can have Gary represent you."

"Before he quits his job."

"Thanks a lot. If I ever run into that chick who wrote the article, I'm going to kill her. I'm telling you, Bel, it was a conspiracy. Maybe Katharine wanted to bring you down—I don't know. But I feel it."

"Of course you think it's a conspiracy—you think everything is a conspiracy!"

"Everything *is* a conspiracy," Joss insists. "I wish you'd open your mind. It's not for me—it's for your own sake. You haven't bothered to read the David Icke books, have you?"

"*Er* . . . yeah, I flipped through them," I fib.

"You're lying. Support the establishment and live a life of lies if you want, but it's your funeral. I wish you'd be more open-minded, that's all."

"Joss! Just because I don't think aliens secretly rule the earth or Katharine roofied my drink to get me to make an ass of myself in front of a reporter doesn't mean I'm close-minded. I saw *The DaVinci Code*. I know about the Illuminati," I say, knowing it'll make Joss fly off the handle.

"Such bullshit," she huffs. "An idiot writer rips off a crackpot theory, and suddenly everybody's an expert on symbology and governmental conspiracies. If only they knew."

"Joss, I have to run. I've been reading magazines for ideas for hours, and I hardly think that constitutes work. I need to impress my new boss."

"I still think you were set up," she says dismissively, "but whatever. I suppose it's water under the bridge now. Do you need a care package? I can send over some candles and body scrubs and get face cream and makeup from the girls on the other teams."

"You're a lifesaver. The closet here—I can't explain to you how slim the pickings are. At this rate, I'm going to run out of my designer products in three months, and then I'll be SOL."

"Can't you just call in the designer stuff? You're still *technically* a beauty editor."

"Yeah . . . I've already tried, and I don't think many publicists are returning my calls—other than you, of course."

"I love you, but after that article, I'm not surprised. I'll only return your calls until my boss finds out. Then I'll have to friend-disown you," she teases.

"Thanks," I say dryly. "Talk later."

"Wait, dinner tonight with the crew?"

"Gabrielle has some movie premiere at eight, so Em's running around town pulling outfits for her to wear. What about tomorrow? Let's go somewhere good and we can make Nick bring his latest girlfriend."

"He's just looking for women to replace *you*—the one that got away."

"You're hilarious. Really." Joss is convinced that Nick is secretly in love with me, based on one drunken evening we had years ago that ended in a sloppy makeout session. Nick *is* attractive, in a sketchy, slutty Mark McGrath kind of way, but I know him so well that the very memory of it makes me cringe. I usually manage to forget the whole thing ever happened, but Joss and Emily revel in bringing it up. He's not my type, anyway—too arrogant, too overtly sexual. Much more Emily's type.

"Later, heartbreaker. Love you."

"Love you, too."

I sort through tears for several hours, jotting ideas down and stopping only to grab a salad from the fridge that I made for myself this morning. Around 2:30, my phone rings. I realize that this is the most uninterrupted work

I've had in years; in my "former" life, the phone rang off the hook.

"Bella, this is Frances. I'd like you to stop by my office immediately, please," Frances says crisply.

"Of course, Frances, I'll be right there." I do a quick check in the mirror next to my cubicle to ensure I look presentable. I've been going for a beachy, Kate Hudson vibe recently, blowing my hair out in the mornings, curling it into fat ringlets, and then running Bumble and bumble cream through the ends to tousle them. My hair is growing out nicely from the orange incident—it's now a subtle shade of honey, hovering between blond and brunette. Very Jessica Alba. Maybe I should start trying to blend in with everybody by putting my wet hair in a bun and wearing clothes from the Gap, but after years of learning and then honing my style skills, I'm just not ready to look like a soccer mom. Besides, I'm the most professional, presentable-looking person in the office, which has to earn at least a few points. Today, I'm wearing a blue flowy Chloé top, a white Calvin Klein skirt that I bought at a sample sale last year, and my favorite pair of tan Jimmy Choo stilettos. My eyebrows are a bit off, however. While reading *InStyle* last night before bed, I decided I liked the look of Drew Barrymore's latest arches and tried replicating them on myself. Twenty minutes later, my eyebrows were practically nonexistent (when Emily popped in my room to say good night, she shrieked, "Did you do that on *purpose*?"), so I was forced to draw them in with powder this morning. Oh, well. They should grow back in a few weeks. . . . I hope.

Once at Frances's office, I knock on the door and she jabs her hand up, palm out, motioning for me to stay in the hallway, instead of coming in.

"Yes, Hal, I told you," she says insistently, standing and leaning over to scribble a note on a galley as she holds the phone receiver to her ear. "Under *no* circumstances do I want you sending out those thank-you notes without my having a chance to look them over first. Are we clear?" Pause. "Yes." Pause. "Absolutely." Pause. "Okay, honey, thank you. I love you, too, see you tonight."

Jesus, she even talks to her husband like a drill sargeant.

"Bella. Rania would like us to go over to her office so you have a chance to meet the publisher. With the upcoming fashion photo shoots, I will not be able to go on many of the sales calls. We'd like to shift this responsibility to you instead."

"Wonderful. I'd be delighted," I say, half-consciously mimicking Frances's speech, even as I realize this puts me in the same category of pretention as Larissa the faux Brit. I rack my brain, trying to remember everything Larissa ever told me about her visits to Boca for CTFA, or her Town Car shuffles around town with the *Enchanté* publisher. I draw a blank—after returning from her sales call meetings, Larissa would usually just moan, "It was *so* ghastly!" and then retreat into her office to treat herself with a manicure. (Beauty girls never go to salons for manicures, unless it's an organized event.) Oh, well, I'm sure they'll explain to me everything I need to know.

We walk over to Rania's office in silence, Frances nodding imperiously at Rania's assistant Lauren as we approach.

"Right on time," Lauren says, waving us in.

Rania sits behind her desk, which is dwarfed by the sheer size of the room. Contrary to expectations, it's a huge, beautiful office, much nicer than many of those at Bonneau-Martray, a fact I'd noticed when interviewing with Rania. I remark silently that, even though the *Enchanté* crowd considers *Womanly World* the very bottom of the barrel, the magazine still holds tremedous sway. Rania's walls are covered with photos of presidents, first ladies, movie stars, television actresses, sports heroes, as well as a few with "real people." In one photo, Rania wears a pretty green silk headscarf that accents her translucent hazel eyes and mahogany hair and stands in the middle of a large group of people. Judging by the similarly beautiful bone structure and round eyes of the women on the sides of her, I guess that this photo is of her family.

"Please come in!" Rania exclaims, moving a stack of papers to the side of her desk and gesturing to seats. "Bella, Frances explained everything to you?"

"Yes. She said I'll be going on sales calls in her place, and therefore she wanted me to meet the publisher."

"Exactly. You'll love James. He's the grandson of Essie Michaels, the illustrious founder of *Womanly World* whose presence graces our hallways, as you've no doubt noticed," she laughs. "Harvard Business School, full of excellent ideas, brimming with the energy the company needs right now." She glances at the doorway and then leans in, whispering, "He's not bad-looking, either."

"Oh, really?" I giggle, stiffening abruptly at a sideward glance from a frowning Frances. Great. She'll probably report us for sexual harrassment.

Rania looks at Frances amusedly and then clears her throat. "In any case, you and James will be spending quite a lot of time together over the next few months as we prepare for the quarterly buying session. It'll be intense, juggling the sales calls with your workload, but I trust you'll manage just fine." She smiles warmly at me.

"Rania?" Lauren calls. "James is here."

Rania stands up. "Send him in, please," she calls back.

James enters the room. He's extremely tall, with dark brown hair slicked back tightly against his head, a strong jaw, ramrod-straight posture, and shockingly blue eyes. He strides in purposefully, and I note the expensive cut and fit of his black pin-striped suit, no doubt bespoke, and the shininess of his black shoes. He's *all business*. I'm surprised by a faint cologne scene wafting off of him—Givenchy Pi by the soapy-yet-spicy smell of it. Expensive taste, this guy. Rania wasn't lying, either: he's very handsome, although his rugged looks are of the subtle, *Hey, he's actually really attractive!* variety, as opposed to the brand of smack-you-in-the-face, *Jesus Christ, he's pretty* girliness particular to male models. And while everybody at Beckwith—with the exception of Frances—has been Pollyanna sweet, James has a frown plastered on his face that's approaching scowl territory.

"Hello, James," Rania smiles, standing up and walking over to the door to greet him. She turns to Frances and me, saying, "You know Frances, of course. And this is our new beauty editor, Bella Hunter, fresh from *Enchanté* magazine."

I step forward to offer my hand, my heart suddenly racing. "Hello! Lovely to meet you!" Oh God, my voice has gone up by an octave. Sexy men have this effect on me. I clear my throat. "Extremely excited to be here," I add in a much lower tone, now sounding like a bad Kathleen Turner imitator.

James shakes my hand briskly. "Welcome. I hope you're enjoying it so far."

"Yes, it's fantastic!" Why can't I stop squeaking?

Rania turns back to James and says, "Since Frances will be out of the office so much on business, Bella is going to be taking over the sales calls duty. Of course, this should be no problem for her, since she did this sort of thing all the time at *Enchanté*."

I did?

Crap! I now vaguely remember something I said in my interview with Rania where I . . . *er* . . . exaggerated the business side of my *Enchanté* duties. There *may* have been promises of sales calls and advertiser pitches on my part. Allegedly.

James turns back to me, nodding several times. "How often did you go on sales calls at your former job, Bella?"

"All the time!" I say brightly, hoping that he won't press me further. "My former editor Larissa was also often at photo shoots—" or shopping at Barneys "—and I frequently went on the sales calls and put together the presentations. Very regularly." Now I'm out and out lying.

His eyes narrow. "I see. What sort of presentations did you make, exactly?"

I swallow, trying to remember any snatch of conversation I'd had with Larissa about the advertiser meetings. "Gathering together clips and tears, explaining our mission, working to bring advertisers on board," I ad-lib. "Very standard."

"You're comfortable presenting to a large group of people?"

Public speaking is one of my biggest fears. "Absolutely."

"Fine. Our first meeting will be with Mode Beauty in just under two months. We've put together a presentation and have all the necessary materials to meet with them, but I'll need some input from you on the editorial side of things. We're going after a younger demographic, so you'll be responsible for explaining our new mission and for bringing it to life through the new pages. Have something to present to me by the end of this month, please. Frances, you should be there, as well." She nods primly.

He turns and starts to walk out the door, nodding briefly at Rania and Frances, but before I can stop myself, I blurt out, "Wait!"

Everybody looks at me. His eyebrow is raised.

"Ahem," I clear my throat, hoping my chest and throat aren't splotchy from embarrassment, "Just to clarify, what would you like me to present to you, *exactly*?"

He stares at me. Is he going to call me out? Finally he sighs, almost imperceptibly. "Would you like to stop by my office to discuss?"

Alone? In his office? Even if he weren't the second coming of Brad Pitt, he's so stiff that the thought of having to carry on a conversation with him one-on-one is terrifying. "If it suits you."

"Fine. E-mail my assistant and she'll set up a time."

And with that he walks out the door.

I feel slightly dazed and realize that I'm staring after James with my mouth agape. Rania looks at me, a tiny smile playing at the corners of her lips.

"James can be brusque at times," she says, "but between you and me, I think it's because he has such a heavy burden to carry. He is really very charming."

"*Such* a hard worker," Frances adds admirably. "You never meet young people like that nowadays."

Chapter 5

I try to focus on article ideas to present to Frances, but my mind incessantly drifts back toward James. When we met, there wasn't an obvious whiff of adventure or mystery about him, but something in his gruff demeanor evoked an old West cowboy facing off against the world alone. James makes me nervous—he'll see right through me. Keep the mask on tight, Bella. You're still new, and you can be whoever you want to be here. Professional! Be professional, for the love of God!

I set a time with his assistant for the following week, at 5:00 p.m. on Friday—the only chunk of time he has free for almost a month—panicking a few minutes before I'm due in his office. At 4:55, I automatically pull out my makeup bag and touch up my appearance in my desk-side mirror, reapplying lip gloss, freshening my blush, curling my lashes, and plumping up my curls. I stare at my reflection critically, turning my head from left to right and quickly checking my nostrils and teeth to make sure the coast is clear. Not bad at all.

I walk to James's office. An older woman, with a honey-colored Barbara Bush hairstyle and 1970s granny glasses, stops me from knocking on his door. "Excuse me, dear. Are you Bella?"

"Yes, that's me. I have a meeting with James at five?"

"I'll let him know you're here," she says, picking up the phone, and then motioning me inside a few seconds later after saying, "Mr. Michaels? Bella is here to see you."

James's office is an exercise in boring, safe taste: a dark mahogany desk with papers arranged in neat stacks, framed black-and-white prints on the walls, and a large bookshelf stacked with expensive, glossy coffee-table reads. It screams: I had an interior decorator do this. There's no personal charm.

"Hello," I say shyly. "How are you?"

"Fine, thanks. You?"

"Wonderful, thank you. Settling in, getting used to the new office culture, coming up with ideas for the beauty pages."

He frowns. "You're not having a hard time adjusting? *Womanly World* is no doubt different from *Enchanté*."

"It *is* different," I admit, "but I'm sure I'll be fine." Huge lie.

"Excellent. Let's dive right in, if you don't mind. I have to finish some work and then run downtown for a dinner." He doesn't wait for me to respond, launching right into his pitch. "Mode Beauty has been advertising with us for years and, luckily, isn't one of the companies whose advertising we're in danger of losing. Regardless, we need to approach every single ad sales call as if it's our most important one. They're still an important, expensive account, and if we *were* to lose their business, it would be grave."

"I see. Treat them like royalty," I say, feigning scribbles in my notebook as I flash a wide smile. I've found it's often easier dealing with men than with women in the workplace, since, let's face it, a woman isn't going to cut you a break because you've got a nice pair or legs or teasingly compliment her on how handsome she looks. James's frown snaps me back into place. No charming this one, apparently.

"Right," he says slowly. "The presentation is essentially set up. You'll wait for me to motion to you, and then you'll talk about *Womanly World*'s beauty format. Explain our different beauty rubrics, talk about future ideas for your column, and explain why our beauty coverage is unique."

"Great." Pause. "How is our beauty coverage unique, exactly?"

He raises his eyebrows. "You have to ask?"

"Well," I say hurriedly, struggling to backtrack, "Of course I know how we differ from, say, *Enchanté,* or even, for example, *O,* but in what manner does our beauty coverage compare to a *Good Housekeeping* or *Ladies' Home Journal* or *Better Woman*?" He should be impressed with my foresight in asking such an important question, no?

"You're the beauty editor," he says dryly. "I suggest you tell me."

"Right!" I laugh nervously. I hope he's being rhetorical and doesn't want me to list differences here and now, because I have no clue. I'll have to do some research before the sales call.

"Any other questions?"

"That's it! You've covered everything. Thank you for your time. It should be a walk in the park. Just like my ad sales calls at *Enchanté,*" I add for good measure, feeling myself moving into babbling territory.

"Can't wait," he says, deadpan.

Back at my desk, I immediately call Joss again, recounting my meeting with James. "And then he was like, 'You're the beauty editor. Why don't you tell *me* how the magazines are different?' As if there's a shred of difference between *Womanly World* and every other boring supermarket magazine. I can't believe I'm stuck here. This place is so *lame.* I really freaking ruined my life, *huh*?"

"Ahem." I turn in my chair, startled, and see that James is standing at the entrance to my cubicle, his face stony. He's

holding my notebook in his hands. "You left this in my office," he says, putting the notebook on my desk.

He *must* have heard me complaining to Joss. "Wait," I say. "I didn't mean—"

He looks at me with a steely gaze and then turns, walking down the hall.

"Bella? Bella?" Joss's voice echoes through the phone. "Are you still there?"

I bury my head in my hands. "For now."

Later that evening, I recount the entire story in vivid detail to a tired Emily, who pulled in connections to dress Gabrielle in a brand-new, never-before-seen Valentino dress for the red carpet. She doubles over with laughter on the floor, unopened psychology books stacked by the foot of the coffee table, clutching a gigantic glass of red wine that threatens to spill everywhere. "Yeah, he definitely heard you. And after you were Masterpiece Theatre–speaking everybody in the office, too! I don't know how you do it, kid. You've got a gift."

"It was terrible!" I moan, sprawling out on the living room sofa and draping my legs over the arm rest. "Should I apologize to him? Or not even bring it up?"

"Calling attention to it would only make things worse. You don't *know* that he heard you—even though I'm sure he did—so better to lie low. The best you can do is show up, give it your all, and prove that you're a good writer. At the end of the day, if you're producing quality work, they won't really care if you like it there or not. As long as you don't go tattling to the *Post*, of course," she adds.

"Emily!"

"And by the way, seriously, stop flirting with him. Put him out of your mind altogether. You don't need to get embroiled in another office scandal. Work, Bella. Work, work, work, work, work."

"Work," I repeat miserably. "But it's so boring there! And I wasn't flirting."

"Oh, Jesus Christ, quit your bitching. A week ago you didn't even have a job, remember? At least you're still in the industry. And the assistant, Mary or whatever, she sounds nice."

"Megan. She is," I agree. "Kind of stalkerish, but . . ."

"See, this is exactly what I'm talking about. What is *with* you? You've always been the positive one. Now you're a spoiled little brat." I open my mouth to protest and she puts her hand up. "Hey, I yell because I love. Remember that sappy book Joss made us read? *A Secret*?"

"The Secret."

"*A* Secret, *The* Secret, whatever. It was all about being positive and attracting things and thinking your dreams into reality—" she flutters her hands in the air as she talks, wiggling her fingers like a deranged magician "—well, you used to be like that, and now you take everything for granted, and all you do is complain, and you don't realize how great you have it. So we need a new attitude." She snaps her fingers in my face, Jerry Springer–style. "Right now."

"You are such a bitch," I say, laughing. "Why am I friends with you?"

"Because I tell it like it is," she says solemnly. "The truth hurts, baby, but somebody's got to burst that pretty little bubble." She swivels her finger in the air, smacking her lips together as she mimes popping an imaginary balloon, then looks at her watch, a diamond-encrusted Cartier Tank Francaise given to her by her father at Christmas last year. "When is Nick getting here, anyway?"

I shrug. "Five minutes? Five hours?"

As if on cue, Nick flings open the door triumphantly, brandishing a brown paper bag, his spiky brown hair sticking straight up and black eyes alight. "I've got the vodka. Who has the tonic?"

★ ★ ★

Two hours later, we're inside Harajuku, the hottest new lounge in Manhattan. Normally, I would feel a sense of guilty superiority for breezing past the long line outside, the bouncer unclicking the velvet rope automatically to let us pass, but it's tempered by the slightest hesitation on the doorman's part. I imagine what he's thinking: "Is she still worth letting in . . . *after* what happened?" My cheeks flush and I rush Emily and Nick inside. We called Joss to alert her to our last-minute clubbing plans, but she'd already committed to dinner with Gary's parents. ("I'm putting an end to this MBA shit right now!" she'd yelled down the phone line before hanging up to board the Long Island Railroad.) There's a massive room with a dance floor and bar surrounded by smaller rooms, each with its own flavor: geisha house, Japanese garden, Shinto temple, and Tokyo street. The general decor is very *Kill Bill*-meets-*Crouching Tiger, Hidden Dragon,* with a huge wooden platform suspended above the dance floor adorned by candy-colored silk curtains. The speakers blast "Whip It" by Devo as gigantic screens suspended from the ceiling play animé cartoons.

"Now this is better," Emily says happily, nestling back on the plush couch in front of our private table and surveying the room as she sips a glass of Veuve. She ordered two bottles of champagne for the three of us so that we could reserve the table, brushing off my protests that Nick and I would contribute to the inevitably astronomical bill. ("Speak for yourself!" Nick said. "If she wants to pay, I've got no problem with that. I'm a modern man.") "Just relax and let the bubbly wash all your cares away. Forget about the fact that your sexy boss hates you—there are millions of fish in the sea and tonight, all the hot catches are here." She pokes me. "What about that one?" I follow her look, noticing a tall, super-skinny boy who looks like he hasn't showered in five weeks.

"Him? The dirty one?"

"*Dirty*? This coming from the girl with the Lower East Side musician fetish?" she says incredulously.

"I don't have a musician fetish, and I don't go for dirty guys. Olivier was always well groomed. Toph was just a special case."

Nick coughs exaggeratedly, waving his hand in front of his face. "I think I can still smell him."

"He smelled great!" I protest. "Very manly! Just because he didn't douse himself in Acqua di Gio like *somebody* I know . . ."

"I wear Chanel Homme Sport, and you know it," Nick says disdainfully.

"My mistake, princess. Testy because Annika wouldn't sleep with you?"

"No," he says, tilting his chin to the ceiling haughtily. "I simply decided she wasn't the girl for me."

"Because she wouldn't sleep with you," Emily corrects.

"Are the details really important? I don't think so. When a man is on his search for true love, he'll inevitably leave some broken hearts in his wake. It'll take her a few weeks, but I think she'll get over me."

Emily starts laughing, then quickly fake coughs as Nick shoots her a dirty look. "Sorry. Must be all the smoke."

"You can't smoke in New York City bars," Nick points out.

"Well, I was trying to let you down easy, but now I don't know what to tell you," she shrugs, smiling at me and adding "Maybe it was the residual Toph smell. Seriously, Bel, what about that guy?" She raises her glass in his direction.

"I told you. He's dirty. *Yes*, dirtier than Toph who I really do not want to talk about, so can we please discuss something else?" This is my not-so-smooth attempt to gloss over any thoughts of my most recent ex, who seemed breezy and hip in the beginning, but then morphed into a clingy hysteric, putting me through six months of late-night phone calls and tears—on his part—begging to give us another chance before he begrudgingly moved on. "I'm not dating him now, thank God, and that's all that matters. It had nothing to do with how nice he may or may not have smelled. The drug habit pretty much killed that one for me."

"Music journalists," she mutters, rolling her eyes. *"Ooh!"* Her gaze lights up on another guy out of my line of sight. "Yes yes yes! Now this one is cute!"

"What does he look like?" I ask, craning my neck to get a better look. "I can't see him!"

"Me neither," Nick says, studying the drinks list intently.

"Nick, you're not even looking!" She pulls me closer to her, leaning away so I can catch a glimpse. "Can you see him now?"

"No. There are too many people in the way." A techno version of "Total Eclipse of the Heart" starts playing.

"I'll describe him for you." She looks excited, taking another sip of her champagne. "You're going to love him—he's exactly your type. A little over six feet tall, light brown hair, kind of shaggy, but not scruffy. Preppy. Clean looking. He's wearing a green T-shirt over a white long-sleeve shirt and he has a red baseball cap on. I think it's an Indians hat. He looks totally jockish, very Abercrombie. Twenty bucks says he smells like soap."

"*That's* what you think my type is? A high school sophomore?"

"Bella." Emily looks at me, her gaze commanding. "Trust me. This guy is hot. I think he's our age, for once, too."

"Oh, good," Nick says. "None of this *is he legal?* business." My face feels warm at their jibes—I went through a slight Mrs. Robinson phase last year before meeting Toph.

"You're one to talk. If he's so hot, why don't you want him?"

"I've told you a million times, I'm not gay, I'm just fashionable," Nick cracks.

"Not you, you moron. I'm talking to Emily."

Emily's face goes grave. "I've sworn off boys for six months. I'm not touching anybody until October. I'm not even *looking* at anybody until then."

"What the hell?"

"It's a *chi* thing."

"Like in *Jerry Maguire*?"

"That's kwan."

"Wait, you're saving up your sexual energy?" Nick asks, suddenly looking interested. "That's hot."

"Thank you, and yes. Men are toxic—I need time to get everything out of my system, get back in touch with me." In her heyday, Emily could have given Warren Beatty a run for his money: she dated Tobey Maguire back when he was just a skinny kid with big eyes and no Spidey skills; she's made her way through several New York Yankees (though never Jeter, to her chagrin); in England, she's something of a celebrity because of her mother and the sheer number of androgynous Brit boy banders she's notched up. There was a never-squelched rumor going around that she secretly married Robbie Williams several years back, when she was only twenty, but it's false. I think.

I refill my glass of champagne and take a sip, still craning my neck for a glimpse of the cute guy. "Joss's New Age stuff is really rubbing off on you, huh?" A girl who looks straight out of the '80s, with pink leg warmers and a shock of crimped fuchsia hair, moves to the side and I suddenly have a clear view of the guy Emily's been talking about. "Wait. I *know* that guy—I went to high school with him! It's Tom Reynolds."

"Who? Are you sure?"

"I'm positive! I was obsessed with him for all of high school.

I can't believe he's here. Move over so he can't see me. I don't want him to think I'm staring at him."

"But you are staring at him," Nick points out.

"I can't help it! Move over! Shit. What is he doing here?"

"Well, Felicity, this *is* New York," Emily smirks. "It's kind of a popular town."

I take a big swig of champagne and stare Tom down. After three months of watching him from afar when he moved to my town the summer after eighth grade, I gathered up the courage to approach him in the hallway during the first week of high school to ask him to Addie Conway's party. He looked at me, cool as Jordan Catalano, and cocked his head, saying, "Sorry, *who* are you?" I'd scurried, away, running through the list of small favors to thank God for in my head.

Number 1: Tom doesn't know who you are, so now you can just go out of your way to avoid him and will never have to see him again.

Number 2: Kelly Pollock told you that Ryan Jackson said your breasts looked like they'd grown over the summer and he thought you looked sort of cute now.

Number 3: You have an October birthday, so you're turning fifteen in just one month and will be *so* over silly stuff like this, because fifteen is old.

The fact that my mother and Tom's mother became fast friends seemingly overnight threw a huge wrench in my plans; I was forced to see him at least once a week for the remainder of my high school career, always turning bright red and inventing excuses never to be alone with him for more than three seconds. He became one of the Big Men on Campus— not surprising, seeing as he was both gorgeous and gifted at football *and* baseball—and I heard through the grapevine that he thought I was weird. My senior year, he once smiled at me in the hallway between classes and said, "Hey, Bella," but that was the most meaningful of our interactions. I obsessed about his greeting for weeks.

As if sensing me, he looks over. A strange expression shades his face, and suddenly he's standing in front of me. "Bella? Bella Hunter?"

"Tom!" I say weakly. I stand up awkwardly and angle my face for a cheek kiss as he leans over me for a hug. I glance over his shoulder and see Emily and Nick exchanging amused smiles.

"Haven't seen you in about ten years," he says in a midwestern drawl, looking me up and down appraisingly. "New York City agrees with you. You look amazing."

"Oh, stop!" I say, collapsing into a fit of giggles even as I despise myself for losing my composure. I slap him on the arm. "You *have* to say that because that's just what you say to people you went to high school with."

"No way," he says, grinning at me, his teeth blinding. "It's the truth. What are you doing here?" Unlike most of our Sweet Falls compatriots, who've grown beer bellies and have started to lose their hair, he is, if possible, ten times more attractive than in high school.

"I'm a beauty editor for a magazine. I've been living here since college. What about you? Are you visiting?"

"*Nah,* I moved here a few months back. Been doing some modeling, believe it or not," he says shyly. "It sounds kind of stupid, but somebody came up to me on the street in Cleveland. I checked 'em out, and it was legit, so I figured, 'What the hell?' People have been telling me for years I should model and Ohio's kind of boring." He shrugs. "*You* know how it is. Bouncing from one adventure to the next."

"Wow! I can't believe you're a model! I mean, I can *believe* it, it's just that it's amazing somebody from our town is doing something so glamorous." My voice is verging on mouse territory, so I clear my throat. "Do you go back home a lot?" Nick stands and stretches casually, looking Tom up and down. This is his game with male models; he always wants to see how he stacks up, heightwise, having acquired a complex over the years at photo shoots. Tom is at least three inches taller, so Nick quickly sits back down, looking disappointed as he reburies his face in the drinks menu.

"Yeah, when I can. Went home just last weekend to see the folks, catch up with some old friends. Good times. Hasn't changed much, you know? Same old small town, same old people doing their same old thing." He winks at me and grins. "Don't know about you, but I think it's a hell of a lot more exciting here in the Big Apple." Something by the bar catches his attention and he puts his hand on my arm. "Hang on one sec. I'll be right back."

Emily waits until he's out of earshot and then grabs my shoulders, looking thrilled. "This is amazing," she gasps. "He's flirting with you. He wants you."

"He's just horny," rebuts Nick. "Who wears a baseball cap to a club, anyway?"

"No, he doesn't," I say, pointedly ignoring Nick. "He's being friendly. I bet he doesn't even come back. I practically stalked him in high school. He's terrified of me."

"Then why is he coming back *right now*?" she hisses under her breath as Tom reappears.

"Sorry. Walked away without paying for my drink. When I saw you, it was, 'Jesus! Bella Hunter! Blast from the past!' Probably the last person I thought I'd see here tonight. Funny how that happens, *huh*?"

"Very funny," I echo, my thoughts racing ahead to the next sentence I can trot out. Dazzle him with your conversational abilities, Bella! Do not get intimidated just because you had a small crush on this guy a million years ago. You are not that dorky high school girl anymore. Keep it together. Pretend he's not insanely attractive.

"Are you dating anybody?" he asks before I can think of my necessary brilliant comment.

Holy shit.

"Nah," I say casually. "You?"

"Nothing serious. What are you doing tomorrow night? Let's grab dinner. Do you live downtown?"

I nod mutely.

"Cool. I know this place, it's down on the Lower East Side. You'll love it. Eight o'clock?"

"Sure! Sounds great." We exchange numbers. As I'm putting his name in my phone, Tom leans over to look at my display.

"It's Tristan now."

"What?"

"My name. I go by Tristan. My booker thought it had more character, you know?" Nick rolls his eyes.

"Oh. Right. Okay, Tristan. Very nice!" I nod, warming to it. "Like *Tristan and Isolde*."

He frowns. "The James Franco movie? Yeah, that and Brad Pitt in *Legends of the Fall*."

"Of course," I say quickly. "A modern classic."

Tom—*er,* Tristan—takes a gulp of his drink and then sets it down on our table. "I still can't believe I ran into you! Crazy! We'll have fun tomorrow." He leans in and gives me a kiss on the cheek, and before I can say anything in response, he's gone.

Emily stares after him lustily. "You can thank me later."

"You mean you can *blame* her later," Nick says grumpily.

I bounce out of bed on Saturday morning. I have a date with Tom Reynolds tonight! Fourteen-year-old Bella would have passed out from excitement at the thought. Of course, I'm not fourteen-year-old Bella anymore. I'm so much older!

Wiser! Definitely more attractive! Oh God, I hope he thinks I'm attractive now.

I've noticed something about girls like me, who were busy studying instead of dating in high school and didn't grow into their looks until later in life. We feel relatively confident about our intelligence, will take on anybody in a game of Scrabble or Trivial Pursuit, and can discuss literature and politics with bravura, eager to prove our brainpower. When it comes to the beauty game, however, our personal history forces us into a perpetual state of insecurity. It doesn't matter if ten men tell me every day until I die that I'm beautiful—it'll be the one who doesn't notice me, or worse, who visibly rejects me, that will crush me and leave an indelible imprint, confirming the middle-school voice in my head.

Tonight, I have to look my absolute best. I decide to make it a day of beauty, dashing to the Bliss salon in Soho for a self-tanning treatment, then giving myself a manicure and pedicure in the afternoon before stopping by George's to have my hair blown out. When 7:30 rolls around, I look more glamorous than ever before in my life: tawny skin, bouncy Victoria's Secret waves, smoky eyes and just a hint of Bare Escentuals Clear Radiance on my face and collarbone for subtle shimmer. Emily lends me one of her mother's red Avignon minidresses and I wear a pair of black Manolo three-inch stilettos that make me a shade under six feet tall.

"Perfection," Emily sighs as I come into the living room and pirouette for her.

"You think?" I ask worriedly.

"Absolutely. He's not going to know what hit him."

"Oh my God, Em, I'm so nervous. I don't look too slutty?"

"You look amazing," she assures me. "You'll be fine! He asked you out, remember? Just be your charming, witty self and he'll be putty in your hands."

"I don't know if I can be charming with him. And forget witty. I'll be too busy worrying there's food in my teeth or that my boobs are going to pop out of this dress."

"Your boobs will be fine," she says firmly. "And if they do, I doubt he'll mind. He's a guy. It'll be like a preview of dessert."

"Emily! I'm not going to sleep with him. Who do you think I am? You?" I grin at her as she throws a couch pillow at me.

"Watch the hair!"

"Okay, Cinderella, get out of here before you turn into a pumpkin. I expect a full report when you get home. Remember, no eating garlic or onions."

"You think he'll try to kiss me?"

"I *know* he'll try to kiss you." Emily settles into the couch and pulls her iBook into her lap.

"What about you? What are you going to do all night?"

"Oh, don't you worry about me. I have an exciting hour of messaging people on a Small World ahead of me, and then Nick's coming over to watch a movie. We'll probably spend all night wondering how the date is going."

"I'll text you updates," I promise.

"Good. Now get out of here!"

Two glasses of wine into the evening, I finally feel relaxed enough to speak to Tristan like a normal human being.

"I was really happy to run into you at Harajuku," I admit shyly, smiling at him across the dinner table. He's wearing dark jeans and a white button-down shirt that shows off his lean, toned arms, with an orange scarf knotted around his neck. The look is slightly too metrosexual for my tastes, but I decide that, if he were to add a pair of aviators and put diamond studs in each ear, the ensemble would be very David Beckham. Tristan picked a chic tapas bar on Rivington Street with killer dishes and even better rioja. Judging from the warm reception given to him by the owner, I've gathered that this is his usual joint.

"Yeah! Talk about the last person I expected to run into. It's been a boring month—didn't get picked for this big campaign I was after, my girlfriend dumped me, my ma's after me every other day to come back home."

"So is mine!" I exclaim, making a mental note to ask about the recent ex-girlfriend later. "She doesn't get that I'm happy here in the city and want to stay. Actually, it's more my father who gets wound up about me—she's just the one who makes the phone calls."

"After your job thingie, I'm not surprised," he says shrugging. "Parents like ours can't deal."

"You know about that?" I ask, stunned.

"Sure. It was on Page Six. Don't feel embarrassed—it happens. Where are you working now?"

"*Womanly World.*"

His face looks blank. "Condé-Nast?"

"*Um* . . . no. It's Beckwith Media. It's also a big company, but their magazines are more . . ." I struggle to find the right word. "Well, crap, basically. They're the only ones who would hire me."

He laughs. "Who cares? At least you have a job."

"Yeah, that's what Emily keeps trying to drill into my head. I don't want to sound like a brat, but it's kind of a hard fall—from the best magazine in the world to this? I think anybody would have a tough transition."

"I'm sure you'll be fine," he says, smiling. God, he's attractive. "Wait. You're going back for your sister's wedding, right?"

"It's my sister! Of course! I'm the maid of honor."

"Cool. I was invited, 'cause of my mom. I never knew your sister that well, but it's sweet she's getting married. Her husband is nice?"

"Harold is the *epitome* of nice. He's so boring it makes my head spin, but Suze is an accountant, so it's not like she's looking for a male stripper or anything. And he's a really good, solid guy."

He winks at me. "That's your type? A male stripper?"

"What? No! Of course not," I sputter, realizing even as I mildly freak out that he's just joking.

"So what *is* your type?" he asks, leaning in. "Am I your type?"

I feel myself go scarlet. "Oh . . . you know . . ." What's a graceful answer to this? Yes, you are my type, and in fact I want to rip your clothes off and have a go at you right here on the table? "I said yes to dinner, didn't I?" I finally respond coyly.

"I like that answer." He stares lustily in my eyes and my tummy goes warm. Check, please.

After dinner, we take a cab back to my place, Tristan not bothering to give the driver two stops. At the front door to my building, I turn awkwardly to him, expecting twenty minutes of banter before he goes for the kiss. Instead, he takes my hand in his, pulls me close and kisses me softly.

"Can I come up?" he asks, gazing at me and stroking the side of my face. His hand is warm and soft, and he smells clean and citrusy, like sea water and lemon.

My knees are buckling. "I . . . *ah* . . . no, I don't think that's a good idea."

"Why not?" he asks, his voice pleading, his breath warm in my ear. "I don't want the night to end."

"*Mmm* . . ." I try to respond, but now he's kissing my neck and it's hard to think clearly with a gorgeous model sucking the life out of my throat. "*Ah* . . . not tonight."

"Tomorrow night, then. Or Sunday. Or Monday. I have to see you again." He pulls me back toward him and kisses me, more authoritatively this time. "Whenever you want."

I have to stop this right now, otherwise I'll cave and let him come up, which is a bad idea on so many levels. "How about Wednesday?"

"Wednesday it is," he says huskily. "I'll call you to make plans." With one last kiss, he's off the stoop and down the street hailing a cab.

I float upstairs as if in a trance, opening the front door to find Emily and Nick watching a movie. They both leap off the couch as soon as I open the door.

"You're home! And without him!" Emily says, throwing a Brown zip-up hoodie over her tank top.

"And *with* the most massive hickey I've ever seen!" Nick exclaims, walking toward me and examining my neck. "Holy mama, that thing is huge. Was he sucking on your neck the entire night, you porn star?"

"Stop it!" I swat Nick away, rushing to the mirror in my bathroom to get a better look at my neck. "Jesus, you're right. It *is* huge." They wander into the bathroom after me.

"Well, it looks like she had a good night," Emily says, cocking her head to the side and looking at Nick.

"And yet she's also home alone," Nick points out, stroking his chin in mock analysis. "With us, and not with Marcus Schenkenberg."

"You know, I'm standing right here. You could both talk directly *to* me, instead of over my head."

"Fine. Spill it," Nick demands, leading me back into the living room. "Was it all amazing and lovey-dovey, and are you going to get engaged but fall for his brother who goes off to war and goes crazy, and then fall for the other brother and kill yourself? Oh, wait, wrong movie."

"Shut up." I laugh, pulling my hand away and plopping onto the couch. "It was good. The conversation was a little stilted, but it got better as the night went on."

"With a face like his, who cares?" asks Emily.

"Conversation, intelligence, opposable thumbs. It's all overrated, really," Nick says.

I shoot Nick a death glare. "We have plans for Wednesday night. I wouldn't let him come up, but he said he has to see me again. And he's *so* cute. You have no idea how in love with him I was in high school."

"Oh, pumpkin," Nick groans, shaking his head sadly at me. "You're in big trouble. Huge."

Chapter 6

Monday mornings are staff meetings. Since I was attacked by Human Resources paperwork during my first week, and was ordered by Frances to take one of her desksides during my second, today will be my first foray into an officewide gathering. Megan brings me a cup of Starbucks, having immediately found out after I began how I took my coffee, and walks over with me, chattering all the way.

"So, how was your weekend?" she asks. "Anything exciting?"

"I had a date. Two, actually. Same guy."

"And? How did it go?"

Tristan called me last night and I agreed to an early dinner, but we quickly hightailed it back to my place; Emily was staying over at Gabrielle's. When I woke this morning, there was a handwritten note on the end table next to my bed: "Call you this week. I want to see you again. xo Tristan."

"Really well, I think. It seems like he wants to go out again soon, but it's always hard to tell with guys in the beginning."

"I know! I've been dating my boyfriend for three years, but when we first got together it was impossible."

"Three years, huh?" I ask, looking sidelong at Megan as we walk into the conference room, sitting in two free chairs at the long, narrow table. "That's a long time. College boyfriend?"

"Yep! We started dating my sophomore year, and we've been together ever since. He's a trader. My fingers are crossed for a proposal this Christmas," she says bashfully.

"Proposal? But you're so young!" My mind automatically drifts to my own postcollegiate hopes for a proposal from Olivier, before everything fell apart and I became incurably cynical about men.

"We've been together forever, though. If we don't get married soon, what's the point?"

I'm about to rebut that she shouldn't rush into anything or look at marriage as the next box to be checked on a list when Ernestine Lumberton strides into the room, closing the door behind her. "Everybody here? Good!" she presses on without waiting for a reply. "Let's get started!"

Ernestine, a big, hulking woman of at least six three, is *Womanly World*'s managing editor, which translates to harassing everybody to turn in their memos and pages on time. After meeting during my first week, I've only seen her around the office twice, and I'm vaguely intimidated by her. It's not just her size; she always has a smile plastered on her face, but seems like the type who would threaten—very pleasantly—to kill your entire family if you were late with a story.

"Everybody has, of course, met our new beauty editor, Bella Hunter. She comes to us from *Enchanté*. Very fancy! Say hi to everyone, Bella!" she commands me cheerily.

I raise my fingers in a small wave, feeling like a deer trapped in headlights. "Hi," I say weakly. I look around at the table of smiling, midlevel faces—directors like Frances, as well as top brass like Rania and James, never attend these meetings—and then back to Ernestine, who is regarding me expectantly. Am I supposed to give a speech? Oh God.

"*Um,*" I clear my throat. Professional Bella powers, *on*! "I'd just like to say thank you to everybody who's been so warm and welcoming to me. I'm thrilled to be here at *Womanly World,* and I'm very much looking forward to becoming a part of your family and working together to bring the magazine to a better, chicer, more popular place. I have a lot of ideas—" lie "—and I'm excited to start implementing them in the beauty pages. If you haven't stopped by my desk yet, please feel free. I'd be happy to give out some beauty freebies!"

I expect my little speech, particularly the offer of free beauty products, to result in wider smiles, but instead, a few of the girls' faces have tensed up into tiny frowns. Shit. What did I say wrong? Should I not have offered freebies? Was that too pathetic, like I'm trying to buy friends?

I look worriedly at Megan, but she gives me a small, encouraging smile as Ernestine says, "Thank you, Bella! Okay, FOB, Home Affairs. How's the piece on DIY kitchen updates coming? Can you have it to me by Wednesday?"

When beauty's turn rolls around, Megan provides the update, her voice and hands shaking slightly, since I'm too new to be up to speed on last month's in-the-well stories. After twenty minutes, fashion, food, features, money, and family having given updates on their sections, the meeting concludes and we all file into the hall.

"That was so nervewracking," Megan confides. "I hate public speaking."

"So do I! Did I say something wrong? Some of the girls seemed annoyed after I finished talking."

We walk down the long hallway, passing a wide yellow cabinet laden with discarded advance-galley books, a slew of fax machines and copiers, and several pastel-colored cupcakes arranged neatly on a tray.

"*Ooh,* cupcakes!" she squeals, pausing by the cabinet to nick one. She takes a bite, swallows, and says, "Aren't you going to have any?"

"No, I'm not hungry," I fib.

"Are you watching your weight?"

I'm surprised by her directness. "Well . . . maybe a little. I gained a few pounds when I was between jobs, and I'm trying to get back down to my fighting weight. I don't feel like buying an entirely new wardrobe!"

"You look great," she says as we move down the hallway toward the beauty department. "You don't need to lose any weight. You could probably gain a couple of pounds." She looks at me worriedly. "I hope that wasn't rude! I didn't mean it like that. I just meant that you're thin, but, you know, well-shaped—"

"It's okay, Megan," I say, and laugh. "Thank you. It's been a while since anybody told me I needed to *gain* weight. You don't hear much of that at Bonneau-Martray."

"Don't worry about those girls."

"The Bonneau-Martray girls?"

"Them, too, but I meant the girls in the meeting. Vicky, Elise, and Shelly. They're just jealous because you're pretty and skinny and look like a model." I blush, but she continues. "I think they were worried you were going to be all stuck-up, coming from *Enchanté*." She pauses. "And you're, like, well-spoken, so they probably just feel really intimidated. But they'll see that you're so nice, and you'll be fine!"

We go back to our cubicles and I sit at my desk, staring blankly at my computer screen. Those girls feel about me the way I felt about the glamazons at *Enchanté* when I started? But can't they tell I'm not like that? I'm a massive nerd! I look down at the outfit I'm wearing today. It's one of my favorite, don't-even-have-to-think-about-it comfy combos—powder blue knee-length Narciso Rodriguez shift, white Nanette Lepore blazer, my beloved tan Jimmy Choos, and a vintage blue-and-white chain-link scarf knotted loosely around my neck, which I picked up for five pounds on Portobello Road with Emily in London. Through somebody else's eyes, I can see how it might look like the kind of outfit a stuck-up label snob would wear. First impressions are key. Is it too late for me to start all over? Can I run by Banana Republic tonight for a quick shopping spree?

Lost in my thoughts, I meander over to the bathroom. Just as I've closed one of the stall doors behind me, I hear the prattle of voices as two other girls enter.

"What did you think of that speech?"

"I was just like, 'What? Do you think you're accepting an Oscar, or something?' I mean, can you be more pretentious?"

I stiffen, holding my breath and silently pulling my legs up so my feet can't be seen underneath the door. A faucet turns on.

"I know! Going on about making the magazine more popular and more glamorous? If you still want to be at *Enchanté*, you shouldn't have gotten fired in the first place."

"Did you read the article?"

"No, did you?"

"Yes, oh my God, you have to read it. I'll Google it and e-mail it to you. She comes off *so* bad. It's sad, actually. I mean, can you imagine being too stuck up even for a Bonneau magazine?"

"She seemed kind of okay when Tammy introduced her around the office. Ridiculous shoes, though."

"Well, obviously, she's not, like, *evil*, but just look at her! You can tell she thinks she's hot shit. Girls like that always do. Homecoming queen, football-player boyfriend. She's a Regina George in *Mean Girls*. Frances didn't even want to hire her, but Rania insisted."

"Why?" The faucet turns off.

"Apparently she's convinced Bella's, like, the second coming and is going to bring in millions of advertising dollars and save us all. I wouldn't hold my breath."

"Yeah." Pause. "I liked her page at *Enchanté*, though. Did you ever read it? It always had good tips, interviews, secret tricks, things like that."

"Oh, sure, she was perfect for *Enchanté*, but that's my point. She's going to *drown* here. Her whole game there was how different she was from the trust fund chicks, but she's exactly the same. She'll never hack i—" The voices fade as the bathroom door closes. They've left. I'm alone again.

The dread creeps over me. What's that Sartre quote? "Hell is other people." What does it matter if *I* know—or think—I'm a good person? Your public perception is your reality and if everybody else sees a snobby one-dimensional bitch, then that's what I am.

The scorn of Shelly and Vicky (or was it Elise? I need to learn everybody's names, stat!) replays itself over and over in my head, distracting me from truly digging into my work. I take out the shoes I wore on my first day of work and put them back in Emily's closet. No more wearing *those*.

My increasingly close relationship with Tristan is the only thing keeping me sane. To say Frances isn't warming to me is like saying Hitler had an image problem. She frowns at me when I pass her in the hallways, makes loud sighing and clucking noises when stopping by my not-exactly-tidy cubicle to deliver manuscripts, and pointedly stares at my outfits whenever I encounter her in the elevator, apparently unimpressed by my Stella jackets and Manolo heels. I've only been at *Womanly World* for a few weeks and already feel that nothing I do is right. Isn't this supposed to be the work honeymoon period? Can't I at least have a few months of blissfully ignorant career happiness before everything turns to dust?

I've been spending a few nights a week at Tristan's apartment in TriBeCa, nervous about bringing him around the apartment to face the full inquisition from my friends. Nick demands a group-drinking session with Tristan on a nearly daily basis, determined to suss out whether he's worthy of my time or "just cheekbones and curls with a penis attached." (His words.) I'm not sure Tristan would pass close inspection, but who wants to admit that their boyfriend—well, *sort of* boyfriend—is little more than a pretty face? Besides, I've put my heart on the line enough times with less-than-gorgeous guys, feeling in some sick way that I was being charitable for personality-dating them. Even the unattractive ones cheat most of the time, and it's not like Tristan and I are engaged. Why shouldn't I enjoy a little eye candy? I get enough banter from my friends. Looks can be *underrated* in a relationship's importance. I deserve a little enjoyment, goddamn it!

When my phone rings one afternoon several weeks after starting at *Womanly World,* I almost decide not to answer it, not wanting to get sidetracked before starting on ideas for the Mode presentation, but my curiosity gets the better of me; surely there's no harm in taking a quick break after working nonstop all day. I gave Frances my first batch of ideas last week, which were quickly returned to me awash in a sea of red and negative comments. After spending an entire day toiling away on changes and improvements, she finally put it through to Rania, which means I'm off the hook—at least until *next* month, when I'll not only have to repeat the entire process, but start working on my first column. It's nearly four anyway, which means I need to leave for my Italiani event in half an hour. The event will be my first post-*Enchanté* appointment, and although I'm terrified to see the other girls, I'm suppressing the panic, having made a deal with myself to enjoy some freak-out time in the car on the way there.

It's Joss, who immediately ropes me into a debate about whether she should spend the money to see Colin Palm, a

Morrison client and the most expensive (and overrated) hair-dresser in New York.

"Joss, listen to me. If you see him, he'll give you bangs, no doubt. You *cannot* let him give you bangs. First of all, they're over, plus they won't look right with your face shape. You know that," I admonish her.

"Why do you think I won't look good with bangs? I had bangs two years ago. When Edward did them? They looked effing fabulous."

"I am telling you this as your beauty guru, but more im-portant, as your friend. Do not get bangs. Just don't. Some people are bangs people, some people aren't. You can rock the long, wavy, sex-kitten hair thing like no other, but the hair around your face needs to be long, so it pulls your face down and makes it look thinner. It is *essential*."

"What are you telling me?" she frets. "Are you saying I have a fat face?"

"Not at all," I say soothingly, even though Joss's head *does* kind of resemble a pumpkin. "It's just that certain hairstyles look right with certain face shapes. You have a round face, so it's either better for you to have an angled bob that brings out your cheekbones, or long layers that start past your collarbone. Take Emily, for example. Her face is heart-shaped. Bangs work fine on her, since other-wise her forehead looks too large. You, on the other hand, have a *beautiful* forehead. Why hide it with bangs that are going to make you break out and will need trimming every two weeks?"

"I still don't see what that has to do with seeing Colin. What is this really about?"

"Nothing! Would I steer you wrong? Colin is a one-trick pony and right now, he's absolutely obsessed with bangs. Did you see that spread in *W* last month where Natalia and Gemma looked like they'd had a run-in with a weed whacker?

That was all Colin." I shudder remembering the tragic photo shoot. "If he gets anywhere near you, he'll be unable to resist. Plus, is he going to comp you?"

She's silent, then finally says, reluctantly, "No. It's fifty percent off. Only editors get the free cuts."

"Joss! Fifty percent off one of his cuts is still six hundred dollars! Are you insane?"

"It's Colin! Can I call myself a beauty publicist if I haven't seen him? You tell me."

"It's your funeral," I say solemnly. "I can understand that you want the Colin experience, but if it were me and *my* hair, I would just go in for a blow-dry. I mean, this is your *hair*. It's not a joke."

"Ahem."

I turn around, startled, and see that James is standing in the door of my cubicle, his features set firmly in a frown. How long has he been standing there listening to me prattle on about bangs and the important of face shape? I've been working nonstop all day, and as soon as I take a five-minute phone break, he catches me. And after he heard me on the phone bitching about the magazine, too. Of all the luck.

"I have to go," I say into the phone in a low voice.

"Wait! Two more minutes! My appointment's in an hour and I've got to decide what to ask for. Layers or angles?" she demands. "Or just a trim?"

"Whatever you think. Go with your gut." I give James an apologetic look, as if to say, *It'll just be two seconds.* He looks back at me, an eyebrow raised.

"I'm debating angles. They'll make my face look more oval, don't you think?"

"Sure. Look, I'm sorry, but I really do have to run." Now James's eyes are roaming, taking in my cubicle. I'd managed to keep it tidy for a couple of weeks, but it's already sliding into did-a-bomb-just-go-off-in-here? territory, with piles of magazines covering the floor and bottles of conditioner, face serum, and nail polish strewn about my desk.

"Layers or angles?" she insists.

"Angles."

"Why?"

"Look, you said it yourself. Angles will help your face look slimmer. Layers are a mistake, anyway. They're impossible to grow out, and then you're going to be stuck going back to Colin over and over, especially since he always gives those really conceptual cut—" I look up at James as I remember that he's still standing there. "Gotta go, call you later, good luck today, bye!"

"Business call?"

"Yes. That was a publicist who needed my professional opinion about a hairdresser she's considering representing," I fib.

"Sure," he says curtly, his expression sour. "I wanted to see what kind of progress you've made with the presentation so far."

"It's coming along great! Really well. Can't wait for our meeting with Frances."

He looks at me carefully. "I see. Can I take a look at what you have so far?"

"Actually, it's at home," I put on my best *Isn't that a shame?* face, wishing I were a better liar. My neck is getting hot and I'm sure that I'm turning beet red. I feel like a kid again, re-membering how Susan used to always tattle, "Bella's lying! Look, she's getting all red!" whenever I'd try to get myself out of a scrape with my parents. "I was working on it late last night, so I took it home with me." What's the point of this lie? Why not just admit that I haven't started working on it yet?

"*Mmm-hmm.* Is it a physical presentation? We just need some ideas on paper. It doesn't need to be fancy; it's about the substance, not the packaging."

"Of course. I have the ideas on paper, but I was . . . just scribbling them down as I worked, then I took the notebook home with me, so they're actually, *ahem,* home right now. On my counter. But, *er,* I can bring them in tomorrow if you want? To look at them?" What the hell is wrong with me? Everytime James sees me, I come across like a twelve-year-old Valley girl.

He pauses a second before shaking his head. "No, I suppose that Monday will be fine as planned. Just come prepared, please." He turns and walks off.

Okay, Bella. Put it out of your head. Come up with something fabulous to present and you'll be fine—James will forget all about your repeatedly moronic encounters and will come to see that you're only an idiot *part* of the time. Much more pressing matters at hand: how are the other editors going to treat me? I have a terrible premonition that I'm going to step out of the elevator at today's appointment and be treated to a wave of pointing and snickering. But surely they wouldn't actually do that. That only happens in the movies. I think.

The event is for the launch of a new foundation by Italiani, held in the penthouse of the Bryant Park Hotel, a popular spot for beauty appointments and presentations. At 4:45, after saving all my work for the day and scribbling a few ideas to follow up on tomorrow on the notepad next to my computer, I hop in a cab. We whiz through midtown and I nervously pull out my Chanel compact. How's my hair? Oh God, it's frizzy because of the drizzly rain. They'll think I've completely gone to pot. I tuck and untuck some around my ears, pulling it forward and back several times before finally digging into my purse for an elastic and scraping it back severely. It looks better, except for a slight cowlick at my crown, which is causing the hair to lay at a strange angle. No good. I take it back down again, but now my hair has a dent all the

way around. Damn it! Of all the days for my hair to mis-
behave! Maybe half up, half down? JLo always looks great
when she wears her hair like that. I slide my fingers all the
way around my head at ear level, pulling up the section and
then securing it in a minibun. Not bad. It needs a finishing
touch, though. Maybe some tendrils near my face? I pull out
a few, but get a little too eager—a chunk falls out on the left
side of my face, giving me a strange Rosie O'Donnell–meets–
Boy George quality. I can't deal with this. I tuck as much of
the weird half-bang behind my ear as I can and decide this
will have to do. A quick check of my makeup reveals that my
nostrils and teeth are clear of any debris, and my eyes don't
have any wayward mascara gunk or eyeliner smudges. This
is as good as it's going to get—I won't be winning any beauty
editor pageants today.

Once at the hotel, I slink through the lobby. Maybe I can
make it upstairs, chat with a PR person for a few minutes,
and then hide in the back, unnoticed. I step in the dark elevator and the doors are just about to close when a tall brunette
smoothly sidesteps through. "Just made it!" she laughs and
then looks at me, her smile fading.

"Bella? What are *you* doing here?" It's Heidi. She clears
her throat and then rolls her eyes, giving me an embarrassed
smile. "I'm sorry, that came out so wrong. I mean—well, how
are you?"

"I'm fine. I'm here for the Italiani event."

"Really?"

"Yes. I'm at *Womanly World* now."

Heidi's eyes are as round as saucers. "*Womanly World*? Well!
Wow! That's great! Congratulations!" Her voice inches into
the stratosphere. "So, *uh,* you're working with Frances?"

"Yep. I just started a few weeks ago."

"Wow. That's a big transition—*Womanly World* is
nothing like *Enchanté.* I don't think I could do—" Her voice

trails off and she pauses awkwardly for a moment. "But, you know, I've heard really good things about the editor in chief, Rania Hassani. She used to be at *Chic*. Everybody loved her."

"Yeah, I know," I say, nodding quickly. We ride the rest of the way up in awkward silence, suddenly finding ourselves intensely interested in our manicures. When the doors open onto the event, we walk down the hallway to the room before Heidi flashes me a quick, toothy smile and then walks into the fray, attaching herself to the nearest PR person.

I stand by the door and take stock of the event. I'm here on the early side—almost ten minutes after the scheduled start time—so there are only four or five other editors there. It's mostly PR people. Suddenly, I feel panicky; what if the PR people hate me, too? I didn't mean to say anything nasty about them, but what if I ruffled all their feathers? You can't be a beauty editor if all the publicists hate you! Oh God, I think I'm finished.

One of the junior PR girls, Kim something-or-other, walks right up to me, however. "Bella! It's so great to see you!" she shrieks, moving in for the obligatory kiss-kiss hug. She grabs my arm and lowers her voice. "How *are* you? Is everything okay?"

"Just great," I say, determined not to be led down this path.

"Are you sure? I mean, I was horrified to hear about what happened to you. I'm so sorry. The way they treated you . . . it's just repulsive."

"Water under the bridge," I say brightly.

"You are so strong." Kim says firmly, gazing at me as if I'm Mother Teresa. "Bravo to you."

"*Um* . . . thanks."

"Okay, so, look," she says, completely switching gears as she conspiratorially beckons me over to a table where fruit and cheese are laid out, "I have *got* to talk to you about something, but you have to promise you won't say a thing to anybody."

"Of course."

"This is sort of embarrassing, but . . . do you think Larissa is going to promote from within for your job, or hire somebody from the outside?"

Okay, *this* isn't awkward.

"I only ask because I've been with Italiani *forever* and I am just so sick of it. Between you and me! But you know how it is. I didn't think I was going to go into public relations, but then I got hired at Morrison out of college, and suddenly I was stuck in PR hell, and then I *had* to get hired somewhere else, so I applied for this position, and before you know it, I've been a publicist for six years! It's a nightmare!"

"Well, *uh* . . ."

"I know that you and Larissa are probably not on the best terms right now, but I'm just wondering if you still happen to have any friends there, or if you hear of anything, could you maybe put in a good word for me? I would be forever in your debt!"

"Sure," I say weakly.

"You're the best! I didn't want to send my résumé without talking to you first, because I know that Larissa and Janelle Morrison are friends, and word travels so fast in this industry." She lets out a peal of laughter. "I don't have to tell *you* that!"

She gives me another kiss-kiss and then hurries off to say hello to two other editors who have just arrived. I skulk around the drinks and food table for a few minutes, sipping a glass of white wine and pretending to be interested in the cheeses. In actuality, I'm scanning the room to see who's here. After a few minutes, I realize that I'm the only person by this table. There's another one on the opposite side of the room, and there are at least seven girls standing by it:

Alanna Doheney from *Chic,* Grace, Mandy, Heidi, and a couple of mid-level PR girls. Normally I would have rated several Hey, Bella!'s by now. They're completely ignoring me. Unless they're over there by coincidence. But what if it's *not* a coincidence? What if my gut is right and they all really hate me and they're talking about how disgusting it is that I would dare to show my face and they're laughing about my downfall and wondering how much longer I'll be able to stay in the industry? Oh God, that's totally what they're talking about. This isn't just me being paranoid. I can feel it. I can feel it in my *bones.*

As the R&D person walks to the front of the room and starts shuffling with notes, whispering frantically to a small man in a suit at her side, everybody sits down. I take a seat on a cushion next to Alanna, giving her a rueful little smile as if to say, "Hey, what's up?" but she immediately averts her eyes and reaches into her purse to start playing with her cell phone.

I shift imperceptibly to the left to see who's next to me and find Mandy, who's, of course, sitting next to Heidi. She's scribbling in a notebook.

"Hey, girl!" I whisper. "How are you?"

Mandy shoots me a tight-lipped smile, then puts her fingers to her lips, pointing cutesily to the R&D person about to begin her presentation.

What the hell? The woman's not even talking yet? Girls all around us are still chatting!

After twenty-five minutes of slides and speeches, the presentation wraps up and I file out of the room in a daze, the girls all twittering excitedly as they compare events for the evening and try to figure out who will be at what place. The elevator is full when I get there, so I take my gift bag from one of the junior publicists and stand awkwardly, trying not to make eye contact with any of the editors inside.

Just then, a voice I can't place whispers loudly: "Can you *believe* the nerve of her, showing her face here after that article?"

A chorus of "I know!" answers as the doors slide shut.

Blow over? Not likely.

Suddenly I hear a soft voice behind me say, "Hey, Bella."

I turn around, startled, seeing Sarah Jeckles, the assistant from *Beauty* magazine. I've never actually talked with her before, but I'm thrilled to have somebody—anybody—speaking to me.

"Hey, Sarah! How are you?"

"I'm fine . . . but how are you? That was so mean," she says, gesturing toward the closed elevator doors.

"Thanks." My face feels hot. I didn't realize Sarah heard it.

"I've only been in the industry for a few months," Sarah says quietly, tucking a piece of blond hair behind her ears and looking around her, "but you didn't say anything that I haven't heard other people say a million times."

"I'm just the idiot who said it to the *New York Post*."

"Don't worry about it. I'm sure it will blow over soon enough. Everybody loves you."

"Ha! You saw what just happened. The only person besides you who's bothered to speak to me is Kim, and that's because she was asking me if I'd recommend her for my old job."

Sarah looks wounded on my behalf. "That's so inappropriate. Besides, Larissa just rehired Delilah Windsor."

"Delilah Windsor? No."

"Yes, I heard it this morning. Today's her first day back there."

"Are you *sure*?"

"Yes, why?"

"Larissa *hates* Delilah," I sputter. "It's—well. Never in a million years—! She would never—!" Words fail me.

Sarah shrugs apologetically, looking vaguely confused. "I guess Larissa doesn't hate her anymore."

The news that Larissa has hired Delilah for my old position officially ruins what was already a terrible week. As if my archenemy winning the most coveted industry job isn't enough, I manage to make a further ass of myself in front of James in the lobby. He stops to say hello as our paths cross and asks if I've had an opportunity to work more on the presentation.

"Yes!" I lie. "Almost done!"

"That's good. If that's the case, can we push our meeting up? I'm free Friday morning."

"Wonderful. Great," I say, silently panicking. I'll have to get cracking on this. "I think you'll love my ideas. I've been working extremely hard on them." Just then, my phone rings. Nick and I have made a game of stealing each other's iPhones and downloading embarrassing ring tones to surprise the other. Nick must have grabbed it last night before I left for Tristan's, because now "Barbie Girl" is blaring loudly, causing the entire lobby to turn and stare. James does not look impressed.

Frances calls an impromptu beauty meeting on Wednesday to gather products for the big September issue. This should be a piece of cake. We were sent all of the best products at *Enchanté,* so I'm familiar with practically every beauty product known to man. I bring my notebook to the meeting in Frances's office, ready to jot down notes about which stories she wants me to formulate.

"Who wants to start?" Frances asks, looking at me expectantly.

"I will," I say, eager to prove myself. I motion to a group of futuristic-looking bottles on the edge of our new product table. "These are all antiwrinkle products available in September. We have a new serum from La Mer, with three times the power of their last wrinkle treatment, and a super concentrated version of the Miracle Broth—"

"Too expensive."

"Right. Okay, scratch that one. Well, next to it is the new treatment from Lancôme. It's designed to work in tandem with their latest line, which is designed for—"

"How much is it?"

I frown, trying to recall the price. I haven't looked at the press release in months, since before I left *Enchanté*. "It's . . . uh . . . forty-five dollars, I think."

"You think?"

"Yes. I'm pretty sure."

"Next time, please come prepared with prices. Megan?" she turns her head, cutting me off. "What about the nail-treatment story you mentioned to me yesterday?"

"Oh! Yes! Well, *er,* our research has shown that our readers really like nail stories, as you know, so I was thinking, maybe, that a small piece on cuticle creams and hand creams and nail strengtheners—you know, all the things you can do at home by yourself so you don't have to spend money at a nail salon—could be really good. *Um,* this one is Sally Hansen—" she picks up a small bottle of clear liquid "—and this one is Orly. They're both, *uh,* under ten dollars and they're also available in September." Megan looks at me worriedly, as if she's afraid she's stealing my thunder. I give her an encouraging smile.

"Wonderful. Thank you, Megan. Let's put that on the roster." She looks at me again. "Bella. Any other suggestions?"

"Yes," I say, taking a deep breath and picking up several pocket-sized lip glosses. "These glosses are all under twenty dollars and are by Stila—"

"Too niche."

"—and also Revlon, Cover Girl, Jane, and Neutrogena. All drugstore," I say pointedly. "The Neutrogena one is particularly amazing. It has SPF, plumpers, and a hint of sheer color, and doubles as a cheek stain."

"A cheek stain?" Frances looks utterly befuddled, drumming her fingers on her desk. "What is the point of that?"

"If you're stuck without any makeup, and you need some extra color, it's designed as a stain, so it won't fade off your cheeks and—"

"I am not sure if lip gloss is right for us now. We just did a story on it three months ago." She raises an eyebrow. "Have you read the May issue yet?" This is the issue currently on the stands, with Hillary Clinton on the cover.

"No, not yet, but I was just going to tackle it today. Maybe we could hold the lip gloss story for next month, or the following, then—"

"Bella, I need you to familiarize yourself with the magazine. Are you telling me you have been here for a month and you have not read the current issue yet?"

"No, but—"

"It has been on newsstands for weeks." She looks thunderous. I realize no excuse will appease her.

"I'm sorry, Frances. I'll read it at my desk the second the meeting's over."

"I do not need you wasting work time reading the magazine. That is something you can do, and should have already done, on your own time." She sighs. "Have you bothered to read *any* of the previous issues?"

Shit. "I read the Diane Sawyer issue," I say meekly.

"And that is it?"

"Yes."

Frances puts her fingers to her temple. "Bella, do you know *anything* about the magazine yet? Any of the basic facts? Tell me, what is *Womanly World*'s circulation?"

Oh, goddamn it. Who knows their magazine's circulation? Actually, I knew *Enchanté*'s circulation by heart—two point five million, and growing. But *Womanly World*? No clue. "Five million?" I guess, praying with all my heart that this number is anywhere close to the reality.

She presses her lips together tightly. "I take it you are grasping at straws, because that is not even close. Sixteen million. Sixteen million women looking to us *every month* for beauty advice. This is your job, Bella. I suggest you take it more seriously, or else."

"Yes, Frances." I have to restrain myself from calling her "ma'am."

The meeting lasts fifteen more minutes, during which four more of my ideas are shot down, and all of Megan's are green lit. As Megan and I walk back to our desks, she says shyly, "Bella? Don't let Frances get you down, okay? She's just cranky sometimes. You're a great writer and those ideas were all really good."

What a sweet girl. "Thank you, Megan."

She looks nervous and takes a deep breath. "*Um,* I know this might be kind of presumptuous, but . . . do you think this week, if you're free—I mean, if you have even five seconds?— you could take a quick look at this piece on hair straighteners I've been working on? I can't seem to get it right, and I know you'd be able to turn it around in two seconds." Her cheeks are pink.

"I'd love to. Hey, why don't we take a look at it now?"

"Now? Are you sure? It's really bad. I don't want to waste your time. I kind of wanted to clean it up a bit first."

"That's okay. Let's take a look at what you have and see if you're moving in the right direction. How does that sound?" I ask kindly, turning around to walk with Megan to her desk.

"Sure! Great!" Megan sits at her computer and pulls up a

Word document, motioning for me to read it. The grammar is off here and there, and the intro is slightly sophomoric, as though a college student has crafted an intro based upon a quick perusal of her favorite magazines, but the descriptions of the products are snappy and succinct, and explain how to help shave time from readers' busy schedules, which I'm sure Frances will love.

"It's good! Nothing to be worried about! The product descriptions are great—very vivid. I like them. My only suggestion is the intro—it doesn't pull the reader in. Maybe you could craft a sentence comparing the time wasted on styling your hair to, I don't know, the time wasted trying to wrestle a kid into its car seat, and explain how learning the right shortcuts will make it all easier. Compare the miracle of bribing your son with candy to the genius of a hair serum applied to wet hair," I shrug, "or something along those lines. That's a bad example, but you see where I'm going. Grab the reader off the bat with an apt metaphor, then segue into the copy. Make sense?"

She nods eagerly. "Yes! That's good!"

"You're being kind," I laugh. "It was crap, and Frances would shoot it down in two seconds. But it's all about the cute hook. Although I sense that *Womanly World* doesn't go for cute so much, huh?"

"Don't listen to Frances," she says firmly. "I mean, you have to listen to her, because she's the boss and all, but don't take it to heart. You've only *just* started working here. You'll win her over. I know it."

I regard Megan for a few minutes, realizing that I've underestimated her. Sure, she's a bit young and naive, and obviously I'm being taken in by flattery, but she's also being sincere, and she genuinely wants me to succeed. I haven't given her a fair chance. "Do you want to grab lunch?"

★　★　★

We walk two blocks to Panera, chatting all the way about relationships and the industry. Not only do I feel happy that I'm building a friendship with somebody in the office, but I'm pleased that she's also the beauty assistant. As I learned with Tasha—or, more obviously, with Delilah—it's difficult, if not impossible, to work alongside somebody you don't like. Megan and I agree to regularly get lunches together; she's only been at *Womanly World* for a year and I sense that she hasn't truly bonded with anybody else in the office, either. I stop by the beauty closet after lunch to freshen up my appearance, wanting to reapply some concealer to hide a stress zit that has popped up on my chin. I grab one of the makeup compacts from the eye shadow bin, opening and placing it on a shelf for mirror access as I dot on Laura Mercier Secret Camouflage with a brush, then set it with some Bare Escentuals Mineral Veil. I hold the compact at arm's length, frowning at my reflection in the mirror. My hair is disastrously greasy; a few sprays of Bumble and bumble Hair Powder should do the trick—thank God our closet has at least a *few* nice brands. I grab a bottle without looking and flip over at the waist, spraying the roots at the back of my head, then flipping over again and spraying around the crown.

"Bella?" I'm startled to see James in front of me, carrying several portfolios, an incredulous look on his face.

"Hello. How are you?" I ask politely.

He shakes his head, mouth slightly agape. "What are you *doing*?"

"For a story," I say quickly. "Just testing out some products."

If he could raise his eyebrows any more, they'd be on top of his head. "A story?"

"Yes. For . . . hair shortcuts. Ways to save time for busy moms."

He opens his mouth to say something else, then seems to think better of it, jamming his hands into the pockets of his suit and pressing his lips together tightly. "Carry on." He walks off.

Okay, whatever *that* was about. James always seems to be lurking about precisely when I don't want him to be. Sod's Law.

I raise the compact back to eye level to make sure the spray is evenly distributed and involuntarily shriek as I see why James was looking at me so strangely. I grabbed the wrong colored bottle; my blonde locks are generously streaked with gummy jet-black powder. Just my luck.

Rania calls me into her office later in the week, which sends me into a tailspin. This is it! They're firing me!

As it turns out, she simply wants to pick my brain about getting involved with American Beauty Women.

"You worked frequently with them through *Enchanté*, didn't you?"

"Yes," I say, relieved that my job seems safe for now. "There's a polo match in the Hamptons that we sponsor every summer, and I acted as the liaison. I'm not sure who's handling it now." *Probably Delilah*, I think darkly.

"I've been toying with the idea of getting on board with that. Polo's popular with several of the advertisers and it could be a good opportunity to prove that *Womanly World* is reaching out to both younger and more affluent readers. What do you think?"

"I think it's a great idea! Edison, Face, Dewy—they're all involved. ABW sponsors a marquee, all of the editors and beauty execs are there, and tons of celebrities. There's always a luncheon, too. Maybe we could work with ABW to have *Womanly World* placed in the gift bags?"

She nods enthusiastically. "I like it. Will you be my point person? You already have the contacts, and maybe we could sponsor a table. We'd need to run it by James, of course."

"Of course," I echo. "I'd love to do it!" Emily introduced me to polo through her father, and while I'm hardly the world's biggest sports fan, it's an undeniably beautiful game. Any excuse to become reinvolved with some of the old *Enchanté* glamour is welcome.

Rania tells me she'll discuss sponsoring a table with James, which relieves me. The less contact with him, the better. My meeting with him and Frances about our Mode presentation is tomorrow, and I've still got *nothing*. I don't just need to kick it into high gear—right now I'm not even in the damn car.

Following a quick deskside with a drugstore beauty company, I spent the entire afternoon working on ideas for the Mode presentation. Frances's admonitions not to skew too young are ringing in my ears, but I also remember Rania's words last month during my interview. She wants to revamp the magazine, right? Rania knows better than Frances, especially seeing as Frances is still stuck in 1991. *Womanly World* needs glamour . . . accessible glamour, of course. Glamour for moms. I can do that. I type furiously, noting ideas to make the beauty section hipper, suggesting a makeover page, a regular feature about the hottest trends and how to wear them, a page where a resident stylist explains how he gives of-the-moment celebrities their hairstyles, and a new front-of-book section highlighting salons and day spas around the country for women on a budget. After I have six pages of notes, I call it a day, satisfied with my initiative. Surely even Frances will be impressed with this.

"So, what have you come up with?" James asks.

Frances and I are sitting in his office on Friday morning, my notes in my lap.

"Well," I say brightly, hoping all thoughts of my black hair powder incident are out of James's head, "I think, based on my conversations with Rania, that what *Womanly World* needs is a shot of adrenaline to make it more appealing to younger readers, which will in turn demonstrate to advertisers that we're pulling in their demos. Compared to the other magazines, *Womanly World* is just *stuck*. There's little that's exciting on the pages and we feature the same few drugstore brands over and over again. I know that our readers have limited financial resources, but variety in the products featured can only be a good thing, especially when it comes to wooing advertisers. I don't think it would hurt to include a smattering of products from specialty lines. Here I have some lists of potential products—"

Frances frowns. "I thought we went through this, Bella. Our readers can't afford expensive specialty items. They *like* seeing the drugstore products."

"I know, but . . . don't you think they'd like to see some glamorous products mixed in, as well? For a balance between real-life and aspirational stuff? For example, after a rough day with the kids, you come home and flip through *Womanly World* and find a really exciting serum from, say, Kanebo, and a feature on a great new day-spa where you can get a pedicure at—"

"Our readers are not interested in hundred-dollar serums and snobby salons," Frances says, shooting James a frustrated look. "I've explained this to you."

I'm flustered by her tone. Why does she have to be so ornery? "Of course. However—"

"What else do you have?" James cuts in.

"Well . . ." I scan my notes. "I was thinking about adding a makeover rubric, featuring—"

"*Glamour* does a makeover. *Good Housekeeping* does a makeover. *Redbook* does a makeover. *Womanly World* readers don't want to see another ridiculous makeover feature where some woman gets a fancy haircut that she'd never be able to afford otherwise and which would take an arsenal of products to replicate. Not us." Frances's voice is rising.

"Yes. I'm sorry." This is not going well at all. "What about a trend page where we show the latest celebrity looks and feature products that readers can use to—"

"Bella," James says with exaggerated patience, "Do you have *any* ideas that aren't stolen straight from the pages of *Enchanté*? Our magazines are different. Our readers are different. What worked there isn't going to work here. I know everybody thinks *Enchanté* is wonderful, but our readers like our formula. You need to take some time and familiarize yourself with the magazine. None of these ideas are right for us."

They didn't even give me a chance! I have six entire pages of ideas here! "Right," I say hesistantly, not wanting to push, but feeling frustrated that my hard work and brainstorming is being completely discarded. "But perhaps you could just take a look at the other ideas I have here. I have a lot of new rubrics and concepts that really *could* work and would prove to potential advertisers that we're trying to move in a new direction."

James drums his fingers on the desk and then glances at his appointment book. "Look, Bella, please clear your ideas with Frances before the next meeting. I don't have time to sit and listen to suggestions that aren't fully fleshed out and which won't work for our pages. This lack of adequate preparation won't be acceptable for our meeting with the Face Group in July. It's very important that we secure their ad dollars," he says evenly, speaking to me as if I'm a five-year-old. He turns to Frances. "Please send Bella the presentation template from last month that you worked on before she arrived. We'll go with that. We'll have to wait until the next pitch to add new ideas."

"Will do," she nods.

"Great. That's all." He swivels in his chair, picking up a pen and crossing off something on a notepad. Meeting adjourned.

"Thank you," I say meekly, following Frances out of the office.

I walk back to my desk, alternating between shame at the reception James and Frances gave me and fury over their abrupt dismissal. They didn't even give me a chance to go through all my ideas! Some of them were very good! So my ideas skew kind of young! So I'm not some forty-seven-year-old mother of nine living in Hickville who only shops at CVS! So I cut my teeth at a glamorous magazine! So what? Beauty is beauty! I'm being persecuted because my ideas aren't dowdy and boring? This is prejudice! Rania was so positive in the interview, I was sure that I'd breeze into *Womanly World* and have everybody love me, but they seem determined to dismiss me as a frivolous moron.

I'm staring at my computer, my cheeks burning at the shame of failing yet *again*, when I hear my name. I turn around and see James standing by my cubicle. Great. More abuse. As if I wasn't embarrassed enough by their tag-team annihilation in his office.

"I . . ." He clears his throat and folds his arms across his chest, cuff links flashing in the light, before continuing, "This presentation is important, so I want to ensure that you were not discouraged by our comments just now. I do appreciate your effort."

Huh?

"Oh, well . . . thank you. Not at all," I say quickly. "I mean, I was disappointed that you didn't like my ideas, but, *uh,* you know, I understand, so . . ." Brilliant, Bella. You are a master of the English language. Excellent use of that degree.

"Good," he says firmly.

Silence.

"Well . . . great," I say awkwardly.

He looks around my cubicle, his arms still folded. "Are you settling in well?"

"Oh, yes, very well, thank you."

"That's good," he says, and nods. As he stands there, his cologne drifts toward me and I catch the scent: Helmut Lang, a sophisticated, sexy fragrance that was discontinued several years ago. *That's* unexpected. He locks eyes with me and for a split second, I feel a sudden flash of lust that makes my cheeks burn. My God, he's attractive. *Bella, don't go there.* He looks away and nods brusquely. "Okay. Please read through the presentation this weekend to make sure it's clear and you're prepared." He turns and walks away.

Did I imagine that? What the hell just happened?

Chapter 7

I leave work at 5:30 to go downtown for an American Beauty Women charity meeting at Cipriani. James has approved the purchase of a table, so it will be me, James, Rania, and five advertisers, with space at the table for two other people, if we'd like to invite personal guests. Frances made clear she would not be involved, muttering more to herself than to me that polo had nothing to do with our readers.

I walk into the restaurant, my stomach nervously clenching as I spot the table of editors and charity board members. Will it be a repeat performance of the Italiani event?

"Well, bless my soul. Look who it is, girls!" a silky voice purrs as I walk up. The hairs on the back of my neck snap to attention. *Delilah*.

"Hello," I say frostily. "It's been awhile."

"Honey, I have been *so* worried about you!" She stands up, gliding over and putting her thin arms around my neck, pressing me tight to her. Her breasts squish against my chest and I can smell her signature perfume—Angel by Thierry Mugler—an old favorite that's been ruined for me forever. "Why haven't you returned any of my calls?"

"You never called me, Delilah."

"Of course, dear." She presses her lips together and looks worriedly at a seated Mandy, as if to say, 'Poor, Bella.' "It's so great to see you. Larissa and I both miss you *so* much. I feel so sad that we're not in contact anymore." The other editors, aware of our history, look back and forth between us worriedly, their heads swiveling rapidly as if watching a tennis match.

"That's funny," I say. "Larissa hasn't mentioned your name once when we've talked." Larissa now calls about once a week to check in and moan—or crow, depending on the tides—about her love life. The first time she called following my Italiani appointment, I confronted her about hiring Delilah, but she'd simply cried, "Doll, I don't want to talk about it!"

"Really? She goes on about you all the time! Of course, she's so worried about you over at *Womanly World*."

"I'm fine."

"Just yesterday," she continues breathily, "we were at the Chanel sample sale—I'd hoped I'd see you there, but of course, I suppose you weren't invited at your magazine—and Larissa said, 'It's a good thing Bella isn't here, because otherwise the *Post* might get wind of it and then it would be canceled!'"

"No, she didn't!" gasps Mandy.

"She *did*. And I said, 'Now, Larissa, that's not very nice—you know Bella didn't mean anything by it! She just speaks without thinking sometimes!' I couldn't stand the thought that Larissa had the wrong idea about you, Bella. I'm in your corner." She grips my forearm, and I feel as though her icy fingers are slicing through my flesh. I find it sickly amusing that Delilah never has any sort of body heat; obviously indicative of her cold, black heart. "Come, sit next to me."

"That's okay." I wrest my arm from her fingers and walk toward a chair next to Kristen Gibson, the ABW polo committee member. "I'll sit here." I can't believe I never recognized Delilah's insincerity when we worked together. Some of my *Enchanté*-era friends questioned why I surround myself with a brash, rollicking group like Nick, Emily, and Joss, but Delilah is a living proof of why one or two tell-it-like-it-is honest friends are infinitely better than popularity with a million sycophants.

Mandy leans over and whispers none too softly in Heidi's ear, "Even after everything, she's nice to Bella. What do you think the real story is?"

"*Shh,*" Heidi hisses, looking nervously in my direction.

"Hi, Kristen," I say, struggling to tune out the whispers that are bouncing back and forth across the table. "Thanks for having me. *Womanly World* is very excited to be part of this."

"I thought polo was supposed to be exclusive, but I suppose *anybody* can get involved now," Delilah says softly, aiming her comment at the ceiling. Mandy looks positively terrified.

"It's for charity," Heidi briskly rebuts. "Any sort of publicity is a good thing."

Kristen is oblivious. "Thanks for coming! I'm happy you'll be involved. After all these years, it wouldn't be the same without you!"

After a few stragglers arrive, the meeting speeds by at breakneck pace, Kristen handing out papers explaining the involvement of each magazine, table commitments, a schedule for the day, and press releases detailing last year's charitable take.

"Call me if you have any questions before the event. And I need you all to e-mail me the names of the people at your table the week before the game, please. Other than that, I think we're done!" Kristen says brightly. The table explodes in chatter, several girls dashing to the bar to order cocktails. I thank Kristen, nod politely at Mandy and Heidi, and gather my things.

"You're not staying?" Delilah simpers. "What a shame. I hoped we'd be able to chat some more, Belly."

I refuse to get drawn into this. "We said it all years ago, Delilah. There's nothing left to discuss."

She sighs. "No need to be *rude*. How often can one person apologize? If anything, I was just as much the victim as you were. That man you were seeing accosted me. It was so upsetting. And then I lost your friendship on top of it—you just cut me out like that without even caring to hear my side . . ." Delilah gently wipes away a tear at the corner of her lashes, casually looking around the table to ensure her performance isn't going unnoticed. Mandy surreptitiously grabs Heidi's wrist, looking ready to hyperventilate from the sheer drama of it all.

"You're a liar, and a bad one at that," I say quietly, calling upon years of Joss-donated self-help books to keep myself calm. "Please leave me alone."

She shrugs, the worried look sliding off her face. "I can only try so many times. *Ciao.*" Her red hair swishes over her shoulders as she pulls out her cell phone and stomps over to the bar, flagging down a bartender.

"She's disgusting," Emily declares.

"Everybody knows she's a liar," agrees Joss.

"Are we *still* talking about Dementor Windsor?" Nick comes back into the room with a fresh bottle of red wine. "Give it a rest! The tramp isn't worth two seconds of your thought. I thought we put the whole thing to bed years ago. She's trash. And wears way too much makeup."

"But why does everybody kiss her ass?" I demand. "I don't get it! Those girls aren't stupid—they see how she is!"

"Maybe they're scared of her," Emily shrugs. "She's at *Enchanté* now, and they know what she's capable of. Why anger the wild, wounded tiger when you can just keep it in a cage and throw meat at it?"

Nick looks at Emily disbelievingly. "That is the lamest

analogy I've ever heard. Did you get that psychobabble from your textbooks?"

"Shut up."

Joss nods. "Emily's right. No offense to you, Bella, but, really, whose side do you think they're going to pick? Nobody likes Delilah, but nobody wants to get on her bad side, either. They're hardly inviting her over for slumber parties. She has working relationships, especially now that she's back at *Enchanté*." Joss pops a cherry tomato into her mouth. Tristan is finally coming over to hang with the full group tonight, and Joss spent half an hour intricately preparing a cheese and crudité plate, harping all the while on Gary's lactose intolerance. Since losing the MBA battle last week, she's been irate, relishing any excuse to complain about him; I think she's more excited about the night with Tristan than I am. "All of the publicists hate her," she continues. "She's sweet as pie until something doesn't go her way, then she's an out-and-out bitch."

Emily puts her hand on my arm calmly. "Forget her. She's not *worth* it."

The door buzzes and everybody springs into action.

"It's Tristan!" My stomach ties up in knots.

"Quick, tidy up!" Joss cries, plumping cushions and putting all the wineglasses on coasters.

"So you were in love with him in high school?" Nick asks doubtfully as I look around the living room worriedly to make sure Nick hasn't "accidentally" left any embarrassing photos out for Tristan to find. "He was the quarterback or something?"

"Right."

"And he didn't know you existed."

"Not so much."

"But now you two are dating."

"In a nutshell."

"And he's a male model."

"Yes."

"He *can* read, yeah?"

"Nick, behave," I warn. "Please."

"I'm just kidding," he says innocently. "I'm sure he's the smartest male model on the block."

"We're almost out of wine! What do we do?" Joss looks bereft.

"There's more in the liquor cabinet," Nick says. "Believe me, we're going to need it."

Emily leans against the living room windowsill, arms crossed, watching us with a look of supreme amusement on her face. "Are any of you going to buzz him in?"

"Oh no!" I scurry to the door, pressing the intercom button. "Hello?" My voice drops an octave into sex-kitten territory.

Nick rubs his hands together gleefully. "This is going to be fun."

"Hey, sweets, it's Tristan."

"Hey," I say smoothly. "Come right up."

I buzz him in, quickly checking my reflection in the mirror by the door. "How do I look?"

"Gorgeous." Joss sets four bottles of red on the table and asks worriedly, "Will this be enough?"

Nick shakes his head. "Definitely not."

"You look very sexy," agrees Emily, who has surreptitiously been smoking and now tosses a half-lit cigarette out the window, waving her hands around to clear the smoke. "I'm quitting, I'm quitting!" she says at the look of fury on my face. "Your hair looks crazy, like a lion. But in a good way. In a 'take me to bed, now' way."

I decide to temporarily ignore the fact that Emily's been smoking again—it can only mean that she and Josie had another fight—and look at Nick expectantly. He shrugs. "Your makeup is smudged."

"Nick! So fix it!" Joss and Emily exclaim simultaneously.

"Okay, okay." He whips out a credit-card-sized pouch, upzips it, and pulls out some Q-tips, moving them around my nose, under my eyes, on my lids and on my lip line in a flurry of activity. He quickly blots my face with an oil-removing sheet and pulls out an O.B.-sized ruby stain, applying it to my lips and cheeks before plunging his hands into my hair, placing the tips of his fingers on my scalp and shaking at the roots to give it volume. "Voilà!"

A glance in the mirror confirms that I look ten times better. "Nick, you're the master."

"I know."

Tristan knocks on the door, and I move to open it but am blocked by Nick, who shoots me a wicked grin. "Allow me."

"Hey! Come in, bro! I'm Nick—saw you at Harajuku!" The two boys slap hands like gang members and Emily starts snickering. "Nick has it in for you tonight," she whispers.

"Dude, can I get you some beer? JD? Jim Beam? Johnny?" Around his guy friends—high school pals from San Diego, plus one or two old roommates—Nick makes a big show of downing pints and doing shots, but we've learned that he's a closeted wine snob and likes nothing more than a hearty glass of red.

"A beer would be awesome, man," Tristan says, engulfing me in a bear hug. "Hey, sweets. You look really amazing."

"Thanks. I'm happy you could come over and officially meet everybody. You just met Nick, of course" (Nick thrusts his chin up as if to say "'Sup, homie?") "and this is Emily and Joss." He shakes hands with both of them, his gaze moving back to Emily.

"Weren't you at Harajuku with Bella, too?"

"I was."

"Thought so," he says, grinning. "You're Emily Tyler, right?"

"Guilty."

"Cool! Bella, you didn't tell me your roommate was a celebrity."

Nick starts coughing, rushing into the kitchen as he gasps, "Swallowed . . . wrong . . . way!" Emily shoots him a dirty look.

"Oh. I guess it just didn't come up."

Tristan plops on one of the couches, throwing one arm over the edge and patting the space next to him with his other hand. I follow suit, perching uncomfortably as he drapes his arm casually around me. I certainly wouldn't be this confident if I were meeting a new gang of people for the first time, but Tristan seems in his element.

"And Joss? How do you know Bella?"

"Well," she says excitedly, "Bella works in beauty, as you know, and I'm a publicist for one of the big beauty firms. Morrison? Don't know if you're heard of them?"

"Sure, sure. You guys handle some men's grooming lines, right? My booker's trying to get me on one of the campaigns. Artillery? Not a huge line, but he thinks it'd be good exposure."

"Artillery! Artillery is one of my clients!"

"Really?" he says eagerly, leaning forward and clasping his hands together. "Any recommendations? What are they looking for?"

Joss sits on one of the chairs opposite and pulls out her BlackBerry. "I don't handle anything to do with advertising, so I don't really know, but I'll put you in touch with someone who does. What's your last name?"

"Reynolds. Tristan Reynolds." Is it my imagination, or is he saying this too proudly? I scrutinize him from the corner of my eye, trying to see him through my friends' eyes: his broad chest, his pretty cheekbones, his softly tousled hair. He's perfect, like a Botticelli painting. He's *too* perfect. Is that possible? Can I really date someone prettier than me? What am I saying? It's *Tom Reynolds*. As far as I'm concerned, he can do no wrong.

"Okay." She frantically writes. "What's your e-mail? I'm sending the advertising director a message to expect your book."

He gives her his e-mail address, saying, "Sweet, thanks, Joss!" He puts his arm around me again and pulls me close. "Your friends are awesome."

"Dude, your beer," Nick says, coming back in the living room and tossing Tristan a Bud Light. "Hope light's okay?"

"Thanks, man. Light's better—keeps me at weight."

"That's what I figured." It takes all my self-control to keep from physically removing the smug smile from Nick's face. He opens his can and takes a sip, shuddering involuntarily as he swallows. "*Mmm*. Beer. Tasty."

Nick, Emily, and Joss grill Tristan for about an hour, Nick tossing beer after beer his way until I finally have to ask him to stop. Nick looks at me innocently.

"No, it's cool," Tristan says. "I'm celebrating!"

"Celebrating what?" I ask.

"I wanted to tell you later tonight, but," he shrugs, looking around at the group, "I guess now's good, too. I booked the new Hugo Boss campaign!"

"Oh my God, Tristan!" I hug him, thrilled that I'm allowed—nay, expected!—to touch him as much as I want. "That's amazing!"

"I know. I'm stoked. It's my first national campaign. Dara, my booker, told me the guy said he couldn't think of hiring anybody else—he thought I was perfect. Sweet, right?" he nods enthusiastically.

"*So* sweet," Nick says. "Dude, that rocks."

"Dude! I know!"

"What does that mean for you now?" Emily asks, settling on the edge of Nick's chair and stealing a sip of wine from his glass. He gave up on beer about five minutes after Tristan arrived.

"We sign the papers, yada yada, and then we shoot next week. It's in the Bahamas. I'm so stoked—I've never been there."

"You haven't signed anything?" Emily looks concerned.

"*Nah,* but it's all set."

I'm feeling more comfortable now as neither Nick nor Emily have yet drawn Tristan's blood. Joss, meanwhile, is gazing at him like he's a young Robert Redford, giggling at his every other word and blushing every time he looks her way. *No worries about* her *disliking him*, I think amusedly. "When do you leave?" I ask.

"Last week in June? Not sure, but I think it's a weekend shoot. I don't know—Dara's taking care of everything. I'll just show up at the airport and look pretty," he laughs. Joss giggles again, flipping her black hair.

"Damn. If it's the last weekend in June, that's the polo match in the Hamptons. I wanted you to come." I had vague hopes of Tristan by my side while facing all the other editors—that would sure as hell shut Delilah up.

"*Aww,* that sucks." He squeezes my thigh. "I would have loved to come. Maybe the date'll change. You never know."

"You never know with a lot of things," Nick says mysteriously. "Who would have known in high school that you two crazy kids would end up getting together?"

I stab him with my eyes and he grins, raising his eyebrows at me impishly.

"The world works in mysterious ways," Tristan agrees. "Buddhism teaches you that."

Nick looks like it's Christmas morning. "You're a Buddhist?"

"*Nah,* not exactly, but my agent gave me a book on it. Heavy stuff. Profound. A lot of good life lessons."

"Buddhism! Buddhism is amazing," Joss says enthusiastically. The two of them enter an animated conversation about reincarnation, Tristan repeatedly mentioning that the concept blows his mind.

"I'm going to grab some more wine," I announce a few minutes later to nobody in particular, standing up and walking to the kitchen.

"'Kay, sweets," Tristan says, turning back to Joss. "But how do they *find* the baby, you know? That's what I want to know."

Emily excuses herself, following me into the kitchen and leaning against the fridge, arms crossed as I uncork a bottle of Syrah.

"So?" I ask, waiting for the other shoe to drop.

"So, nothing. He seems really sweet."

"And?"

"And, nothing! Why are you so convinced I'm going to hate him? I met him that night, remember? I like him. I think he's a good distraction from all your work stuff."

I peek around the corner of the kitchen into the living room. Nick has unearthed an old bottle of Jäger and is offering it to Tristan insistently.

"He is a good distraction," I admit, swiveling my body back around to face Emily. "But I think that's all he is."

"What the problem with that? You don't have to marry the guy. Come on—*nobody* marries somebody who looks like that. You'd need bodyguards for the rest of your life just to keep him from getting attacked by horny women. I think he'll go far; he has the right look."

"I might as well enjoy the ride while it lasts, *huh?*"

"Exactly."

I'm silent for a few seconds, then I start grinning. "I still can't believe it. Tom Reynolds. Tom Reynolds!"

She laughs. "So what are you doing in here with *me*?"

All doubts are erased from my mind when Tristan and I are alone in my bedroom later that night after Nick and Joss have left. He's in the bathroom for about ten minutes while I worriedly tidy up the room, tossing dirty underwear and my good luck teddy bear onto the floor of my closet, and quickly checking my appearance in a compact mirror to make sure no makeup has migrated onto my cheek. When he comes back in the room, he's only wearing jeans, the top of his gray boxer-briefs hugging his hipbones, his pecs and arms defined as if Rodin himself chiseled them. The light from the hallway casts a halo around him. He enters the room, closes the door, and I have to stop myself from squealing in excitement as he grabs me and throws me on the bed.

Chapter 8

Tristan and I spend what feels like the entire weekend under the covers, so I'm obviously disappointed when I have to reenter the world of reality on Monday morning. My presentation with James is this morning. I tried to talk to Tristan about it yesterday, but the conversation kept turning back to his excitement over the Hugo Boss campaign. He's probably right: I *don't* have anything to worry about. I'm feeling very Pollyanna—if I give it my all, surely I will succeed, right? No mistakes! Turn on the charm! Hard work and perserverance will win the day.

I have a split-second flash of worry that I'm being wildly overconfident and that I've done nothing to prove myself yet and that I'm going to fall flat on my ass today, but I quickly banish it from my mind. No negative thoughts.

For luck, I wear my favorite blue silk skirt, a blue, white, green, and yellow striped Missoni shirt that shows off my waist, and white straw espadrilles Emily picked up for me the last time she was in Spain. I then spend fifteen minutes staring at myself in the mirror, wondering if I look too Bonneau-Martray. Should I try to look more Beckwith? Should I change into khaki pants? I want to look attractive—but not because of James or the tension—imagined tension?—we had in my cubicle. Only because looking attractive is always good when going into meetings, of course. I'm dating one of the hottest men in Manhattan. James has nothing to do with it.

I agonize over my outfit, changing back and forth between the skirt and the new J. Crew khakis Emily has loaned me until I realize that I'm going to be late for the meeting and decide to go with the prettier of the two: the blue skirt. Surely even at *Womanly World* khaki is not appropriate for big meetings. Luckily, my hair and makeup—two things I can practically do in my sleep—are picture perfect.

James shot me a brief e-mail last week saying that he'd pick me up at my house this morning. It read:

> *I will pick you up at 8:30 a.m. Monday outside of your house for the meeting. Please respond with the address and let me know if you will be unable to make the appointment for any reason. Many thanks.*
>
> *James Michaels*
> *Publisher*
> Womanly World

So cold! Couldn't he have at least signed his name, rather than using the default signature?

Well, fine, if he's going to be all weird and stiff, I'll be the same. My response was equally curt:

> *Very well. My address is 457 West 14th Street. I will meet the car outside at 8:30 a.m.*
>
> *Best,*
>
> *Bella Hunter*
> *Beauty Editor*
> Womanly World

Of course, I didn't know how to use the signature feature on my e-mail, so I'd been forced to type in the full section of my name and title, but he wouldn't know that, would he? It would just look like that was part of *all* my e-mails, like I couldn't be bothered to sign my name, either.

I look at my clock. It reads 8:34 a.m. Damn. I'd planned to be down there at 8:30 on the dot to avoid any disparaging comments about a Bonneau-Martray work ethic, or some other such nonsense.

I grab my Louis Vuitton Speedy, give myself a last glance in the full-length mirror opposite my bed, remembering one more time the attraction I'd unexpectedly felt toward him in my cubicle, and then fly out the door, running down the three floors to the street.

He's already there.

I immediately slow down, smoothing my hair as I approach the Town Car, but trying to do it in a manner that says, "This is a professional hair smoothing to ensure that I look polished, not because I actually care about what I look like to you." The driver steps out of the car to open the door for me and I slide in.

The door closes behind me with a loud *thud* as I look over at James, expecting him to archly comment on my lateness. His navy blue suit is as natty as the last time I saw him, but something is different now. The dark hair is smoothed back, but an errant wisp that escaped the hair cream peeks out from behind his ear. His blue eyes are cloudy, impenetrable. He looks like he hasn't slept; faint shadows are visible under his eyes. He looks vulnerable. He looks sexy.

Oh God. Is it wrong that I find him insanely hot right now? My old therapist would have had a field day with this. Ever since Toph—and *really*, even before that, since Olivier—I've had my nose to the grindstone, practically oblivious to men.

But now that the floodgates of male interest have opened
again, I'm like some horny fifteen-year-old boy.

"Hi," he says lightly.

"Hi."

Silence.

"Are you ready for this?" he asks.

"Are you?"

"Yes. This presentation is crucial."

I nod silently, trying to gauge his mood. Okay, I'll be honest—I'm also kind of afraid of my voice cracking with lust.
Bad, Bella. Very bad.

The car drives along Fourteenth Street and we head
crosstown without speaking. My heart is pounding. Why is
he being so strange? Why isn't he talking? The cold James
I met in Rania's office is preferrable to this uncomfortable
silence. Is he a jerk? Shy? A deaf-mute? What's the deal?

At Sixth Avenue, he clears his throat and then says, "Did
you go over the presentation this weekend?"

"I did," I say.

More silence.

Damn! Why is this so awkward? What is he thinking?

I sneak a glance over at him. He's staring thoughtfully out
the window, fingers drumming on the door handle. I have a
weakness for nice hands, and his are definitely attractive—
with long, well-shaped fingers and neatly trimmed nails. I
once broke up with a guy because I hated his thumbs. A lifetime, or even a year, of entwining my fingers with his stubby
little nubs was just too much for me to handle. (Everybody
has a deal breaker.) James's are nice, though. Not perfect—
the nail is ever so slightly too oval for my liking—but good
nonetheless. Our hands could have a grand romance together.
In theory. If the owners ever got around to actually convers-
ing with each other, that is.

Maybe I should just say something and break the tension.

I didn't imagine the look he gave me at my cubicle; he's attracted to me . . . isn't he? And seeing as I'm the most transparent person in the history of the universe when I like somebody, he must be aware that, despite myself, I'm attracted to him, too, which is why there's this crackling awkwardness between us right now. Yes, he's my boss, but he also can't be more than three years older than I am. If we weren't encumbered by our work circumstances, surely we'd be more relaxed around each other. *So make a joke, clear the air, and then it'll be like nothing ever happened*, I tell myself.

James's BlackBerry buzzes, jolting me from my reverie and bringing me back to the present. I sneak another glance at him as he runs his thumb over the dial, brow furrowed as he reads e-mails. I want to send him one telepathically:

Dear James. I think you're hot. Do you think I'm pretty? I liked talking to you on Friday when you let your guard down for a second, and I like your cologne, too. I know you're my boss, and I'm dating somebody, and for all I know, you have a girlfriend, but can we make out and see where this goes? Love, Bella. P.S. Your thumbs are actually pretty nice.

But that would be weird, of course.

His phone rings, causing an annoyed look to flash across his face. "Hello? Hi, Mom." Pause. "I don't know. Probably. I'll stop by tonight after work." Another pause. "I've told you five times already. I can't make it at seven. You know I never leave the office before eight thirty." I hear a woman's high-pitched voice chattering on the other end. "Look, I can't talk about this right now, okay? I'm in the car with somebody." Pause. "It's eight forty-five! I'm working." His brow is knotted in a frown. "Well, you should have thought of that sooner." Sigh. "Fine. I'll do my best." He shakes his head. "Yes, Mom. See you at seven." He hangs up, looking out the window again. "Sorry," he mutters.

James has put his BlackBerry away and is back to drumming his fingers on the door handle.

"*Uh,* so, listen, James . . ."

"*Mmm?* Sorry?"

I clear my throat. "Nothing. I just wanted to say . . ."

He nods and then turns toward me, leaning in ever so slightly as he focuses his attention. His cologne drifts toward me. He's wearing the Givenchy again today. It smells amazing. "Yes?"

He looks at me, and all the words fly out of my head. What would I possibly say? Are you crazy, Bella? Same age or not, this guy is your *boss.*

"*Uh,* nothing."

"I'm sorry?"

"I'm ready for this presentation. We're going to do just fine. Better than fine! We're going to rock it!" I cringe inwardly at my voice. I sound like a deranged cheerleader.

He furrows his brow. "Okay . . . that's good. Good attitude." He pulls out his BlackBerry again and begins typing furiously. "I hope you're right."

In the elevators, James fiddles with his tie and looks nervously around at the walls. His anxiety is starting to make me nervous. I've never done an ad sales meeting before. I don't even know what to say! I'd been planning on following James's lead, but it's obvious from his jitteriness that he's feeling on shaky ground as well. I hope *he's* done an ad sales call before.

"So, make or break, huh?" My lame banter makes me cringe internally.

James seems startled, as if he forgot that I was in the elevator with him. "Yes. We can't afford to lose their business."

"Why don't they think they should place with us?"

James runs a hand through his hair and sighs, looking

upset. "Classic stuff: our readers are too old, they're trying to go after younger women, they just started advertising in *Flash,* and a new magazine on the scene means fewer dollars to go other places. We need to show them that we're still players, that our magazine isn't irrelevant."

I'm nodding. This is doable. "So, I should be charming and youthful and cute, right?" I say, sort of teasingly.

"We need to be as professional as possible," he snaps.

Whoa, buddy. So much for an imaginary spark.

The elevator reaches the twenty-sixth floor and we step through the doors, our arms laden with portfolios. Jack walks up to the receptionist and says, "James Michaels to see Steven Schmidt, please."

"He'll be right with you. Have a seat."

James sits stiffly on the edge of his chair, then pulls out his BlackBerry, clicking through it. *That thing is like a freaking security blanket*, I think. I look around the room, trying to gather my composure for this meeting. I went through my presentation documents last night, trying desperately to soak up Frances's memo. I don't agree with half of it, but that's not my job right now: today, I am a trained puppy—no more, no less. I realized while studying the outdated ideas that Frances doesn't have any grasp of the current state of the beauty world. She may or may not be a fashion genius—I think that point is debatable—but how can you expect somebody who has used Olay products exclusively for the past twenty-five years (and still insists on calling it Oil of Olay, even though the company name changed several years ago) to be able to relate to the current, dynamic beauty industry? My new ideas, as well as my first column, are due to Frances soon and I'm hoping to come up with a fresh take on *Womanly World*'s beauty section that will appeal to Rania but that's also acceptable to Frances, in order to avoid another fiasco like the one in James's office recently.

A man strides into the waiting area, his hand outstretched. His suit looks just like James's; they are Important Business-people clones. "James, wonderful to see you."

James jumps up, looking alive. "Steve! How are you? May I present our new beauty editor, Bella Hunter."

"It's nice to meet you, Steve," I say crisply, hoping my low voice implies: *This girl means business! She is a serious person! She is not-at-all frivolous and is extremely professional and definitely does not have an inappropriate crush on her weird, stiff boss! Give* Womanly World *your money!*

"Likewise," he says, shaking my hand and smiling warmly.

"Bella comes to us from *Enchanté,*" James says. "She was one of their most popular writers. Has an excellent grasp of the youthful beauty market." *Ahh,* I see what he's doing.

"Wonderful! And how are you liking *Womanly World* so far?"

James shoots me a look, as if to say, *Don't you dare blow this.*

"It's fantastic," I say, cheerily. "It's such an American icon and our readers really have a connection with us. We have a ton of new ideas, so I'm very excited to start implementing them!"

"That's great," Steve says, gesturing to the door and leading us down the hallway. "That's what we're here today to discuss! We're looking forward to hearing all of your thoughts."

"How's Jenny doing?" James asks.

"Oh, she's splendid, thanks for asking! We went to Scarsdale last weekend to visit the folks. You can imagine how that turned out." Steve starts laughing and James and I politely join in. Jenny who? "And what about you, my boy?" Steve says, clamping a hand on James's shoulder. "How is Elizabeth doing?"

"*Err . . .* we broke up," James says. "In the winter."

"Oh no! I'm sorry to hear that. What happened? You seemed so happy at CTFA last year." CTFA: the annual beauty industry conference in Boca Raton. Mind-numbingly dull.

James clears his throat and shrugs slightly, not looking at me. "You know how it is. It just wasn't . . . right."

Steve nods. "Do I ever. Jenny and I broke up and got back together about three times before we finally got married. How long were you together? Five years?"

James looks down at his portfolios uncomfortably. "Yes."

"Well, I'm sure you two will find each other again soon, if it's in the cards," Steve says, gesturing toward a doorway. "Shall we?" The three of us walk into a conference room off of the hallway where a team of three men and one woman are waiting.

"James Michaels, Bella Hunter, this is Lucy Brightly, Dave Gelson . . ." Steve goes around the table and introduces us, everybody shaking hands before settling back down to begin the presentation. Facing a group of people, no matter how small, immediately makes my heart pump faster with nervousness.

James removes a stack of papers from his briefcase, setting up the presentation boards outlining our editorial strategy for the coming year. The presentation includes a selection of *Womanly World* articles from the past few months designed to show our new youthful message, as well as a selection of the prettiest photos from recent *Womanly World* beauty shoots. We sit around the table in a circle as James begins talking.

"As I'm sure you're aware, *Womanly World* has been the number one women's magazine in the country for the past thirty-five years. We are the number four magazine in the country in any category, and a recent independently conducted survey of American women readers indicated that seventy-one percent consider us an American icon. There's no doubt that *Womanly World* is immensely popular and still enjoys tremendous cultural force, but what about cultural *relevancy*? I know that's the watchword on everybody's lips, and we're here to demonstrate that our magazine's new editorial mission will continue to impress existing readers as well as draw in newer and younger ones." James turns to me. "Bella?"

I open my mouth, but nothing comes out. My mind flashes back to eleventh grade, when I had the part of Electra in *Gypsy*. I was on stage for all of three minutes with two other girls, singing "You Gotta Get a Gimmick" together. During my solo, however, I completely froze up, forgetting my handful of words ("So I *uh*! And I *uh*! And I *uh, uh, uh*! But I do it with a switch!"), standing on stage stupidly while Christina Lawrence, who played Tessie, shimmied by in time to the music, hissing, '"But I do it with a switch! *But I do it with a switch,' Bella!*" My mouth is bereft of moisture. Dear God. After a prolonged pause, I manage to squeak, "Thanks, James." Pause. "I don't know if you all know my background, but I'm the former beauty writer from *Enchanté* magazine. *Enchanté* and *Womanly World* are obviously . . . very different. The, *uh*—" My mind has gone blank again. I know I'm supposed to do something with the numbers at this point. I look down at my notes, fumbling through the pages. "Sorry, *uh* . . ." I spot a statistic James has highlighted for me to read. "*Enchanté* is aspirational and only twenty-three percent of their readers will buy products featured in the pages. *Womanly World,* on the other hand . . ." I peer at the paper again. My heart is pounding; I *hate* this. I read aloud the sentence written on the paper. "By contrast, *Womanly World* readers have a personal, real, tangible connection with the magazine, and sixty-nine percent of our readers will buy products advertised or featured in our pages." I look around the room. Lucy and Steve are nodding enthusiastically, as if saying, "C'mon, little Bella! You can do it!" James's face is thunderous, which only makes me more nervous. I should have prepared more. I mentally curse my own arrogance. *How hard can it be?* I'd thought. So much for that. "So, *uh* . . . as you see, we are a true industry leader. Whereas our competitors, such as . . . *um* . . ." Who? "Our pages are set apart from our competitors thanks to . . ." My voice falters again. What are our pages? What is the magazine about? I have no clue.

"We've prepared these charts for you to see our numbers," James interrupts smoothly, passing a stack of papers around the table with numbers and graphs displaying every conceivable number about *Womanly World* and its readers. He shoots me a look that reads: *keep your mouth shut for the rest of this presentation.* "As you can see from this first chart . . . ," James continues talking and I'm impressed with how calm and cool he is now. The nervous Nellie I'd seen in the car and in the elevator has disappeared. Thank God he's here. I'm pissed at myself; I've blown it.

The presentation concludes twenty minutes later, the group visibly swayed by James's presentation. After my disastrous monologue, I have not uttered a peep. We shake hands with everybody and then walk silently into the elevator. As soon as the doors close, he lets me have it.

"I cannot believe how unprepared you were for that. It was disgraceful."

"James, I'm so sorry. I'm terrible at public speaking. I should have told you."

"It had nothing to do with you being nervous. You don't know anything about the magazine. This isn't some beauty party where you can get by on looks and charm. It's *work.* You have displayed the most unbelievably cavalier attitude since day one. I know you think *Womanly World* is beneath you, but I don't give a damn. If you don't want this job, there are plenty of others that would. Stop flitting around the office in a daydream, complaining to your friends about how boring it is and playing with your hair every fifteen minutes, and shape up. Otherwise, just get the hell out. You aren't doing us any favors with your golden presence."

James storms out of the elevator and strides across the lobby. I scurry after him and get into the waiting Town Car.

I'm too cowed by his outburst to argue. Sure, I've been trying, but I've been reactive, not proactive. He's right. I've been so up on my high horse about the magazine being beneath me that I'm barely doing my job. We ride back to the Beckwith building in silence.

I stare out the window, mentally willing the driver to go faster.

The driver turns the radio on low—it's AM talk radio. Suddenly, James asks, "Why did you come here?"

"I'm sorry? You told me that I was supposed to come with you today."

"I meant, why did you come to *Womanly World*?" he says stiffly. "Why did you leave *Enchanté*?"

"I had an incident there, and my bosses decided that it wasn't the right fit anymore."

"The *Post* article."

"Right."

"I see."

"I'm very grateful for the opportunity."

"No, you're not," he says automatically.

Whoa. Is he going there?

"Yes," I say firmly. "I am."

"Okay. If you say so."

"What does *that* mean?"

"Come on. We both know you hate it here. You think the magazine is beneath you, you think that *Enchanté* better, and you're only biding your time until you can quit and go to a 'cooler' magazine."

"Well, you said it, I didn't," I shoot back without thinking.

"Excuse me?"

"Nothing! I'm sorry."

"Typical. Instead of substance, you offer an insincere apology and a smile. The poor-me, dumb-blonde card is played out," he scoffs.

"*What?* Dumb blonde? You don't know anything about me."

"I know that you show up at the office late everyday. Not a single one of your ideas has made it into the magazine yet. You make lazy, half-assed attempts at your beauty column. You stare at yourself in the mirror every chance you get. You have no idea what our circulation is, who our readers are or what makes us differ from the competition. I have never heard a coherent thought come out of your mouth. And you have a habit of spilling secrets to reporters. How's that for knowing you?"

My gasp echoes throughout the car and the driver looks back at us nervously in the rearview mirror. "I cannot believe I thought even for a *second* that you were nice!" I spit. "You are, without exception, the rudest, most obnoxious, most mean-spirited man I have ever met. Where the hell do you get off yelling at me? I'm not your child. You have no business speaking to me that way—I don't care if you are the publisher." He opens his mouth, eyes flashing, but I cut him off. "I am *not* through. For your information, I had a 4.3 GPA and an 800 on my SAT verbal. I graduated from Northwestern. I volunteered at a soup-kitchen for three years in college. I was on the Academic Team in high school, for Christ's sake. You think I'm some stuck-up, stupid, untalented bitch, but you don't know a damn thing about where I come from, who I am, or what I can do. No, I haven't taken to *Womanly World* like a fish to water. Yes, I speak in a high-pitched voice and wear lots of makeup and have blonde hair. Yes, I giggle when I'm nervous and say 'like' a lot. No, I haven't pushed myself to my full potential here. I regret that, and you can be damn sure that's going to change from this moment forward just so I have the pleasure of proving your ignorant ass wrong. But don't *ever* demean my intelligence, talent, or work ethic again." I jab my finger in his direction. "You want to judge a book by its cover? How about you? I've got you pegged. You're a poor little rich boy who's only here to make your daddy proud. You've never worked an honest day in your life. You don't know what it feels like struggling to make ends meet, or worrying about the rent not getting paid on time, or having to live and die by your manufactured public image because it's the only thing keeping the money coming in. And you hate your job just as much as I do, so don't you dare throw that in my face. At least I have a *personality*."

The car pulls up to the Beckwith building and I grab my purse, stepping out of the car and slamming it behind me as I storm up the pavement into the building.

Emily is at Gabrielle's that evening, going through outfits for a party later in the week, so I call Tristan and ask him to come over for moral support. He's unenthusiastic.

"I don't know if I can, sweets. I'm feeling down."

"Why? What's wrong?"

"My booker called. Hugo Boss is going with somebody else."

"But I thought it was a done deal!"

He sighs heavily. "Yeah, me, too. I'm so bummed right now. Some of my boys are over and we're watching the Indians game. Tomorrow night?"

"That's fine," I say, disappointed. "I'll call you tomorrow."

"Okay, baby." He hangs up and I stare blankly at the receiver for a few moments before automatically dialing Nick.

Forty-five minutes later, Nick's at my door with Joss and a very harried-looking Emily in tow. "I made them," he says.

"Much more important than Gabrielle," Emily agrees. "Damn diva."

Chapter 9

"He said *what*?" Emily demands.

"'Instead, as usual, you're playing the dumb-little-girl card,'" I repeat sarcastically. "Then he proceeded to tell me he'd never heard me say anything coherent and that I go about my job half-assed. Stupid jerk. I let him have it—I'm probably going to get fired now."

"Do you want me to beat him up?" Nick calls from the kitchen.

"It's completely unprofessional, first of all. And is it *legal* for him to yell at you like that?" Emily asks.

"You should sue him," says Joss. "We can have Gary represent you."

"No lawyers. When he called me a dumb blonde, I went mental. The worst part, though, is that he's right about the other stuff. Kind of. I *have* been half-assing it."

"Well, obviously."

"But to jump down my throat like that! Uncalled for!"

"Son of a bitch," Joss says. "You've got to prove him wrong."

"As usual, you girls can't read men," Nick says, walking back into the living room with an open bottle of Pinot Noir in his left hand and three wineglasses in his right. He sets the glasses down on the coffee table and pours us each a generous amount. "The guy is either crazy or in love with you. Personally, I think crazy is more likely. He could be bipolar."

"I doubt that," I say, downing half of my glass in one gulp. "He's not crazy, he's just an uptight asshole. He hasn't given me a fair chance! He automatically hated me right off the bat because I came from *Enchanté*! And he's judging me for the way I *look*! How unfair is that?"

"It's not fair," admits Emily, "but, really, can you blame him for being on his guard? All he knows is what he read in the papers, and that your choice was *Womanly World* or unemployment. You never would have gone there voluntarily."

"He *did* hear you slagging off the magazine," Nick points out.

"And you *do* stare at yourself in the mirror every chance you get," Joss adds, a smile playing at her lips.

"Thanks a lot," I mutter.

"Maybe he has a drug problem," Joss volunteers helpfully. "He could be a total stoner. Or a cokehead! Have you been around when he suddenly gets really twitchy?"

"He's not a drug addict! He's always perfectly sober. He's too sober."

"He's been perfectly sober *once*. Or twice—however many times you two have been in the same room together. That could be his MO—no drugs at the office, but then he goes home and binges. It would explain the bad moods. He's jonesing for his next fix. Didn't you learn anything from Toph?"

"And where is Tristan exactly?" demands Nick.

"I already told you," I say wearily. "He didn't feel like coming over because he didn't get the Hugo Boss campaign, after all. He's watching baseball with some friends."

"Baseball," he scoffs. "Is that what the kids are calling it these days?"

"Stop it," I warn. "I have enough problems without worrying about my non-boyfriend, too. He can do whatever the hell he wants. I don't care anymore. Men are pigs."

Nick looks wounded.

"Why are you looking at her like that?" Emily laughs. "You're the biggest pig of them all, you hypocrite!"

"Only *sometimes*," he mutters, blushing. "You girls are so harsh."

Joss flops down on the couch next to Nick and kicks her shoes off dramatically, accidentally spilling some wine on his sleeve in the process.

"My Paul Smith!" he gasps, setting the wineglass down carefully and hurrying into the kitchen, clutching his arm as if he's been shot.

"Are we *sure* he's straight?" Emily asks, her eyes skyward. "Nick and his ridiculous shirts. That's what happens when you blow your entire salary on a button-down."

I giggle and then quickly pull the corners of my mouth back down. "No, we shouldn't laugh. Nick loves those shirts. He thinks they make him look older."

"If he wants to look older, he should stop wearing pink," she counters.

"And maybe start dating women who have already graduated from high school?" Joss adds.

"I can *hear* you!" Nick bellows from the kitchen.

We dissolve into fits of giggles. Nick pokes his head around the kitchen wall, glaring at us. "I will have you know that pink is *extremely* in right now in London, Emily, which you'd be aware of if you actually answered your mother's calls every once in a while or shopped somewhere other than H&M and the Salvation Army."

"*Ooh,* snap! No, you didn't! Hit me where it hurts, Nick!"

"And as for *you*," he says, looking at me, "are you seriously mocking my taste? Right now? When we're discussing your moony romance with Bipolar Boss?"

I stop laughing. "Are you kidding me? It's not a romance. We hate each other."

"Riiight," he says, retreating back into the kitchen to finish furiously rubbing at his shirt.

"Bella wouldn't be stupid enough to get into an office romance, anyway," Emily says, raising an eyebrow reproachfully at me as she walks across the living room, opening the window and lighting a cigarette. "And besides, she has Tristan."

"What the hell is wrong with you?" I demand, charging over and tossing the cigarette onto Fourteenth Street. "Are you trying to get cancer? Should we install a sun bed in our kitchen next?"

"We can play this game for hours," she says languidly, brandishing her pack. "I have about fifteen left."

"You said you were trying to quit!"

"I *am* trying to quit. I didn't say I'd succeeded."

"Nicotine is a very serious addiction, Bella. Emily is powerless in its grip," Nick says, returning to the living room with a huge wet patch on his sleeve and a mournful look on his face.

"Thank you for that after-school moment, but you're one to talk. One week you're a smoker because model A thinks it's cool, the next week you're president of the local American Lung Association chapter because model B's father died from emphysema. Do you have *any* morals, or did you shag them all away?"

He screws up his face, as if pondering the question seriously. "I probably had morals before losing my virginity. It's been so long that I can't remember anymore. I think every woman I sleep with makes me dumber, somehow."

"No arguing there," Emily cracks, lighting another cigarette.

"Jesus Christ!" Joss yells at the same time I shout, "Oh, come on!"

"Kids, I've had the month from hell, and I want to unwind with a cigarette and some wine. I don't use drugs and I'm sure as hell not screwing my tension away, so chill. And it's my body and my lungs—" ("Although it's also my living room," I mutter) "—and when I meet my maker, whether it's tomorrow or in seventy years, I will be secure in the knowledge that I lived it well and did it right and enjoyed every last second. And right now, that means having a cigarette, you fucking fascists."

I don't agree with the particulars, but I love Emily's unwillingness to bend, even when championing an unpopular—or ridiculous—viewpoint. "Fine, it's your funeral. At which we'll play 'My Way' at full volume, okay?"

"Thank you," she says, leaning against the window and exhaling rapturously.

"I can't watch," Joss frets. "I can't watch. Does she not understand that she is creating wrinkles *right now*? It hurts me. It physically hurts."

I go into work early the next day, feeling like it's time to make some major changes. First up: my cubicle. If I'm being perfectly honest with myself, it's disgustingly messy. I have tears from *W* and *Chic* and *Vogue* all over the place, and several back issues of *Enchanté* are in a pile on the floor. Purses are strewn about under my chair and an extra pair of black Manolos lies carelessly in the corner, in case a major event pops up at the last minute. I realize that my cubicle is almost an exact replica of my area at *Enchanté*. It would be funny, if it weren't so pathetic. I remember James's words in the car. I *didn't* come here willingly and I'm not putting my heart into it. It's time to get over it.

I feel like today is the first day of school. It's a fresh start! It's a whole new Bella! There's no more room for all of these *W*'s and *Enchanté*s and *Vogue*s. Why does an editor from *Womanly World* need to be reading *Vogue,* anyway? I should be scoping out *Good Housekeeping* and *Midwest Living*. I gather all of the magazines and dump them into the large trash bin outside my cubicle, then spend the next twenty minutes rearranging my desk. This is *way* too cluttered. No wonder my ideas have been all jumbled up. Joss would say that I've been blocking the feng shui of the place with the negative energy that I brought over from *Enchanté*.

Once I've finished cleaning up, I gaze around my cubicle with a renewed sense of purpose. Gone are the magazines, the photo tears from fashion spreads, the jumble of purses, shoes, and "emergency" going-out tops. I've neatly folded the clothes and arranged the accessories in a bin under my desk, then tidied up the beauty products normally cluttering my cabinet. Now the entire area is bare, with only a potted plant on my desk, a phone log, a notebook, and a jar full of pens. The walls of my cubicle are empty, save for a photo I have tacked up of Joss, Emily, Nick, and myself. It looks almost like nobody works here. Perfect.

No more Chloé pants and Christian Louboutin heels. No more esoteric articles that would fit right in place at *Enchanté*. I need to embrace my inner midwesterner, learn to live like a *Womanly World*-er. For better or for worse, I'm here to stay, if for no other reason than to prove that bastard wrong.

The following Monday, I breeze into the office in my new outfit: beige Express slacks, a long-sleeved blue-and-white-striped button-down from Banana Republic, black pointy-toed flats from J. Crew, and—at Emily's insistence ("It makes the outfit!")—a sturdy black satchel with silver buckles from Kenneth Cole. I followed my normal makeup routine this morning (Bare Escentuals Bare Minerals foundation, Bobbi Brown bronzer, NARS blush in Orgasm, NARS lipstick in Dolce Vita, Lancôme Fatale mascara, Tarte eyeliner, and Vincent Longo eyeshadow), but instead of spending an hour parting, blowdrying, sleekifying, and styling my hair, I spent only thirty-five minutes quickly blowing it out before brushing it and pulling it back into a low ponytail. I'm so low-maintenance now! I feel really good about the whole ensemble. I look stylish *and* like I belong at *Womanly World*. Who says I have to look like crap in order to fit in? These ladies are still hip. They're still with it. Well, they *want* to be with it, and that's really all that counts. And I finally look the part, so now everyone will be forced to see me in a new light and everything else will fall into place. I can just feel it. (Plus, my daily Astrology Zone for Libra said this morning that it would be a red-letter day, and Astrology Zone is *never wrong*. It's eerie.)

Midmorning, Frances marches by with a pen in hand, stopping dead when she passes my cubicle, a confused look in her eye. "Bella? What's going on? Are you quitting?" She sounds vaguely hopeful.

"No! Just tidied up a bit. You know, out with the old and in with the new."

Frances looks at me suspiciously, one eyebrow raised. "I see. Well, carry on." She continues down the hallway, shaking her head as she walks.

I sit down at the desk and open one of the notebooks, which has writing on only the very first page: a to-do list that I'd made several months back after ordering the notebooks at *Enchanté*. I'd decided on a whim that I would make a daily to-do list. This resolution lasted one day. But no longer will I make resolutions and not stick to them! Now I will *definitely* make a daily to-do list. And I'll even try to get most of the items on the list done, too.

I tear out the old page with the writing and look down at the now-empty notebook, picking up a pen and letting it hover over the page. So? What do I need to do today?

I spend all afternoon working feverishly on the End of Summer makeup story that Frances has come up with. She stopped by my desk this afternoon, asking me to whip up a few paragraphs for the body of the story, and reminding me that Rania wants an ideas memo for next month by Thursday. ("Do you think you can handle *all* that?" she asked, eyebrow arched. I replied eagerly, "Yes! Absolutely!" Load it up, boss!) After three hours of tweaking existing copy and adding new lines, I have something I think Frances will be happy with. It's snappy, but helpful, young-at-heart while still recommending *Womanly World* "appropriate" products.

When I walk by Frances's office, she's sitting at her desk, studying galleys quietly. I knock before entering.

"Hi, Frances. Just wanted to give you the End of Summer story for your approval."

"Thank you. Everything good?"

"Yes. I edited the copy, and inserted about eight extra lines to make it fit. After reading it and looking at the makeup you suggested, I thought a sidebar on the best foundations and concealers could be cute, so I added five products each for you to look at, with prices and website availability."

She takes the paper-clipped papers from my outstretched hand, surprise etched across her face. "Oh. Thank you, Bella. I'll take a look and let you know."

"Great!" I start to walk back to my desk before remembering something. "By the way, I took out three of the eyeshadow compacts because they're limited edition and probably will only be in stores for the first part of September. I figured our readers might not like seeing products they can't buy, so I substituted possible suggestions. Drugstore, of course."

Frances just stares at me, her eyebrows practically reaching her hairline. "Wonderful."

I float back to my desk, passing a picture of James's grandmother, Essie Michaels. "Lazy, my ass," I mutter.

"Who on earth are you talking to?" Vivian demands, materializing out of thin air.

"Vivian! Jesus! You scared me."

"Well, you scared me, too, walking down the hall whispering to yourself as if you had an imaginary friend," she laughs. "If you're not careful, people are going to start spreading rumors that the new girl is crazy."

I lean against the wall. "Am I still the new girl? I've been here for two months!"

"Has it really been that long? Lordy me, I can't believe that. So, how's it going? Is Frances treating you okay?"

I turn around and peek my head over the divider, checking to see if Frances's door is open. It's not—she must be on the phone.

"She's fine," I whisper, "but I don't think we're going to be buying friendship rings anytime soon. I've never met anybody so prickly in my entire life." *And she's not the one here I'm having problems with*, I think darkly.

Vivian shakes her head. "Then you've obviously never met Ken, my ex-husband." She cackles merrily. "A divorced relationship-advice columnist. *So* Dr. Phil, right?"

"Or Dr. Laura."

"Please! Don't compare me to that hag. I'm much younger and prettier than she is, anyway."

"And your advice is so much better," I grin.

"Is that sarcasm?"

"No! I really do like your column. I think your advice is perfect, and it's never too sugary or preachy—just smart." After Frances reamed me out, I've now read all the back issues of *Womanly World* from the past three years.

"You're such a sweetheart." Vivian pats me on the shoulder. "So, tell me, is there any relationship advice I can give the beauty expert in exchange for eyeshadow tips?"

"Well . . ." I pause. Should I tell Vivian about James? What's to say? No use in bringing up a crush—I'm sorry, a blink-and-you'd-have-missed-it *former* crush. And Tristan is barely worth mentioning. Even in my besotted-over-his-hotness state I know that "relationship" is going nowhere. "Nothing," I finally say. "No men."

"Darn," she says. "I really was hoping for makeup advice."

"Vivian, I'll give you makeup advice, no strings attached!" I exclaim. "What do you want to know?"

"Jeez, where to begin? My hair, my foundation, my eyeshadow, my lipstick. I'm not beauty savvy, but even I know that I'm stuck in the nineties. I haven't worn much makeup since Ken and I got divorced, but now that I'm dating again—"

"You're dating?" I interrupt. "Who? Tell me!"

"It's embarrassing . . ."

"You've got to be kidding me. If there's one person in the world who will never judge when it comes to embarrassing stories, it's me. Spill it."

Vivian looks at me for a second as if sizing me up. She smiles sheepishly, and I remark to myself how attractive she is. With the right makeup and haircut, she could look five years younger.

Finally she blurts out, "Match dot com."

"That's the big secret?" I shrug. "So? That's not embarrassing! Everybody I know has used some type of Internet dating service at least once."

"Really?"

"Of course! How else do you think people meet nowadays?"

"I don't know anymore. My friend Ruth's daughter says that the gym is a real swinging pickup scene, but that makes me nervous." She gestures to her attractive, curvy figure and says, "I'm hardly a gymgoer."

"*Eh,*" I say dismissively. "The kind of guys you'd find at the gym aren't your type, anyway. Most of them are twenty-one and total narcissists."

"What makes you think that's not my type?" she laughs, adding, "I'm just kidding!" when she sees my surprised expression.

"For a second there, I thought you were serious!"

"Hey, if Demi Moore can go there, so can I. Heck, she's older than me."

"Really?"

"Lordy. That's not a good sign."

"No! I didn't mean—"

"It's okay, honey. I know I look older than I really am." She smiles ruefully. "You wouldn't know it now, but back in the day I was a real looker."

"You still are!" I exclaim truthfully. "On my first day here, that's one of the very first things I noticed—how beautiful you are."

"Especially for somebody my age, right? That's the unsaid part."

"No, no, not at all," I protest.

She waves her hand in the air. "No harm, no foul. That's what Ken would always say. I'm not in my twenties anymore. And that's okay! I shouldn't have to feel bad that I'm getting older. It's part of life, right?"

I nod, impressed by her attitude. "Vivian, you're one cool lady."

She winks. "You're not bad yourself."

"Okay!" I say, clapping my hands together. "So tell me all about this Match dot com thing. Who's the lucky guy? When's the date?"

She gestures toward my computer screen. "Do you want to see a picture of him?"

"Sure!" We enter my cubicle and I motion for her to sit in my chair. She logs onto Match, scrolling through her account until she pulls up a photo of an attractive older gentleman, with salt-and-pepper hair and kind, crinkly brown eyes.

He looks like a cross between Tommy Lee Jones and James Brolin.

"His name is Walter," she says proudly. "Isn't he cute?"

"Vivian, this guy is gorgeous!" I exclaim. "Look at you, bagging the hotties!"

"I know!" she giggles. "Our first date is in two weeks. He's taking me to Gramercy Tavern."

"Excellent taste, too," I say, and nod approvingly. "I'm definitely liking him. So what's the problem?"

She wrings her hands nervously. "Well . . . the photo I sent him is a little . . . old."

"How old?"

"It was taken in 1995."

"I see. So you're afraid that he'll be expecting a thirty-year-old."

"Exactly."

"Doesn't your profile say how old you are?" I ask.

"Yes, but I'm scared that when I show up on Saturday night he's going to take one look at me and walk right out of the restaurant."

"Never," I say firmly. "You are a gorgeous, intelligent woman and any man would be lucky to call you his. Don't put yourself down for even one second by thinking that you're not worthy."

"Aren't you sweet," she says, patting me on the arm as if she's trying to reassure me. "I do appreciate it, Bella, but I'm past my prime. The fact is, I'm forty-three, and a lot of men just don't want women in their forties. They want newer models. And me . . . I look kind of *old*."

"Okay, so we change that. A new dress, a new haircut, some great makeup techniques. I can have you looking thrity-five years old on Saturday night, or I don't deserve to be called a beauty expert."

"Really?" she asks dubiously. "How?"

"Well, first things first. We'll take you to see my stylist George—are you free Saturday morning? I wrote a huge article about him in *Enchanté* right before I left, so he owes me a favor. He's the best colorist in the industry, and he gives a pretty great haircut, too. A few layers around your face with a razor to make it hip, some buttery highlights by your crown, maybe some cutting to make some of the ends flip up. He's genius. Then," I say, gazing at her thoughtfully as I try to put the pieces together, "some different eye makeup, less harsh, more impact. Plummy shadow, maybe, and brown mascara instead of black. You have such a lovely, fair complexion—too much makeup just overwhelms you and makes you look older. Then definitely NARS Orgasm—"

"What on earth is *that*?" she exclaims.

"It's the best blush in the history of the world. Trust me. You'll love it."

"I can't ask you to go to all this trouble for me!" Vivian looks as though she might cry.

I give her a hug. "This isn't trouble, this is fun! I love doing things like this! Just think of it as a down payment on the relationship advice I'm inevitably going to need from you later."

"I *knew* you had a guy in your life," she says triumphantly.

"*Er . . .* yeah, well . . . *mmph,*" I mutter.

"That bad, huh?"

"You have no idea."

My fight with James still flashing through my mind, I work on my column for three and a half hours. I'd been planning on writing something about manicures and pedicures, but I realize that this might not be very *Womanly World*. What could I do that would be more boring and would appeal to Frances? Maybe something on *at-home* manicures and pedicures? I nod to myself. Cheap, do-it-yourself, democratic. What's not to like?

★ ★ ★

"Bella Hunter."

I answer the phone absentmindedly, my mind focused on coming up with ideas for the September hair story that Frances assigned me. It's been two weeks since my disastrous sales call with James and I've been putting in 100 percent effort at the office in the hopes of proving to everybody that I can succeed. Frances left me a voice message earlier this morning—for once, I came in at 9:25 today!—telling me she wanted a meeting at 2:00 p.m. to discuss, so I've been jotting down notes and pulling out tears from competitive magazines to illustrate the direction I think we should go in.

"I'm finished," says a low male voice awash in self-pity.

"Huh?"

"I can't effing believe this. I'm moving back to San Diego."

"Nick?"

"Goddamn plastic diva," he mutters. "Was I supposed to send her out looking ugly?"

"Back up. I have no idea what you're talking about."

"The Jessica Cartier movie premiere? C'mon, Bella."

"Sorry, not ringing any bells . . ."

Loud sigh. "I *told* you last week at Balthazar. I did Jess's makeup for her premiere last night. That stupid movie about in-laws and divorce. Remember? She cried on the phone for an hour about getting old and needing a new look and how nobody thought she was sexy after the split from Lon Price?"

"That was Emily."

"What?"

"You had dinner with Emily, not me. I had to work late that night, then went home and watched *The Office* with Tristan. Emily told me all about it after she left dinner."

"Oh." He's silent for a second. "Well, you . . . Emily . . . whatever."

I smile into the receiver, amused. "Anyhow. So, what happened?"

"I went to her apartment to do the makeup and it took me three full hours—she bitched the *entire* time. Finally, I said 'Listen, Jess, *I'm* the makeup artist, so are you going to trust my professional opinion or not?'"

"Okay." I'm now flipping through *Allure* while listening to him. Nick's become awfully crisis ridden as of late.

"So she relaxes and lets me do my thing, but makes me promise that the whole look will be very dramatic and beautiful. As if I haven't been doing her makeup like an effing genius for years. She begs for lots of color, lots of style. I'm over that bronze-skin, pale-lip thing, so I decided to go big eyes, big lips, with a hint of pink on the cheeks. Very classic. 1920s." His voice is increasingly panicky as he recounts the story.

"*Uh-huh.*" I love this Aveeno ad with Paulina Porizkova. How does she manage to stay so young looking? I hope I'm even half as pretty—hell, even a quarter as pretty!—when I'm in my forties. Maybe I should start adding some more antioxidants to my diet.

"And she loved it! Effing loved it!"

"Nick, that's great!" I say halfheartedly. Why is he calling me about this? He must have had a fight with Annika or Cheryl or whatever the hell his latest twelve-year-old model-girlfriend's name is. Nick never calls us during the day to talk about work. He'd rather we call *him* with *our* problems, so that he can retain a sense of superiority.

"And then those stupid blogs started ripping apart her look this morning and she lost it! Fired me! After five years of working together, she fired me without even thinking about it. No remorse. It was *her* idea to do that makeup, not mine. I love the makeup I've been doing on her, obviously."

This snaps me back to attention. "Wait, what? She fired you?"

"Haven't you been listening?" he demands. "She would be nothing if it weren't for me!" I keep my mouth shut and refrain from telling Nick that, without him, Jessica Cartier would still be a multimillionaire actress . . . just one with a different wisecracking, sex-addicted makeup artist.

"Honey, I'm so sorry. That's terrible!"

"I'm going to *US Weekly*," he growls. "People hate her after she stole Len from Amelia Gage. Wait until everybody finds out about her pill addiction. America's sweetheart, my ass!"

"Nick, that's a bad idea."

"Why? She deserves it. I'm going to ruin her before she ruins me."

"First of all, she hasn't ruined you. You're a fantastic makeup artist and everybody knows it. All the bookers know that she's completely bonkers and they're not going to hold this against you. Secondly, if you go squealing to the tabloids, that *will* kill your reputation, and that's half of what you've got going in this industry."

"That's all I've got going for me?" Nick's voice has gone up by three octaves.

"Oh, calm down. You know I adore you—and you know exactly what I'm saying. And we both know that you're not going to go crawling off to *Star* or *US*."

He's quiet for a moment. "You're a know-it-all today."

"I've been on the other end of this conversation with you too many times. I'm just surprised that it's *you* having the nervous breakdown, not me. You're normally so cool."

"I know," he says miserably. "Arabelle dumped me. I'm not the same." Nick's voice is awash in melodrama and self-pity.

"Which one is Arabelle?"

"English. Personal trainer. Gorgeous."

"I'd expect no less."

"She treated me like crap."

"But you love that."

"I know," he sighs. "I miss her."

"Bella?" I turn in my chair to see Megan poking her head in my cubicle. "Oh, sorry!" she says, seeing that I'm on the phone. "Frances wants to meet with you at one, not two," she whispers. I mouth back, "Thank you," as she scurries away.

Time to wrap up this little chat with Nick.

"Nick, I'm so sorry. She's not worth it. You're too good for her. You'll meet somebody else before you know it." Any more clichés I can throw out to make him feel better?

He makes a little tutting noise.

"Okay, this is what we're going to do. I've been telling you for years that you need to sign with a major makeup company. You've done literally everybody in the business. There's no reason that you shouldn't be in the same league as the Pat McGraths and the Gucci Westmans."

Nick doesn't say anything.

"Nick . . ."

"What if I go to all the houses trying to get hired and nobody wants to ink a deal with me? Humiliating! Better to just be freelance, don't you think?"

"No," I say firmly. "I don't think. Maybe they'll slam the door in your face and tell you to piss off, or maybe they'll hire you and sign a multi-million-dollar contact, but you won't know until you try. Personally, I think the second scenario is a heck of a lot more likely. You're *Nick Darling*. You're a beauty industry institution." I can practically hear Nick puffing up with pride through the phone, so I continue. "Listen, I'm going to sniff around and find out from my contacts if any of the houses are hiring. I think as soon as we put the feelers out there, you'll get snapped up in a heartbeat."

"I suppose . . . ," he says, and sighs.

"Okay, good. Now, not to be totally insensitive, but I have to run. I have a meeting with Frances in exactly three minutes and I don't want to be late."

"Look at you," he says wonderingly. "You're trying to get to a meeting on real-people time, instead of on Bella time?"

"I know. Pretty crazy, huh?"

"It's a completely new Bella."

Buzz.

"She's here!" I exclaim as our buzzer rings, running over to the door and pressing the button. "Come up, Vivian!"

"I feel so sorry for this poor woman. She has no idea what she's getting herself into." Emily stands behind me, glasses on, hugging a psychology book to her chest. She's in her standard "studying" outfit—sweats and a Columbia T-shirt—with her hair pulled back and no makeup on. Of course, she looks absolutely adorable. I so wish I could pull off that whole "no makeup but still gorgeous" look. Me, I have on my favorite espadrilles and about two pounds of makeup. But makeup is fun! I don't mind putting it on.

"Hush up," I admonish. "That's not nice; Vivian is going to think you're serious. She's nervous enough as it is about her date."

"Who says I'm *not* being serious? Just don't send her out tonight looking like a hooker, please."

"What does that mean?"

"It means you can be a little heavy-handed with the eye makeup and lipstick and blush. I worry that she'll leave here looking like a lady of the night, that's all."

"That was harsh." I pout. Maybe I *am* a little creative with makeup, but that doesn't mean I give people hooker face.

Vivian knocks on the door and I swing it open, giving her a hug.

"Vivian, I want you to meet my roommate, Emily. Emily, this is my coworker Vivian."

"It's great to meet you!" Vivian exclaims. "I'm so excited about this." She turns to me and squeezes my hand. "Bella, I can't thank you enough." Last weekend I took Vivian to see George and he gave her subtle highlights and a killer shag; tonight is her first date with Walter, so I'm doing her makeup.

"What are friends for? I'm excited to see the finished product!" I gesture to the gym bag Vivian is carrying on her arm. "Can I see the clothes you brought?"

Vivian walks in the room and puts the bag on our couch, unzipping it and pulling out numerous items on hangers. "I didn't know what to bring so I just brought most of it," she says sheepishly, laying down top after top, skirt after skirt, jacket after jacket. "I'm also wearing my favorite jeans," she says, gesturing down at her legs, "in case you think that's the best look. My daughter tries to get me to wear jeans when we go out to dinner, but I feel much better about myself in a skirt."

"We'll try different combinations until we find something you're comfortable with," I say soothingly. "By the way, Emily here is a real fashionista, so she'll be able to help you with your outfit choice, too." I try to keep myself from giggling when I see the annoyed expression on Emily's face.

"Wow! That's great."

"Bella's just kidding you," Emily says, shooting me a stern look. "I'm not a fashionista."

"Don't be modest," I prod her. "Emily's a psychology student, but she has better fashion sense than anybody I've ever met. She helps her sister with her wardrobe a lot. You could say it runs in the family."

"I'd love your opinion, Emily, but please don't feel obliged to help," Vivian says. "Lordy, I feel terrible enough as it is taking over your apartment for a few hours."

Emily's features soften into a smile. "No, please, Vivian, it's no trouble. I'd love to see what outfits you brought."

Vivian gestures toward her clothes awkwardly, as if to say "Go ahead," and Emily moves forward, slowly picking up piece after piece.

"Okay, let's see. No . . . maybe . . . *ooh,* this is cute . . . definitely not . . . very nice . . . maybe . . ." Emily works her way through the pile, spreading the clothes around her.

"I like that one!" I say, pointing to a printed top Emily is about to put into the no pile.

"Are you kidding me?" she asks. "Not right for a first date *at all.*"

"Why not?"

"First of all, it's way too high cut. Vivian has a sexy collarbone and should be showing it off. Secondly, the colors don't work with her complexion. There's too much lime green. I think she'd be better with something light pink, blue, or yellow. Like this!" She grabs a yellow three-quarter-length scoop-neck top and holds it at arm's length, as if judging how Vivian will look in it. "With a knee-length skirt, maybe those kitten heels? Perfect."

"Wow," Vivian says. "I'm impressed."

"Told you she was good," I say smugly, sticking my tongue out at Emily playfully when she rolls her eyes back at me.

After spending fifteen minutes picking out an outfit, we move into the bathroom for the makeup application. I grab a chair from the living room and plant Vivian on it, eschewing the small makeup bag she brought in favor of my massive beauty arsenal.

Twenty minutes later, I'm done. I stand back and admire my handiwork. "What do you think?" I've evened out Vivian's ruddiness with Armani foundation that practically melts into her skin and warmed up her complexion with light Guerlain bronzer. Then, a few dashes of soft gray and violet M·A·C shadow, Lancôme mascara, and NARS blush complete the look.

Vivian looks in the mirror and her hand flies to her mouth. "Oh my God, Bella, I look amazing."

"You're gorgeous!"

"I can't believe this. How did you . . . ?" She stares at herself in wonder, gently touching her fingers to her cheeks and inspecting her eye makeup. "You made my eyes look blue!"

"Your eyes *are* blue."

"But they always look so dark, you can hardly tell! And my skin! It's . . . glowy!"

Emily leans in the doorway, nodding approvingly. "Vivian, you're beautiful."

She stares at herself for almost a full minute and then turns to us, hugging and kissing our cheeks. "I don't know how to thank you girls enough."

Five minutes later, she's on her way out the door, rushing downstairs to catch a cab back to her apartment, where Walter is due to pick her up at 8:00.

After a second flurry of hugs and kisses, I close the front door and sit on the couch next to Emily, who has already reopened her psych textbooks and is busy scribbling notes in the margins, her Lisa Loeb–style glasses sliding down her thin nose.

"That was a really nice thing you did," Emily comments, flipping back and forth between pages.

"Vivian's a doll. Did you see how happy she was? Plus, she and Megan are basically my only friends in the office. *You* did an amazing job."

"Whatever, it was easy," she says dismissively, looking up at me and resting her book in her lap. "Three months ago you wouldn't have wasted five minutes on an older coworker unless she invited you to spend the weekend at her house in

Bridgehampton or something. You did it just to be nice. Good for you."

"Don't throw it back at me. You should think about setting up shop as a fashion stylist, Em."

"And quit my masters program?"

"Well . . . yeah. Look, you know I'm the first person to be pro-education, but you're being silly. If your mother weren't *your mother,* you would have pursued this ages ago. Who cares if you're Josie Tyler's daughter? You have talent, and any idiot can see that. Nobody would accuse anybody of using you just because of your name."

"God, Josie would be thrilled." Emily and her sister both call their mother by her first name, which is something I find incredibly weird. My father would disown me if I dared to show either of my parents such disrespect. Then again, Josie literally gets *angry* when Emily and Gabrielle call her Mom, pouting that it makes her feel old. Emily shrugs. "I'll admit that I've been tempted to leave school; my classes are a nightmare and I can't see myself actually becoming a psychologist." She wrinkles her nose. "Can you imagine anything more depressing?"

"Not for you."

She nods, tapping a pencil on her textbook. "We'll see. I'll think about it."

Weeks later, I have a meeting with Rania, Frances, and Megan to go over the reader numbers for our latest issue—the issue featuring the first column I wrote. It's been four months since I started at *Womanly World,* and I'm getting into the groove: Megan and I take regular lunches; Vivian stops by my desk for chats; Shelly, Vicky, and Elise no longer seem to hate me, thanks to the regular beauty bounty I supply them with. Things are coming together. Even the other beauty girls seem to have forgotten my spectacular flameout from *Enchanté,*

chatting with me—insincerely, but hey, it's conversation—
at events. The only sore point is that my relationships with
James and Frances are still frosty, but I suppose you can't win
'em all. Maybe Tristan's laid-back come-what-may attitude is
finally rubbing off on me. (It's not the only thing. Our interactions are almost purely physical, both of us having silently
realized, I think, that there's not much of a mental connection
there. I only slightly mind—stimulating banter doesn't keep
you warm at night.)

I rush over to the large conference room by the stairs, where
Rania, Frances, and Megan are waiting for our meeting.

"You're late," Frances says primly.

I look at the clock on the wall. It reads 1:01. She's got to be
kidding.

"I'm sorry."

"No problem," Rania says, waving her hand in the air dismissively. "We've only been here for a few seconds ourselves.
I'm still waiting for Lauren to come over with the beauty
results from the survey."

"How do you think we did?" I ask.

Frances looks at me sharply. "Haven't you read them yet?"

"No . . ."

She presses her lips together in disapproval. "I left you a
note about it on your desk last week. I put the note right next
to your computer, where you *should* have been able to see it,
assuming your desk wasn't such a mess."

My desk is about a million times cleaner than it used to be,
but I suppose Frances, like my father, considers anything less
than white-glove-worthy cleanliness to be slovenly. *If Frances used e-mail like any normal person*, I think darkly, *maybe I
wouldn't have missed seeing a random note.*

I don't say anything. Megan looks terrified, as if it's her
fault that I missed the memo. I smile at her and give her the
most imperceptible of winks.

Frances shakes her head and scribbles a few notes on the yellow legal pad she always carries around with her. I hate that thing. It drives me crazy wondering what she's writing. Maybe: *Bella is the worst employee ever?* Or: *I hate my job, I hate my life, I hate this magazine?* Perhaps. More likely it's something along the lines of: *Bella is very forgetful and disorganized. Discuss this in her review.* God, she's so anal.

Lauren walks into the room carrying a stack of papers. "Here you go. I organized it from back to front, so the most recent issue with the beauty statistics is on top."

"Thanks, Lauren," Rania says, taking the stack and passing Frances, Megan, and me one copy each. She flips through the statistics booklet, pausing on the third page. "Bella, I know you haven't had a chance to look through this yet, but Frances and I have already had several discussions about this in the past week. I have to be honest; the beauty numbers were not what I'd hoped. Overall impression, quality of writing, interest in topics, likelihood of reading again—they were all distressingly low. I know that you've been putting in a lot of effort with the pages, especially recently, but we're simply not going in the right direction."

She pauses to flip through more pages and Frances jumps in. "Your page received the lowest marks out of any in the magazine."

The news sinks in. *My* page was the lowest? Lower than the stupid article about flats? And the boring financial advice? And the who-actually-re-creates-these-dishes-anyway food tips? My page was always one of the most widely read, popular features at *Enchanté*! How can it be such a bomb here when it was such a hit there?

"I . . . I don't understand," I say haltingly. "People always loved my page at *Enchanté*. I thought . . ."

"Well, that's just it," Frances interrupts. "You are not *at Enchanté,* you are at *Womanly World*. You cannot expect to take the same formula and stamp out your pages without making any sort of connection to the reader. It's irresponsible and they can see right through it."

"I think it's a matter of taking some time and finding the *Womanly World* voice," Rania says soothingly, taking a different tack from Frances, who looks completely annoyed with me. "You wrote the column when you'd only been here a few weeks. Your page was beloved at *Enchanté,* but we have to accept that the readers are completely different. What readers responded to there might go over the heads of our readers." She pauses. "Or vice versa."

Yeah, like the food articles, I think. *Enchanté* readers don't cook; they *have* cooks.

I nod. "I can do that."

"I do not think you are taking this seriously enough," Frances snaps. "These readers hated your column. You need to think long and hard about what that means for your future here when your only major contribution is universally panned. You cannot talk down to the readers. If they hated this one, they are bound to hate the next two columns, too, and those are already set to print."

Frances is probably right. Maybe I need to get it through my head that, horrifying as it is to me, these readers *are* Frances. I'm not writing for twenty-four-year-old socialites and Sherrell Aston facelift patients and de Rothchilds anymore. I'm writing for late-middle-aged women who wear mom-jeans.

I'm geniunely cowed. "I'm sorry, Frances. You're right. It won't happen again next month." Jesus, this is becoming my mantra.

"Good," she says, looking suspicious but slightly appeased.

Rania wraps up the meeting with lots of uplifting talk and positive cheer and I walk back to my desk, annoyed at myself for letting my feelings for Frances get in the way of my job. Megan tries to pep talk me. Frances might be ornery, but she genuinely means well . . . I think. She does have an affinity for the readers, after all. At some point I'm going to have to swallow my pride and follow her lead—it's not as simple as changing my outfit and being chummy with my coworkers, apparently. I'm not going back to *Enchanté*—that much is clear. It's do or die time, and now I'm fighting for my very career survival.

famous dermatologist in France before moving his practice to the United States. His waiting list for "real people" is over eighteen months long, but I was able to get in with only two weeks' notice, thanks to the magic of publicists. I try to ignore the fact that my previous trips to see Dr. P, for IPL and zit-shrinking cortisone injections while at *Enchanté,* were booked only the day before.

As I walk through the doors, the receptionist smiles. "My, my, Bella Hunter. What a pleasant surprise!"

"Hi, Birdie! How are you?"

"Just wonderful. But how are *you*? My God, what a scandal maker you are!" she giggles. Birdie is in her late thirties and has been working for Dr. Patrice for years—at least as long as I'd been at *Enchanté.* She's one of those cheerful, pleasant people who lets everything roll off her back and never seems to have a bad day. She is, in fact, Dr. Patrice's polar opposite, which explains in theory why they get along, but still doesn't really make sense to me. I don't know how she puts up with him—five minutes in his office, and I'm ready to bolt. But he's the best—and it's free—so you do what you must.

"I'm at *Womanly World* now. *Enchanté* gave me the boot."

"You're telling me this as if I didn't read all about it on Gawker," Birdie admonishes, shaking a finger at me. "Hon, you're infamous now."

"Don't remind me."

She pulls out my file and reads through it quickly. "So . . . Botox, *mmm?* Aren't you a little young? Surely you can't have wrinkles *already* from that whole fiasco?"

"It's for a story. Botox at the derm versus all the at-home wrinkle-relaxing creams."

"Those creams aren't too expensive for *Womanly World*?"

"Not as expensive as Botox with Dr. P!" I laugh, conceding, "Those creams *are* usually pricey, so we're focusing on the drugstore alternatives."

Chapter 10

A week in the life of a beauty editor is an exercise in variety: no two days are the same. One day might find you chained to your desk, researching and writing a story; the next might be spent in the back of a Town Car, being escorted around the city from Cornelia Day Spa to Soho House. I can never decide whether I prefer staying in the office or being out and about—it's nice being away from your desk, but the price is to be paid in uncomfortable interactions with fellow editors and publicists. Before my *Post* scandal, I'd felt nervous around the other girls, who I considered colleagues and chums. Now, despite our tentatively friendly interactions—Delilah notwithstanding—my unease knows no bounds.

Today I have an appointment with a dermatologist on Park Avenue. Frances and Rania have accepted my latest column proposal (Botox versus over-the-counter antiwrinkle creams—for cheap, of course), and so I'm heading to see Dr. Patrice Lefabré for my first ever Botox injections. I think I'm too young at twenty-eight to even be *contemplating* Botox, but several of my editor contemporaries (and everybody at *Enchanté*) have already jumped on that bandwagon, so I at least know what to expect.

The office entrance is just off Park on Seventy-sixth Street, with a small plaque next to the door reading Dr. Patrice Lefabré. Dr. P, as everybody calls him, was the most

She peers at me. "And . . . how do you feel about that?"

"Do I have a choice?"

"Good point! No point in crying about what you can't change." The phone rings and she winks at me before answering it, motioning for me to have a seat.

I settle into one of the plush chairs and gaze around the waiting room. Even though I've been here several times, I always feel a thrill at the Louis Quinze–style gold chairs, the Persian carpeting, the cascading chandelier and soft, warm lighting. It's practically as opulent as one of those furniture rooms at the Met. (I *love* those rooms. I like wandering around and pretending that I'm an eighteenth-century European princess and everything in the rooms belongs to me and my handsome, strapping prince husband, who looks vaguely like Colin Firth in *Pride and Prejudice*. Does that make me weird?)

Just then the door swings open and a fit blond woman wearing a blue tracksuit strides out in a cloud of Dior perfume, her face obscured by a blue Kangol cap and giant Gucci shades. "Thanks, darling," she calls over her shoulder in a clear voice, her accent unplacably mid-Atlantic. "Next month as always!"

As she breezes past, I suddenly realize who it is. I look at Birdie wonderingly, as if to say, "Was that . . . ?" and she nods slightly, a smile playing at her lips. So *that's* how she manages to look so young! It's been rumored for years that she's a client of Dr. Brandt's, something they've both vigorously denied. Right client, wrong doctor, apparently. *Aging naturally, my ass.*

Suddenly, Dr. P appears at the doorway, his hands clasped together.

"Bella! *Mon cherie! Quelle plaisir!* It 'as been a long time, *non?*"

"Dr. P! Way too long. Great to see you!"

We kiss-kiss-kiss (he likes to give three; two on the right and one on the left). I look him in the eye and, as always, have to paste the smile on my face to keep from letting the horror show. As one of the foremost Botox experts in the world, Dr. P has decided to turn himself into a human guinea pig, injecting every last inch of his face until he resembles a bad copy of a wax statue of himself. It's one of the industry's biggest wonders: how can somebody who's so gifted at making everybody *else* look natural walk around himself looking like the Cat Lady? Wonders never cease.

He stares at me searchingly, his eyes sweeping my face. I have no doubt that, if it were humanly possible, his brow would be furrowed right now. Alas, it's as smooth as a baby's bottom. "Yes," he says, "It is good zat you are finally coming to me for zee Botox. I did not want to say anythin' before, *mais,* for you . . ." He presses a clammy finger to my temple, then touches another finger to where my crow's feet would be, if I had any (which I don't). He sighs. "All youth must come to an end sometime, *non?*" He shakes his head as if I look seventy-five years old and pats my shoulder reassuringly. "Not a moment too soon."

What a jackass.

In his office, a degree from some French university I've never heard of is quietly hidden on the wall, dwarfed by the framed magazine articles and glossy photo shoots: Dr. P in *New York* magazine's annual Best Doctors list; a huge piece in *W* magazine; a three-page spread in *Tatler;* an *Enchanté* story that I wrote almost five years ago; as well as about twenty others.

He sees me looking at the articles and smiles warmly, gesturing to a piece from French *Vogue.* "*Ahh,* yes. Zat was one of my fav-oh-reet. Wonderful story." His voice is as loving as if he were talking about one of his children.

"Wonderful," I repeat, nodding emphatically before switching gears. "I don't know if Petra—" his publicist "—told you exactly what I'm doing, but it's a story comparing Botox to all of the new antiwrinkle creams. We—"

"*Bof!*" he interrupts. "I 'ate those creams! Zose creams are not Botox! Only Botox is Botox! It is insulting to sink zat a stupid little cream could make your wrinkles go away like *magique. Impossible!*"

"Well . . . yes. Anyway, our readers can't all afford *real* Botox, so it's necessary to do the comparison to give them—"

"What? Your readers? Your readers are the most affluent in the world! *C'est folle!*" he chuckles.

I realize that Petra must not have told Dr. P that I've switched magazines.

"Oh, I thought you knew. I'm at *Womanly World* magazine now. I've left *Enchanté.*"

"*Womanly World?*" he repeats uncomprehendingly. "What is zat?"

"It's, *um,* a magazine. For women."

"It is like *Enchanté?*"

"No . . . not *exactly* like *Enchanté.*"

"Well, what kind of articles does it do, zees *Womanly World?*"

"You know, the same sort of stuff, really," I say vaguely. "The best products," . . . for cheap . . . "the chicest ways to decorate your home," . . . on a budget . . . "the hottest fashions" . . . from Wal-Mart. "Basically no different."

"*Fantastique, eh!* Well, per'aps after we do the Botox, we can also do a little Restylane, to write about in zee story? And some laser treatments, *non?* I didn't want to say, but you really need to do some'seeng about z'ose nasolabial folds. And your frown lines! Zere is no reason! When you leave today, we will 'ave you looking beautiful again."

I clench my fists as I tightly squeeze my mouth into a smile. "Aren't you sweet, Dr. P. But maybe just the Botox today. I know our readers are dying to hear all about Restylane and lasers and everything else, but we have to save something for our next issue, after all!" *You know, in case* Womanly World *ever does a 'Blow your child's college savings at the dermatologist' piece.*

"Fine," he says, looking a little forlorn. "No Restylane today." He sighs.

When I leave the room twenty-five minutes later, my face feels tingly, but otherwise normal. Dr. P warns me that the effects of Botox will take a few hours to appear, up to five days to fully take effect, and that I need to remain upright until this evening. "So no upside sex, *eh?*" he leers, leading me down the hallway.

I laugh nervously. "I'll try." Perv.

Birdie sends me off in a flurry of hugs and makes me promise that I'll return soon. "Just to say hi," she whispers, "not because you need anything else from him, 'cause you don't." I love Birdie.

Out on Seventy-sixth Street, I'm heading toward Lexington, trying to decide if it's faster to hop in a cab or take the subway when I realize that my favorite shoe boutique is just two blocks east on Madison. It's only 3:45 p.m. and I told Frances I'd be back to the office around 4:30. Surely I can squeeze in five minutes of shopping?

I dash over to the store and happily try on pair after pair of shoes, finally attempting to decide between a practical-yet-chic pair of pointy black Marc by Marc flats and orgasm-on-heels red Christian Louboutin stilettos. The Marcs are $250 on sale, which is about three times as much as what I want to spend. But then again, I'd wear them every single day, so in a way, they're actually really cheap! When you divide $250 by 360—since I would *definitely* live in these shoes—it's less than fifty cents a day. It's a total bargain! The Christian Louboutin stilettos are much more difficult to justify—I have absolutely no use for them, and they're $850. I don't even have an appropriate dress to wear them with. But what if Emily lends me a dress, and then it's the perfect dress to wear to an event *and* the perfect dress to wear with these heels, but I don't have these heels, and then I have to pair ugly and inappropriate shoes with the dress and then I look completely out of place? That *always* happens. Not the inappropriate dress-and-shoes combination, but, rather, cheaping myself out of buying a really fantastic something because I feel like I don't have enough money, and then I kick myself for years because I didn't throw caution to the wind and bypass Starbucks soy lattes for two months and buy the thing instead. I will not do that to myself any longer. I am worth *more* than that! I deserve designer red stilettos! I must have them.

I'm not justifying anything, I tell myself firmly. In a weird way, it's extremely practical. I slap my card down.

Back out on the street, I swing the bag back and forth happily as I walk, feeling like a modern-day Mary Tyler Moore. I glance at my watch. Crap! It's already 5:30! It's not possible that I spent nearly two hours in the store deciding between only two pairs of shoes.

"Hello, Bella."

I look to my right and physically start when I see James carrying a briefcase, looking sleek in a navy suit, white shirt, and navy, green and red striped tie, his hair smoothed back behind his ears. "Jesus! You scared me! *Er* . . . I mean, hello, James."

He glances at the bag and then looks up at the store I just exited from. "Working hard as always?"

"I was just going back to the office!" I say, perhaps a bit too defensively. The *one* time I play hooky from work, I get caught by the very man who thinks I'm a lazy airhead. Goddamn it! Can I not catch a break?

"Mmm-hmm." He doesn't look convinced in the slightest.

"I had an appointment with Dr. P, the dermatologist—I mean, a work appointment, that is, not a personal one—and he gave me Botox and it was just a block over, *uh,* on Fifth, so, when I walked by this store on the way to the subway, I decided to stop in. For a new pair of work shoes," I fib.

"I see," he says, looking at me incredulously. "You had Botox?"

"For a story," I say firmly. "Work related."

"For our magazine?"

"What *other* magazine would I possibly be writing stories for?" I ask, exasperated, before I realize that I'm nearly yelling. I lower my voice and take the sarcasm down a notch. "Yes. For *Womanly World.* I suggested doing a beauty column comparing Botox with antiwrinkle creams so our readers could decide for themselves if spending all that money was worth it or not. I test out the treatments for them—their guinea pig."

"Not bad." He glances down at the bag again. "You picked up a pair of shoes, too? For work, of course."

"Of course," I say uncomfortably.

"Can I see them?"

What? This is totally inappropriate. He's only asking to see them because he knows I'm lying. Damn it.

"I don't really . . . I'm not sure . . ." I shift back from one foot to the other, offended that he's even asking, but trying to think of a way to get out of this without being (a) rude and (b) found out. "I'm sorry, but I have this thing about not showing anybody my shoes before I wear them. It stems from childhood. It's bad luck." What a moronic story; couldn't I have come up with something better on the spot?

James coughs and puts his hand over his mouth as if trying to suppress laughter. "I understand. My brother has the same compulsion, but in reverse, and with underwear. It's gotten him in trouble countless times."

Huh? Is he . . . joking? Does he know how to joke?

"*Er* . . . yeah. So, anyhow, I need to be getting back to work, to finish up this column I've been working very, very hard on. All week. Bye." I spin on my heel and start to hurry away, but my shoe gets caught in a crack and I trip over myself. James reaches out and grabs me by the arm, keeping me from falling.

"*Whoops,*" I say, involuntarily giggling nervously as I brush the dust off my pants. I feel like crying from humiliation. "That was a close one. Thanks."

"My pleasure," he says, gesturing at the ground. "Hope that doesn't bring you more bad luck, though." I look down and suddenly realize that I dropped my shopping bag when I tripped—the red stilettos are sprawled on the concrete.

"It wouldn't be humanly possible," I mutter, kneeling down and stuffing them in the bag, my cheeks flushed. The only people wearing *these* shoes to work would be strippers.

"Those look perfect for the office," he says, his face deadpan.

"*Er* . . . they're not really for the office, per se. More for work events. Dinners, obligatory beauty parties, things like that."

"Right."

"Okay, so you caught me!" I burst out despondently. "My appointment was actually on Park, but I'm absolutely obsessed with that store, and it was only a block away, so I decided to run in for just two seconds. I really *have* been working like a dog all week and I've been trying for months to get into the spirit of *Womanly World,* but no matter how hard I try nothing I do is right and I've been going crazy! I thought there would be no harm. Just for a second! But then I saw these shoes *and* another pair of shoes and I couldn't decide between the two of them, so I spent two hours in the store and then I blew all of my money on these and now I've completely missed half of the workday. Are you happy?"

He stares at me for several seconds. Is he going to fire me

now? Right here on Madison Avenue? Who will hire me after this? Two magazines in four months? I can already see the Page Six headline now: LOOSE-LIPPED BEAUTY WRITER CANNED FOR SHOPPING.

"Are you going to fire me?" I whisper, close to tears.

James presses his lips together and I see a small dimple at the corner of his right cheek that I've never noticed before. Small wonder—I don't think I've ever seen him smile. He's trying to hold back laughter! The bastard! He thinks my misery is funny!

"No," he says. "Not today. Let's not make a habit of this, though."

"Okay. They really *are* for work. Kind of."

"Of course."

We stand there facing each other and I feel extremely vulnerable. I realize that this is our first real conversation in ages, since our fight in the car. I've never been a sex kitten, but I usually can at least attempt to fake flirt my way through an interaction with a guy. James completely unnerves me, however. Mostly because, despite what I yelled at him, I sense he *sees* me, unlike most other people.

"Well, bye," I say awkwardly. "Back to the office."

"Wait. Listen, my car is just over there. I'm heading back myself. Do you want a lift?" he asks politely.

"Oh. Sure. *Um* . . . thanks."

We walk across the street to his waiting Town Car and get in together, the driver shutting the door behind us. I notice with relief that it's not the same driver who witnessed the meltdown last time.

"So . . . ," I say, racking my brain for some thread of conversation, no matter how inane. "Busy day?"

"Incredibly. I've had three appointments today and have been going back and forth, uptown and downtown. I haven't eaten yet."

"You haven't eaten?" I ask incredulously. "All day?"

"Nope. Not once."

"Oh my God, I would die. I can't make it two hours without having something to eat." I pause, then add, "Not that I'm a cow or anything." Why am I incapable of having an intelligent conversation with this man? "I'm actually hungry myself, so I feel your pain."

He's quiet for a second then looks at his watch. "It's nearly six. There's not much point in going back to the office now and Frances has probably left for the day. Why don't I have my car drop you off at home?"

"Are you sure? I won't get in trouble?"

"If you do, you can blame it on me. How's that?"

"Oh! Sure."

"Actually," he says casually, "if you truly are hungry, I was planning on stopping for a bite to eat. Do you want to join me? We could go over the July presentation for the Face Group. If you don't have plans this evening and don't mind doing a bit more work, that is. I know you've had a busy day."

My cheeks flush. "Right. Yes, that sounds great. It would be good to get a head start on the presentation."

"Excellent. Restaurant suggestions?"

"Leviathan? I've been dying to go there."

"Their food is great, but it's impossible to get in at the last minute. What about Chez Michel-Antoine? Have you been there? It's a fantastic place in the West Village, not far away from where you live. Great Mediterranean food."

How does he know where I live? *Ahh,* yes, he picked me up for the last presentation.

"Sure, sounds good. It's a date." No! Not a date! Take it back, take it back!

James pulls out his BlackBerry and clicks through it for several seconds as I stew in my own embarrassment. "Here it is. I'll call to make sure they have a table."

"Great."

I can't believe I just called our dinner a date. But isn't that kind of what it is? My stomach is fluttering with excitement and nervousness. Oh my God, how did this happen?

He calls to make a reservation then hangs up. Immediately, his BlackBerry starts ringing and he answers it. "Hey! What's up? Where were you last weekend? I tried calling."

My curiosity is piqued. Girlfriend? Despite myself, I feel jealous. *Why are you jealous? You have a boyfriend. A hot model boyfriend. With the IQ of a peanut.*

Silence, then hearty laughter on his end. "Yeah, like that's going to happen. You know how she is. Never satisfied." Pause. "*Nah,* not much. I have to finish up some work on that presentation I was telling you about last week, but other than that should be pretty chill." Another pause. I hear a girl's voice chattering through the line, but I can't make out her words. "No, it's fine that you missed it; he bailed at the last minute. I was pretty pissed about it—he knew how important it was for us. Whatever. That's Simon. Typical moody Brit. Still, can you believe it?" Pause, then laughter. "Thanks Nance, I will. Love you, too. Tell mom I say hi. Okay, bye."

Ahh, it's his *sister.* That explains the uncharacteristic warmth in his voice and his relaxed tone. Interesting. So he's close to his sister, and he talks to her like a human being. And there's some Brit dude named Simon who screwed him over. Valuable tidbits, all.

"Your sister?" I ask casually.

"Right," he says, putting the BlackBerry in his suit pocket and settling back in the seat. "How'd you know?"

Um, because I was listening intently to your conversation and dissecting every word . . . *obviously.* "Oh, at the end, you said something about your mom, so I figured . . ."

"Right. Yeah, her name's Nancy. She's eight years younger than I am, so I almost feel like her dad sometimes. When she was in high school, half of the time it was me freaking about her coming home late, instead of my parents. My brother could disappear for three days and turn up at the front door naked, and nobody would bat an eyelash, but Nancy . . ." He laughs at the memory and looks out the window, his smile fading. "We became a lot closer after my dad died."

"I'm sorry." I remember my comment in the cab after my failed presentation that he was working at *Womanly World* to please his daddy and my cheeks flush.

"Plane crash. He died instantly. In a way, I think that's better than wasting away from cancer or . . . you know. Quick and painless. End of story."

"So, was *that* the reason you came to the company? Because of your dad's death?"

He looks out the window again, his face blank. "Right. Basically."

Okay, there are obviously a lot of issues here. I can work with this. He's in *pain*. That's why he's always so moody and mean. And he's not a total robot. Just in the last few minutes, he's sounded like a normal thirty-year-old guy, instead of a seventy-five-year-old grandpa. There's a real guy lurking in there somewhere, dying to let his hair down—I can *feel* it.

We ride in silence for several minutes, each looking out the window. I wonder what's going through his mind. Is he thinking about me? Work? His sister? Simon the Brit dude? I would give anything to crawl into his head for a few minutes.

Maybe he senses me thinking about him because he looks at me and says quietly, "Listen. I'm sorry about what I said to you in the car last month. It was way out of line. I hope you don't hold it against me."

I'm touched by the sentiment. "Thank you. I'm over it now. I guess I can't stay mad after you let me play hooky, right?" I'm teasing him, but I have no idea how he'll react. Every time I attempt to inject some levity into one of our conversations, he freaks out and gets very proper, as if the Uptight Police will arrest him for cracking a smile or something.

He doesn't say anything for a second, but then chuckles. "I guess not."

It's not quite Academy Award–screenplay worthy conversation, but it'll do. At least we're making some progress here.

Half an hour later, we're sitting by the window of Chez Michel-Antoine, tucking into a massive shellfish platter. We've spent twenty minutes touching on the finer points of the upcoming presentation.

"I guess that's all," he says, sipping a glass of Chablis. "Let's hope the presentation goes smoothly."

I slurp out the juice from an oyster and gaze at him thoughtfully. I get the sense that he's putting on an act to hide the real him, like an evening in a rowdy pub with cans of PBR and a group of brazen, scantily clad babes would immediately force the normal thirty-year-old out of him. Something about the whole uptight worker-bee James thing doesn't sit right with me.

He looks at me quizzically. "What?"

I realize I've been blatantly staring at him. "Oh. Sorry."

"Why are you looking at me like that? Do I have something on my face?"

"No." His paranoia makes me smile.

"Why are you smiling?"

I laugh. "No reason! Chill out!"

"You must be staring and laughing at me for a *reason*."

"No reason. Not really."

"Not really?" He makes a tiny face. "Okay. That's how you want to play it."

"I'm not playing anything!" I giggle.

"Never mind the fact that you *do* actually have something on your face."

My hands fly to my cheeks. "I do? Where?"

He cocks an eyebrow. "Not so fun anymore?"

"No, seriously. Do I really?"

He shrugs. "Maybe."

"Damn it!" I dive into my bag and pull out my Chanel compact, discreetly staring into my lap to see if there actually is anything on my face. There isn't.

I look back up at him, torn between embarrassment and annoyance, and he laughs, rocking back in his chair like a little kid. "You're gullible."

"I'm not gullible!"

"Actually," he says, nodding slowly, "you *do* seem kind of gullible."

"You have got to be kidding me. How on earth would you know if I'm gullible or not?"

"I don't know. You just have a gullible air about you."

I cross my arms, shaking my head.

"In a good way," he adds. "It's sort of childlike."

"My boss thinks I'm a naive toddler. Awesome. I'm making a great impression at work," I say sarcastically.

He takes another sip of wine and smiles at me. My glass of Cabernet has gone to my head and I'm feeling a little tipsy.

"You know, you look like a teenage girl drinking that glass of white," I blurt out. "Are you sure you wouldn't be more comfortable with a rosé? We could stop at the convenience store down the block after dinner and get you some pink wine in a box if you'd prefer."

He raises his eyebrows slowly and stares across the table at me incredulously. As his eyes burn into mine, I feel the heat slowly creeping across my neck and into my face. I cannot believe I just said that. I break into a guilty grin. "Sorry."

He's still staring at me. He's still not saying anything. Why isn't he saying anything? Crap. I crossed the line. I thought we were being flirty, and now all he's thinking is how inappropriate I am, and probably remembering the fact that I was totally flaky today and skipped half the day to buy hooker heels and that he thinks I'm a terrible employee. Why did I let my guard down like that? For a second, I thought of him as a normal, sexy guy I was having dinner with. I actually forgot I was flirting with my boss! *Flirting* . . . with my . . . *boss*. Words that should never, ever be in the same sentence together. Stupid, stupid girl.

I stare back at him, begging him with my eyes to get me off the hook for my lame joke.

He looks conflicted, like he's struggling with his emotions. He's probably torn between telling me off for being rude and feeling pity for how lame I am. Finally he finishes the glass in one gulp, puts it down on the table and crosses his arms. "I didn't realize it was a drinking contest, but next time I'll bring the tequila, how's that?" He smiles to let me know he's joking. Oh, thank God.

I'm suddenly grateful that James is so overly polite. Frances is equally proper but probably would have reamed me out for my inappropriateness. James, on the other hand, seems determined to keep the mood pleasant at all costs—that's probably why he apologized so profusely for being rude in the car a few weeks ago.

I smile back at him. Maybe it's the wine, or maybe it's the fact that, thankfully, he still hasn't fired me, but I'm beginning to like him. Professionally, of course. "Sorry, I was making a joke. Kind of silly."

The waiter refills his glass and James shrugs, smiling slightly. " 'S'okay."

"I know you think I'm . . . tightly wound," he says out of nowhere.

I blink, surprised. *"Uh . . ."*

"No. It's fine. I am. Well, rather . . . I am at the office." He sighs. "It's a job. Or, it's *the* job. I'm young . . . I took over for my father . . . there's a lot riding on everything . . . I have to behave a certain way . . ." He stares down at the table. "Do you understand?"

I want to, but I'm completely baffled why he's telling me all this. "Sort of," I say tentatively, not wanting him to stop talking.

He looks at his hands and then looks back up at me. "I just . . . I'm *thirty years old* and I never would have this job if not for my family. It's easy for people to dismiss me because they don't take me seriously. I can't kick back and take it easy. People expect me to fail. I have to prove them wrong."

"But you can still be yourself while doing a terrific job," I say gently.

"It doesn't work that way," he says, shaking his head. "I can't be myself. Myself is . . ." he looks around the room wildly, as if searching for a comparison, finally shrugging. "That's not the real world. People expect things from you, and if you're not a certain way, you're screwed."

I sit back in my chair. "That's pretty pessimistic. People expect things from you, but I think they expect what you *teach* them to expect. Take the way I've seen you in the office compared to how you were on the phone with your sister earlier. You were completely relaxed—normal! Maybe you can't joke about personal stuff during work meetings, but you don't have to be totally mummified to be competent. Personality goes a long way." I rap my fist on the table in mock emphasis.

The waiter refills James's glass and he takes a deep sip, drumming his fingers on the table. "I really shouldn't be discussing this with you. I'm sorry. I didn't mean to—"

"Don't do that!" I shriek. "I know you're the boss, but Jesus, you're only two years older than I am."

He looks offended. "Well. I—"

"Come *on*," I say boldly. "Be normal! Act your age! I'm sitting here having dinner with you and I don't know anything about you, other than the fact that you're chronically uptight and grumpy." I take another swig of wine, aware that I'm getting myself back into trouble. But I can't take this! Surely he's a little tipsy, too. *In vino veritas.*

We stare at each other. My head is starting to swim. Maybe it wasn't a good idea to refill my glass of wine. Did I just call him uptight and grumpy?

"Okay," he says. "What do you want to know?"

I like this game. "Where did you go to school, for starters?"

"Harvard."

"Major?"

"Econ."

"Where were you born?"

He takes another sip of wine and gives me a tiny smile. "Here in New York. You know, these are pretty easy questions. I could go all night long."

I try to remember a novelty book that Susan bought me when I was in college called *The Book of Questions.* "If you were out hiking with your mom and your girlfriend and they both got bitten by a rattlesnake at the *exact same time* and you only had one vial of rattlesnake antivenin, and whichever person you didn't give the medicine to would definitely die, but whichever person you did give the medicine to would definitely live . . . who would you choose?"

"What?" he laughs. "What kind of crazy question is that?"

"You said my other questions were too easy. This is a thought provoker!"

He rolls his eyes. "You're weird. Okay, have I been dating the girl for a long time? Are we engaged?"

"I don't know. You tell me."

"Fine," he sighs. "If the girl and I are engaged, or I'm planning on asking her to marry me, I'd pick my girlfriend. But if she's somebody I've only recently started dating, then I'd pick my mom."

"You'd pick your mom over your girlfriend? That's so Oedipal."

"Come on! The woman who raised you versus some girl you've been on three dates with? I think it's a no-brainer."

"Remind me never to go camping with you." I blush as I suddenly realize the implications of what I've just said.

He laughs at the look on my face. "Okay, what about you? We've already established that you went to Northwestern, as you so delicately yelled in my face a few weeks ago. And I know you were an English major. So, where were *you* born?"

"Fayetteville, North Carolina," I say ruefully.

"What's with the face? What's wrong with North Carolina?"

"I don't know," I shrug. "It's hardly the most glamorous place on earth. I was an army brat; there was a base there."

"Nothing wrong with it, though. North Carolina is beautiful. My mom had a ranch there growing up. The people are much friendlier than New Yorkers."

"I love New York! I could live here forever. There's always something to do, there's so much culture, the energy is palpable. It kills me. It's amazing. Hardly anybody's *really* from here, but everybody makes it their own."

"Where's your family? Are they here now?"

"They're in a suburb of Cleveland and harass me daily to move home. My sister is getting married in three weeks, so I'm going back for the wedding, and they'll probably bribe me to stay. It's impossible for them to wrap their minds around the idea that I've left for good."

"Don't you miss them?"

"I do," I admit. "More than they realize. But I'm just not a Clevelander. I was meant to be in New York. This feels like home. I only lived there for about six years, anyway—I don't feel a connection to it. Home is where you make it."

"You have a lot of courage," he says, shaking his head. "I don't know if I could just pick up and leave my family. It's amazing."

"Amazing in a good way or amazing in a 'this chick is crazy and has no business working in my office and I'm firing her first thing tomorrow morning' kind of way?"

"Amazing in a 'this chick has no business working in my office . . . but I'm glad she does' kind of way."

"I can't tell if that's a compliment or not."

"It's a compliment." He gives me a tiny smile. "So," he says. "Are you finally settling into the office, or are we still way beneath you?"

"Hardy-har," I say sarcastically. "I'm settling in. Frances and I aren't exactly best buddies, but I finally have some friends there, and I'm working hard on my column and—" I shrug. "I don't know. Things are better now."

"Frances has been pleased with your efforts recently."

"Really?"

"Yes, we were discussing it last week. She thinks you have a lot of room for improvement, but that you've grown leaps and bounds since you started."

"Oh! Well. That's nice to hear. I wish she'd tell me that to my face. I feel like she hates me."

"She doesn't hate you," he assures me.

I study my glass for a few seconds before asking, "What about you?"

"Does she hate me? No, I think she likes me very much." He smiles mischievously to let me know he purposely misunderstood the question.

I roll my eyes. "Fine."

"I don't hate you, Bella. I feel terrible about how rude I was to you last month. You *were* completely unprepared, and I'm not saying it was acceptable, but I know you've been trying, and I think I can understand how hard it's been for you to adjust to our office. Don't give up on us yet." His eyes are fixed on mine.

"Thank you. It *has* been hard," I confess. "I feel like nothing I do is right—I felt the same at *Enchanté,* but at least there the column was popular. Here, it seems that no matter how hard I try to fit in and do the right thing, I can't. At least I have a few people in the office who like me for me, not what everybody seems to expect me to be."

"Maybe you should relax. Stop trying to be what everybody wants you to be, and just be yourself. And other clichés, as well," he says, smiling self-consciously.

"Yeah, but that'll just expose all my flaws. Of which there are about ten million," I laugh.

"Your flaws are what make you charming. You should embrace it."

"You think I'm charming?"

"Of course you're charming." He smiles warmly at me and I feel as though a nest of butterflies has just built a village in my tummy.

The waitress comes with the bill and James slaps down his corporate card before escorting me out of the restaurant. Outside, the sun has gone down and there's a slight chill in the air. We begin walking toward Seventh Avenue and I shiver slightly. The temperature must have dropped at least 20 degrees since this afternoon.

"Are you cold?" he asks with concern.

"It's a little chilly," I admit. "I can't believe what a mild June it's been so far."

"Do you want my jacket? Here," he says, taking it off and draping it around my shoulders before I can say anything.

I wrap it around me, hugging my arms to my chest. "Thanks," I say shyly, his citrusy, musky scent wafting up at me from the fabric. This is so intense! I wonder if he's going to kiss me at the end of the night. Probably not, since this is only our first date, and it's not a real date, since he had to ask me out under the guise of work. But now we're strolling through the West Village and the lights are all twinkly and it's a chilly night so I'm wearing his jacket which smells just like him and it's all so sexy and I don't really know how he *would* be able to resist kissing me. Maybe if I kind of lean into him and pretend to stumble again, then he'll grab my arm, and that will quickly morph into him linking his arm through mine or grabbing my hand. And once he's holding my hand, we'll come to a street corner, and I'll turn to him and the light of the streetlamp will be shining through my hair and making my eyes look really green and intense, and he'll look at me and murmur something sexy, like, "This is so wrong, but I can't help myself." And then we'll have our first kiss! I smile in anticipation. It's going to be amazing.

He looks at his watch. "I can't believe it's nine already. Dinner sped by. Good thing I ran into you and we were able to discuss everything. It'll make next week much easier."

I frown. Why is he looking at his watch? Why is he talking about work? This is not romantic. This is employee-boss banter.

"Right," I say uncertainly. "Well, thanks for dinner. It was unexpected, but lovely." I try to lower my voice slightly, to give it a sexy edge. For the millionth time in my life, I rue the fact that I have such a boring, normal, unremarkable voice. It's not deep and throaty. It's not thin and breathy. It's just girly. And I'm convinced I have a slight Drew Barrymore lisp, too, although Joss, Nick, and Emily insist I'm being silly. I think they're simply being polite. I toss my hair, to make up for the unsexy voice. "It was nice seeing a different side of you." I look up at him through my side-swept bangs. Well, at least my hair is kind of sexy. You can't win 'em all.

He doesn't say anything. We keep walking.

"Bella," he says, turning to me, when suddenly I spot Tristan walking out of a bar across the street.

"Shit."

"Is there a problem?"

"No. No problem. I just saw . . ." I can't bring myself to finish the sentence and call Tristan my boyfriend. He's hailing a cab when he looks up and sees me.

"Baby!" he calls, his face surprised. He jogs across the street and puts his arm around me, kissing me deeply. He smells like beer. "What are you doing here? Who's this?" He looks at James, somewhat accusingly, then down at his jacket, which is still draped around my shoulders.

"Tristan, this is my publisher, James. James, this is Tristan."

"Her boyfriend," Tristan says, his arm still around me.

"Nice to meet you." James sticks out his hand and the two shake stiffly. James looks at me, his face impenetrable. "I should really get going," he says. "I need to do some more work before the presentation next week. Great meeting." He spins on his heel.

"Wait! Your jacket!" I take it off my shoulders and hand it to him.

"Thanks," he mutters, hailing a cab and quickly taking off down Seventh Avenue.

"Your publisher?" Tristan says. "Why were you two having dinner together?" He watches the cab drive away suspiciously.

"It was a work thing. It's nothing."

Chapter 11

There are few things that strike more terror into the heart of beauty editors than the words "beauty sale." A beauty sale is a once-or-twice yearly exercise in pandemonium when the beauty department rounds up the old contents of the beauty closet and sells them to the rest of the magazine employees at a deep discount—typically, every product for a dollar. At *Enchanté,* the offerings were obviously more glamorous than those at *Womanly World,* but cheap makeup is still cheap makeup. All the proceeds go to charity. This fact, however, does not seem to stop otherwise warm-hearted, generous women from behaving like spoiled, me-me-me! toddlers. The conference room is crowded with assistants and editors, all frantically pawing through the products on the tables. Megan scuttles back and forth between the beauty closet and the conference room, replenishing makeup, face creams, and shampoos. One woman, who I don't recognize and who I'm absolutely certain does *not* work at *Womanly World,* snatches a lipstick out of the hands of Lauren, Rania's assistant. "That's mine!" she exclaims nastily. "I just put it down for a second. *I'm* buying it."

Our art director Debbie Shaney, a bespectacled woman with shaggy shoulder-length brown hair, walks over to me. "Since this eye shadow is crumbled, can't I just pay fifty cents for it?" she pleads.

I look at the shadow. Vincent Longo. It retails for around thirty dollars.

"That's a really popular shade. I think we have a few more of them there," I say, pointing to a small table against the wall.

"Yeah, but . . . I'd rather just take this one and pay less for it."

I want to scream, *It's one dollar, you stingy cow!* Of course, I don't. That would be rude, not to mention would completely flood my system with cortisol because of the stress of yelling. I refuse to age myself with free radicals because of silly people. I take a few seconds to compose myself. "Debbie . . . it's for charity. You can pick whatever shadow you want . . . but it will still be a dollar."

"Fine," she pouts, heading over to the table and picking up a fresh compact. She peers at it as if she's inspecting the flaws on a diamond. "I guess this is fine. I'll take this one."

"Thanks." I manage a smile and take her dollar, silently seething.

Another woman walks up to me sheepishly. It's Shelly. "*Um,* Bella? I'm just wondering, is this stuff going to go on sale in an hour?"

"I'm sorry?"

"You know. Are you going to sell the stuff you can't get rid of later this afternoon for, like, ten items for a dollar? That's what they used to do at *Glamour* when I worked there."

"I don't know yet. I guess we'll have to see how well this stuff sells," I say grumpily. "I'd rather not discount it . . . seeing as it's *for charity.*" These people are slowly sucking all the goodwill out of me.

"Riiight," she says slowly, looking around the room thoughtfully. "Well, I guess I'll come back in half an hour. You know, just to check."

"Fine." I turn away from her and busy myself cleaning up one of the tables holding fragrance and body products. Luckily nobody's yet had the balls to try and barter me down to, say, seventy-five cents for the products that normally cost seventy-five dollars. Yet.

I pull out the envelope I have stashed in my purse and count the money we've made so far. Three hundred and sixty-three dollars. Not terrible, but nowhere near the bounty we used to pull in at *Enchanté*. My personal best for a beauty sale, the second year I was an assistant, was about eighteen hundred dollars. Then again, we charged higher prices and people there bought beauty loot like they were at a sample sale, which means there was plentiful shrieking along the lines of: "Oh my God, I can't believe you're selling Chanel and Marc Jacobs perfume for only fifteen dollars! I'll buy ten!"

Frances walks in the room and stands in the doorway, arms folded. "How are we doing?"

"Not bad. A little over three hundred and fifty dollars. It's not great, but I'm planning to run the sale for at least another hour and a half."

She nods her head approvingly. "Good. Let's try to kill two birds with one stone—make money for charity and also clean out our beauty closet. God knows we have enough clutter in there."

"Okay." What does she *think* I'm doing? Standing here for my health?

She stands in the doorway for several more seconds, surveying the scene, then turns to me. "Don't forget, I need your new column the day after tomorrow."

"I know. I hope to have it to you before then. Just plan on finishing up this sale, then I'm going to go back to my desk to start working on it."

"Good. Maybe this try you'll get it right."

Ouch. My eyes feel tight and I force myself to hold back unexpected tears, blinking several times and looking discreetly at the ceiling to allow them to drain.

I feel Frances's gaze on me. "Well, carry on," she says, walking out of the conference room.

The mystery nonemployee walks up to me, carrying a bottle of Donna Karan body lotion. I mentally note that it retails for about forty-five dollars, since I know exactly what she's going to say before she opens her mouth. "This is only half full," she says. "Can I have it for fifty cents?"

Three hours later, I've closed down the sale with Megan's help, after running a clearance with ten items for a dollar. Even after slashing the prices, there are still about fifty-odd products on the table, from makeup to shampoo to skin care. I know it's snotty, but I find it amusing that the "rejects" on the table include massively high-end but obscure products like Alterna Caviar Shampoo, mini Z. Bigatti face cream jars, and Kanebo cleanser, while the Avon, Elizabeth Arden, and Olay were all snapped up instantly. I suppose there was a time when I thought La Mer was the ultimate in luxury, too. Live and learn.

"What should we do with the rest of these products?" Megan asks, gesturing toward the half-full bin she's carrying. We walk back to her desk and I place a bag of makeup on her counter.

"We should send them to Dress for Success. They'll pass everything on to women in crisis."

"Perfect. I think I have their number somewhere; I'll take care of it."

"Thanks, Megan." I lean on the side of her desk. Megan's cubicle is twice as neat as mine, which is hovering somewhere between tidy and disorganized two months after de-*Enchanté*-ing it, but she has a bulletin board with scores of photos and tears tacked up. I find it surprising that most of her favorites are edgy brunettes with a downtown, Misshapes, club-kid vibe. Before seeing the wall, which she updates weekly, I'd have pegged Megan as a Gwyneth Paltrow–lover, not Fifth Element–era Milla Jovovich–type. "How are things with your boyfriend?" I ask.

She blinks several times before responding, her face tightening. "We broke up."

"Oh no! I'm so sorry! Do you want to talk about it?"

Her lower lip trembles. "It happened this weekend. He told me he didn't love me anymore and felt trapped. The thing is I don't feel the way I used to, either. But I thought we could make it work."

I put my hand on her arm. "Whatever you need. Drinks, dinner, a band of hooligans to go beat him up. I'm your girl."

She giggles, rubbing her eyes. "Thanks, Bella."

I go back to my desk. It's time to start my column—Frances approved the at-home manicure-pedicure concept, moving Megan's piece to next month. My mind is completely blank, and I know what's going to happen, anyway. I'm going to write something that I think is fantastic, and which Larissa would have absolutely loved, but which Frances and Rania are going to loathe, and then that's going to be the end of it. I'm finally feeling comfortable at *Womanly World,* socially, at least, but I just can't seem to get my head in the right place—why can't I understand these readers? They like cheap products, and I'm surrounded by cheap products all day. Surely *Enchanté* didn't so *completely* warp my perception of reality that I can't even write a relatable article after four months. This is ridiculous. I'm stuck on the first sentence.

Far be it from me to impune anybody's beauty sense, but few things are as tacky as French manicures.

No. This is all wrong.

In a hectic life, treating oneself to a manicure and pedicure can be a blessed luxury. Unfortunately, few of us can find the time.

And with the added distractions—and strain on the wallet—of children, husbands, college, and groceries, a trip to the nail salon is often simply not in the cards.

Ugh. Terrible. It's like a high school parody of what a magazine article should sound like. What would Frances write?

Salon manicures and pedicures can be two of life's small luxuries. With hectic schedules and often-steep prices, however, learning how to mani/pedi can save both time and money.

This is so boring, even my mother would slit her wrists reading it. Besides, Frances would never use the term *mani/pedi.* The real problem is that I can't get James out of my head. What was he going to say to me? Was it my imagination, or did we have a connection that night? If only I hadn't run into stupid Tristan, is it possible that James would have kissed me, or am I being crazy? I should really end it with him. Who changes their name to Tristan, anyway?

I'm still procrastinating on the day the column is due. I've managed to write something passably decent, but it's not good enough. I want to *wow* Frances and prove that I do belong here. What's the point in being a so-called good writer if I'm only a one-trick pony? Shouldn't I be able to write well in any style, at any magazine?

I wander by Vivian's desk, eager for a distraction.

"Hey, sweetie!" she says. "Working hard or hardly working?"

"Definitely the second. What about you?"

She's sitting in front of her computer, open letters from readers sprawled in a pile around her keyboard. "The same. I'm trying to come up with answers to these questions, but I'm not feeling inspired. How can I concentrate on these negative romantic problems? I'm in love! All I can think about is Walter!"

"Viv, that's great! So, things are going well?"

"More than well. He's a dreamboat," she smiles happily.

James walks by, his brow furrowed, carrying a big dossier of papers.

"Hi, James," I say tentatively, leaning on Vivian's cubicle and putting my hand up in a small wave.

"Oh. Hello, Bella." He looks at Vivian and nods. "Hello, Vivian."

"Hi," she says, suddenly quiet.

"How was your weekend?" I ask.

"*Er* . . . it was fine. Thank you. Yours was nice, I trust?"

"Very nice." So, we're back to awkwardness. I press on. "Went to a movie with my roommate, then had a dinner with some friends. It was at a restaurant close to the one we went to. Brompton something or other. You should try it. It's great."

"Thanks for the recommendation. I'm sorry, but I'm swamped—I have to run. I'm scheduled to go over some things with Rania. About the presentation you and I discussed during the business dinner."

Is it just me, or is he going out of his way to make sure Vivian knows that our business dinner was a *business dinner*? Okay. It was business. Thanks. We get it.

I paste a smile on my face. "Oh, good. Hope she likes it."

"We'll see," he says, before nodding brusquely at us and striding off down the hall.

"Are you okay?" Vivian asks.

"Huh?" I snap back to reality.

"Your face is kind of . . . purple."

"Oh? Really? I wonder why," I say, feigning ignorance.

She stands up, peering over the top of her cubicle to look at James, who's now in Rania's office. "That was odd. I've probably spoken to James Michaels once in my life, at the Christmas party last year. I'm surprised he even remembered my name. He usually doesn't speak to me when he walks by." She looks back at me. "You two had dinner together?"

"Business," I say quickly.

She nods, smiling knowingly.

Should I confide in Vivian? She *is* the resident relationship expert, after all. But wouldn't that just make me look pathetic and desperate? I mean, who *actually* falls for their boss? It's so tacky and '80s. I feel like I'm letting down an entire generation of postmodern feminists.

I decide it's best not to say anything. I hate that feeling when you confide in other people, knowing full well how stupid you appear, but powerless to keep the words from tumbling out of your mouth, only to feel like double crap afterward when you feel them silently judging you for how obviously wrong you are.

I mean, he didn't ignore me, right? That's . . . something. Then again, he was hardly hugging and high-fiving me. I'm suddenly seized by the uncontrollable urge to barge into Rania's office and confront him. I'll yell, "You led me on! I'm a woman, and I know when a guy is flirting with me, and you were doing it!" and Rania will look up knowingly and say, "I *suspected* there was something going on. James just hasn't been the same since you've been here. You've changed him somehow," and then James will look at me sheepishly and confess, "I know, I was a total jerk. I just can't help how I feel about you. You make me weak in the knees," and then we'll stride across the room and start making out. Meanwhile, a crowd will have grown around us, and everybody will watch as we kiss. Maybe Vivian will start cheering. It would be wonderful.

Oh my God, I'm such a freak show. Here and now, Bella. Get it together.

On Monday, I drag myself out of bed at 8:15 a.m., trying to ignore the fact that I can't remember the last time I hit the gym. What's the point? I make it to the office by 9:20—forty minutes early!

Frances is already in the office and has laid a stack of papers on my desk with a handwritten note: *Bella, I need your ideas memo by the end of the day.*

The ideas memo! It completely slipped my mind. I'll make it top of list today. I have a 3:30 appointment for a new makeup line presentation at the Hotel Rivington and I'm feeling particularly cranky—not in the mood for fake schmoozing. Surely I can finish the ideas memo before 3:00 p.m.?

After two hours of typing, erasing, tweaking and editing, I have several ideas that I think even Frances will find acceptable. We're currently working on the September issue, which means the requisite roundup of fall makeup and hair trends. Since Frances has made plain that she doesn't want to be beholden to the beauty companies and unwearable trends, however, I decide to eschew a story on what's new in favor of a safe "Getting Ready for Fall" feature.

Getting Ready For Fall

The weather is turning crisper and the family beach towels have been stowed. As you get the kids ready for Back to School, you also need to tend to your hair and skin, which will start to undergo seasonal changes. Colder air means more frequent exfoliation for skin and more conditioner for hair. Here, the six classic hair and skin products you'll need to help you transition.

I reread my list of products and nod, satisfied: L'Oreal, Face Group, Olay, Dove, Pantene, John Frieda. All under ten dollars, all available in the drugstore, and all (by-the-by, even though Frances doesn't care) advertisers. Perfect.

Fifteen minutes later, I'm sitting in Frances's office as she reads through the printed-out memo, her brow furrowed.

"This is it?" she asks.

"Yes," I respond, confused. Why isn't she *thrilled* by this? Isn't this what she wants?

She flips through the pages again, her lips pursed. "Bella . . ."

I wait for her to finish the thought, but she doesn't say anything and sighs, taking off her glasses and pressing her fingers to her temples.

"What's wrong?"

"I think you're confused by what I'm looking for here. These ideas are boring, frankly. What's new or fresh about "six hair and skin products for fall"? There's no concept. There's nothing about it that says '*Womanly World.*' This could be a throwaway piece from any women's magazine in the industry."

"But I thought . . . you said my other ideas were too *Enchanté,* so I was trying to come up with items that had lots of drugstore stuff our readers could afford."

"*Enchanté* doesn't *officially* hold the patent on clever stories, you know," she says dryly. "We can write interesting articles featuring drugstore products. Our readers aren't morons."

Why is it that every seventh word out of Frances's mouth is "our readers"?

I stifle a sigh and agree that I'll give the memo another go-around. I'm actually *trying* now. Why can't I get this right?

Chapter 12

All throughout June, before the polo match, Tristan buzzes with excitement, pumping me for information about which celebrities will be there and reconfirming at least three times that we have passes for the VIP enclosure. We take a Town Car out to Bridgehampton, with him chattering the entire time about how one well-placed photograph with a celebrity will pay dividends for his visibility ("Preferrably an A-lister; B-lister is still good, and I'll even take a C-lister, but if some totally pathetic hanger-on is there wanting their picture with me, I just don't know if I can do it. You have to make yourself scarce, you know?").

Tristan is seated next to me during the luncheon, but spends most of his time talking to Rania, who is seated on his right and seems both charmed by his good looks and outgoing personality and bemused by his self-centeredness. I'm on Tristan's left, next to one of the Face Group advertisers, while James is across the table, scrunched between Ben Wales and Charlie Ridge, two Face Group honchos. James barely looks at me through the entire lunch, which features a delicious lobster risotto that I have to restrain myself from scarfing down (Tristan's remains untouched, much to my hungry tummy's chagrin) for fear of my stomach bulging too much from my white pants and skin-tight blue Chloé top. The whole gang is here, with Mandy and Heidi seated at tables with their respective magazines, an Armani-clad Grace holding court at the *Catwalk* table, and Larissa and Delilah whooping up a storm with the *Enchanté* advertisers.

Finally, the match begins: the real reason for all the action. Eight players take to the field on some of the fastest, most expensive mares in the world, the players all wearing white pants and brown knee-high riding boots, decked out in colored jerseys advertising the names of their teams. As they gallop up and down the field, the sound of the horses hooves audible as they tear up the dirt and aim like freight trains toward the white goalposts, the players loosening their reigns to let the ponies take off at full speed, I look around the box to see if everybody is as enthralled as I am. Both Rania and James are watching avidly, but Tristan is yammering away on his cell phone, and I notice that most of the crowd is too busy socializing to pay attention to the action on the pitch. The lone ten-goaler makes a spectacular near-side neck shot to whip the ball between the posts for the first goal and I lean excitedly toward Tristan.

"He's one of the best players in the world. Argentine. I met him once in England with Emily when we were there for Cartier Da—"

"I'm on the phone with my booker," he says, frowning as he puts his hand over the mouthpiece. "We'll talk at intermission, okay?"

"Halftime," I correct sourly, folding my arms and settling back into my seat to watch the rest of the first half quietly.

During halftime, Tristan is still talking on his phone, so I walk alone onto the field to tred in and take an offered glass of free champagne from one of the waiting Hummers, which have been driven in by the managers of Bridgehampton Polo Club to satiate the crowd's thirst and up the glamour quotient. I spot several celebrities: Jessica Simpson, Hilary Duff, Jessica Alba, Ivanka Trump, Karolina Kurkova, and

Stephanie Seymour. Tristan will no doubt be thrilled by the wattage.

The second half unfolds at breakneck pace, with one of the teams—sponsored by a well-known New York City hedge funder—winning by six goals, a sizable margin. Both teams line up on a raised trailer as champagne is passed, trophies are presented, and the Best Playing Pony award is named.

I'm happily and quietly watching the scene when I feel a pair of strong arms engulf me in a bear hug. I look over my shoulder and see Tristan, who has buried his head in my shoulder. "I'm so sorry, baby. Dara wouldn't let me off the phone, even though I kept telling her it was so rude and you were getting pissed off. You're a rockstar."

"It's okay," I say reluctantly, his musky smell briefly alleviating the irritation I'd felt.

"Are you having fun?" he asks worriedly. "I know you were trying to explain the game to me. I'm sorry. Horses just aren't my thing, you know?"

"I know. I guess it would be the same if you took me to a basketball game," I admit. I love polo, I love baseball, I tolerate football—at least, during Super Bowl season . . . for the commercials—but I inexplicably have zero patience for basketball.

"Exactly." He swivels me around and puts his hand on my chin, bringing my face up as he presses his warm lips to mine. "*Mmm,* you taste good. Like candy." Despite myself, I giggle. He looks pleased.

We watch for a few minutes, his arms wrapped around me, until the players step off the platform and begin mingling with the crowd. Several photographers start yelling for Jessica Simpson, who has presented the trophy for Most Valuable Player; Tristan's body tenses with excitement. "Sweets, I'll be right back, okay?" He dashes away, standing by the ropes, his eyes locked on Jessica.

I decide to take the opportunity—he'll obviously be awhile—to head to the bar inside the VIP enclosure to get a drink.

"One Pimm's, please."

I take the glass, tip the bartender, and turn around, but Tristan is now nowhere in sight.

Heidi walks up next to me and leans down the bar. "I'll have a Pimm's cup, please." She catches my eye and smiles. "One for me, one for my twin."

I laugh as she inclines her head in Mandy's direction and rolls her eyes.

"So, how are you, Bella? How's everything at *Womanly World*?"

"It's going well. Much better, actually," I say honestly. "It's taken a while, but . . . it's good."

Heidi nods, tipping the bartender and taking a sip, holding Mandy's drink in her other hand. "I'm glad to hear it. If you ever need anything . . . just call me, okay? You know we're all still here for you."

I don't know why this surprises me. Maybe I've been too harsh in my judgement of Heidi. "Likewise," I say, immediately feeling silly for intimating that *I* could have any favors to pass on to her from my lower perch.

We walk back into the fray, well-formed, dark-haired men in muddy whites and knee-high riding boots milling around. Several tall, skinny women with long, glossy dark hair and tawny complexions carry babies or hold the hands of chubby toddlers.

"Where is he?" I say under my breath, craning my neck for a view of Tristan.

"Who?"

"Oh, my . . . boyfriend. Tristan."

"Tristan Reynolds?"

I look at her, surprised. "You know him?"

"I haven't met him, but I know who he is. He's a male model, very up and coming. *Very* sexy," she giggles. "I saw him two seconds ago, having his picture taken with Jessica Simpson." She nods approvingly. "You're dating him? Wow!"

"Yeah, it's fabulous," I say sarcastically, drinking my Pimm's a little faster than is socially appropriate.

"There he is," she says, putting her hand on my arm. "Over there, by all the photographers."

Tristan stands about ten feet away, his right arm clenched firmly around Jessica Simpson's waist as the two lean into each other and grin for the cameras. Every few seconds, Jessica and Tristan both turn their heads and chins in a different direction as they reangle their stances. It looks ridiculous in person—but no doubt makes for a fabulous picture: the Homecoming King and Queen, all grown up.

"Who does he think he is, Paris Hilton?" I mutter.

"Heids! My drink!" Mandy cries from several feet away, where she's busy cooing over a chiseled TDH (tall, dark, and handsome) polo player who moonlights as a Ralph Lauren model.

"I'll catch you in a few," Heidi says apologetically, sidling over to Mandy and handing her the Pimm's, leaving me standing to watch Tristan preen happily.

I wonder how much longer I need to stay here. Now that both the luncheon and the game are over, is it rude for me to sneak out? All I want is to go home, wash off all my makeup, put on a pair of pyjamas, and watch my season two *How I Met Your Mother* DVDs. If the shit-eating grin on Tristan's face is any indication, however, he'll be posing until the sun has set. *Well*, I think darkly, *he's a big boy. He can get home by himself.*

"Enjoying yourself?" I look to my right and see James, his hands in the pockets of his khakis, wearing a tucked-in blue-and-white-striped Oxford shirt with the sleeves rolled up.

"Is it unprofessional to say no?" I say sourly.

"*Nah*. I'm not really enjoying myself, either. This is hardly my scene."

I take in James's preppy boating-in-Nantucket ensemble from head to toe—he's wearing brown loafers with no socks, for the love of God!—and have to restrain myself from rolling my eyes. It looks like *exactly* his scene.

We stand side by side silently, watching the throngs of chattering people wandering around the pitch. Tristan's voice rings loud and true. "Tristan Reynolds. T-R-I-S-T-A-N. Tristan Reynolds. I'm with l'Homme Management. Do you want to see one of my cards?" He's talking to two photographers, both older gentlemen eyeing him with great interest.

I let out an involuntary *tut* of disgust and James looks at me. "Everything okay?"

"What, with me, or with me and him?"

He pauses. "Either."

"Yeah. No. Not really. He's just . . ." I pause. "Well, look at him."

James nods, quiet for a few moments. "I wouldn't put you with a guy like that."

"Really? Who would you put me with?"

"I don't know. Somebody with a little more . . . substance, maybe?" he shrugs.

"Tristan has substance," I respond defensively. "It's just of the . . . less obvious kind. He's not bad, once you get to know him. He's actually very intelligent. In a not-book-smart way."

"I see."

"He's good at sports," I offer. "He was captain of our football team *and* our baseball team."

"In high school?"

"Yeah . . . ," I say lamely.

"Oh, I see. So, you're high school sweethearts?"

"God, no! Nothing like that. We've only been dating for a couple months. It's pretty casual, actually. Not serious at all," I hasten to add.

He nods again.

Tristan notices me staring at him and winks, then sees James standing next to me. He immediately disentangles himself from Jessica and lopes over, putting his arms around me and dropping me into a deep kiss that leaves my arms floundering at my sides.

"Did you see that?" he asks excitedly. "The photographers were all over me! Dude, it was awesome. That one I was just posing for is a *Post* photographer. Fingers crossed me and Jess make Page Six tomorrow, okay?"

"Fingers crossed," I repeat.

"Hi, I'm Tristan Reynolds," he says, offering his hand to James and shaking it firmly. "I'm Bella's boyfriend. You are . . . ?"

"James Michaels. We've already met. We were sitting at the same table at lunch. And I met you on the street a few weeks ago."

"Oh yeah? Sorry, I meet so many people, it's hard to remember."

"Of course." James turns to me. "I should go. Nice seeing you Bella, Tristan." His eyes lock with mine for a split second and then he turns and disappears in the crowd.

Tristan waits until James is a safe distance away and then squeezes my hand. "Okay, I'm going back in. Meet you in, like, an hour?"

"An hour? Tristan, I'm ready to go."

"Well, I'm not," he pouts. "Don't you see all those photographers? I need to get some more pictures to make sure I get as much coverage as possible. And I met this woman earlier who's in advertising for Calvin. She gave me her card but I want to schmooze her some more. You never know where it might lead." He winks at me. "If you want to go, that's totally cool. I can text you later tonight."

I throw my hands in the air. "Whatever you want. Do your thing. I think I'm out of here, though. Call me later."

"'Kay, Sweets. Thanks for being understanding. You're the best." He gives me a peck on the cheek and then dashes back into the throng like a little kid let loose at Toys "R" Us.

As I walk away, sidestepping girls in sundresses and men in chinos, I wonder how it's possible to feel so sour on such a beautiful day. *You're at polo, Bella! Everybody here is having a fabulous time, and it's for charity. Just lighten up.* I can't, though. I'd thought it would be possible to breeze by on the exhaust fumes of Tristan's good looks, but even I'm not that shallow, and I hate the feelings of contempt I have for him— it's not fair to either of us. This relationship is flogging the life from me.

Just as I'm about to step off the field, I see Delilah, wearing a red sundress crisscrossed with gold threads. She flashes me a smug smile and raises her fingers in a triumphant little wave, rushing over.

"Hi, doll face," she coos. I stiffen at her use of Larissa's trademark pet name.

"Delilah." I continue walking.

"Wait a minute," she says, putting her hand on my arm in a viselike grip. I wrestle it away, but before I can walk away she calls, "'Riss! Here she is! It's Bella!"

Larissa swoops down, appearing out of nowhere in a white linen dress, white espadrilles, and a monstrously huge diamond-encrused watch that must have cost as much as my parents' house. "Doll face! I've been looking for you everywhere!"

"I've been here," I say a bit too defensively, on edge with Delilah flanking Larissa. "I was at the luncheon, then watching the match afterward."

"Polo," Larissa says, throwing her hands up in the air, one of which is holding a glass of champagne, sweeping them around grandly. Droplets of champagne splash down on us. "Isn't it divine? You must be in heaven. I know you and Emily love going to matches. Look at you! You're growing your hair out! You look amazing!" She lights up a cigarette and sucks on it deeply. "How's Rania? Isn't she fantastic?"

"She's great. Honestly, she couldn't be friendlier—she's gone out of her way to make me feel welcome there. Where's she from, anyway?"

"Jerusalem. Or Lebanon, I think. Or India. She's to die for! But you! Who were those hotties I just saw you with?"

"Oh. *Er* . . . my boyfriend . . . and my publisher."

"Yummy, double yummy. You're a lucky girl."

"Didn't you like my little surprise, Larissa?" Delilah quickly interjects.

"Like? Love! It was fabulous! I don't know how you pulled that off!"

"It was nothing," she says, beaming. "Daddy is good friends with Joe Simpson, so he put a call through, and Joe said he'd be *happy* to have Jessica sing at your wedding! The publicity will be huge, and Katharine already wanted Jess for the cover, though Joe didn't know that, of course. Mutual back scratching."

"Genius," Larissa says, swaying slightly as she tosses her cigarette on the ground and pulls out another. "Damn shoes! I should have worn flats like you, Bella." She gestures to the Chanel ballet flats Emily gave me as a Christmas present two years ago. I wonder how many glasses of champagne Larissa has had. She's teetering a bit too much to blame on high heels.

"Wedding?" I ask. "You're getting married? Who's the guy?"

"Maurice," she says, smiling happily. "The love of my life. He's divine, Bella."

"What's his last name?"

"Oh, I can never pronounce it. It's something weird and German like Schlitzeldorfer or Dusselfurter."

"And this is the love of your life?"

"He really is," she says, hugging herself.

"I'm so genius for introducing the two of you," Delilah exclaims. "I just *knew* you'd hit it off." She wags a manicured finger in Larissa's face. "But I expect maid of honor duties in return, boss."

"Done," Larissa says, swaying again. I realize she's not just drunk—she's plastered.

"Oh, I can't wait!" Delilah says, throwing her thin arms around Larissa and shooting me a triumphant look.

"Well, it was great seeing the two of you," I say loudly. "I'd better take off."

"Bye, Belly," Larissa says, fumbling in her bag for a lighter as Delilah clings to her like a crab.

"Here, darlin', let me." Delilah speedily disentangles herself to produce a lighter, smiling at me as if to say: She's *my* friend now. *My* boss. *My* magazine. *My* life.

The next two weeks pass smoothly and without incident. I'm about to head over to Frances's office to give her my latest beauty memo when I see James walking down the hallway. I steel myself to say hello to him as we pass, mentally wondering how my makeup and hair look, but he suddenly spins on his heel—it is my imagination, or did he look at me first?—and starts walking the other way. What the hell? Did he see me? Did he suddenly forget something in his office? I can't help but feeling that he's avoiding me, which makes my chest hurt in a strange, tight way.

Our presentation is scheduled for two weeks after I

return from Paris, with the Face Group. It's going to be a huge challenge, with Face representing one-fifth of our total advertising budget. Larissa informs me through the beauty grapevine that they're secretly planning to pull their advertising, although when I tried to mention this to Frances, she scoffed and told me not to be ridiculous. The only minorly bad thing that happens to me is a freakish self-tanning incident that leaves my brand-new white Lacoste polo shirt (a gift from Ring Communications along with their summer product mailings) stained brown around the collar. With the millions of times I've used self-tanner, you'd think I would remember not to wear a white shirt mere hours after using a bronzing lotion. But, you know, everybody has bad days. It just happens to me more frequently than most.

Susan's wedding is the first week in July, days after I mentally decided that I need to end things with Tristan, who achieved his heart's desire and landed a small picture in the *New York Post* with Jessica Simpson. I don't think it's my imagination that James was a little jealous after encountering us together—twice. After he iced me in the hallway, I don't see him for several more days, until one Friday when I'm riding up in the elevator after lunch, my mind fixated on the curt, error-rife text Tristan sent me this morning ("Sorry din't cal u back last cople days. Realy busy. CU at airport 2nite 4 flite?"). What bothers me more than not seeing—or even speaking to—Tristan in a week is the fact that we've started texting each other instead of phoning, and his texting skills are roughly the same as a drunken ninth-grader. Sure, I know that most people abbreviate their texts nowadays, and that "CU L8R" has become an acceptable means of communication, but hasn't anybody ever heard of predictive text? It's not like it takes more than three extra seconds to let your phone spell out the full words. Really. It's just laziness, not to mention ruining the English language. Jesus. I feel like Frances.

As I'm crankily ruminating, James steps through the doors and visibly stiffens when he sees me. We're the only two people in the elevator.

"Hello," he says.

"Hello." If he's going to be formal, two can play that game.

With every passing second of silence, I become more ornery. What the hell is wrong with him? Did we not have a fabulous dinner where we bonded and drank like college kids? Was I foolish in thinking we opened up to each other? How on earth are we back to stiff avoidance?

"You're well?" he asks.

"Yes, I'm *well*, James," I snap.

He looks taken aback. "You don't have to be rude."

"I'm not being rude!"

He sighs and looks skyward. "Okay," he says sarcastically.

"What the hell is going on? You've barely said two words to me since we had dinner together. A *business* dinner, as you kept saying all over the office." Even I know this is hardly fair, but I'm so hurt by his coldness that I don't stop myself.

He opens his mouth then closes it again, shaking his head. "Whatever. It's not worth it."

"Apparently not."

The doors to our floor open and we both stomp out in opposite directions.

Tristan and I meet at the airport in the early afternoon and board the plane together, barely speaking throughout the flight home to Cleveland. There's no animosity—we simply have nothing to talk about. Our interactions are limited to me offering him gum and his asking to borrow my *Glamour* to study the ads.

As we're disembarking, I nervously check my reflection in my Chanel compact.

"You look hot," he says reassuringly.

"I don't want to look hot; I want to look presentable for my parents." I'm wearing a knee-length fitted jean skirt, a white oxford shirt with the sleeves rolled up, and a pair of black ballet flats. Chic, but not too fashiony or snobby. It says: I care about my looks, but I'm not a label snob and I haven't forgotten where I came from.

My mother squeals when we finally make it through security and charges forward, nearly knocking me off my feet with her force, even though she's only five foot three and barely weighs a hundred pounds. I notice approvingly as my face is buried in her hair that she's lightened the color and cut it into an appealingly wispy bob: very Ellen Barkin. I disentangle myself from my mother's bear hug and look at my tall, stiff-backed father, who's standing behind her in crisp black dress slacks, his shoes so shiny I can see my reflection in them, salt-and-pepper hair neatly parted and combed. His expression is gruff, but relaxes into a small smile.

"Hi, Dad," I say tentatively.

"Sweetheart," he says, moving forward and patting me on the back, then turning to look at Tristan. "This must be the Sweet Falls boy your mother told me about."

"Tristan Reynolds, sir," he says, putting his hand out and shaking with my father. "Colleen's son."

"How exciting!" my mother chirps, linking her arm through Tristan's as we walk out of the airport carrying our hand luggage. "My baby and Colleen's baby. Who ever would have thought? The two of you never spent any time together in high school! Colleen and I always wondered why, since we both thought you'd be just adorable together, but sometimes it takes a bit of time and distance for people to come together, *hmm?*" she beams up at Tristan, who grins down at her and tosses his hair. "Now, Susan is back at the house, Izzie. She feels terrible she couldn't come to pick you up at the airport, but you know how stressful all these preparations are. We had to change the seating places just yesterday because your father's cousin Bill decided at the last minute that he *was* going to come, after all, even though he RSVPed 'no' months ago. But I suppose, as long as it's family, it's not a chore. You haven't seen him in about ten years, Chuck, so I don't know if that makes it better or worse that he's suddenly deciding to show up for Susie's big day. Susan was a bit put off, of course, because you know how she prides herself on—"

I catch my father's eye as my mother prattles on, and we share a small, imperceptible smile.

Driving in the family Dodge minivan into our subdivision, Oak Park, and up the shady, tree-lined streets I spent my middle school and high school years on, I stare out the window, remembering little snatches of history. That two-story brick house with green shutters, Kelly Pollock's, is where I had my first kiss, in ninth grade with Ryan Jackson during a game of truth or dare. I was still saddled with braces, which marred the entire experience, although I had the foresight to pop a piece of Bubble Yum in my mouth beforehand to ensure I had fresh breath. Five doors down is Joey Harris's, who used to carpool to school with me and Caroline Granger, my high school best friend. I learned to drive a stick shift in Joey's driveway, after an hour of stripping his gears as he shrieked in frustration. Underneath a large oak tree in his backyard under cover of night, I had my first *real* kiss—beer-fueled, of course—with Michael Lyons following a game of I've Never on the night of our high school graduation. (Michael, a peace-loving Dead Head in my AP English class, was horrified by my admission that I'd never had a true kiss and set about to rectify the situation, flirting with me all night until we ended up in the dark backyard, leaning against the tree for hours as other couples smooched and sighed in the grass and on the trampoline.) The car turns left, entering our street, and we pass Caroline's old house. Between the late-night slumber parties, the drunken senior-year Saturday nights, and the hours we used to spend primping for Friday night football games, I must have cumulatively logged months in that house. Despite our promises to be best friends forever, our friendship was limited to phone calls, e-mails, and one visit during our freshman year of college, then dwindled to occasional e-mails every month or so during our sophomore year. By the time I left for Paris during the second semester of my junior year, I hadn't spoken to Caroline in nine months. I don't even know where she lives or what she's doing now. It's funny how the bonds that once sustained you can loosen so easily.

Finally, we're in front of my parents' redbrick house. With two leafy, gnarled trees carving out real estate on our front lawn, rose bushes, a large, prominently displayed flag, and white shutters on all the first and second floor windows, it's a typical all-American Cleavers-type home. A wide driveway slopes along the left side of the house, leading into the back, where our garage is no doubt still full of golf clubs, tennis rackets, lawn mowers, and gardening tools.

"Bella!" Susan exclaims as we enter the house, Tristan carrying both of our bags, my father holding the back door leading from the garage open. She's obviously been waiting for us and engulfs me in her arms, her familiar smell of Elizabeth Arden Green Tea lingering in the air over our heads. "You're finally here! My God, how long has it been?"

"Seven months. Not since Christmas."

She releases me, holding me at arm's length and looking me from head to toe. "I wish you'd bite the bullet and move back to Ohio. We miss you so much. It's not the same around here without you." She squeezes my hand and herds us into the kitchen where she's set up cookies and crackers on the table. She opens the fridge and automatically pours a glass of milk, handing it to me, then turns to Tristan. "Tommy, what would you like? Milk? Water? Soda?"

"I go by Tristan now, actually," he says. Susan looks at him blankly. He continues, "A beer would be awesome, if you have it. Light?" He sits on one of the seats at the kitchen table and surveys the room, saying "Man, I haven't been here in like ten years." I look around our bright kitchen, painted cheerful yellow and cream, with knickknacks and potted plants scattered around the room, a large vase of lilies in the middle of the kitchen table, a fridge covered with takeout magnets and photos of our beloved, departed family cocker spaniel, Roger, and an assortment of family photos in frames decorated with words like "Love" and "Happiness." A Norman Rockwellesque plaque saying "God Bless Our Happy Home" hangs over the kitchen door that leads outside to the backyard. This is where I spent every morning and every afternoon for nearly a decade of my life, but it feels alien now, as though another family I've never met has moved in and taken up residence.

"Beer?" Susan frowns, pushing her glasses up her nose and blowing her dark blonde bangs—newly cut for the wedding—off her forehead. The bangs accentuate her heart-shaped face and watery blue eyes, making her look like an older, less glamorous Reese Witherspoon. "I don't know if we have beer."

"We do," Harold says, entering the kitchen from the living room and enveloping me in a warm hug. "I bought some yesterday. I suspected Bella's gentleman friend might want it."

"Harold!" I exclaim. "You're the best! How are you?"

"It would be unwise of me to complain just now, lest your lovely sister take it as an insult. I'll just say that wedding preparations are more than I bargained for." He smiles warmly at Susan, who now has a scowl affixed to her face and her arms crossed. "To celebrate our love in front of friends and family will be a blessing, but the true blessing will be spending the rest of my days with my soon-to-be-wife. It makes all of the decisions over flowers and invitations and songs to be played

worthwhile." Harold is such a nerd, but I adore him. He reminds me of Matthew Broderick in *The Producers* . . . but not
quite as Ferris Bueller all-grown-up attractive.

"Oh!" my mother sobs, fumbling in her pocket for a crum-
pled up tissue. "I'm so happy! It's a dream come true!"

"Yes . . . well . . . thank goodness one of us is getting married. It may be the only chance you've got!" I joke, foisting
myself up on the kitchen counter and gulping my glass of
milk as I sit cross-legged. Some vodka would be really nice
right now.

"Bella, don't jinx yourself," Susan scolds.

"I'm not jinxing myself. If I get married, great. If I don't,
whatever. I'm happy. I'm focusing on my career, and there
are too many things I want to do before I settle down. I want
to travel, I want to get a puppy—" ("Both of which you can
do while married," Susan says pointedly) "—I want to finish
sowing my wild oats." At this, my father frowns, and I blush,
continuing. "I just don't think I'm going to meet anybody now
I'm certain I'll want to spend the *rest of my life with*. People
rush into marriage too quickly. It's why the divorce rate is so
high."

"When did you become so cynical?" my mother gasps.
"After college, you were dying to marry Olivier! You told
me on at least three occasions you thought he was going to
propose!"

"People change," I mutter. "It's called being realistic."

"You know," Tristan pipes up, "I agree. Everybody has to
get married sooner or later—but later's better. Gives you a
chance to, you know, be selfish before you have to take care of
a family and all that stuff."

"You don't want to get married, Tommy?" my mother
asks, looking horrified. "Does Colleen know this?"

"Oh, sure I do, Mrs. H. It's just that I want my marriage
to last forever, you know? Like my parents'? Right now, the

modeling thing is going good, and it would be unfair to put it on the back burner. Gotta think about myself. It's like, you know when you're on airplanes, and they tell you to put your mask on before you put on your kid's? It's the same thing," he concludes sagely, looking around the room.

Susan looks confused, her pale eyes sweeping my face.

"I do understand where you're coming from," Harold says seriously, nodding. "Of course, it's mostly timing. Had Susan and I met ten years ago, well, things might have turned out differently. She was only just beginning her CPA degree, I was in the middle of my own and up to my ears in work. I didn't have the time necessary to devote to a potential mate. Luckily for me, we met at exactly the right time." He grabs Susan's hand, and they look at each other adoringly. Geek love. It's a beautiful thing.

"I *believe* in marriage," I reassure my family. "In theory, when and if you find the right person. Suze and Harold are perfect together—you two complement each other. He's laid-back, you're the doer, but you share the same interests. If I ever find somebody like that myself, I'll probably marry him, too."

"Sooner rather than later, I hope," my mother says, a wistful look on her face.

"Mom," Susan admonishes. "Don't rush her. Better to be alone than with the wrong guy." She shoots a surreptitious glance at Tristan and opens the fridge again. "More milk?"

My father places Tristan's bags downstairs in the patriotically themed guest room just down the hall from my parents' room, obviously to discourage any late night hanky-panky. My room is upstairs, at the very end of the hallway opposite the stairs, which are lined with framed photos of Susan and me, showing our progression through the years, next door to a communal bathroom I shared with Suze while growing up. There are fifteen minutes until the rehearsal dinner, which is taking place just down the street at our family's favorite restaurant, so I change into a yellow sundress and quickly blot the oil on my face before carefully applying eyeliner, lip gloss, and blush. My room hasn't changed since the day I left for Northwestern ten years ago: Pearl Jam, the Who, and No Doubt posters on the blue-and-white walls, shelves of AP English books, framed photos of Caroline and me on my dresser. A black stuffed dog I call Roger Two sits on my white bedspread, bought by Susan to comfort me after Roger died.

The door of my room swings open and in walks Tristan, dressed in a slim-cut suit, his wet hair falling carelessly—perfectly—around his handsome face. "What do you think?" he asks. "Too dressy?"

"No, it's just right. Harold said he's going to wear a suit, too, and you *know* my dad'll be in one. Any of your friends coming to the dinner?"

"Nobody tonight. A ton of people from high school are coming tomorrow. I didn't know Susan was so popular!"

"She wasn't exactly popular; she was more *smart* popular. I mean, she was her class president," I point out.

"Oh yeah." Tristan walks over to my bed and plops on it, bouncing up and down several times, causing Roger Two to ricochet off the bed. "Do we have time?"

"Time for what?" I ask testily, picking up the stuffed dog and placing it on my dresser.

"You know." He grins at me suggestively.

"No. I don't think so." I stare into the mirror, brushing my hair and then twisting the ends into a loose bun.

"I don't like it like that," he frowns. "It looks better down."

I ignore him, turning my head from right and left and examining the style. "I think I'll keep it like this."

Susan's rehearsal dinner is full of speeches and tears from her closest friends, mostly chums from Sweet Falls High that

Susan has held onto over the years. My mother cries through the entire dinner. My father does not. When we drive back to our house, my parents quickly go to bed, bidding Tristan, Susan, Harold, and me good night. After Susan and Harold have given us kisses on the cheek, Tristan looks at me inquisitively, standing at the foot of the stairs looking up. I'm already on the fourth step. "So, should I, like, stay in my room? Your dad is kind of intense."

"Yeah, I think it's for the best," I agree, wondering why Tristan didn't stay at his own parents' house.

"No worries," he says, and shrugs. "I sleep better by myself, anyway. See you tomorrow morning?"

"Okay." We give each other a quick peck on the lips and then walk to our respective bedrooms, turning out the lights.

Susan's big day speeds by; before I know it, Susan and Harold are kissing at the altar, my mother sitting in the front row weeping messily. At the reception, Susan and my father dance to "My Girl," my father stiffly swaying from foot to foot as he clenches Susan's hands. My mother forced him to agree to dance lessons beforehand, all in preparation for this moment. Finally the time comes for my speech, and I stand up, hands shaking, glancing at my lilac bridesmaid's dress to make sure I haven't spilled any food or wine on it. I didn't trust myself to memorize anything, so I wrote the speech on a notecard. I've decided to keep it short, bland, and joke-free, which is how I know Susan would want it.

"I'm Bella, and as most of you know, I'm Susan's sister. When Susan asked me to be her maid of honor, I was both nervous and thrilled. Nervous, because I was worried I'd make her special day harder, not easier! And thrilled, because Susan has found her perfect match in this world, and I'm honored to be with her as she and Harold pledge their love to each other for the rest of their days. Theirs is a true love, full of respect, loyalty, warmth, laughter, and happiness. We should all consider ourselves blessed if we manage to some-day find something even half as genuine. I can't think of a better man for my big sister, and I'm proud to call you my brother, Harold. Everybody, please raise your glass: to Harold and Susan!"

"To Harold and Susan!" everybody echoes, holding their glasses aloft.

I sit down, feeling a rush of adrenaline; I didn't blow it! It certainly wasn't the best maid-of-honor speech in history, but at least I didn't cause all the silverwear on the table to come crashing down or lose my dress or do something similarly idiotic.

After an hour of oldies and wedding classics, the DJ switches to modern music, pumping out Beyoncé. I look at Susan, surprised. How did *this* end up on her playlist? Does she even know who Beyoncé is?

"What?" she asks. "People want to dance! And Beyoncé's popular, right? Some girls at work gave me a list. I never got yours," she says somewhat pointedly as I realize I promised to send Susan my song suggestions ages ago.

"Of course!" I say quickly, glossing over my forgetfulness. "No, I mean, it's great! I love this song!"

Susan smiles, satisfied, and turns back to Harold. "We should go mingle." They stand up, hand in hand, and walk to a table seating several members of my mother's extended family from North Carolina.

The room is full of people I went to high school with, several of whom I haven't seen in nearly ten years. I wasn't close friends with any of them, and I find it particularly bizarre that a few members of the football team are here, apparently having married girls Susan became friends with after moving back to Sweet Falls.

Another glass of champagne has appeared on the table in front of me. I take it and move to the balcony at the back of the room, stepping outside into the warm air. The Sweet Falls Country Club overlooks lushly manicured lawns and has steps leading down a lit walkway to a large fountain. The air is redolent with the scent of hyacinth and jasmine, and the cacophony of people dancing, singing, and talking in the ballroom carries out onto the balcony in a pleasing hum.

"Bella Hunter, right?" A stocky guy who looks about my age is a few feet away on the balcony smoking a cigarette, his tie and top few shirt buttons undone.

"That's me. Did you go to Sweet Falls?" I can't quite place him.

"Yeah. Jordan Irwin. I was on the football team with Tommy."

"Oh, right. Nice to meet you." I reach my hand out and we shake. His calloused hands engulf mine as he pumps enthusiastically.

"So, you're dating Tommy, *huh?* He's sitting at my table. Was just telling us all about you and how great you are."

"Really?" This surprises me. For some reason, I'd assumed Tristan was as apathetic about our relationship as I am. Now I feel guilty for being such a bitch to him these past few days. "Yes, we're dating," I add. "We ran into each other at a bar a few months back, by chance."

"Crazy." He shakes his head. "My wife, Lori, is friends with your sister. They do some charity thing together. I don't know, I can never remember which one."

"It's okay. I can never remember, either." I smile conspiratorially at him.

"So, you're living in New York, *huh?* What's it like? Different from here?"

"Very different. You can get a hot dog at three in the morning, walk out your front door and catch a cab, go to a different restaurant or bar every single day and never experience them all. It's the most exciting city in the world."

"It sounds awesome. Don't you miss home, though? Your friends and family? Your parents?"

"Sure," I say cautiously. "But it's only a short plane ride away. I was at work for most of the day yesterday, hopped in a cab to the airport, and then was here two hours later in time for dinner. It's not so bad."

"That's cool," he says, nodding as he takes another drag off his cigarette.

I look around. "Where is Tris—*uh*—Tom, anyway? I haven't seen him since the reception started. You guys are seated across the room from the bridal table."

"I don't know," he shrugs, looking confused. "Maybe in the bathroom? If I see him, I'll tell him you're looking for him."

I thank Jordan and reenter the ballroom, my eyes darting back and forth as I look for Tristan. I should put more effort into this. If we're dating, then we're *dating*—no more of this halfway crap, I've decided.

It takes me nearly twenty minutes to make my way across the ballroom, aunts, cousins, and various family friends all accosting me with bear hugs and chatty inquiries about my life in New York. My uncle Vern takes a picture of me with my Aunt Kathy and I give her my e-mail address, she demanding that I keep in touch and promise to let her know when I finally decide to move back to Ohio.

The band switches back to wedding favorites, playing "Twist and Shout," and a collective squeal goes up as the majority of my relatives make their way onto the dance floor. A short, sweet-faced girl in a pink cocktail dress rushes by me, but then stops, spinning on her heel. "Bella? It *is* you!" I recognize Olivia, one of my almost thirty cousins on my mother's side. My mother, being one of six, has countless nieces and nephews, whereas my father was an only child. Olivia is just two years younger than I am and moved to Sweet Falls from

North Carolina as a freshman when I was a junior. Though we haven't spoken in years, she was always one of my favorite cousins.

"Ollie! How are you? I missed you!" We exchange fierce hugs.

"You look amazing! Oh my God, you're so gorgeous!" she squeals, holding me at arm's length. "And, am I losing my mind, or did I actually see you show up with Tom Reynolds? Are you two *dating*?"

"We are! I ran into him a few months ago in New York, and it happened really quickly. It's kind of surreal, actually."

"I'll say! Didn't you have the biggest crush on him in high school?"

"Yes," I admit, embarrassed. Did *everybody* know?

"Don't blush, so did all the girls!" She giggles. "So, how's it going? Wedding bells for you two next?"

"God, no!" She looks taken aback by my vehemence. "No, it's just that . . . I don't think either of us are really the other's type. We're more just having fun. You know how it is."

She nods sagely. "Do I ever. I was dating this guy in Cleveland off and on for ages, and then we broke up, but then I missed him, so—" she waves her hand in the air. "Whatever, it's old news now. Where's Tom?"

"I was just coming to look for him, but I keep getting roped into conversations with the fam."

"Don't let Aunt Tina see you, otherwise she'll spend the entire evening trying to introduce you to eligible men. She saw you with Tom and spent five minutes complaining about how stuck-up he looks!"

"Great!" I laugh. "Thanks for the advice."

We exchange e-mail addresses, and I plead with Olivia to come visit me in New York. "You'll love it! I'm telling you, one week visiting me and you'll never want to leave."

"I don't know how cool the 'rents would be with that. They

had coronaries when I moved to Cleveland, and it's only down the road. You're so lucky that your mom and dad are okay with you living there."

"They're hardly okay with it, but they know there's nothing they can do. I mean, none of us are toddlers anymore. We *are* actually old enough to make decisions for ourselves!"

"I wish I had your courage," she sighs. "I dissolve into puddles of tears when they get mad at me. I promise I'll at least try to visit." We hug again, then I continue my dance floor search for Tristan. I find it oddly amusing that my family and Sweet Falls compatriots seem to think of my leaving home as brave. Are we still living in 1960?

There's another balcony on the other side of the dance floor, and I see Tristan standing in the center of a group of people we went to high school with. My heart sinks—it's the *popular* kids. I feel fifteen again. Do I have to go out there and talk to them? I'd like to think we've progressed beyond high school labels, but I can't help worry that they're all going to look at me with surprise and disgust as I walk onto the balcony, as if a giant flashing neon sign proclaiming "Nerd Alert!" is suspended over my head. I decide to enter the balcony from the side, so I can approach the group quietly from the back and blend in unnoticed.

Tristan's voice carries across the balcony as I approach. "Dude, I know! But it's cool, she's okay now. Still a *little* weird, but she's pretty—nice, too—and one of her friends is a booker for this big men's line, so I'm working that angle."

I freeze. You've *got* to be kidding me.

"Remember how obsessed with you she was?" a girl that I vaguely recognize as a former cheerleader says.

Another guy laughs. "That's right! She used to stare at you in the cafeteria. I'd forgotten that!"

"She looks fucking *hot* now, though," another guy pipes up. "Nothing like she did in high school."

"I think it's plastic surgery," one of the girls sniffs.

"Jill, shove it, she didn't have plastic surgery," Tristan says. "She, like, grew into her looks. I see it all the time. Send a guy to the gym, put him on a high-protein diet to gain twenty pounds of muscle, the right haircut, a tan, some dental work, and you can turn any geek with good bone structure into a model. It's the same thing with girls." He smirks. "None of *you* were models in high school."

"You're such an asshole!" Jill shrieks.

He shrugs. "It's not like either of us is gonna get hurt. We're pretty much using the other until something better comes along. She's not in love with me. And I'd be stupid to dump her. She has, like, mad connections, even after she got fired from that other magazine. Her roommate is Emily Tyler, did you know that?" he says proudly.

"Screw you," I say, walking up, my voice low with fury. "You're a fucking pig."

Tristan's jaw falls to the floor. "Baby, wait—"

"Don't *baby* me. We *have* been using each other, and it stops now. You're shallow—the only thing you care about is getting yourself in the papers and being seen with cool people. I'm not wasting more time on you. Later." I spin on my heel and walk away, my hands balled into fists.

"Wait!" Tristan pushes one of the guys out of his way and grabs my hand. "Bella, wait." He spins me around and pulls me to him, putting one hand on my face and the other around my waist. "I didn't mean that. You know how it is—I was just showing off for the boys. All I've been talking about all night is how amazing you are and how I'm falling in love with you."

"Yeah, because you've been surrounded by my relatives all evening, and this is the first time you could let your guard down!"

"It's not like that," he says, eyes wide. "Bella, I think . . . no, I know. I *am*. I'm falling in love with you."

I can't help it. I burst out laughing. "Tristan, you're not in love with me."

"I am! I think I am!"

"You're embarrassing yourself." His friends have all edged several feet closer and are blatantly eavesdropping. "You're in love with being on Page Six and with the fact that my roommate is semifamous, and with the fact that my friend handles a men's grooming campaign. We haven't been alone together in weeks, and neither of us honestly cares. So, spare me. You're a handsome guy. You'll find another woman soon who can help your career. I've got better things to do."

As I stomp away, he says weakly. "Don't tell your mom, okay?"

The clock is creeping toward noon when I walk downstairs the next morning to find my mother in the kitchen, sipping a cup of tea and staring out the window onto the back garden. *The View* hums in the background on the kitchen TV.

"Good morning," I say, giving her a kiss on the cheek, my vision still blurry from too much champagne and not enough food.

"Morning, honey. Sleep well?"

"I slept like a baby," I say, and yawn, popping a piece of bread in the toaster and pulling a tub of butter out of the fridge. I feel relieved now that I've dropped Tristan's dead weight. He spent the remainder of the reception shooting me wounded looks and sitting at his table, pounding back beers while I danced with Susan, Olivia, and my cousins. Susan could barely contain her relief when I confessed before she and Harold fled for their hotel that I'd broken up with Tristan.

"That's nice," my mom says. She smiles at me, but her face looks blank, as if her thoughts are somewhere else.

"What's wrong?"

"I'm thinking about Susie. It's hard to believe she's married. Now both of my babies are gone."

I pull up a chair and sit at the table across from my mother. "We're not gone. Susan and Harold will be back from Hawaii in a week, and they live only ten minutes away. And I'm still here," I shrug. "I don't think you'll be losing me to marriage any time soon, at least not at the rate I'm going."

She swallows hard, her eyes tearing up. "I know Susan will be back soon, but it won't be the same. And we lost you years ago, Izzie-Bear."

"Mom." I reach across the table and pat her hand, looking at her earnestly. "Just because I don't live here doesn't mean you've lost me."

She sniffles, then puts her hand to her face embarrassedly, holding it there for a few moments. "I'm sorry. I know that, sweetheart." She looks back up, wiping away a lone tear streaking down her cheek, and smiles. "Look at me! I'm being so silly."

My toast pops up, and I butter it, facing the window, purposefully giving her some time to compose herself.

"So, I have some news and I'm not sure how you'll take it," I say finally, sitting back down and taking a small bite of toast. "Tristan and I broke up last night."

"What?" she gasps. "Why? He's such a handsome boy. Colleen and I always hoped you'd come together. We spent at least half an hour last night talking about you two!"

"I couldn't let my guard down around him. He's just too damn *pretty*."

"Izzie," she admonishes. "Don't swear."

"Sorry."

She sighs, taking another sip of tea. "It did seem off, I suppose. You didn't have the same spirit that you did when you were with Olivier." My mother was crushed the day I informed her we'd split. "I guess you want somebody smarter? You and your father were always the intellectuals in the family. Now, don't get me wrong," she says, putting her hand up, "Susan is very intelligent and a very hard worker. But you and Chuck are so . . . lofty? Is that the right word? You've both got your heads in the clouds, learning things for the *sake* of it. Susan and I—we're more practical."

"I don't feel very intelligent sometimes. And Dad is the epitome of practical."

"Not always. And don't you put yourself down. You're the smartest girl I know."

"Thanks, Mommy." I smile. I haven't called her Mommy since I was twelve.

I take another bite of toast, chewing thoughtfully. "I'm a lot like you, though."

"I hope so! You're my daughter, too," she says, and laughs softly. She reaches across the table, stealing a piece of my toast and then cocks her head to the side, looking at me carefully. "Is there someone else?"

"What? Someone else? No. Nobody else. Why do you ask?"

My mother looks at me impishly, a twinkle in her eye. "I think you're protesting too much."

"Nobody else!" I cry again. "At least . . . well, not really. It's complicated."

"What does that mean?"

"It means . . . I work for him, for starters."

"Oh, Isabella," she says disapprovingly, the smile sliding off her face. "That can only lead to trouble."

"I know! Do you think you're telling me something I don't know?" I cluck in frustration. "It's not going to lead anywhere. Half the time, it's as if he hates me. He's cold, he's uptight, he's concerned with what everybody thinks of him."

She raises an eyebrow. "And the other half of the time?"

I think of James's wry smile, his dimple, his eyes boring into mine with interest and concern. "Well. The other half of the time, he's . . . different. Not like everybody else. I think he might care for me. I think, maybe, he feels . . . what . . . I feel," I say haltingly.

My mother looks taken aback. "Oh, my."

"What?"

"Nothing. I just . . ." She takes a sip, looks out the window, then looks back at me. "I haven't heard you talk about anybody that way since Olivier."

My mother and I talk for two hours—I confess everything that's happened during the past several months, and she reassures me that, no matter what happens at work or what decisions I make in my personal life, she'll support me. ("Even if you decide to shack up in one of those strange Goldie Hawn and Kurt Russell nonmarriages," she sighs.) Eventually, the conversation turns to my father.

"He worries about you, Izzie."

"He never calls me."

"Honey, you know your father. Emotions aren't his strong suit. He talks about you all the time."

"Really? He does?"

"Why do you sound so surprised? It's your father! Do you think he doesn't care?"

I shrug. "I know he *cares*. I just didn't think he . . . He always seems so disapproving."

My mother looks sad. "He has high expectations for you girls. You especially. You're more like him than either of you realizes."

I've inherited my nervous loquaciousness from my mother, but it's true that I have the same emotional temperament as my father, which is to say: avoid confrontation; avoid emotion; avoid any sort of interaction that gets too close; explode if somebody breaks those rules. But people change, don't they? The family persona you get trapped into at age eleven shouldn't be the one you're saddled with for the rest of your life. My therapist—not to mention my friends—has helped me to feel comfortable owning my emotions (her words, obviously, because who *actually* speaks like that?). A father-daughter chat is long overdue.

"Dad?" I say, knocking on the door of his study. War memorabilia dots the room. The entire right side of the room is wall-to-wall books, at least 75 percent of which are devoted to earth-shattering conflicts. One third, closest to his massive cherry wood desk near the window overlooking the rose bushes, is devoted to books on World War One. The second third, in the center of the wall, is filled with tomes on World War Two from every conceivable perspective—American flyboys, marines, and POW perspectives, of course; English accounts of the blitz; German dissections both pro- and against Hitler, including Hitler's prison penned autobiography *Mein Kampf* ("Nazi son-of-a-bitch who'll burn in hell, but you have to read about the devil to understand him, you see?"); the plight of displaced Jews; numerous volumes devoted to French resistance fighters—a particular favorite; the Japanese ("Always thought they were damn cowards to sneak up, but I did enjoy the Clint Eastwood film. Insightful."); and the Russians. The remaining space is filled with discussions of what went wrong in Vietnam, accounts of the Crimean War, three Napoleonic War shelves, and a small but growing corner devoted to September 11.

I expect dad to be frowning over a newly acquired book, maybe yet another tell-all from one of George W. Bush's former cabinet members detailing what went wrong, perhaps a cigar burning in the crystal ashtry—though it's been nearly twenty years since my mother forbade my father to smoke in the house, he delights in asserting his independence within the confines of his study—but instead I find him leaning back in his chair, watching TBS reruns of *Friends* on the small TV to the right of his desk, chuckling heartily.

"Sweetheart," he says as I enter, looking briefly at me before turning to the television again. "Have you seen this one?" Rachel is doing cartwheels across the room in a cheer-leader uniform and emerges with a swollen lip. He chuckles again.

"Oh yes! It's one of my favorites." I motion to the seat in front of him. "Dad. May I sit?"

"Of course." He turns the volume low on the TV and swivels to face me. "Nothing wrong?"

"No! No, of course not. Nothing wrong at all. I figured . . . I'm home so infrequently, and we hardly talk on the phone. I thought I'd come by your office so we could speak for a few minutes." My voice involuntarily stiffens and prunes itself of all *likes* and *you knows* whenever I talk to my father.

He regards me expectantly. *A little help over here, please!* I think.

"Well, I just . . . *er* . . ." I'm at a loss for words. I don't actually have anything to *say* to him.

"How's the new job?"

"It's going well," I respond with some relief. "My coworkers are all very nice, and I'm working hard on my new column."

"And your boss? Everything fine there?"

"She's . . . okay. She's a bit tough. I'm doing my best and trying my hardest, but she seems to think I'm not in the right mindset to relate to our readers."

"So get in the right mindset," he says, jaw set.

"I'm trying!"

He shakes his head stubbornly. "Try harder."

"I've read through all the back issues, I keep writing and rewriting my column, and I'm working as much as I can, but my boss didn't like me right off the bat, and the publisher doesn't like me, either—in fact, the editor in chief is really the only one I have in my corner—and it's just tough. It's demoralizing."

My father taps his fingers on the desk impatiently, reminding me of Frances. "They're not there to hold your hand, Isabella. You're out for yourself; nobody will do you any favors; nobody will fight for you. If you fail, there are plenty of other girls who'd be happy to fill your shoes. So don't fail."

"Right," I say disappointedly. "Good advice. Thank you, Dad. *Er* . . . I should go pack for my flight." He *is* right, of course, but I feel let down. Maybe I was secretly hoping that, in the wake of Susan's wedding, his guard would be down and we could attempt to bond, for once.

I smile brightly and give him a tiny nod, standing up.

"You won't fail," he says, regarding me from behind his small black eyes. "You're already there, you see? Twenty-eight years old, taking the city by storm. You're made of different stuff than all the rest. Show 'em what sets you apart." He clears his throat and nods curtly. "I know you can."

"Thanks, Dad."

He picks up the remote control, turning the volume on the television louder. Conversation over.

Chapter 13

I go to work early the Monday after returning from Cleveland, feeling strangely recharged from my interactions with my parents and my strength in chucking a model I'd elevated to God status during high school. I don't have anything to prove to anybody, whether the other beauty girls, Frances, or James. Now's the time to prove my talents to *myself*.

At my desk, I turn my cell phone off and set my work phone to automatically forward all calls to voice mail.

Okay. What am I writing about here? I can't write about my Dr. P experience until next month because several of the drugstore creams we want to feature won't be available until October.

An idea flashes through my head; it might be a little too colloquial, but maybe the readers can relate. What if I write about making Vivian over?

Everything else has bombed. *So this probably will, too—but at least I'll enjoy writing it*, I think.

It's worth a shot.

At noon, I call Megan to take a rain check on lunch and instead nibble on nuts and raisins from a container on my desk. I work straight through until 4:00 p.m., when I feel I finally have something presentable. It's not perfect, by any stretch of the imagination, but it's better than the feeble attempts I've submitted the past couple of months. While reading it, I actually laugh out loud twice—which either means that it's good or I'm simply irredeemably lame.

I reread the column twice, double-checking for errors. (Few things in the world give me such profound enjoyment as proofreading.) Finally, I print it out and head to Frances's office, also printing out a list of ideas for the upcoming months I've been working on over the last few weeks. She's hunched over a galley, red pen in hand. I knock softly on the door.

"Frances? I have the first draft of my column for you, as well as a new ideas memo."

She looks up and puts her pen down. "Bella. How was your sister's wedding?"

"It was lovely, thanks. Both nice to see my family, and kind of stressful at the same time," I admit.

Her face relaxes into an amused expression. "Yes, I can imagine."

I offer her the pages in my hand. "Here's my column. I hope you like it."

She picks up the pages and sets them on the side of her computer without looking at them. "I will read through everything tonight and let you know. Thank you for getting it to me early."

"No problem." I pause. "I tried a different tack. I thought the readers might enjoy reading about something they could, maybe, personally relate to." I don't say the dreaded word *makeover* to her. I'll let her read it for herself.

She looks at me without saying anything, finally nodding. "Fine. I will give it a look."

"Thanks," I say. Time to start making edits on the August galley waiting on my desk.

"Hang on. While you are here, I would like to have a quick invite meeting. I want to coordinate our schedules for next week, since I will be in the Bahamas for the fashion shoot and you will be in Paris. What day is the trip?"

"Wednesday."

"I see. Well, that's not optimal. I leave Monday and am not back until Thursday." She drums her fingers on the table in frustration. "That means there will be two days that you're here without me. Knowing this photographer—we're using Fernando—it could run even longer. He made us wait two days on the last shoot because he insisted on changing models. It was the height of unprofessionalism," she says, glowering.

I state the obvious. "I think I'll be fine for two days without you, Frances. If there are any emergencies, I'll call you on your cell phone and can fax you any galleys at your hotel."

"I suppose," she says reluctantly. "If that's the best we can do."

What's the alternative? Me flying to the Bahamas with pen and paper in hand to let her sign off on everything? I just nod. "Everything will run smoothly, I promise."

She looks at me dubiously and nods. "Okay, then."

I mean, things *should* go smoothly, right? *What could possibly go wrong?* Don't ask yourself that. That's just an invitation for everything to go awry. Okay, *many* things could go wrong . . . but the new Bella Hunter will handle them. It's going to be fine. It has to be.

On Friday, Frances stops by my desk and hands me a stack of papers.

"Here's your column back with my changes. Could you have them to me by the end of the day, please?"

"Sure," I say, taking the papers and flipping through them. My words are awash in a sea of red, which would normally be daunting. I'm thrilled, however, because instead of comments like: "All wrong!" "Not for us!" "Who are you talking to?" and "Needs a complete revamp!" I have: "Right track; more explanation." "Too expensive, pls substitute." "Grammatically incorrect," and "Needs to be about fifty words longer."

From Frances, the mildness of the criticism is the equivalent of a gold star!

Finally, July 27 rolls around. I leave for Paris tomorrow! I float through the day, counting the minutes until I can go home and pack my bags. Just before 6:00 p.m., I take a few minutes to write a to-do list in my Smythson notebook (last year's Christmas gift from Bobbi Brown) of things I must accomplish while in Paris:

1. Photograph self in front of Eiffel Tower, Arc de Triomphe, Notre Dame, and Sacré Coeur.
2. Check out cafés where Hemingway and Fitzgerald hung out (I have my tattered copy of *A Moveable Feast* in my carry-on luggage and plan to dog-ear notable pages for later sightseeing use)
3. Buy something fabulous at Louis Vuitton. (It's cheaper in Paris, right? Must be; after all, Louis is French!)
4. Find a cute French boy to kiss while walking along the Seine. Screw Tristan, and screw James.

"Have a blast!" Vivian says, stopping by my desk. Megan is sitting on my product counter, having brought over Starbucks five minutes earlier. "I'm jealous. Take lots of pictures for me, okay? Walter mentioned last night that we should take a trip together. Maybe we'll go to Paris, too!"

"So things are still going well?" Megan asks.

"Unbelievably," she gushes. "He is such a gentleman."

I smile. "Vivian, that's fantastic. You deserve it."

"But what about you? Do you know that you've never once mentioned a guy to me? You must have somebody in your life. A one-night stand? A jilted lover? A hot crush? Your sister's husband? Anybody?"

"You've been watching too much *General Hospital*," I say, and giggle.

"You're changing the subject," Vivian says, wagging a finger at me. "We'll let you off the hook, but I want you to kiss a Parisian man for me! Have a romantic moonlight walk on the Seine! Anything to add a little spice to my column!"

"Your column or your life?" I tease.

"Honey . . . I've *got* a boyfriend now," she grins. "My personal life doesn't need any more spice."

"I'll take some spice," Megan moans. "Being single is boring."

"I can't promise any moonlight walks, but I'll do my best to at least flirt with a cute Frenchman, and maybe get a picture."

"Say hello to Jean-Pierre and Gaston for me," Vivian says, she and Megan giving me warm hugs before I turn off my computer and set my phone to automatic voice mail. I give my desk the once-over and then flee. Nick's coming over to the apartment tonight for some wine as an incentive to help me pack. Emily insists that she's too busy with studying to help, but I know her—as soon as Nick and I go into fashion mode, she'll take over and shower us with her brilliance. The girl just can't help it.

"You should be locked up. You were planning on going to Paris with only three pairs of shoes?" Emily demands that evening.

"What's wrong with that? A pair of Pumas for walking around, my black Burberry flats for events and meetings, and my new Christian Louboutins for dinners and parties."

"That's absurd!" she hollers. "You can't get by with just one pair of party shoes. What happens if the heel snaps? And those flats aren't going to go with everything. You need a pair of black or tan heels, at least three pairs of sandals, probably some flip-flops—it's sweltering in Paris now—a great pair of boots *just* in case the temperature goes down in the evening, in black and maybe tan—"

Nick stands in the doorway with his arms folded, a Jack and Coke in hand. "You're going to send her with enough shoes for a month. I'm telling you, the tan wedge Michael Kors are all she needs. They go with everything." After years of doing makeup at photo shoots, Nick has decided his expertise extends to fashion as well. Like most men, however, he thinks women should only wear high heels and dresses—the taller the heels and the shorter the hemlines, the better.

"Nicolas, my darling, this is *Paris*," she says, shaking her head. "She needs . . . eight pairs of shoes, minimum."

"Eight? Are you nuts? She'll be there three days!"

"Four days."

"Whatever. It's not Fashion Week. She doesn't need to bring a shoe store. Her dresses are much more important."

"But it's her first press trip with the other editors, and she needs to let them see she hasn't lost it."

All of this backing and forthing is making me anxious. "Forget it. I'll bring an extra pair of casual shoes, and if I have room in my suitcase, I'll bring an extra pair of dress shoes, but that's it. I don't need my entire wardrobe for a couple of days, Emily—I'm not Gabrielle for Christ's sake—and I can't just bring dresses, Nick. I need some black pants and jeans, too. Maybe a skirt. And I was thinking some cute Marni tops? Oh, and my Stella blazer."

"Suit yourself," she sniffs. "Don't call me crying if you're at dinner and are wearing the completely wrong footwear. I put up with enough of that shit from Gaby."

"I'll try to restrain myself. Now, what about the outfits?"

"How many jackets are you planning on bringing?" Emily asks. "That's the crux of your wardrobe. You need a few good jackets that will go with your jeans and flats during the day, but that you can throw over a dress at night."

"Well, the Stella blazer, for sure. I have that cute Nanette

Lepore one, and the pink Cacharel that's part of the suit—but I won't bring the shift dress—and I really want to bring the blue Thakoon—"

"*Whoa,* girl. So, you'll bring seventy-five blazers, but no shoes?"

"Excuse me," Nick says. "I'm the one helping her here, remember? Aren't you busy learning about Freud and how all boys are in love with their mothers, or something?"

"Well, I just thought I could *help* . . ."

"Sick of your homework already?" I ask teasingly.

"Fine! Forget it! I'll leave you two alone to ransack my closet and mispack Bella's suitcase with all of the wrong things." She stomps off into the living room.

"Emily! Come back!" I poke Nick in the ribs and motion for him to help me.

"Yeah, I was just kidding!" he calls, shaking his head at me and cheekily mouthing, *"No,* I wasn't."

A few moments later, she wanders back into the room, looking defeated. "It's fine," she says, and sighs. "I should really read this . . . this . . . manifesto, or whatever it is. Maslow's hierarchy of needs is much more important than Marni versus Matthew Williamson."

"Now you're just being silly. Your expertise is not only appreciated but necessary. If you don't help, Nick is going to send me off with thirty-two different hooker outfits, one for every five hours! I'll be like Lindsay Lohan at an awards show!"

"It's chic to change outfits at different times of the day," he mutters, turning red.

"Are you sure?" Emily asks. "I don't want to break up the party."

"Oh, will you shut up and help?" Nick says. "You're going to fail that class anyway, so you might as well spend time doing something you're good at."

"Nick!"

"It's true. She hates her classes. She has no business being in grad school. Just give in and become a designer, Emily. Then you and I can join forces and start a house together—you'll dress them, I'll do their makeup, and then Bella will write about us every day and make us millionaires!"

"Let's put that scheme on the back burner for now," she says dryly, coming back in the room. She clears my bed and places the open suitcase on the floor. "I'll help, but I don't want any bitching, okay?"

"No promises," says Nick.

Forty-five minutes later, I have ten outfits laid out on the bed in front of me. Emily has set aside three jackets, two dresses, one skirt, one pair of pants, two cashmere sweaters and six tops, all designed to be mixed and matched together. She lays out jeans, a crisp white top, a pashmina, and Chanel ballet slippers for me as my "traveling outfit" and places all of my carry-on items (iPod, mini makeup bag, contact solution, glasses, Elizabeth Arden Eight Hour Cream, face wipes, oil-free moisturizer, a toothbrush, and the latest book from Jane Stanton Hitchcock) in a large Louis Vuitton duffel she's lending me. It's all so chic, I could die.

I survey the outfits. They're perfect: glam *and* comfortable. Sure, maybe the Christian Louboutins aren't the best choice for sore feet, but Em's right—it is Paris, after all.

"Do you realize that this is about a quarter of what I packed for my trip to Arizona last year?" I say. "And that was only for two days!"

"Yes, but you have everything you need here," Emily insists. "You don't need to pack tons of clothes. It's about combining the right outfits, that's all."

"Who needs millions of clothes when you have the proper ones?"

"You've been so brainwashed by the establishment. I never,

ever thought I'd hear those words coming from your mouth," Nick says. "You, who used to be so obsessed with wearing the perfect outfits to fit in?"

"Who am I trying to kid? I'm just me," I say earnestly

Nick guffaws. "Okay, Pollyanna. You might be 'just' you, but let's not get stupid. You're hardly the poster child for the Mall of America," he laughs.

"The Mall of America has some really upscale stuff!" I protest, remembering a trip I took there with my family in high school.

"Gross," Nick sighs. "Who *are* you?"

"Shut up, Nick. Who else is going on this fantasyland cruise, anyway?" Emily asks.

"The usual suspects: Grace, Heidi, Alanna, Mandy. A few others. And . . ." I can barely bring myself to say the word. "Delilah."

"Forget Delilah," Emily says dismissively. "She's disgusting."

"I can't help it! She refuses to admit she did anything wrong. She has balls of steel. You'd think she'd feel remorseful or embarrassed or *something*! And you should have seen her at the polo match. She was sucking up to Larissa like it was her job."

"Babe," Nick points out, "it *is* her job."

"I was never like that with Larissa," I say haughtily. "If she drove me crazy, I'd tell her so to her face!"

"Delilah is a big fake and everybody knows it," Emily says soothingly. "How many times has Joss told us that none of the publicists can stand her?"

"Yeah, because they see her evil side when she reams them out for not sending gifts or forgetting to include press releases. Larissa has succumbed to her spell. It's bizarre. She used to hate her."

"Deep down, she remembers what Delilah is like," Emily

says. "It's only a matter of time before she sees her true colors again. Anyway, it doesn't have anything to do with your relationship with Larissa, or with any of the editors. Let Delilah do her fakey-fake thing and just steer clear. You should think of it as a compliment. She only hates you because she's obsessed with you."

"Me? What the hell are you talking about?"

"It's obvious. Single White Female. She hates you because she wants to *be* you."

"Or maybe be *with* you?" Nick adds eagerly.

"You're a pervert. She doesn't want to be with Bella."

"Every woman has a little bit of lesbian in her. I've seen it many wonderful times." He smiles dreamily.

"I'm sick of talking about Delilah," Emily says, pointedly ignoring Nick. "She bores me. What's the James scoop?"

"Nothing."

"Nothing?"

"Nothing. We can't be in the same room without snapping at each other. He's been avoiding me like the plague."

"Didn't he try to talk to you last week, though?" Emily asks.

"Yeah, in the hallway at work, and in the kitchen, and once in the lobby . . . ," I mumble.

"And you didn't say *anything* to him?" Nick looks at me pityingly.

"What am I supposed to say? I have a crush on you? I mean, rather, I *had* a crush on you, but now I think you're a big jerk? He's so confusing. If you like me, be nice to me. If you hate me, ignore me. But don't keep blowing me hot and cold! One minute he's all, 'Hi, Bella! Let's have dinner!' Then the next he's running in the opposite direction as far as his legs can carry him, moaning and rolling his eyes about what a jerk I am."

"You certainly can pick 'em," Nick marvels.

"Excuse me, but we are not having this conversation," I say. "To the best of my knowledge, none of my other male friends have had girlfriends show up at their apartments banging on their door, threatening to sue them for emotional distress because of trysts with said girl's mother *and* said girl's sister."

"I've told you, it never happened!" Nick protests, his cheeks turning pink. "Leslie's entire family was crazy. Diana—*er*, Mrs. Sinclair's not even hot, so like I'd go there, and I may or may not have kissed Katie, but I'm *certain* we never slept together." He pauses, eyes narrowing as though trying to retrieve a memory. "No, definitely not."

"Can't remember?"

"I'm *pretty* sure we never slept together."

"I cannot believe what a tramp you are," Emily says.

"Pot. Kettle. Black," he replies. She flips him off in response.

"I'm just saying, those who live in glass houses . . . ," I continue.

"New topic. You're going to Paris tomorrow! How many frogs are you going to snog?"

"With my track record? Negative three."

"That's not even possible."

"You should be a mathematician."

"Children, children! *Arrêtez!* Bella is going to Paris and she's going to make out with as many boys as she can and she's going to stop thinking about James, and that's that," Emily declares. "And Nick didn't bang Leslie's entire family, either," she adds.

"I didn't," he says, eyes wide. "Honestly."

"And I'm going to pass psych," she says wryly.

Chapter 14

James is kissing me. Oh my God, James is kissing me. I accidentally left my passport at work, so I had to go in early this morning to get it, before the car arrived at my house to pick me up. It was still dark outside when I got to the office, and I was sweating because I was in a panic—terrified I wouldn't be able to find the passport, and then would spend hours looking for it, and then would get stuck in traffic on the way to the airport, and then would miss the flight. At my desk, I cursed myself for being so stupid as to leave my passport at work the morning of an international trip. Only me.

Just as I yanked open my drawer to find the passport sitting there waiting for me, I heard James behind me.

"What are you doing here so early?" he said. He looked scruffy, like he hadn't slept. His hair was twisted this way and that, his button-down shirt was wrinkly, and there was faint stubble growing on his chin and cheeks. Had he not shaved? Was he here all night? Did he sleep at work on his leather couch? Poor guy. No! Not poor guy! Mean, confusing jerk!

"I, *uh,* accidentally left my passport here," I said, too startled by the sight of him to remember that I'd promised myself to avoid him for the rest of my natural-born life.

"And you need your passport now? At—" he glanced at his watch "—seven thirteen in the morning?"

"There's a press trip this morning. To Paris. My flight leaves in four hours, and I still have to go home and get my bags. The car is picking me up to take me to the airport." My voice was scratchy, with the sleep still clinging to it.

He shook his head. "Why am I not surprised?"

"I don't know, why aren't you?" I said, offended.

"It just seems very . . . you."

"And how exactly would you know what 'me' is?" I asked boldly. "Are you some sort of expert on me?"

He moved closer. I could smell him. It was that mixture of sleep and guy and something else, something more primal. Instinctively, I stepped toward him.

I expected him to back down. But he didn't. "Yes," he said.

"What?" I said, shocked. My heart started thumping so loudly, I wouldn't have been surprised if he could hear it.

"You heard me." His eyes were locked onto mine, not backing down. He didn't move. He didn't look away. I felt more vulnerable than I'd ever been in my entire life.

I had to diffuse the situation with a joke. "Are you still drunk from last night?"

"No." He was still staring at me. "Why?"

"You're being . . . different."

He stepped a tiny bit closer. "Different good? Or different bad?" Now we were less than a foot apart. Barely any room for the Holy Ghost, as Miss Gleason used to say at the middle school dances.

"Just . . . different," I mumbled, my words failing me. This was not happening. Was this really happening? Here? Now? I couldn't even begin to wish it, for fear that something would make it all stop.

"Bella," he said, his voice gruff. The way he said it, it sounded like a growl.

"Yes," I said. It wasn't a question.

And that's when he kissed me.

Now. He is kissing me right now.

As I lean into him, I feel my breath catch in the back of my throat as his arms tighten around me. He smells so nice. His scent is soft and clean, with the faintest hint of musk. He tastes like candy, like saltwater taffy. I could stand here, at my cubicle, in the early morning before work, kissing him forever.

I let out a tiny involuntary sigh of pleasure. He stops kissing me and looks me in the eyes, his face inches from mine.

"I've wanted to do this since the moment we met."

"You have?" I ask, shocked. "But I thought you hated me."

His index finger traces the outline of my face softly, running over my lips, my cheeks, my eyelids, my temple. He slides his other hand up my neck, then gently pulls it through my hair, sending tingles shooting down my spine. "I didn't hate you. I was scared of how you made me feel."

"Really?" I say, feeling so pathetically hopeful that I could cry.

"Really," he mumbles, pressing his lips against mine again. "I know this is so wrong, but I just can't help it."

Wait a minute.

Hasn't he said that to me before?

Am I . . . ?

Damn it!

Of course. I'm dreaming.

My eyes fly open and I find myself in my bed, alone, drenched in sweat. The clock reads 4:13. My alarm is due to go off in two minutes. I prop myself up on my elbow and look across the room. There, sitting on top of my suitcase, is my passport. So much for that one.

It's swelteringly hot and my fan is only on low, but I lay in bed until the alarm goes off, sleepily replaying my dream over and over in my mind. It felt so real! I could actually feel his lips on mine! By the time I'm in the shower, however, washing my hair in water as cold as I can stand, the sharpness of the dream is already becoming fuzzy. I have to strain to remember exactly what he said to me, how his arms felt.

The car comes at precisely 4:45, and by then, it's all a distant memory.

As my driver pulls my bags out of the car and deposits them on the sidewalk in front of Signature Flight Services at Newark, the night still enveloping us, I peer through the glass doors, trying to see who's here already. I've never been on a private jet before—I'm so excited! Even though several of the highly coveted "PJ" trips came up while I was at *Enchanté*, either Larissa saved those for herself ("It's not as good as it was with Concorde, but at flying PJ is *so* much better than going first-class commercial," she often declared) or they were exclusively reserved for beauty directors, anyway.

I thank the driver, picking up Emily's Louis Vuitton duffel and rolling suitcase and walking into the small waiting area. It's so tiny! I don't know what I expected, but it's no bigger than my apartment. And this is the *entire* terminal for all private jets coming in and out of Newark? Wow. Even more exclusive than I realized!

A man in uniform comes over to check my passport and take my luggage from me. "You packed it yourself?"

"Yes."

"No explosive devices?"

"*Uh,* no," I say nervously. Even though I'm obviously not packing any heat, I always feel as if they're going to think I'm lying. I have a similar sense of irrational panic when bouncers check my ID at bars. I'm several years past twenty-one, yet still have that deer-in-the-headlights, "Are they going to find me out?" feeling.

"Any liquids in your carry-on?"

"No." Nazis.

"Thank you. Have a nice flight," he says, taking my baggage and depositing it on a large rolling cart with other Louis Vuittons and T. Anthonys and Tumis and Diane Von Furstenbergs.

That's it? A two-second security procedure? I have *so* been flying the wrong way my entire life. Private jet is the way to go.

Only a few girls are here so far, including Heidi and Alanna, both wearing matchy-matchy candy-colored Juicy Couture dresses and Havaianas flip-flops, with Chanel sunglasses perched on their heads and Gucci totes tucked into the crook of their arms. Of course, all of the items were gifts at one time or another, which explains why most beauty editors roam around looking like carbon copies of each other. The fact that it's so brutally hot today accounts for all of the (faux) bronzed limbs flying about.

The exception is Grace, who's sitting on a chair away from the group reading a copy of the *Financial Times*. As befits a beauty director at a highbrow publication, she's not wearing anything gifted or too beachy, instead settling for cream-colored pants, Chanel ballet flats, and a crisp white button-down shirt, her brown leather Mulberry purse lying on the floor at her feet. She looks me up and down haughtily and then buries her head in the paper again, taking a sip of her coffee. A few months ago, this would have embarrassed me to no end, but now it just makes me feel sort of worldweary. I can't believe I ever thought she was cool. What a classless cow.

I catch the eye of Samantha Mills, a slim, doe-eyed editor from *American Woman,* and give her a small smile. She smiles back and walks straight over. Her honey-colored hair is tossed up in a messy bun.

"Are you excited?"

"Incredibly," I say. "I haven't been to Paris in years, and never by private jet, and never staying at the Ritz!"

"I've never been to Paris at all," she says. "I studied abroad in college, but went to Buenos Aires, so I didn't have a chance to do the traveling around Europe thing."

"Paris is to die for. You're going to love it."

She fumbles around in her purse for a stick of gum and pops it into her mouth, then offers the pack to me. "Want some?"

"Sure! Thanks."

"So, you're at *Womanly World,* right? How's that going?"

"Pretty good, you know. Can't complain," I say noncommittally.

She pauses for a second and then says, "The way you landed on your feet—it's very cool. You should feel proud."

I blink. "Thanks."

"No, seriously. This bunch, they're tough. You've kept your head held high and you're just working now and doing your thing. It's a good example for the younger girls. Half of them are too busy worrying how many Christmas presents they're going to get from the publicists to just *work.*"

Samantha and I have never had an actual conversation before. I'd always written her off as boring based upon the fact she was at *American Woman.* I'm embarrassed by my own prejudice, especially when I've been getting mad at other editors left and right for doing the same thing to me these past few months.

"Thanks," I say quietly. I add, "I can't believe you and I have never chatted before. I mean, really chatted."

She shrugs. "It's okay, I know how it goes. *Enchanté* and *American Woman*—they don't exactly mix. We were rarely at the same events, anyway."

"Sort of like *Enchanté* and *Womanly World,*" I say, pointing out the obvious.

"Well . . . exactly. Are you friends with the same editors now that you're at *Womanly World*?"

"Not so much. Our friendships before, I realize now that they were pretty superficial."

"It's not just you. I don't hang out with any of these girls outside of work, either. If I were at *Vogue,* I'd be in the clique with Grace and Alanna, too. It's all so silly. You can't take it seriously."

"Everybody else seems to think that the sun rises and falls based on what magazine you're at and how many years you have under your belt."

"It's not much different in other industries," she says. "Trust me, I know. I spent two years as an advertising assistant, three years at the *New York Observer,* and one year at the *New York Times.*"

"You left the *Times* for *American Woman*?"

"Don't sound so surprised!" she laughs. "*American Woman* is a fantastic magazine! So is *Womanly World*. They sell about ten times the copies of any other magazine in the industry."

"I know, but . . . the *Times*? That's a whole different league."

"*Eh,*" she says dismissively. "It has boring people and silly rules and stupid hierarchies just like any other newspaper. I wanted a chance to do some writing that was more fun and creative but less stressful. So, I went to AW."

"You know what's strange? In a way, I find it *more* stressful being at *Womanly World*."

"Why's that?"

"I don't know. I feel like I'm always looking over my shoulder now. I didn't feel such a need to prove myself before."

"Frances can be tough, too."

"Yes! You know her?"

"She's good friends with my director, Alicia. Just so you know, she means well. She thinks you have a lot of potential."

"They've been talking about me?" I groan.

"You didn't hear it from me," she grins, putting her fingers to her lips. "I saw your last column, by the way. Good stuff."

"Frances doesn't seem to think so. Neither do our readers. It's been the lowest rated page in the magazine the past three months running. And that's just the three issues that have been rated—I still have two others to print that the readers haven't had a chance to bash yet."

"It takes a while to find your voice," she says, and shrugs. "You haven't even been there six months. It took a full year before my editor at the *Observer* stopped yelling at me! You're your own toughest critic."

I nod. "My best friend keeps telling me the same thing, but it's still nerve-wracking. I feel like an idiot for not immediately being overwhelmingly brilliant."

"You're human! You had a long way to fall, but now you can build yourself back up without anybody noticing. Sometimes it comes in handy to be out of the loop. Everybody's too busy freaking out about who's going to get the job at *Chic* or which island Dove is sending them to next month, anyway."

Suddenly the air is broken by a series of high-pitched squeals. "Hiiii!" exclaims Mandy, who has just walked through the door and spied Heidi and Alanna. "How *are* you?!"

"Oh Jesus," Samantha groans. "I can't deal with five days of this."

After everybody checks in and loads their luggage onto the carts, we're shuttled on golf carts over to the steps of the plane, which is waiting for us on the runway. I feel like I'm in some sort of 1950s movie, back when air travel was still new and glamorous and everybody stepped directly onto the plane from the tarmac stairs.

I gasp as we enter. The plane is cavernous, decorated entirely in white, tan, and blue, with royal blue carpeting, glossy butter-colored wood paneling, and white leather seats, couches and love seats scattered about, as if in a living room. There are three cabins: the first has a large flat-screen television mounted against one panel, with two couches and several chairs facing it; the second cabin has seats and couches on opposite sides of large tables, similar to the setups on European trains; and the third has individual seats spaced far apart, presumably to allow people to sleep. A quick glance around reveals at least four bathrooms and two kitchens.

Several editors make a beeline for the individual seats in the back and immediately pull out eye masks and earplugs. On a normal day, most of us would still be asleep for hours. I decide to sit in the middle cabin, with the tables. Maybe I can do some work and read a little of my book on the way over. There's no need to sleep, since when we get to Paris, it will only be early afternoon in New York.

A few minutes later, everybody is settled in a seat and the plane is almost full. The seat next to me is empty, but nobody has bothered sitting in it, apparently because the other editors are all five years old and I have cooties. Sam apologized for not sitting next to me, opting for a nap in the last cabin. "I went out for dinner last night and am still hungover," she offers up. "How sad is that? I need to get it through my thick skull that I'm not twenty-two anymore. Let's sit together tonight at dinner." She's not a regular beauty girl, I note happily—a total breath of fresh air.

As I look around, I notice several men sitting on the plane in casual Docksiders-chinos-and-blazers outfits. Who are these guys? Why are they coming to Paris with us? There are only three male editors in the entire beauty industry and none of them are coming on this trip so . . . are these husbands? Some companies allow editors to bring guests with them, like on the recent Edison trip to Palm Springs, or the legendary Dewy week in South Africa. I've only been able to have guests a handful of times, and almost always bring Nick,

since he "gets" the industry, can shoptalk with other editors, and inevitably drags a handful of us out clubbing after the beauty presentations and dinners are over, hitting on every girl in sight. I feel a momentary twinge of nostalgia for the old days when I felt popular, but it passes quickly. Better now that I know where I stand.

Grace stands up and walks from the front of our cabin to the back, where one of the men is sitting. "I read through the presentation and made a few notes. The second part is still lacking, as it doesn't give a feel for where we're taking the pages," she says tonelessly. "Thoughts."

The man takes the portfolio and looks through it, frowning. "The products don't grab you. These pages are full of Lauder and Arden. Can't we throw some Shu and Ole and SK-II in the mix? A little more obscure? I saw you flipping through those tears earlier. Let's put those in here." He's attractive in a bland all-American way, as though he should be working at a bank in Minnesota. He does *not* look like the kind of man who would know his Shu Uemura from his Ole Henriksen, let alone his Dove from his Olay. He obviously works in the industry. I'm completely baffled.

As Grace walks back to her seat, presumably to grab more tear sheets for Handsome Beauty Man, I see three more people stepping through the doors at the front of the plane.

"Sugar, we are *so* sorry we're late. I was just terrified y'all were going to leave without us!" It's Delilah. She's wearing a tight fire-engine-red halter dress covered in tiny white polka dots, with high-heeled white espadrilles. Her massive boobs are practically touching her chin. Subtlety is not her strong suit.

Hattie, the head publicist for the Face Group, rushes forward and engulfs Delilah in a hug. "Sweetie! I'm so glad you made it! You're the last three."

"Oh my *goodness*, that is *so* embarrassing."

I peer down the aisle to see who the other late editors are, but Delilah and Hattie are standing by the door chatting, blocking my view.

Kay Buchman from *Simple Elegance* squeezes around Delilah, shooting her a dirty glance, and then takes a seat at the front of the plane. I thought we were only expecting ten.

"Well, luckily I had Jamesie here to keep me calm," Delilah prattles on, steadfastly unaware that the rest of us are waiting for her to sit down so we can take off. "I was practically hyperventilating! But he was so soothing and understanding, I felt fine in no time." She reaches back and pulls forward by the arm a man wearing long khaki cargo shorts, a short-sleeved blue-and-white-striped button-down over a white T-shirt, and blue flip-flops. "He is *such* a doll," she says, stroking his arm possessively. Delilah looks down the plane aisle and catches my eye, shooting me a wicked grin. "C'mon, Jamesie, let's go find our seats. I think I see some in the middle."

Delilah walks into the middle cabin, her claws firmly gripping this guy's arm, and I finally realize that the man she's using as a scratching post is James. *My* James.

"Hi," she coos at me before pointing to the two seats directly opposite the aisle. "Why don't we sit here, Jamesie?"

"'S fine," he mumbles, tossing me a quick, "Hi, Bella," as he takes the seat next to the window. He won't look me in the eye, which isn't surprising.

Delilah floats down next to him, leaning across the aisle and whispering at me, "I think this is going to be the most fun trip *ever*, don't you, Bella?"

Two hours into the flight, I realize that I've read the same page of *Jane Eyre* about three times without comprehending anything. Emily, Joss, me, and a few other random friends started a book club last year, and we meet once a month to read things that are either at the top of the best-seller list, or novels we always wanted to read when younger, but never got

around to. We alternate between literary works and fluffy-but-well-written confections, which means that the past few months have seen the latest books by Plum Sykes and Emily Giffin alongside *On Chesil Beach* by Ian McEwan and *Middlemarch* by George Eliot. As a former English major, I normally relish the chance to add to my book checklist, and I'm embarrassed to admit that I sometimes scroll through the MLA's list of the century's top hundred books, just to see what I've missed. (I'm hovering around half, which isn't great, but isn't terrible, either.) *Jane Eyre* somehow escaped me in both high school and college, and so far, I've been completely engrossed, sneaking in a few chapters here and there before going to bed. Today, however, I just can't concentrate.

I sneak a glance over at Delilah and James. He's intently reading a copy of *Blink* by Malcolm Gladwell, which I can't help feel smug about, since I devoured that years ago. Delilah, on the other hand, is flipping through a copy of *Star,* smirking at the photos of celebrities with cellulite on their thighs.

Are they dating? How does he know Delilah? And what could he possibly *see* in her? Well, other than the fact that she's beautiful, of course . . . but she has no inner beauty! She is a troll dressed up as a beauty queen!

Why did they come together, anyway? When Delilah opens her mouth, I try to drown out the noise, but I think I remember her saying something about the two of them coming together. It was all, "*We* came together," and "*We* are so sorry that *we're* late." Am I remembering incorrectly? No, she definitely said they shared a car over, since she was going on and on about missing the flight and how James calmed her down. Does that mean they spent the night together? Why would they have shared a car? How did she know he was coming to this event and I didn't? Why is he even here? I'm so confused!

I glance over at him again, trying to be stealth, but just

then he lifts his head from the book and catches my eye. I quickly bury my head back in *Jane Eyre*, feeling my face redden. When was the last time we spoke? It was in the lobby recently, I think, when he tried to speak to me and I pretended I didn't hear him. I'm not going to look at him again, since I don't want him to think I'm suddenly interested now that Delilah has her claws in him. Mostly, I'm just annoyed that I was anticipating this lovely trip to Paris, and now I'm going to feel awkward and jumpy all weekend, always looking over my shoulder to see if James is there. This is terrible.

I feel thirsty, so I try flagging down one of the flight attendants—there are five, even though there are only twenty of us in total!—but they're huddled in the back of the plane whispering. None of the attendants can be a day over twenty-three, and they're all perky blondes or sultry brunettes—straight from private jet central casting. I stand up and walk through the back cabin, where all of the windows are down and everybody is sleeping.

"Excuse me? Hi. May I have something to drink, please?" I whisper to one of the blondes, peeking my head through the heavy royal blue curtain.

"Sure!" she squeals, motioning for me to come back into the kitchen. She readjusts the curtain so that light won't bother the sleeping beauties and then leads me into a small room where two of the attendants are busy preparing trays of cheese, fruit, meat, salad, bread, olives, paté, and vegetables to bring out to the first two cabins. "Do you want some wine? Prosecco? Champagne?"

I look at my watch. It's eight-fifteen New York time. "Just an orange juice for now, thanks."

"Suit yourself! There's plenty of champagne to go around, though, so you should come back later and have some!"

Champagne sometimes gives me a headache, and I know that drinking while flying compounds the effects of altitude and dehydration. I give her a little nod and smile, though, saying, "Okay, sure. Maybe. Thank you."

"Good!" She opens a carton, pouring it into a tall glass with ice, and then hands me a glass. "If you want more, just press the call button and I'll bring it to you."

"Thanks."

"We're bringing the food back soon, but do you want anything now to nibble on? Some brie? A little paté and toast? There's a lot of salmon, and prosciutto and turkey, too, and we have nice Greek olives dipped in—"

"I'll just wait," I say hastily. "I don't want to make you go to any trouble. Thank you."

She opens her mouth to protest but I rush back through the curtain before she can force more luxuries on me. If I were to bring a plate full of food back into the cabin, everybody would immediately start eyeing it, and then think that I headed back there like a diva, demanding food. Yes, yes, I know that I shouldn't care if all the other girls think that or not—but I do. I'll admit it.

Once on the other side of the curtains, however, I realize that the last place I want to be is next to James and Delilah. I stand in the back of the plane, sipping silently. I feel annoyed that James and Delilah are here together—or that Delilah is here at all—but I try to force myself to keep a positive attitude. There are about a billion worse scenarios in the world, right? So your archenemy is on this trip. So your awkward-Bella-inducing boss is here, too. So they're here *together.* You're still flying to Paris! On a private jet! And, inevitably, you're going to take home mounds of glam beauty loot with you. And this is your *job.* You get to play with makeup for a living and write about it and make a difference in how the women of America look and feel. Not too shabby.

I smile, aware that I'm basically manipulating myself into feeling better, but at least it's working. It's hard to feel like such a sourpuss when I force myself to put things into perspective.

I stand there for a few minutes, finishing up my OJ, then head back through the curtains to ask the flight attendant for more.

"Back again?" she says, and smiles.

"Sorry, I just didn't feel like sitting down right away," I admit.

"Stay back here as long as you want! Would you like more?"

"Please," I say, holding my glass out for her to refill.

"Why don't you come back here with us?" she says, gesturing to a small seating area off the kitchen with a table and several chairs. "I know it's awkward to stand around in the middle of the plane. You feel like everybody is looking at you."

"Thanks," I say gratefully. I walk back in the room and perch on the edge of the table. I lower my voice and confide, "There's another girl in there I don't really get along with, and she's sitting very close to me. I think she did it on purpose."

"That's terrible! Is she trying to pick a fight?"

"Probably."

"Is it the girl in the red dress?" she whispers.

I nod ever so slightly, rolling my eyes. "She's a piece of work."

"I could tell," the girl says. I look at her name tag and see that her name is Bethany. She sees me looking and holds out her hand to introduce herself. I introduce myself in return, and she says, "Pleased to meet you! I thought when you came on that you were one of the nicer ones."

"Really? How's that?"

"You meet so many people doing this, you pick up on little cues. You can tell how someone greets you or how they ask for food or where the bathroom is if they think they're better than you. You're polite—which is rare, trust me—and you tried to be nice a few minutes ago by pretending that you were going to have champagne later, even though you didn't want any."

I'm amazed that I was such an open book. "Were you a psych major in college or something?"

"College of life," she grins.

"Impressive!"

"If you watch people, you can tell when somebody has that spark or when they're just trying to make everybody *think* they have it. That red-dress chick? She's just playing at it. Although her boyfriend is really sexy," she giggles.

"Yeah," I say. "I guess he is sexy."

She looks at me carefully. "There's something you're not saying."

"I . . ." I shake my head. "I don't know if you're a mind reader or just the most intuitive person I've ever met."

She smiles. "I knew there was something. You got this weird look on your face when you said he was sexy. Do you know him? Do you like him?"

"He's my boss."

"*Ahh . . . very* interesting. So how is he with her? Why? Is that why you two have issues?"

"If they're dating, it's news to me. I didn't even know he was coming on this trip."

"No! Are you serious? And she just shows up with him in tow? As her date?"

"I have no idea. Nobody would be brazen enough to—" Bethany's eyes widen suddenly and she interrupts me, "Can I help you, sir?"

I turn to see James standing in the doorway, looking sheepish. "I was looking for the bathroom."

Bethany smiles. "It's in the back. What would you like to drink when you return?"

"A coffee would be fine," he mumbles.

"One coffee, coming right up!" She winks at me so that James can't see and then rushes into the kitchen, leaving the two of us alone in the small seating area.

James stands there, his hands shoved into his pockets and his posture slightly hunched, as if he's trying to make himself disappear. I cross my arms and look at him frostily. He doesn't say anything, so I finally break the ice.

"Well, this certainly is a surprise."

"What do you mean?"

"I mean, what are you doing here?"

He looks confused. "I'm here for the Face Group press trip. Isn't that what you're here for?"

"Yes, but I'm a *beauty editor*. You're just here for fun? For the free ride?"

"No . . . ," he says slowly, as if speaking to a child. "I was invited, like all of the publishers. George from *Chic* is here, and so is Annabel from *Beauty* and Stefano from *Catwalk,* and a couple of others. You honestly didn't know I was coming?"

"How would I? You didn't bother telling me."

He looks frustrated. "Maybe I would have if you'd stop when I try to speak with you. We can't have a working relationship if you won't talk to me."

"You could have e-mailed to let me know, at least," I say, annoyed that he's right.

He rolls his eyes. "Fine, whatever. In any case, yes, I'm here for the trip. Face wanted all the publishers to see their new products and is having a separate meeting with us outlining their advertising strategies for the upcoming year. The head of marketing called me last week to let me know that he'll be able to have a quick meeting on Saturday to go over our new positioning, which I've been *trying* to tell you. It'll be more relaxed than the meeting we originally had scheduled for a few weeks from now. If we're lucky, it might be the push we need to secure their ad dollars for the next year and a half."

"Am I supposed to be at this meeting?" I ask.

He shrugs. "I don't know. I guess I wasn't planning on it."

I let out an abrupt sigh. "Let me rephrase. *Shouldn't* I be at this meeting?"

"Yes, frankly, you should. But like I said, you've been too busy sulking around the office to allow me to discuss it with you."

"*Errgh!* You are so *annoying*!" I shriek.

He rubs his temple with his hand. "You're worse."

"Here's your coffee!" Bethany says brightly, walking directly between James and me to give him the mug.

"Thanks," he mutters.

Bethany stands there for a second, looking worried. "Is there anything else I can get either of you?"

I shoot her a quick glance, as if to say, *This is such a mess*, but I shake my head. "No, thank you. We're fine."

"Okay, good. I'll be in the kitchen if you need anything. Anything at all, just ask!"

As soon as she walks out, I turn back to him. "I'm going back to sit down. If you need to discuss anything business related during the trip, please do not hesitate to let me know," I say with exaggerated politeness. "I am primarily concerned with the well-being of the magazine."

"Likewise. Obviously."

"Good. Fine. Enjoy yourself."

"Fine. You as well."

I start to walk through the curtain, then turn around. I know I shouldn't say anything, but I can't help myself. "But . . . Delilah? Just watch out."

"What are you talking about?"

"She's bad news. That's all I'm going to say. I mean, hey, it's your life, but . . . *Jamesie*? Seriously?" I shrug and then walk back to my seat, my heart pounding. James follows a few seconds later, picking up his book again as he sits.

"Where have you *been*?" Delilah gushes. "You were gone forever! I missed you!" As she slobbers all over him, she playfully slaps his forearm.

I can't take this. "I'm going in the front to watch the movie," I announce to nobody in particular, standing up and walking to the front cabin where *Harry Potter* is playing. Can I maybe avoid the two of them for the *entire* weekend? It'll be a challenge, but I'm certainly willing to try.

At 6:25 p.m., we arrive in Paris. Chauffered Mercedes are waiting to shuttle us to the Ritz. The sky is still filled with daylight, but the lights of the city are already illuminated, winking to us as we drive along the Seine, under the gilded bridges, down the tree-lined Champs-Élysées and finally to the Place Vendôme. It reminds me of that famous Oscar Wilde quote: "When good Americans die, they go to Paris." As I drink in the scenery, feeling that, no matter the minutiae of my life, all is right in the world, I can see what he meant. Maybe it's not going to come in the form of a mysterious TDH, but I have the sense that this coming week is going to be magical all the same, despite James's presence and Delilah's determination to get under my skin.

We pull up to the Ritz and pile out of the cars, gathering in the lobby like a herd of sheep as we wait for our next instructions. After a clipboard-wielding publicist swathed entirely in black does a head count to make sure we're all accounted for, the vice president of marketing, Ben Wales, a tall, pale man with sandy brown hair and a few extra pounds on his beefy frame, steps forward to deliver a brief speech.

"Welcome to the most beautiful city in the world! I'm so pleased to have you here for the next five days, and I promise that we have a whole host of surprises and delights in store. For those of you who don't know, I'm Ben Wales, vice president of marketing for the Face Group, and I'll be your cruise director for this trip." Everybody laughs politely. "Kim has already checked you in," he says, pointing at a short brunette standing on the edge of the group, "and all you need to do is speak with her to get your room keys and itinerary. You have the next hour free, so please relax, shower, walk around the hotel, or have a drink at the bar. Let's meet back here at 8:30 p.m. See you all then!" He waves us off, and, one by one, we collect our welcome package from Kim.

When I get to my room, I gasp—it's massive! I have a small but lovely suite with a garden view, a queen-sized bed, and a sitting area. My bags are already there, lined up neatly at the foot of the bed, and there's a bottle of Bordeaux and a fresh plate of cheese and fruit sitting on the table in the sitting room. A card next to the food and wine reads:

The Face Group welcomes you to Paris! If you need anything during your stay, please don't hesitate to call Kim or Lana at any hour. Enclosed is a copy of your itinerary, a pass for the spa, and two hundred Euros, in case you did not change money before arriving. See you at 8:30 p.m. at L'Espadon!

Holy crap, they're actually *giving* us money? This is standard practice on press trips to Las Vegas, where you'll arrive to your room at the Bellagio or Wynn to find a bag full of gambling chips waiting for you, compliments of the publicists, but I've never heard of companies simply handing over money for the hell of it. It's better than Christmas!

I unpack my suitcase and then take my toiletry bag into the bathroom, neatly arranging the cosmetics and products— which easily take up a third of my suitcase—on the marble counter before taking a shower. I'm surprised that I'm not tired, but it's always easier taking day flights abroad than the red-eye. And, of course, the whole private jet thing helps, too. I shower quickly, slap on some makeup, and then decide to air-dry my hair. I know it looks better when I blow it out to make it sleek, but I really can't be bothered. It's not like I have an image to maintain now, anyway. I neatly comb it around my ears and then squirt a few spritzes of Bumble and bumble Styling Spray in it before leaving it alone. It's beachy, but presentable.

Our itinerary calls for a group dinner downstairs at L'Espadon before giving us the night off. I haven't decided yet if I want to go out afterward. On the one hand, it's only about three in the afternoon in New York, but on the other, I did wake up at the crack of dawn today. Maybe after a glass of wine or two at dinner, I'll be dying to explore the Parisian nightlife. Or maybe I'll pass out for eighteen hours. We'll play it by ear.

I soon discover that the entire trip is meticulously planned, from the seating at dinner to the order of the introductory speeches to the amount of time between courses to the wines we are served. Sam and I want to sit together, but I am instead placed in between Grace and Sarah Ross from *Primp* at a table with the junior publicist from the Face Group, the head of R&D, a male publisher from one of the magazines and Yasmin Elhassan from *Sweet Life*. I notice darkly that Delilah is sitting next to James at a table with Ben and Hattie. As soon as James looks up to see me scowling, I quickly turn my frown into a serene smile and look slightly away, as if I'd just been glancing around the room in a reverie. I'm sure that, rather than looking casual, I probably look lobotomized.

The dinner is blissfully short, considering we're all completely jet-lagged. After a short presentation and welcome speech from Ben, we're left to eat and chat. I have one glass of Burgundy, then cut myself off, not wanting to exaggerate the effects of flying.

Just before 9:30, the evening breaks up. As we file out of the dining room, Delilah falls into step beside me. "My, my, honey. You're certainly looking . . . rustic," she simpers. "Didn't you have time to shower?"

"Excuse me?" I say, looking down at my outfit. I'm wearing one of the skirt-and-jacket combos that Emily laid out for me, with the Christian Louboutins to give it a little extra *oomph*. (The fact that dinner was downstairs fifty feet away from my room aided in my decision to wear three-inch stilettos.) The very *last* word I'd use to describe myself right now would be rustic. "What the hell are you talking about?"

"Oh, nothing!" she laughs breathily. "It's an interesting departure for you, that's all."

I look her dead in the eye. "Delilah, I have no idea what you're babbling about."

"Your *hair*, honey. Did you forget to bring a converter for your blow dryer?"

Oh. She's referring to the fact that I didn't straighten my hair as usual.

"No. I'm wearing it like this on purpose."

"It's darling! Really!" She giggles nastily.

"Thank you. I agree. By the way, if you need a recommendation for a good colorist while you're in Paris, I know tons personally. Oh, unless you're purposely going for a brassy orange look?" I say innocently. "Is it for a story?"

Her hands fly to her head. "My hair *isn't* orange," she hisses, adding, "Then again, you would know."

I shrug and start walking away, not caring how she found out about my orange locks moment. "Whatever you say . . . honey."

As Delilah fumes, I walk back into the main lobby, feeling a surge of triumph. For once in my life, I stood up to her! And lordy, did it feel good. I haven't just been prattling on about becoming a changed Bella—I *am* a changed Bella! A whole new woman! I take no prisoners, and I suffer no fools.

As I pass by James on the way to the elevators, I decide it's time to put my newfound confidence into action with him, too. I've been acting ridiculous. Am I one of those silly women who fall apart when they are having problems with a man? No! I am strong! I am independent! I am perfectly reasonable and liberated! I simply need to clear the air with James. Just, *um,* maybe not tonight. He averts his eyes but I stop and say, "I'm going to bed, but I'm free tomorrow after the massage to go over the presentation, if you'd like. I think you're right—it *is* important for me to be there with you."

"Oh," he says, looking surprised. "Yes. Good. That would be excellent."

"Okay, good. I'm exhausted, so I'm going to bed. See you tomorrow."

"'Night," he says.

"'Night, James." There, now! That wasn't so hard, was it?

Chapter 15

Mmm, this is the life. I wake up in the huge bed and hug myself as I look around the room. It's phenomenal. My suite looks like one of those antique, dusty salons you'd find in a museum, where the furniture is blood red and royal blue and the rooms are filled with gilded mirrors and ornamental clocks forever frozen in time. I feel like I've stepped into the eighteenth century.

I look at the clock. It reads 11:13 a.m. Holy crap, I slept for almost twelve hours. Then again, it's only 5:13 a.m. in New York, so I suppose I shouldn't feel too bad about sleeping in. The presentation is in forty-five minutes, but I'm absolutely starving and want to grab a quick bite beforehand. You can never count on the food at beauty presentations to fill you up, since they normally consist of a small salad, a dollop of salmon (good for the skin!), and a bread plate that nobody touches. Luckily, my hair has settled from the previous night into soft, messy waves, as if I'd purposely styled it that way, so all I require is a quick shower and then a bit of makeup. As I put on the clothes that Emily had designated for my first morning, I mentally thank her for having the foresight to pick out all my outfits beforehand. Otherwise, I'd probably go downstairs looking like a color-blind toddler.

A few of the editors are sitting downstairs in the breakfast room, sipping cups of green tea and chatting with each other.

I grab a croissant, a coffee, and prepare a fruit and cheese plate before going to sit by myself.

At five to twelve, James wanders in the room to grab a cup of coffee. His hair is wet and flopping around his face, as if he's fresh from a shower, and he's wearing a long-sleeve blue-and-white-striped collegiate-style button down T-shirt with khaki shorts and brown leather flip-flops. As always, he looks delectable. He smiles at me tentatively as he walks over. "Mind if I sit?"

"Sure, go ahead." I motion at the chair opposite from me. "I can only stay another couple of minutes, anyway. We have our first presentation at twelve. All about nanotechnology."

"Sounds riveting," he jokes.

I take a sip of coffee and peer at him surreptitiously over my cup. "You're very . . . touristy."

"What?" He looks down at his outfit. "What else should I wear? A suit? Jeans? It's about eighty-five degrees out there! I thought the shirt classed it up a bit. I don't have any meetings until tomorrow."

"No, no, it's fine. I mean, *I* wouldn't necessarily wear shorts and flip-flops on a business trip but, you know, to each his own." I smile to let him know I'm only kidding. He smiles back. So far, so good. Neither of us has drawn blood yet. It's progress.

Several of the editors stand up from their chairs to leave for the presentation. "So, what else is on your agenda today?"

I pull my itinerary out of my pocket. "Twelve o'clock product presentation, then three o'clock scrub and wrap followed by a massage," I read. "And then a five thirty walking tour of the Right Bank, *Île Saint-Louis* and *Quartier Latin*."

"Nice accent."

"I do actually speak French, you know."

"I figured as much. Us Amer-uh-cans normally just call it the Latin Quarter," he says with an exaggerated Yankee accent, taking another sip of coffee. "Massage, though, *huh?* That doesn't sound very business-trip-like to me."

"It's a beauty press trip! They have to find a way to throw a spa treatment in there somehow. It's par for the course."

"I think I'm definitely on the wrong end of this bargain here."

"I think you're right."

We smile at each other across the table. James suddenly looks at his watch. "It's almost noon. You'd better go or else you'll be late for your meeting. Are you still free to meet around five to discuss our presentation?"

I almost say, "It's a date," but stop myself, remembering the embarrassment it caused me the last time. "Five it is."

After a mind-numbingly dull presentation all about antiaging, nanotechnology, and the unique ingredients in the Face Group's newest cream, the editors are set loose to enjoy relaxing treatments in the spa. I have a scrub and wrap and "wet and dry" massage scheduled, which I absolutely can't wait for. There are few things in this world that beat a professional massage—maybe chocolate ice cream and the thrill of kissing somebody for the first time, and that's about it. I promise myself that I will have some chocolate ice cream while in Paris. Hey, two out of three ain't bad.

My massage technician is a tiny brunette woman named Juliette who spends the better part of an hour exfoliating my body from head to toe before beginning the massage. As I lie facedown on the table, I want desperately to enjoy the massage and just fall asleep. My mind begins to wander, however. I'm glad James and I have started to put our silly differences behind us. He was very pleasant this morning! I think we're on the right track. If we can keep building our working relationship, maybe eventually I'll be able to look at him without either wanting to kill him or sleep with him. That would be some serious progress.

"*Allo?* Bella?" Juliette's soft voice floats in my ear and I realize that I must have drifted off to sleep at some point during the massage. "*C'est fini.*"

"*Ah, merci beaucoup. J'ai,* uh, *bien dormi. Très fatiguee.*" I try to explain in my crap French that I was tired and fell asleep.

"*Eh, aucune probleme. Bah, donc, j'ai utilisé cette fluide fabuleuse qui vous donne une radiance extraordinare et rend la pelle douce et souple. Il faux le utiliser avant de—*"

"Um . . . *Anglais, s'il vous plaît?*" I smile sheepishly as I ask if she can explain everything to me in English. I think she just said something to me about skin and radiance, but with her rapid-fire French, I might as well require subtitles.

"I zee. Okay. So, I am saying zat zees creams is giving zee skin a *radiance et,* uh, softness, *non?* You must use eet s'ree time a day *pour* one month to get zee full benefits. *Tu comprends?*"

"Yes. I mean, *oui.*" Three times a day for a month? Yeah, right. She'll be lucky if I use it three times a day even *once.*

I stumble out of the massage room clutching my complimentary beauty products and head back to the spa bathrooms, where I catch a glimpse of myself in the mirror. I don't have that relaxed, naughty, "Wow, what has *she* been doing?" glow. Instead, I look as if I haven't washed my hair in a month and slept facedown on a waffle iron. Not sexy.

Delilah walks out of one of the bathrooms sporting a full face of makeup, her wet red hair neatly combed and braided, and bursts out laughing.

"Oh my goodness, sugar, you look *terrible!*" She smirks. "Too bad."

I stare her down. "Don't you have any animals or children to terrorize? Or are you just following me around on purpose, on the off chance you can make a snide comment?"

"You *wish* I were following you around."

"*Um,* actually, no I don't, 'cause that's stalking and it's just creepy. But if that's your thing, hey, don't let me keep you—"

"Let me tell you something. You think you're so great, but you're not. In fact, you're *nobody.* Nobody likes you. You're *over.* "

I laugh loudly. "Is that the best you can come up with, Delilah? What, are you taking insult classes from fourth graders now? Or do you just keep watching *Mean Girls* repeatedly?"

She glowers. "You're jealous."

"Of what? The Wicked Witch of the South?" I take a step closer to her and look her dead in the eye. "You're a nasty person, on the inside *and* the out." She gasps sharply, probably caring more that I insulted her looks than her personality. "There's nothing to be jealous of. I actually feel sorry for you. I mean that."

"How *dare* you! I will *ruin* you!"

I sigh and roll my eyes, turning away. "This conversation is over. Please don't speak to me again. I really can't—I mean, you're pathetic. Grow up."

"You're jealous because I got Jamesie."

I stop and turn back around. She's smirking again. "See? I knew it."

"First of all, I couldn't give a crap about what you do with my publisher. Secondly, his name is James, not Jamesie, get it?"

"Oh, I got it. And he's *very* good. You know how he pretends to be buttoned-up? It's just an act. Not that you'll ever get to see the real him, anyway." She smiles coyly. I want to grab her by the hair and stuff her head into the toilet. That would be wrong, right?

Breathe, Bella. Don't let this cow get to you. She's just trying to push your buttons.

"Whatever, Delilah. Just leave me alone."

"Bye!" she calls in a singsong voice as I storm out of the bathroom. "See ya later, doll face!"

I cringe. I'm furious at myself for storming off. I should have stayed and said something calm and mature to show that she wasn't getting to me, like, "James's personal life does not interest me, and neither does yours," or "Delilah, I think you need serious professional help," but instead I ran away like a schoolgirl getting taunted on the playground. *Ooh,* she winds me up.

After returning to my room to shower all the oil out of my hair and put on a small amount of makeup (just my Bare Minerals foundation, Lancôme Definicils mascara, NARS Orgasm blush, and Vincent Longo eyeshadow), I head back downstairs to the lobby to meet James. He's sitting in one of the gilded chairs, Delilah leaning over him and giggling as her cleavage falls in his face.

"Oh my gosh, Jamesie, you are so *funny!*" she squeals, putting her hand on his arm and rubbing it back and forth.

He sees me walking toward them and stands up, papers in hand. "Hi."

Delilah glares at me and doesn't bother to say anything. I return the favor, pointedly ignoring her. "Hi, James. Ready for our meeting?"

"Absolutely. Shall we go into the Palm Court?" He looks down at Delilah, who's sitting on the armrest pouting up at him. "We have business to attend to. Can I catch you . . . later?"

She brightens up. "Sure thing, sugar pie. I can't wait." She winks suggestively. I roll my eyes.

"Okay!" I say loudly, walking away and talking at the same time, so that James is forced to follow me. "So, what exactly is this meeting about?"

James falls into step with me, looking uncomfortable. "Wait. *Uh* . . . about that . . ."

"The meeting?"

"No. Delilah." We walk into the Palm Court and a waiter leads us to two chairs at the far end of the room, away from everybody else.

I wave my hand dismissively. "It's your personal life. You don't need to explain anything." Wow. That was calm and mature on my part. I'm dying to know what's going on, obviously.

"No, you don't get it. I mean, *I* don't get it. I barely know the girl. It turns out she and I live in the same building, so Face sent one driver to pick up the two of us. She wouldn't shut up the entire way there, and by the end of it, she was calling me Jamesie and acting like I was her boyfriend. It's creepy."

I burst out laughing, secretly feeling relieved. "Are you serious?"

"One hundred percent. You know what's funny? When you're around, suddenly she's all over me. Just now? She was sitting in the lobby, reading a magazine, and then came over and sat on the armrest next to me. But it was only when you stepped out of the elevator that she started swinging her boobs in my face."

"Poor baby. What a misery that was for you, I'm sure."

He grins. "I'm not saying it was painful, but still. The whole thing is odd. She mentioned something in the cab about seeing us together at the polo match. Do you two have history?"

Ahh, now it makes sense. "We worked together years ago and she hooked up with my boyfriend at the birthday party she threw for me, if that counts as history." James's eyebrows fly off his face. "And we just got into a catfight in the spa bathroom an hour ago. She told me I was jealous and I called her the Wicked Witch of the South."

"I can think of worse things to call her, but I'll keep silent so you'll think I'm a gentleman," he says, and smiles.

"A gentleman? Where? I don't see any gentlemen here, do you?"

"About as many ladies as *I* see here," he retorts.

"*Ooh!* What a diss." I laugh. "Seeing as I'm so unladylike, just let me know if you need protection from her. I'll rough her up good."

"Thanks," he says dryly. "I'll keep that in mind, killer."

There's only one moment of tension—as we discuss the presentation and he dismisses Larissa's Face Group intel as pure rumor—but it quickly vanishes.

That night at dinner, James and I are seated on completely opposite sides of the room, so we have no chance to chat. During breaks in our conversations with our tablemates, however, we shoot each other silly faces. We finally stop when I catch Grace shooting me a look of utter disdain, Delilah sitting next to her looking like she wants to kill me.

After a forty-five minute product presentation the following morning, the group gathers outside the Ritz to pile into the cars bound for Versailles. "There are ten cars available, so please get into whichever one you'd like!" Hattie says.

I motion to Sam to follow me as I hop into the third Mercedes and am pleased when James slides in after me. I'm less pleased, however, when Delilah also squeezes in on the other side of him in the remaining seat. Sam shrugs apologetically, pointing at another car and miming that we'll meet up once we arrive.

"Room for one more?" Delilah asks sweetly.

"*Uh* . . . sure," James answers, even though he's now squished in firmly between the two of us on the small hump seat.

I almost start laughing at Delilah's moxie. Nobody can accuse her of being timid, that's for sure.

The ride to Versailles takes about half an hour and is a beautiful journey through Paris's nicer suburbs and then the rolling countryside. James and I chat for most of it, although Delilah peeps up every once in a while with comments that I do my best to ignore.

We're almost at Versailles when she grumbles, "This press trip is so stupid. We haven't had any time for shopping yet!"

"I think it's lovely," I say. "It's been one of the nicest trips I've ever taken."

"I'll second that," James says. "All expenses paid to Paris on a private jet and staying at the Ritz? What's not to like?"

"Well, I mean, it's not *horrible*," Delilah sputters, correcting herself. "But it would be a lot better with more shopping." She looks over at me nastily, pointedly staring at my outfit. I'm wearing jeans, paired with a white tank top and a powder blue J. Crew cashmere sweater tied around my neck. "Some people on this trip could totally do with new wardrobes. Who wants to see a musty old house?"

"I do," he says.

"Me, too," I second. "Versailles isn't a musty old house. It's the grandest palace in the world! It's living history. It's a monument to Louis the Fourteenth's court as a force to be reckoned with. And it saw the demise of the French monarchy, the rise of democracy, a revolution—"

"What*ever*," she grumbles. "Boring."

James and I look at each other amusedly, sharing tiny smiles.

Five minutes later, our cars pull up at the foot of the gates. Even with all the time I've spent in France, I never once made it to Versailles. I'm psyched!

Our cars drop us off, and several editors gasp as we make the long trek up the cobblestones to the foot of the palace. I've never seen anything so grand in my life. The Château is a vision of baroque majesty, with wings extending on either side of the courtyard decorated a warm amber color, accented with ornate gold detailing. Throngs of tourists stand at the

entrance and scatter around the yard, peering at their guide-
books, posing proudly for photos, and gazing wistfully up at
the massive structure. I've recently read Antonia Fraser's bi-
ography of Marie Antoinette and try to envision it through
her eyes: a young girl from another country seeing this splen-
dor for the first time knowing this would be her permanent
home—not knowing this country was her death sentence—
and feel a palpable thrill travel up my spine.

"It's *huge*," I murmur.

"You're never been here?" James asks as we stroll together
up the cobblestones. I discreetly look around and note with
satisfaction that Delilah has joined Grace and Alanna. She's
talking animatedly and shooting me dirty looks.

"Never. Have you?"

"Of course. You can't come to France and not see Versailles!"

"Sorry," I shrug. "Never had the chance. I was busy in college. You know, places to go, people to see."

"Bars to visit," he adds.

"Well . . . yeah. It was *college*."

"You're just lucky you're getting to see this with me. I'm
something of a Versailles expert."

"What? I thought you were a business major in college.
How does that translate to being a Versailles expert?"

"How did you know what my major was?"

"Because you told me?"

"I did? When?"

I feel myself involuntarily blushing slightly, embarrassed
that I recall the conversation and he doesn't. Does it make me
look pathetic, like I've been hanging on his every word? "I
don't remember," I lie. "At some point, on our way to an ad
sales call, maybe."

"Oh. Anyhow, my major has nothing to do with my pas-
sions. I'm extremely interested in old French châteaux. I've
read hundreds of books on the subject."

"Really? That's fascinating!"

"Yep. Like, see that gate we just walked through?" he asks, pointing back to where the cars dropped us off. "Its name in English translates to the Majestic Gold Entry Gates."

"The Majestic Gold Entry Gates?"

"Exactly. And see that alcove right there?" He points to three arches along the right side of the courtyard. "That's Les Portes Glorieuses. It translates to "the Glorious Doors." It was only allowed to be used by Louis when he sneaked out of the main house to see his mistress."

"Uh-huh," I say, doubtfully.

"Few people know that Louis—"

"Okay, you can stop making stuff up now."

"Who's making stuff up?" he says innocently. "I told you—I'm a Versailles expert!"

"Of course you are, sweetie," I say patronizingly. "I didn't know you spoke French, though. Your accent was pretty convincing a second ago."

He smiles. "There's a lot you don't know about me."

"Well . . . likewise," I say, raising an eyebrow.

"Such as . . . ?"

"Such as . . . I also speak Spanish and German."

"I already knew that," he says smugly.

"What? How?"

"It's on your résumé."

"How have you seen my résumé?"

"What do you mean?"

"I mean . . . *why* have you seen my résumé? I didn't meet you until about two weeks after I was hired."

"Oh. Well . . . you know . . . official office stuff."

I scrutinize him. "I suppose." I wonder if he's telling the truth—it's plausible that he'd need my résumé to craft a bio for ad sales calls—or if he was simply looking at my résumé because he was curious about me. I hope it's the second. "So, what about you? What's something that I don't know?"

"For starters, I'm a drummer in a band."

"What?" I shriek. "I *cannot* picture you in a band."

"I knew that would surprise you," he grins. "You have a much different picture of me than how I actually am."

"You mean boorish and uptight?" I ask sweetly.

"Don't give up your day job to pursue stand-up comedy anytime soon," he shoots back.

I stick my tongue out at him as we're directed into the entry hall.

A squat woman wearing a calf-length black skirt and Mary Janes and carrying a small St. George's Cross flag booms nearby in a twangy northern English accent, "Versailles was built in 1623 as a hunting lodge for Louis the Thirteenth, the father of Louis the Fourteenth, otherwise known as the Sun King. Young Louis carried out his own renovations in 1661, which lasted for over—"

"What's your band called?" I ask, turning back to James.

"I don't want to tell you," he says, blushing. "It's embarrassing."

"Come on! You have to tell me!"

"You'll make fun."

"Probably."

He laughs. "I'd expect no less. It's called Animal House."

I stop walking and put my hand out, grabbing his arm in surprise. We've been ushered into a small chapel-like room. "Let me get this straight. *You*—Mr. Uptight and Proper— are in a band called Animal House. What kind of music does this band play?"

"The usual. Polka, folk, Chuck Berry–era rhythm and blues." I cross my arms and shoot him a look and he continues, "Well, what do you think? It's rock, obviously. A little punk, some Brit-pop and new wave. It's a cross between

Kaiser Chiefs, the Cure, and Nirvana," he says animatedly, obviously enjoying the conversation. "Our lead singer Simon quits and rejoins daily, just to keep the drama level high. He's holding out hope that we'll get signed."

"And you don't think you will?"

"I'm keeping my expectations realistic. There are so many bands in New York City—what are the odds? We're good, if I do say so myself—" ("Of course you do," I interrupt, smiling) "—but it's a one in a million chance. We plays gigs two or three times a month around the city."

"I'd love to see you play!" I exclaim, mentally noting that James's sexiness quotient has gone through the roof. A drummer? Yummy.

"*Shh,*" Grace appears next to us, frowning. "Will you stop babbling. We're trying to listen."

"The tour guide is twenty feet away, over *there*," I say, pointing across the room to the woman I'd noticed a few seconds ago. "If you want to listen, I suggest you walk by her and stop bothering us. It's not a library." I look at her defiantly.

"Well!" she huffs, her cheeks turning pink.

"Who is she again?" James asks as she storms away.

"Grace Donovan, beauty director of *Catwalk*. She's essentially the most important editor in the industry. Just don't let Larissa hear you say that."

"And she's obviously not used to anybody standing up to her."

"Hardly."

"Good. She seems like a bitch. There's no excuse for that."

"You don't think I was too rude?"

"You were a little rude," he concedes. "But it's okay. I think it was justified."

"Good," I nod, satisfied. "I've spent so many years kissing

up to these jerks that it feels great to finally tell them off. You know she asked me to send her my résumé only a week before I ruined my life with the *Post* article?"

"You're being too hard on yourself. Not to mention insulting to *me*. Coming to my magazine ruined your life?"

"No!" I sputter. "That's not what I mean! I mean, it's just that, you know, I made such a public spectacle of myself and then was *fired*—and nobody wants to be fired—and I like being at *Womanly World* now, but it's not necessarily something I would have *chosen* for myself, you know, back then, even though I'm happy now, and—"

"Chill . . . ," he says, and laughs, putting his hands on my shoulders to steady me. "In and out. Deep breaths. *Therrre* you go. Nice Bella."

"Oh, stop," I say huffily, throwing his hands off my shoulders.

"You're okay? Not going to have a nervous breakdown?"

"No."

"Too bad. I think that'd be kind of fun to see. I've already seen the beginnings of about ten of them."

I gasp. "That's not true!"

He puts his hands in the air innocently. "I'm not saying you would have finished cracking . . . but I've witnessed one or two episodes."

We walk up a giant carpeted staircase lined with portraits, trailing behind the group. I'm so engrossed in our conversation that I barely notice the beautiful surroundings.

"Name one," I demand.

"When you begged me not to fire you for going shoe shopping during work," he responds automatically.

"What? That wasn't a nervous breakdown."

"You practically started crying."

"You were *laughing* about it, you bastard! It was horrible!"

"Time number two: when I met you in Rania's office and

you pretended you knew all about ad sales calls and then had to cover your ass."

"That's not fair," I protest. "That was hardly a nervous breakdown. And, I wasn't pretending . . . ," I say, fibbing as my cheeks start burning.

"Then there's the time you—" he continues.

"Okay, I get it! I'm a spaz. Fine, lovely, whatever. Moving on."

"So you admit I'm right?"

"I'm sorry?"

"I said, 'So you admit I'm right?'" he says exaggeratedly.

I roll my eyes. "You have issues, dude."

We catch up to the group, which has congregated inside a hauntingly beautiful chapel with tall white columns, a cool marble floor and a painted ceiling. "Might have issues . . . but I'm still right." He smiles at me. "I *see* you, Bella Hunter."

Our group spends nearly two hours inside Versailles, enjoying a guided tour through the Palace, including a walk down the famous Hall of Mirrors, which is lined with gold statues, filled with chandeliers, and features a breathtaking view of the famous Gardens and fountains outside. When we leave the Château, Hattie guides us down the massive back steps into the Gardens, which look big enough to dwarf Central Park. We walk for five minutes, to an open green near the Grand Trianon, where Kim and Lana are waiting for us with a picnic and several bottles of local wine for a tasting.

I grab a glass of white, load my plate with cheese, bread, and paté, and settle on one of the blankets next to Sam. James follows suit, and soon the three of us are engrossed in conversation about the differences between France and America.

"I adore the French," Sam says. "They're so straightforward. If they don't like you, they'll either ignore you or tell you so. No smiles to your face while talking behind your back."

"When I studied here, everybody always told me that I was too smiley," I comment.

"You *are* too smiley," James says.

This is a sore point for me. "Are you kidding or being serious?"

He thinks for a moment. "Maybe a little bit kidding, a little bit serious."

"Why do you think I'm too smiley?" I ask quietly.

"It's not that you're too smiley, but you have a bubbly personality. You're an intelligent girl, but that can get obscured in the first impression."

"Smart people smile," I protest.

Sam nods. "You know, I understand what he means. Not about you, Bella, but in general. People take others more seriously when they're all stern. They assume you're an airhead if you smile a lot."

"But it's just being friendly! It's spreading cheer through the world! I think people are entirely too *mean* to each other. I hate seeing everybody walking around all day with frowns on their faces. It pollutes the atmosphere. It's just rude. And besides, it's going to give them terrible wrinkles later in life."

"It always comes back to beauty, doesn't it?" James says, winking at me. I hate to admit it, but his wink sends a shiver of pleasure down my spine. It's very sexy. *He's* very sexy. It's nice to see him relaxed.

"You're so chill here in Paris," I say, aware that I'm changing the subject, but not giving a flip. "It's fab."

"How is he normally?" Sam asks.

"Oh my God," I groan. "Unbearable. He dresses like somebody's snobby grandfather, in these tweedy bespoke suits and silk ties."

"Pretentious?"

"Very. And he's always rushing around, never smiling,

always frowning—totally polluting the environment, by the way, like I was just saying—barking commands at people—"

"Terrible!"

"It is. I mean, he can really be a world-class jerk."

"Of course."

"But thank goodness we've forced him out of his stuffy suits and into normal people clothes. He even sounds like a regular guy. Kind of."

"Can't you two wait until I'm gone to bitch about me?"

We dissolve into fits of giggles.

Sam sighs with happiness and leans back in the glass, stuffing a piece of bread in her mouth. "I'm so glad you're here, Bella. You're fun. This trip would be awful without you."

James looks at me, smiling. "I'll second that."

Three and a half hours later, the group is back in Paris, freshly showered and changed into evening clothes for a cruise down the Seine. As we step onto the Bateau-Mouche, I can't help but feel I'm in some sort of movie. The sky has a faint purplish glow as the sun sets and the lights twinkle around us. Looking behind to my right, I can see the tip of the Eiffel Tower; in front of me, stands one of Paris's famous bridges; to the left is the faint outline of the Louvre on the banks of the Seine and, beyond, the proud, strong silhouette of Notre-Dame. With a view like this, how could tonight be anything but amazing?

After a quick speech from Ben, we're set free to enjoy dinner and drinks. For once, our evening isn't completely scripted—the meal is buffet-style and the bar is open, allowing us to eat and drink downstairs, outside on the deck, or at one of the tables. I take a plate and head for the buffet, but the line is already massive. I decide to grab a drink and wait for the crowd to subside instead.

"*Champagne, s'il vous plaît,*" I ask the barman.

"*Bien sûr, mademoiselle.*"

"What are you drinking?" James asks, walking up to me.

"Champagne. Do you want one?"

"Sure," he says, signaling the waiter to bring two flutes. "It's been a gorgeous day, hasn't it?"

"The best! I've enjoyed this trip ten times more than I thought I would. And I was already looking forward to it *so* much."

"I've had a nice time, myself." He chuckles. "And thank God you've been around to keep me safe from Delilah."

"You know, I'm almost embarrassed for her." I giggle. "Almost."

The bartender hands us our glasses and I raise mine in a toast. James follows suit. "To Paris!" I exclaim.

"To Paris," he repeats, holding his glass aloft. "And to new friends."

"And burying silly arguments," I add, smiling, locking eyes with him.

"I'll drink to that." We clink our glasses and each take big gulps.

I sigh happily. I haven't eaten in several hours and the champagne goes straight to my head, but it's a pleasant, slightly fuzzy feeling. "I think this is going to get me drunk!"

"Lightweight," he teases.

"I will have you know that I was a *fantastic* drinker in college. All the frat boys were scared of me."

"I very much doubt that."

"It's true! I could out-chug anybody! Nobody ever beat me."

He puts a finger to his lips. "I don't know if you should run around advertising that at a work event. Being an alcoholic isn't exactly a talent."

I punch him hard in the shoulder. "Oh, shut up."

He shrugs. "I'm very sorry, my friend. The truth hurts."

"I bet you had two beers and then would pass out. In fact, you probably didn't even drink in college."

"Keep thinking that," he says dryly.

"Oh, so *you* were the alcoholic? Somebody's being a hypocrite?"

He smiles. "I drank my fair share. Of course, that was about a decade ago. I probably couldn't handle more than three or four beers now. How quickly the mighty fall."

"Excusez-moi?" I call. *"Deux verres plus de champagne, s'il vous plaît!"*

"Please tell me I misunderstood you just now."

I shrug coyly.

"Did you actually order more champagne?"

"Maybe."

"I don't know if that's a good idea. I haven't eaten yet. Have you?"

"Okay, grandpa," I say, downing the rest of my champagne and then handing him a new glass. "Drink up."

An hour and a half later, James and I are outside on the balcony of the boat, telling each other stories as the ship cruises down the Seine, monuments floating on either side of us.

"See that?" he says, pointing to an area on the banks of the river. "I came to Paris in college with a bunch of my friends and we were standing there, taking photographs, when all of a sudden my friend Brian fell in and almost drowned." He giggles like a little girl. "It was awesome. He smelled like sewage for two days."

I laugh. "You're sick."

He leans against the railing, smiling at me. "You have no idea."

"Ew!" I exclaim. "Whatever that means! I don't want to know."

"That didn't sound very good, did it?"

"No. It didn't. Now I'm wondering if you troll the Internet for young boys or have a serial-killer past."

"Serial killer? No. Lady-killer? Yes."

"Lame."

He shrugs sheepishly. "A guy can try."

"Okay. Give me your best pickup line."

"Pickup line?"

"Yeah. Let's say you're in a bar and the woman of your dreams walks by. What do you do?"

"Probably just watch her walk away and then decide she's not my type."

"No! You have to play along. C'mon. Woman of your *dreams*. You've been waiting for her your entire life. It's now or never, buddy. Make the move. What do you say?"

He thinks for a second. "Does, 'Hi, I'm James,' count as a pickup line?"

"Definitely not. I'm beginning to think you're beyond saving."

"Fine. In all honesty? If I wanted to talk to her, and thought I had a shot, but was still feeling nervous? I'd probably say something like, 'I'm sure you get this all the time, but you could be Charlize Theron's twin.'"

"That's not bad. Kind of cheesy, but also sort of sincere and shows that you think she's gorgeous. But, is she?"

"Gorgeous?"

"Charlize Theron's twin. That's your type?"

"I think that's every guy's type," he quips. "Tall, sexy, and beautiful, with a sick body? Yeah, I'll go out on a limb and say that's my type."

"Dream on, buddy. She's way out of your league." Actually, she wouldn't be—James is so sexy, he could easily be with somebody who looked like a supermodel. "What did your last girlfriend look like?"

He looks up at the sky, as if straining to remember. "Fiancée, actually. I don't know. She was pretty. Sort of the girl-next-door type. She had a bad attitude, though. Always looking to trade up for something better. We weren't right for each other; I think my parents liked her more than I did."

I assume this is the girl Steve mentioned during our disastrous sales call. "She wanted something better than *you*?" I ask, shocked, realizing too late that I've inadvertently delivered a compliment.

He sighs heavily. "I know it's hard to believe. She wanted somebody better than the Golden God that is myself." He grins to let me know he's kidding.

"She sounds high maintenance."

"Oh," he groans. "Everything was a huge production. Nothing I did was ever right. After a while, it's impossible to live like that."

"Are you the one who broke it off?"

"It was mutual."

"It's *never* mutual."

"Okay, it was mostly mutual. We'd been unhappy for months. Years. I was too nervous to break up with her and disappoint everybody, and then she had a fling right before the wedding—cold feet, I guess. When she told me, I was actually relieved because it gave me a way out. She wanted to get married anyway, but . . . we didn't."

"Do you two speak anymore?"

He shakes his head. "She got married about six months later to somebody else. The new guy owns a hedge fund and is the jealous type, so I've heard. I sent her a congratulatory card, but that part of my life is done. I wish her well, I'd say hi to her if we passed on the street, but I'd honestly be happy never seeing her again."

"That's intense."

"What about you? Do you have any crazy ex-boyfriends lurking?"

"No crazy exes. Just jerks. I haven't had a truly serious boyfriend since college, and he was completely controlling and then cheated on me. We dated my senior year and then for a while after I graduated. There was one guy after college, but I never felt the same about him as he did about me. The college boyfriend did a number on me, though."

"That's a shame. I'm sorry."

"Have you ever cheated on anybody?"

"I haven't," he says simply. "When I'm single, I'm single, but once I make that commitment, I'm in it. My parents had a bad marriage and I saw what cheating does to a relationship. I just don't have it in me."

I feel relieved for some reason. "That's fantastic. I mean— that's rare nowadays."

"What can I say? *I'm* fantastic. I am, in fact, the most fantastic guy to ever walk the earth."

"Let's not get ahead of ourselves. You're okay." I lean against the railing next to him, grinning. As he looks down at me, a huge smile spreads across his face, making him look insanely attractive.

"You're very cute when you smile," I blurt.

He wiggles his eyebrows at me. "I know. Didn't we just go over this? I'm a total catch."

"No, really. You are. I can't believe I wasted all that time fighting with you. You're amazing."

I lean in and stand on my tiptoes to give him an impromptu kiss on the cheek, resting my hand on his chest. Even in my heels, he towers over me by several inches, and I wobble precariously, putting my other hand on his chest to steady myself. His hands close over mine and we are suddenly inches from each other's faces, our hands and torsos clasped together, standing at the edge of the boat with the city stretched out on either side of us. I can feel his heartbeat racing. I'm light-headed. Is it the champagne—how many glasses have I had now? Five?—or the proximity to James? I'm not sure.

Neither of us says anything. Neither of us moves. I know this moment is fragile—the teeniest thing could shatter it, and we'd never have it back. Our lips are so close. I could just lean in . . . just a fraction! Inches away! But I can't kiss him first. I have to know that he likes me. I have to have proof.

I close my eyes. I'm afraid my knees are going to buckle. I inhale softly, hoping he doesn't notice that I'm trying to drink him in. It's all I can do from jumping on him and wrestling him to the ground. I silently will him to kiss me, to put his arms around me, to touch my cheek, to run his fingers through my hair. Anything.

Our breath is rising and falling in unison. I open my eyes and see that he's looking at me, his eyes searching my face. I turn my head a fraction of an inch to the right and lift my chin slightly. If he would just do the same, we'd be kissing. I have to kiss him. I can't wait any longer.

"Bella," he says hoarsely, his breathing shallow, his eyes locked onto mine.

"Yes?" I murmur.

"I . . . I can't. I'm sorry."

I take a deep breath and then exhale sharply, whispering, "Why not?" His heart is still pounding. I unclasp my right hand from his and place it at the nape of his neck, feeling the softness of his skin and running my fingers up through his hair. "Why?" His eyes are still glued to mine.

He swallows and closes his eyes for a fraction of a second as my fingers trace their way back down his head, along his neck, over his shoulder, and down his arm. I clasp his bicep with my hand, rubbing my hand over it softly to feel his strength. He tenses and then steps back, his hand dropping mine, his eyes clouding over.

"I'm sorry. I can't." His voice is resolute.

I refuse to let him get away this easily. I'm not crazy. He does like me. "But you wanted to."

"What?"

"If I didn't work with you. If I were just a girl . . . would you kiss me?"

He shakes his head. "I don't . . . I have no . . . I can't answer that question."

"James, I'm throwing myself at you! I don't understand. You don't like me at all?"

He looks trapped. "Bella . . ." He sighs, sounding defeated.

"Fine. Business only. I get it. See you tomorrow to go over the presentation." I start walking back inside, then turn, spitting out furiously, "But next time, maybe you should decide beforehand whether you're going to lead somebody on or not. You know. Just to save her a lot of confusion."

I march back into the bar, angry tears blinding me. Sam is standing there, laughing as the editors dance around tipsily in a circle, singing along to a Madonna song at the top of their lungs.

"*There* you are! It's like a junior-high dance," she says, her face becoming concerned when she sees my tears. "Hey. What's wrong?"

"Men are stupid, is what's wrong. And I'm stupider for letting one get to me." I lean against the bar for support, staring at my reflection in the mirror opposite. For once, I actually look kind of pretty—no hairs out of place, no runny makeup (thank God for waterproof mascara!). My nose is slightly red from my tears, but it's barely noticeable in the dark room.

"James?" she asks softly.

I don't say anything, looking down at my hands.

"I saw the spark between you two this afternoon. I don't know what happened, but I'm sorry." She motions to the bartender. "You need a drink."

I can't believe I begged James to kiss me. I want this feeling of mortification to go away, pronto. "Make it a double."

Chapter 16

The next morning, I'm jerked out of a dream—where, mysteriously, Jessica Simpson and I are best friends—by a shrill noise. What is it? What's going on?

I'm blind! I can't see anything!

No, wait. No, it's just that I'm wearing an eye mask. I push the mask away, sitting up quickly as I look for the source of the ringing, when I'm thrust supine again by spasming pains shooting across my forehead.

Oh my God, my head is killing me.

I glance at the clock. It's 2:00 p.m. Why did I sleep so late? Where am I?

Slowly, Bella, slowly. Let's piece this together. At least the noise has stopped.

A quick look around the room yields nothing. Am I in a museum? Why are there gilded chairs and gold mirrors everywhere?

I'm in a hotel. Some sort of fancy nightmare.

I peek at my nightstand for clues, careful not to move too much for fear of disturbing the fragile peace I've brokered with my throbbing head. Just as I suspected, there's a small notepad next to the lamp; it says Ritz Paris.

Ah. Yes. It's all coming back to me now.

I'm at the Ritz in Paris for the Face Group press trip. Oh, no—the press trip. If it's 2:00 p.m., I've doubtlessly missed several hours of organized meetings. Why am I so hungover? Oh, God, what did I do last night? Something about James is lurking at the fringes of my mind. This is not good.

I stare at the ceiling. Well, I obviously drank more than I should have last night. That much is clear. I summon all my powers of memory and form a fuzzy picture at the fringes of my mind: me, plastered, calling Nick in desperation and leaving a rambling message, then going to my window, throwing open the curtains overlooking the magnificent view, and weeping, forehead pressed against the glass.

People can be *so* melodramatic when they're drunk.

My brain cells have finally started working again; I realize that the ringing which jolted me out of my teen-queen reverie was, of course, my cell phone. I call to check my messages. Just one, from Nick.

"Where are you? Are you okay? I got a weird message from you on my phone last night. Are you drunk? Why were you awake so late? I bet you have nasty circles under your eyes now. I hope you brought the Nickel gel like I told you to. You'll never snare anybody if you're in sloppy, homeless-Bella-mode—" pause, *click,* long pause, another *click,* "Gotta go, it's Arabelle. We're back together! I think I'm in love. Don't forget the eye gel." *Click.*

The evening comes back to me in a sudden, horrific flash. I feel like I need a cigarette, and I don't even smoke.

By the time I finally drag myself downstairs, it's 3:15. I've taken a steaming hot shower and done my best to slap on makeup, but I still look like something the cat dragged in. I pile my hair into a wet bun and wear my largest sunglasses, hoping they'll cover as much of my blotchy, gray face as possible. The meeting with James and Ben from Face Group is scheduled for 5:30, so I have about two hours to sightsee. Oh God—James. I can't believe I threw myself at him.

When I get downstairs, however, I don't see anybody. I

pull a tattered copy of the itinerary out of my purse and re-alize that everybody is out and about on walking tours. I've completely missed out on the product presentation and have missed the group leaving for the tours, as well. Should I wait here for people to get back or just go off on my own? The thought of solitude is appealing; I don't want to see anybody after last night's fiasco. I hope I didn't say or do anything too embarrassing around the other editors.

I walk for fifteen minutes until I reach the Seine, then cross over onto the Left Bank, marveling for the hundredth time at the beauty of Paris. It's almost enough to soothe my feelings of mortification and make me feel better. Almost.

Strolling along the Boulevard St.-Germain, I decide to have a completely indulgent kind of afternoon. Screw it! I've already been bad today by sleeping in and accidentally ditching the presentations. Why not treat myself a little more? I pass by the Sonya Rykiel boutique and decide that I'm going to go inside and buy something. Forget Louis Vuitton—I can get that anywhere. I want something uniquely Parisian! Inside the shop, however, the prices give me pause. I don't have six hundred Euros to spend on a shirt. I could rationalize it away, but I'd just be fooling myself. There's self-indulgence, and then there's pure folly, after all. Instead, I settle on a small but lovely scarf.

A few doors down from the shop sits the Brasserie Lipp, a touristy spot popular with conservative politicians. I stop in and have a cup of coffee and a croissant, relaxing at one of the outdoor tables so I can watch the world pass by. As the buttery flavor passes over my lips, I realize just how famished I am. No wonder I got so drunk last night—I didn't eat dinner! My cheeks feel pink remembering my desperation. I completely lost all self-respect and threw myself—threw myself!—at my boss. Pathetic. I bury my head in my hands, feeling physically ill with regret.

I shouldn't be so hard on myself. Everybody makes mistakes. And I think we've established that James isn't going to fire me. Hell, he's so conservative, he's probably worried I'll sue him for sexual harassment, or something. Oh God. Could he sue *me* for sexual harassment? He wouldn't do that, right? Then everybody would think I'm some sort of horrible lecher who throws herself on unsuspecting, perfectly innocent men and who tries to seduce her boss on romantic cruises in Paris! The shame!

But, hold on a minute. He's not that innocent and you're not crazy—he *was* flirting with you. He held my hands against his chest for much longer than is appropriate in your average boss-employee relationship. He looked into my eyes. He murmured my name. If Frances had been on the cruise and I had tripped into her, I very much doubt that she would have clasped my hands to hers and gazed deeply at me for a full fifteen seconds. He was definitely into me.

But he stopped himself. I'm not stupid—I know the fact that he's my boss makes the whole thing . . . delicate. But not impossible. Why is he holding himself back? Why can't he admit that he likes me and allow himself to try? Am I that unlovable? Aren't I worth a shot? I am. I'm worth dozens of shots! I'm a catch, damn it!

I order another cup of coffee and lean back in my chair, watching the tourists walk by. One of my favorite games while abroad is Spot the American. Whether it's due to our sneakers, sporty clothing, shorts, or tendency to wear too much makeup, Americans stick out like a sore thumb in Europe. The whole notion that French women are inherently sexier and more stylish than Americans really riles me up, however. If Americans only drank coffee, smoked cigarettes, and ate enough to feed a baby hamster, we'd be stick-thin and able to wear quote-unquote chic clothing, too.

A larger-than-life middle-aged blonde walks by wearing

tan shorts, Reeboks, and a roomy blue polo shirt. She calls in an American accent to her young children running ahead of her, "Bobby! Jodie! If y'all don't stop this behavior, you can forget dessert tonight! And I mean it this time!" I watch her thoughtfully as she walks by and it strikes me that she's the exact reader *Womanly World* is reaching out to. She's very attractive, but her hair, her makeup, and her clothing are just *there*—they don't accent any of her positives. She has a friendly, adventurous look about her. I bet if we showed her the right makeup that fit into her family budget and hair tricks that didn't take away from her time with the children, she'd be more than willing to improve herself. This woman probably can't afford all of the stuff at Bloomingdale's or Macy's, but I bet she wouldn't care if her face cream came from a department store or the drugstore, as long as it had a pampering feel and worked. *Duh.* This is exactly what Frances has trying to get through my head for the past several months.

Suddenly, everything becomes crystal clear. My problem with James is exactly the same problem I've been having at *Womanly World* with my writing: we've both been trying to be things we're not. I'm not some stuck-up steel heiress who has millions of dollars and looks like Rebecca Romijn when I wake up in the morning. I'm a mess. My eyeliner smears. My hair gets frizzy. I can only afford expensive beauty products because I work in the industry. I guess, in a way, I *am* the *Womanly World* reader . . . just a few years younger. As for James, he insists on putting on this "Master of the Universe" front, but it just makes him seem like a robot and runs counter to who he really is. He's in a rock band, for the love of God! And I've seen him when he lets his hair down. He drops the stuffy language! He downs shots! He looks at me lustily! He really *is* a normal thirty-year-old guy. If he could just somehow stop being so concerned with what he *should* be and behave as who he really *is*, then maybe we'd have a shot. Or maybe he'd still reject me, and then I would have no excuse but to be completely and utterly mortified and go into hiding forever. Or become a freelance writer. Toss up.

Half an hour later, I'm walking along the dusty cobblestones on a narrow street near the Pantheon when I spy some of the editors and publishers about a hundred yards ahead of me, laughing and chatting loudly. I duck onto a side street, hoping to avoid them. They're walking in the opposite direction, but I don't want to take the chance that one of them happens to look behind and see me. Despite its beginning, today is lovely and I want to prolong it as long as possible.

I get back to the hotel with just enough time to change my clothes. My head has gone completely blank. I can't remember what James and I discussed a couple of days ago for the presentation. How will I be able to work with him again? My God—I actually *begged* him to kiss him. I'm still mortified.

When I head to the fourth floor and see him waiting by the elevators, he looks miserable. "Bella—"

"Hey," I say casually. "How are you?"

"Fine," he says, looking distracted. "Can we talk for a second?"

I put my hand up. "James, listen, let me just get this over with. I'm really sorry about last night. I was *completely* drunk. I barely remember what I said or did, but I know that it was beyond inappropriate."

He blinks, looking surprised. "Oh. Well . . . it wasn't completely your fault. I apologize for my behavior. You're right that I, *um,* perhaps, let my guard down in a matter that was not befitting an employer. I just want to make sure you're . . . okay?"

"Okay? *Oh,* I see. No, no." I laugh loudly, waving my hand dismissively. "James, I was seriously wasted. No offense."

"Sure. Of course," he says quickly. "Good, no offense taken. I'm just glad we cleared everything up."

"Let's get this thing done," I say, motioning to the hotel door where Ben is waiting. We knock and Ben calls that the door is open.

"James, Bella, hello," says Ben, standing up from a chair in his sitting room and striding forward. "I know a Saturday afternoon isn't the most opportune time for a big meeting like this, so thanks for coming."

"No, thank you," I say. "We know you're busy. We'll be quick."

"Don't want to rush you," he laughs, "but that's always good to hear." He motions to the coffee table in front of his chair. "Please. Why don't you set up here?"

"I don't have any materials," I say simply. I decided on the way to the elevator that Face doesn't need to hear more BS. They already have their minds made up about where the ad dollars are going next year—that is to say, not with us, however much James wants to delude himself—so why waste the time? I'm going to try a new tactic, and I don't care if it makes James upset or not. "You've already seen all of our charts and figures. You obviously know the magazine. I think we should cut to the chase."

James looks stunned and holds up the portfolios in his arms. "*I* have some materials here," he begins, but I cut him off.

"I don't think it'll be necessary. Listen, Ben. The reality is this—" I gesture to the chair. "Can we sit?"

"Sure," he says.

"Thanks. Okay, so, the reality is this. Face Group is the most important advertiser in the business. *Womanly World* is the oldest and most highly respected women's magazine in America. It seems like it would be a natural fit, but you're more likely than not hesitant because our readers are older."

James opens his mouth to protest, but I keep talking. "We don't have fifteen million teenagers reading us. We have fifteen million moms, with some grandmothers, and, yes, some twentysomethings thrown in. But we both know that you're pulling your advertising with us. Am I right?"

Ben looks bemused. "If we're being frank . . . yes. Our strategy for the upcoming year is to start advertising in magazines that skew slightly younger." James looks stunned by this revelation.

"Exactly. So, I could sit here and waste twenty minutes of your time on charts and graphs explaining what we both already know, since you've been an advertiser for years, or I could cut to the chase and explain why you *should* stay with us—no BS."

"Okay," he smiles warily. "Why not?"

"I came from *Enchanté,* which you probably know. So, I have a pretty good idea of the type of demographic you think you want. You're looking for a woman in her late twenties or early thirties, who has the money to spend on your products, but who you can hook young and retain as a customer for life. She doesn't want a hundred-dollar face cream, and frankly, she doesn't have the money for that. But she's not interested in drugstore products, either. Her beauty regimen is her luxury, so she's willing to spend money on products that work. But by pulling your advertising and going exclusively with magazines like *Glamour, Chic* and *Enchanté,* you're completely cutting yourself off from the woman you *should* be wooing, which is our reader."

He nods, as if to say, "Go on."

"Our readers are your natural customers. The girls who read *Chic*—they're simply too young for you. Those magazines claim to be for twentysomethings, but it's all high school girls with after-school jobs and no cash. You can pump your millions into their magazine all you want, but at the end of the day, the ones who can afford more than drugstore products are only going to be buying stuff like Dewy and Tarte and the niche brands. When they do have money to blow, they're going to spend it on Chanel or Dior, not Face. I *am* a

late-twentysomething girl—I know. It's just the way it goes.
You know when they're going to start buying your cosmetics
and skin care? When they're in their thirties . . . after they
stop reading *Chic* and have moved onto *Womanly World*."
Ben smiles and I shrug my shoulders. "It's true! You have a
chance to advertise with the women who would actually buy
the products and sway them away from developing loyalty to,
say, Edison or Estée Lauder, who are your biggest competitors, and who *do* still advertise with us."

Ben raises an eyebrow and looks at James. "I must say, this is
the most unconventional ad sales call I've ever experienced."

James puts his hands up and shakes his head. "Ben, I'm
very sorry. I had no ide—"

"Well, wait a second. Let her continue. I'm finding this
interesting."

I ignore the surprised look that James gives me and press
on. "When I started with *Womanly World,* I thought it was
completely beneath me, and I couldn't find my voice at the
magazine. What I realized, though, was that I had been
trying too hard at *Enchanté* to be something I wasn't. It took
a while to get over this mentality. I think I'm only just realizing it now. *Womanly World*'s strength is in the fact that we're
not cool. We're practically dowdy, to be honest. And Face is
the same, by the way, like it or not. But *Womanly World* tells
it like it is, and we know what our readers want, and need,
to hear. We give it to them. As a result, they know they can
trust us and that we're never going to steer them wrong. I
could give you lots of numbers and figures about how, when
we speak, our readers listen and buy in droves—and it's all
true. That's probably what you'd be interested in, since it's
a "bottom line" thing. But at the end of the day, what we
have over our competitors is credibility and consistency. We
don't change with the trends. We stick to our message that
value and quality never go out of style; if it's expensive, but

it's the best, we'll feature it. If it's cheap, and it's the best, we'll feature it, too. But we'll never put a product in our magazine to kowtow to advertisers, or just because it happens to be the item of the season. So, when *Womanly World* readers see Face in the magazine—either in the advertisements or on our actual pages—they know that it's quality. They know that it's a brand that's in line with their values, because no matter how you try to spin it to woo younger girls, Face stands for the same thing: value and quality. Our readers will buy your products for their daughters as their first makeup or skincare purchase. And then they, and their families, will use it for their entire lives. That's the beauty of shunning the trends; if you're just seeking what's new and young and cool and hip— that stuff goes out of style. But *Womanly World,* and Face, and quality, and consistency: it's always worthy."

My improptu speech finished, I sit back in my chair, out of breath. James's eyes look ready to pop out of his head. Ben clears his throat. "My, my. That was . . . impressive."

"I don't mean to be rude, or flippant, Ben, but I just figured—you know, here's a guy who has smoke-and-mirrors presentations crammed down his throat all day long. For once, maybe you'd actually like to hear the truth. I meant every word of it. And I really do think it would be pure folly to pull your advertising just because our readers are older."

"It certainly sounds like it," he says, smiling hesitantly and then looking at his watch. "It's nearly time for the group to leave for the Eiffel Tower. Do you two . . . have anything else to say . . . ?"

James stands up. "I think Bella has pretty much covered it." The tone of his voice makes clear that he'd actually like to substitute the word "covered" for "ruined."

"Great. Unconventional . . . but nicely done. I'll speak with my team and get back to you next week. See you in a few minutes downstairs?"

"Of course," James says smoothly, heading to the door and holding it open for me.

Once we're in the hallway and safely out of earshot of Ben's room, James turns to me. "What the hell was that?"

"What?"

"You just completely disregarded everything we worked on."

"I thought it was a better tactic."

"A better tactic? Bella, Face is a multi-million-dollar account. The future of our magazine could well depend on their business. Do you realize what you just did? You completely blew it."

"I didn't blow it. They were going to pull the advertising and put it in a hipper magazine like *Chic* or *Flash,* anyway. Why do you think Ben was meeting with us alone? They couldn't care less. I may well have just *saved* it."

He groans in frustration and puts his hands to his head. "I should have you fired for this. *I* am in charge of the presentations. You cannot pull a stunt like that."

I glare at him, folding my arms. "What's the worst that can happen?" I know I'm being pigheaded, but I'm convinced I'm right.

"Wha—? The worst that can happen is we lose the business. And when Face pulls their advertising, other companies follow suit. And then our ad pages continue to plummet, and eventually we have to shutter the magazine. It's not unrealistic. It happens all the time. This business is incredibly volatile. I shouldn't have to tell you that."

"First of all, there's no way in hell Face was going to advertise with us based on your boring, safe presentation. They were almost certainly going to pull their advertising. At least now maybe we have a shot. And do you really care? You hate it there. I can tell you can't stand your job."

"That's ridiculous."

"I don't think so. When was the last time you did something you *wanted* to do, instead of what you were expected to do? I looked you up online recently. You did go to Harvard—but for your MBA. You actually went to Central Saint Martins in London as an undergrad so you could study film and music."

He looks at me in disbelief but doesn't say anything, so I press on. "You're terrified what your family will do if you leave the magazine that your grandmother founded, but by staying, you're killing yourself. Maybe not physically," I shrug, "but emotionally. I've never met an older, unhappier thirty-year-old in my life. Screw the magazine. Take a good look at yourself."

He looks at his watch. "I don't have time for this conversation. We're running late for the dinner."

"Fine, whatever." I throw my hands in the air in frustration. "Later," I say, stepping into the elevator and watching the doors close as he stands there, alone, his posture rigid and his face angry.

The Jules Verne restaurant on the second floor of the Eiffel Tower has spectacular views of Paris, lights blazing, but I'm too grumpy to notice or care. I'm replaying my last conversation with James in my head over and over, convinced I was right. If we had played it safe, we'd be kissing the Face business good-bye.

I'm leaning on the railing, trying to make out Sacré Coeur in the distance, when James appears by my side.

"Hi," he says quietly. "Can we talk?"

"I don't think that's a good idea."

"Come on, Bella. I've been thinking about what you said."

This gets my attention. I turn away from the railing to face him. "And?"

"And . . . you're right. I *am* wrapped up in doing what's expected of me. But I don't know any other way to live."

"You can't have always been like that. Didn't you ever rebel? Do something your parents absolutely forbade you to do?"

"Going to Central Saint Martins pissed them off," he offers.

"Then what? How do you go from studying the arts to getting a Harvard MBA?"

"Dad went to Harvard," he says quietly. "When my grandmother died, he was upset and he threatened to cut me off if I didn't make something of my life. He made it clear that I had to join the family business and follow in his footsteps, or else. My family is very conservative and my younger brother is the wild one—which doesn't seem to bother anybody, for some screwed-up reason. But me . . . I have to set the example."

"Your dad's not here anymore," I gently point out. "Making yourself miserable to honor his memory, or whatever you're trying to do, isn't going to bring him back. Surely he'd want you to be happy? *Are* you happy?"

He looks pensive. "I don't know. I guess."

"That's convincing. Come on!" I say, grabbing him by the shoulders. "You're still young! Life is too short. *You* could die tomorrow! Do you want to spend your last moments on earth doing something you don't love, which doesn't make you feel fulfilled? I mean, what do you have? A fancy title, a heavy wallet, and that's about it. You're not married, you broke up with your fiancée, you don't have any children, and you hate your job. Fun life, James."

He looks hurt. "I . . ."

I look at him expectantly. "Yes?"

"My family wanted me to marry Elizabeth. And I didn't. It's the one thing I ever stood up to my parents about. They weren't thrilled by Central Saint Martins, but at least it's a great school, and they figured it was a phase, anyway. But Elizabeth . . . her parents were old family friends, we'd known each other for years, it was a good match. It was just expected. But it wasn't right."

"Your life could use more decisions like that. Go after what you want. Don't let anything stand in your way!" I'm warming up to my own speech. Maybe I should become a motivational speaker. I think I'm pretty good at this! "Life is about passion," I continue, thinking of Emily and her willingness to grab life by the horns. "You have to live it with your arms wide open. Be honest with yourself about what you want and need. Why don't you worry less about what's appropriate, and stop trying to please everybody? The fact is you can't live by other people's rules. Believe me, I've tried. It doesn't work."

"I'm falling in love with you," he says simply.

My heart skips a beat.

"What?" I whisper.

"You heard me." His chest is rising and falling heavily. He looks scared. "I can't get you out of my head. Last night, I wanted to kiss you. Being close to you is torture. And I don't know if you feel the same way about me. I don't see how you could—sometimes it seems like you literally hate me. But I think about you constantly. And it doesn't matter, because even if you *did* feel the same, I can't be with you."

"What? Why?"

"You know why. Beckwith has a policy against employees dating each other."

I didn't know. "But . . . but . . . that's ridiculous!"

He shrugs. "It's the way it is."

"Then why did you bother telling me?"

He looks pained. "I shouldn't have. Forget I said it. I'm your boss. It wasn't appropriate."

"Who gives a shit about what's appropriate?" I explode. "You can't do that! You can't tell a girl you're falling in love with her and then take it back!"

"I'm sorry," he says, looking pained.

"No, I'm sorry," I say furiously. My eyes fill with angry, hurt tears. "I'm not going to chase you, James. I deserve more than that. I deserve somebody who tells me they're in love with me and *means* it."

"I do mea—"

"Stop!" I say, holding my hand up. "It's not fair. You can't say that, and then tell me it's never going to work. Either you want me or you don't. Figure it out. But don't want me just because you can't have me." I walk away looking around wildly, my eyes blurred with hot tears. The whole of Paris stretches out in front of me, but all I see is a hazy, dark, twinkly mist.

The next day, I spend the entire plane ride back to New York getting a head start on next month's column for *Womanly World*. I'm taking my own advice—not to mention a cue from my last column, which seemed to be on the right track—and am trying to be completely true to myself, writing in a conspiratorial tone about a styling mishap with a flatiron, and explaining how to easily—and properly—heat style your own hair at home. Gone is the haughty tone I had with my *Enchanté* columns. No more boring topics. No more talking down to the reader.

I don't look at James once during the flight.

I hand my column back to Frances first thing upon returning to the office.

"Thanks," she says, setting it on her desk. "How was Paris?"

"Oh, it was fine," I say dismissively. "Some great new products from Face that we can go over whenever you'd like. Our readers will love them. But do you have a second to take a quick glance at this now?"

Frances eyes me curiously and then picks up the printout. "What's this?"

"It's next month's column. I felt inspired."

She motions for me to sit. I wait nervously while she reads it, glancing at her face every few seconds for signs of like or dislike.

When she's done reading it, she looks up at me and says, "Well done. Very well done. The tone is perfect."

I let out a sign of relief. "Thank goodness."

She picks up the paper again, her eyes quickly scanning the sheet. "Last month's was good; this is better. I'm pleased." She smiles.

The next month is a dream. Frances talks easily with me in her office following product meetings, green-lights ideas and sends back memos with hardly any corrections. One day, she even *calls in sick for work,* asking me to inform Rania that she's taking a personal day and assuring me that I'll be able to handle anything that comes up. It's as if Frances's body has been snatched and replaced by chill, groovy hippie aliens.

About three weeks following the press trip, I see James for the first time when he gets on an elevator I'm already in. Being so close to him after weeks of no interaction makes my stomach lurch and my heart begin pounding.

"Hi," he says tentatively.

"Hi, back." I lick my lips nervously and peer at him sideways through my lashes, quickly looking back at the elevators doors as his head swivels toward me. I don't know whether I should will the elevator to go faster or slower.

"I was going to call you," he says.

"Oh?" I look at him sharply.

"Yes. We, *uh,* just got news today. Face is not only renewing their advertising with us, but increasing their buy by ten percent. I can't claim any responsibility for that. It's thanks to you."

"Oh," I say disappointedly. "That's great." I was hoping James meant he was calling me about *us.* But . . . what would he possibly say? We work together, and he's a whore for the rules. End of story.

"I know."

We ride in silence down to the lobby, my mind racing at a million miles a minute. What would James do if I simply threw him against the wall and kissed him? Would he finally kiss me back? Push me away in disgust at my impropriety? Shriek like a little girl and run screaming through the lobby?

The doors open and I step out, James following me. Impulsively, I turn back to him, not quite sure of what to say but instinctively wanting to prolong our interaction, and he runs into me. A thrill of lust travels up my spine as our fingers accidentally brush and we stand face-to-face in the elevator bank, our eyes trained on each other. I have to remind myself to breathe.

"Why, hello, you two!" It's Rania, walking purposefully toward the elevators, carrying a massive Hermès Birkin. The two of us immediately step back from each other and turn toward Rania. "Bella, James told me the good news this morning!"

"Yes!' I clear my throat. "He just told me himself! Very exciting."

"It's more than exciting. It secures the future of the magazine for at least another year. I agree with James; you're the best thing that's happened to *Womanly World* in a very long time."

"Really?" I look sideward at James, who is fiddling with his tie. "What a nice compliment."

"I meant it," he says brusquely. "Have to dash. Meeting in fifteen minutes downtown and I'm late."

He hurries away and Rania looks at me curiously, eyebrow raised and a smile playing on her lips. "You're certainly under his skin."

"What?" I ask quickly. "What do you mean?"

She doesn't respond, stepping into the elevator, and chuckling to herself as the doors close.

"It's so Romeo and Juliet," sighs Joss, dipping a carrot stick in a jar of ranch dressing and chomping loudly. Nick sits on the couch sipping a Jack and Coke and looks over at us, frowning.

"It's not Romeo and Juliet. It's just stupid. You like him; he likes you. So, what's the big problem?"

"Allow me to explain," Emily interrupts, sprawled on the floor with designer lookbooks and notepads surrounding her. She's finally thrown in the towel on her would-be psychology career, taking a leave of absence for the fall semester to instead focus on "dressing" Gabrielle and establishing a name for herself as a stylist. "Bella, you see, has too much self-respect to throw herself at a man who can't demonstrate a willingness to be with her." Her tone is loud and pointed. I blush at Emily's choice of words, remembering that I did, actually, throw myself at James in Paris. Details. "She's also not going to quit her job, obviously. So, she and James have to work together peacefully until one of them moves on—either to a new job or a new person—or until Bella breaks him down and makes him see the sense in sleeping with her."

"Emily!" I exclaim.

"Well, in a nutshell," she says, shrugging.

"What if you *tricked* him into sleeping with you?" Nick asks helpfully. "Or maybe you show up at one of his gigs and get him drunk, then pretend you lost your house key, so you have to stay at his house—"

"You disgust me," Emily says. "How you get women is beyond me."

"Why don't you tell me?" he shoots back.

She buries her head in her notebook and shakes her head, huffing, "In your dreams."

"You don't know the half of it," he drawls.

As Joss loudly crunches on a carrot stick, I eye the two of them suspiciously. Emily and Nick? Never. They must be joking.

It's the middle of September when Frances drops a bombshell. We're in her office, having just finished sorting through products for the December gift guide (who can focus on Christmas when it's only September?) and Megan has carted a bin of products to her desk to begin calling in prices. "I have some news, Bella," Frances says. "I'm leaving *Womanly World*."

"Frances! No!"

"It's time. I've been here too long and I'm out of touch with the readers."

"What are you talking about? You know these readers like the back of your hand. I would never have been able to get in the right mindset if it weren't for you."

"You're doing just fine. Each column you've submitted has been better than the last, and Rania was thrilled with your most recent memo, as I'm sure you know. You can still improve, of course, but there's nothing here for me to teach you."

"Who will take your place?" Please don't say Delilah. Anybody but Delilah.

"Well . . . I'd planned on suggesting you for the job. If you want it." She looks at me as though I'd be crazy to turn it down—which I would.

"Frances—I don't know what to say. I'm stunned."

"You don't need me to hold your hand. I've been in the industry for over thirty-five years, I'm tired, and my husband thinks we should travel. Says I've become too serious." She cracks a small, wry smile.

"Never," I say feebly, attempting a joke.

Frances picks up a bottle of the Neutrogena hand cream next to her computer and absentmindedly rubs it into her cuticles. "I'll stay for another three weeks, to help ease your transition. Rania has great confidence in your abilities, however, and she'll be here after I leave, of course, if you feel you are stumbling." She regards me, chin aloft, raising an eyebrow inquisitively. "What do you think?"

"I think . . ." I take a deep breath, remembering the day I was fired from *Enchanté,* when it seemed my world was crumbling around me. Fast-forward less than a year: beauty director at twenty-eight years old? Unheard of. "I'm honored. And for once . . . I think I'm ready."

Chapter 17

Three months later, as part of my new Monday morning routine, I open up the e-mail in-box attached to "Ask Bella," planning on answering a few questions and printing out e-mails to use as ideas for future columns. My in-box is flooded, mostly with subject lines like:

"I love the new issue!"
"So funny!"
"New issue rocks!"
"Your column is great!"
"Love your page!"

I click through a few of them. Judging by these gushing e-mails, the readers hands down loved my page! This is so exciting!

One of the e-mails reads as follows:

Hi, Bella! I LOVE the new column!! I was cracking up reading about what happened to your hair! It sounds like something I would do! Anyhow, my question is about wrinkles. I'm doing my best to prevent those dreaded fine lines (I'm 33) and wonder what the best creams and serums are that I should be using. I can't afford expensive stuff, so maybe something under $20, please? If that exists? Is there anything you recommend? Thanks so much!

Pam, Bakersfield, CA

Another e-mail says

Bella, Your page is so funny, it's my favorite in the magazine! You don't take yourself so seriously but you still give really good beauty tips. So, thanks! If you have time, I have a quick question: what's the difference between a ceramic flatiron and a regular one? Is it worth the extra money? I read some article last month in another magazine about ceramic products being better for the hair, but it didn't explain why, and my husband would get angry with me for spending $200 on one! Thanks! Can't wait to read the next issue!

Jenna L. from Des Moines

Still another reads

Dear Bella,

Help! What on earth is a peptide?? I keep reading all about how I'm supposed to be using them in my skin creams, but I have very sensitive skin and a little bit of adult acne (I went to one dermatologist who diagnosed me as having rosacea, but another dermatologist told me I didn't have it, so I'm confused), and I'm worried about peptides irritating my skin or making it break out. Are retinols better? What really is a retinol, anyway? Or an antioxidant, for that matter? When did beauty get so confusing? It's like I'm back in high school chemistry! Any help would be so, so appreciated. Thanks!

Cindy, Scranton, Pennsylvania

Several months ago, I would have been impressed by the questions—I hadn't realized the women of America even knew to *ask* about peptides and retinols and ceramic flatirons—but now it's par for the course. Since Frances left, the readers and I have embarked on a full-out mutual love affair, and I feel fulfilled with my job in a way that I only could have dreamed about at *Enchanté*. The job success is even enough to keep me from thinking about James.

Well, almost.

It's an old New York City adage that you'll never simultaneously achieve the triumvirate of happiness in your apartment, career, and love life; at least one of the three big factors will always be out of whack. My house situation is aces—not only do I have a great West Village apartment, but I've got Emily, whose career as a stylist is taking off at lightning speed—and my career is progressing beyond my wildest dreams. All the other important things, like my health and my finances, are in check, too, and of course, I have my family, which might soon be expanding. Only a few weeks after Susan and Walter returned from their honeymoon, my mother called me to report that Susan had put on some weight and shunned alcohol. She'd never say anything—even to me—before the three-month mark, so we're all waiting with baited breath. Aunt Bella! It has a nice ring to it.

So why do I still feel like there's something missing? After all, as Suze so pointedly mentioned before her wedding, and as I discovered with Tristan, it's better to be on your own than with the wrong person. I'm happy with me. I like me! Me is good! Women are strong, damn it, and I don't need a man, and I don't even know if I believe in marriage, and I'm *pretty sure* that I don't want kids.

All of these realizations and affirmations only make me feel weaker—like I'm letting womankind down—because I have to admit that I think about James every day.

I don't think it's about simply wanting a boyfriend, or needing security, or not wanting to be alone. It's a case of finding that right person for you and not feeling complete without them.

Oh, well. Two out of three ain't bad, right?

Look on the bright side, I tell myself. Just yesterday, there was a front-page article in *Ad Weekly* about how *Womanly World*'s pages have been up 25 percent from last quarter—the *only* woman's magazine in the industry to post a gain, with several companies following the Face Group's lead and increasing their ad buy. The article included a small blurb about how the gain was due in large part to *Womanly World*'s "impressively revamped" beauty pages. *Hey, that's me!* I thought.

I spend an hour and a half reading through, printing out, and responding to e-mails, placing copies of the best questions in a folder next to my desk. I'm going to propose a monthly question and answer page to Rania, so all the readers can benefit from my responses, not just the ones who write in. Another idea struck me last night while I was scrolling through Jezebel to catch up on my online gossip. What about a beauty blog? It seemed silly at the time, considering that our readers aren't of the Facebook generation, but reading the scores of e-mails I received just today, I think it's a solid idea. If *Womanly World* set up some sort of online beauty page, I could post daily questions, tips, and product suggestions. Most of the other women's magazines have recently started beauty blogs, and it's time for us to follow suit. It would be a great way to reward our readers with fresh content, plus it would prove to our advertisers that we *are* hip (kind of) and are doing our best to draw in a younger demographic.

Who knew? I'm actually enjoying my job!

One day, my phone rings as I'm absentmindedly eating a salad from Hale and Hearty Soups and scribbling a list of products to have Megan call in for a story.

"Hello?"

"Darling! It's Riss! How *are* you?"

"Larissa! It's good to hear from you. I'm fine, thanks. Actually, I've never been better."

"Really? Is it a man?"

"No, it's not a man. It's the job—everything is finally falling into place. Rania likes my writing, I'm happy with my column, the readers are eating it up, our ad pages are going through the roof. It's fantastic!"

"*Mmm*. That's nice. But, surely, you miss the glamour of a magazine like *Enchanté*?"

I pause, reflecting on how I feel. "I do miss some of the perks, like invites to all the exclusive press trips and sample sales, and the really sick gifts. But the reception from these readers is like nothing I've experienced in my life. I'm making a difference for them. They actually *care* about what I have to say!"

"*Uh-huh,*" she says doubtfully. "Well . . . good for you, I suppose."

"You sound weird. What's up?"

"Well . . . ," she says, and sighs heavily. "It's just that I was calling to offer you your old job back. But, you know, if you're so happy at *Womanly World* and all . . ."

"What?" I shriek. "Are you kidding me? Why? What happened to Delilah?"

"Fired. *So* fired. Not only did that skanky bitch hit on Gene at the *Enchanté* Christmas party last week—"

"Wait, who's Gene?" I interrupt.

"My fiancé. He's divine! Oh, that reminds me, I need to have Julie send you an invitation to the wedding."

"You're getting married to Gene? I thought you were engaged to some guy named Maurice. Love of your life? Don't you remember? Jessica Simpson was going to sing at the reception?"

"*Maurice*? Oh, honey, no no no. We broke up *ages* ago. Jessica's still booked, of course, but it'll just be a different groom! Anyhow, what was I saying? Oh, right, Delilah. So, there she is, being a total whore and hitting on Gene while she thinks I'm outside, and I pulled her away from him and told her, 'You'd better watch it, trashy, because not only is your writing so terrible that even Katharine is hating it, but don't think for a second that I forgot what you did to Bella.' Katharine was basically looking for a reason to fire her, anyway—*finally*. So, on Monday, Julie's working late and she walks into the fashion closet, and she catches Delilah stuffing her bag with diamond earrings and necklaces from our last ice queen photo shoot. I mean, can you imagine? How tacky! So, long story long, we fired her." I can practically hear her smiling through the phone. "The office energy is *so* much better now that she's gone. But we need to hire somebody to take her place, obviously, and I thought, 'Who better than my favorite little editor ever?!' That's you, of course. I know you're a beauty director now, but it's at *Womanly World*. Being an editor at *Enchanté* is so much more powerful, as you remember. Plus, I might not be here forever, and then you'll get my job—maybe sooner than you think! The budget is a teensy bit tight, so we couldn't offer you a *ton* more than you're making now. I'd say about ten thou more. I mean, room to negotiate, obviously, but give or take. You know."

"I don't know what to say."

"I knew you'd be thrilled! So, listen, if I were you, I wouldn't say anything to Rania until after you meet with HR here. It's just a formality, but you know how silly Bonneau-Martray is about all their red tape, and because it's only been about a year since you left, I'll have to pull strings to get you back on board. Katharine is so desperate for a good writer, though, I know she'll let me have you back. I mean, they're *my* pages anyway. Plus, it's sort of a good PR move for the magazine, don't you think? It makes us look really charitable, like, you know, forgive and forget, live and let live. All that."

"But, Larissa . . . ," I swallow, unable to believe I'm actually saying this, "I'm not one hundred percent sure that I want to come back."

"What? Are you crazy, child? Of course you do! You were just telling me how horrible *Womanly World* is and how you never get invited to anything and about how ghastly all your presents are. Don't you remember how worshipped you were here? The voice in your column was fab! Everybody loved it! You were one of the most popular girls in the industry!"

"Thanks, Riss. But . . . at the risk of sounding like a cheeseball, I feel like I *belong* here. The people here are so nice, Rania actually listens to my ideas, the readers are loving my column—"

"Does this have to do with your hot publisher that Delilah was yammering on about?"

"What? James? No."

"Are you *sure*?" she asks doubtfully. "Because if you're giving up on the most fantastic opportunity of your life because of a guy, I will murder you. I mean it. You're smarter than that."

"It's not like that—"

"The hell it's not like that! Do you know how many times I've seen smart girls turn their backs on their careers because of their boyfriend or husband? Do you think *he* would give you the same courtesy? He'd accept the new offer in a heartbeat, then come home that night and inform you—not ask you, but inform you!—about how he's made a life-changing decision without consulting you. Why? Because that's the way it should be. You need to live for you! Not for anybody else! Do what makes *you* happy!"

"Larissa," I explain patiently, "James has absolutely nothing to do with it. We've barely spoken in months. He declared his love for me on the Paris press trip, then told me it could never work because there's a company policy against it. If I wanted to be with him, it would actually make *sense* for me to come back to *Enchanté*. I just . . . he's not a factor, at all. In the slightest."

She's silent.

"Riss?"

"Just think about it," she says finally. "Please? I understand that you think you're happy there, but consider what it will do for your career staying at *Womanly World*. Here, you were in the spotlight. People who *matter* were reading your column. There, it's just housewives and dental hygienists."

"You're wrong! I mean, it is housewives and dental hygienists, but it's also teachers and entrepreneurs and young moms and old moms, and, and . . . everybody! This magazine is huge, Larissa. It has quantity as far as readers go, but it has *quality*, too. These people care about the magazine. It's not just some rag that they read and then throw away."

"*Enchanté* is not a *rag*!" She sounds horrified.

"That's not what I'm saying. What I mean is, these women archive our issues, and then save them for their daughters. They collect our beauty articles and take them to the drugstore with them. They look to us—to me!—for guidance. It's a huge responsibility. I can't help it. It makes me feel really proud."

"God, you've been totally brainwashed," she says, and sighs. "Fine, it's a fabulous magazine, everything about it is fabulous, the readers are all fabulous. But, you know, you could make a difference here, too. Maybe you could make it more democratic, inject a little heartland into it or something? I don't know, whatever. I need you, Bella! And, don't forget, I'm not going to be here forever, either. After Gene and I get married, well . . . who knows if I'll even be working."

"Didn't you just spend five minutes lecturing me about women giving up their careers for their husbands?"

"Well, that doesn't apply to *me*, love. I've already made my mark! I'm a legend in the industry! What else can I do here? It's like Marilyn Monroe—you quit while you're ahead, and then people love you forever!"

"She didn't quit while she was ahead, she died of a suspicious drug overdose. When her career was on the way down," I point out. "And, are you honestly comparing yourself to Marilyn Monroe?"

"Whatever. The point is, Gene is fabulously wealthy, and if I decide to leave my career to be a full-time shopper and citizen of the world, that's my *choice*." She giggles. "If you don't take the job, you're mad. But even if you go temporarily insane and decide to stay there—*blech*—maybe we'll still work together again, sooner or later," she says cryptically. "Sooner, I hope. Just promise me you'll think it over."

"I promise."

Her tone becomes serious again. "You have to let me know by the end of the week. HR is already sending me résumés—you wouldn't *believe* how ghastly they are—Katharine wants to hire somebody immediately, we have to start preparing for the spring shows. I can't wait around forever."

"By the end of the week," I echo.

"Good," she says. "I can't wait to have you back!" In Larissa's mind, it's already a done deal. Maybe I *should* go back. Isn't this what I wanted for months? And I know Larissa is all over the map, but what if she actually does leave the magazine . . . and then they promote me to beauty director? Beauty director of *Enchanté*? It would be, literally, a dream come true. But I'm happy here. I never, ever thought I'd feel this way . . . but I have a sense of belonging. I'm home.

Chapter 18

I spend a few days wondering if I'm making a mistake by staying at *Womanly World* before finally deciding that I need to trust my gut. I was never truly happy at *Enchanté*. I don't care if it's an ostensibly better and cooler magazine, and I ignore the fact that, at least technically, leaving would mean that James and I could finally give ourselves a chance. *Screw him*, I think. I've obviously been taken in by years of chick flicks, but somehow I feel that, if he truly wanted us to be together, he'd find a way. He's the freaking grandson of the magazine's founder! Couldn't he bribe people to change the rules, or something? Well, what's done is done. I told Larissa that I was staying at *Womanly World*, and she ended up hiring Sam from *American Woman* on my recommendation.

And today, things are getting really interesting.

I walk into the office to find my in-box flooded with e-mails, all referencing some item about me on Page Six. *Again*, I think? But I haven't *done* anything! I spent the two weeks of my Christmas and New Year's vacation at home in Cleveland with my parents, Walter, and an increasingly pregnant Suze (they're having a girl!), feeling simultaneously both five years younger, and, for the first time in my life, like an adult. (I'll admit the word still makes me shudder . . . but I'm coming to terms with it.) I race to the art department and grab a copy of the *Post* from the communal newspaper rack.

"Is it true?" asks Sy Jones, the art assistant.

"Huh?" I'm busy flipping through the *Post*, looking for the item. Suddenly, I spot it: on the top left-hand side of the page—primo real estate. It must be a slow news day.

Bella of the Ball

Nearly a year after getting fired from top magazine **Enchanté**, beauty writer **Bella Hunter** is reportedly taking a lucrative consulting gig at the **Face Group** as the head of their new beauty brand, working underneath former boss Larissa Lincoln, whose hiring was formally announced yesterday. Word is that Face honchos were impressed with Hunter's work at **Womanly World**, where she's credited with single-handedly revamping their beauty pages and pushing the magazine's ad sales revenues through the roof. Face executives are champing at the bit to award a six-figure contract to Hunter, who one exec, speaking on the condition of anonymity, declares as beauty's "golden girl."

"What?" I whisper in confusion. I have *no* idea what this item is referencing.

Sy's looking at me with interest. "That's bizarre. You don't know? You haven't been talking to Face Group people?"

I shake my head. "No clue." But I know who will.

"Surprise!" Larissa chirps over the phone.

"Are you *insane*?" I demand, clutching the phone in my office with the door closed so nobody can overhear me. "What is this? And why didn't you tell me you were leaving *Enchanté*?"

"Honey, I did tell you. It's not my fault if you can't read between the lines."

"Larissa, you can't just announce in the newspapers that I'm taking a job I know nothing about! What about *Womanly World*? What about Rania? I could be fired for this!"

"Oh God, could you be more *melodramatic*? *Womanly World* won't fire you—they'll be thrilled! It's not like you have

to quit your job; it's just a consulting thing. It's great publicity for them, trust me. I know Rania. And are you telling me
you *don't* want to make millions of dollars with the biggest
company in beauty and set your career for life? 'Cause I can
easily hire somebody else . . ."

"Let's not be hasty," I mutter. "I didn't say I didn't want it."

"There's my girl! Okay, so you'll sign the papers, *blah-di-
blah,* all that boring stuff, then we'll get started! Julie's coming
over with me, and we'll need to hire a derm and a makeup
artist, then we need to start brainstorming about everything.
So, I was thinking something very high end, but for the mass
market. What would make women really *love* it? Of course,
it'll be popular. Everything Face does turns to gold. But it has
to be iconic. It has to be the kind of brand that women *must*
use because they adore it. Fifty years from now, girls will still
be buying it; grandmothers will still be using it; mothers will
be recommending it to their daughters. It has to be epic, for
all ages, all women. You know, a—"

"*Whoa.* Slow down. It's not that easy."

"Bella, you are so literal and linear sometimes. Yes. It is.
I'm offering you the job. Do you accept or not?"

"Yes, but—"

"Done! It's that easy! I know you. I trust you. More important, I know where you live, and I'll tell Gene to have one
of his people take out a contract on you if you steal my concepts and go to another beauty company behind my back,"
she cackles, adding, "Only kidding, of course."

"Of course. But . . . what would I do for you exactly? I don't
know anything about the business end of cosmetics and skin
care."

"What, like I do?" she cracks. "Doll face, it's not going to
be you and me sitting in a room dreaming up a brand and
doing spreadsheets. We have the entire Face Group behind
us! When you combine your experience at *Womanly World*

with the masses, plus your *Enchanté* background—and my intuitive beauty genius—we're golden!"

"But I don't have any brand experience. I don't have a marketing background. What if I screw up the whole thing? What if my ideas are terrible and I drive it into the ground?"

"Then I'll fire you again." I can hear her shrugging through the phone. "And you've already been there, done that—plus you have a day job with that *Womanly World*—" she says it like a disease "—so what's the harm in it happening twice?"

"I'm serious."

"So am I. You're perfect for this and you know it. Why should we hire some marketing slave who only knows bottom lines and number crunching and focus groups? Our buyers are your reader. Think about it—everything you learned at *Enchanté*, everything you're learning at *Womanly World,* it'll all come together. Plus you know me, so you'll be able to work with me without immediately quitting because you think I'm a diva—"

"No promises on that one," I say, warming to the idea.

"And you're only a consultant, so it won't consume your life. Well, not completely, anyway. Look back on this moment, kid, because your life just changed." She pauses. "And stop rolling your eyes."

She knows me too well.

The planets must be aligned—I actually read my Astrology Zone column for February three times in a row, looking for clues as to how my life is going so well—because Larissa was right: it really *is* that easy. I clear everything with a visibly thrilled Rania, sign the contracts with Face honchos, and am officially announced as the consultant for the new Face line in the span of three weeks.

I'm feeling high on my new position when I walk by James's office. He's sitting at his desk, staring at something on the wall. Should I tell him my exciting news?

He makes eye contact with me, and I pause in my tracks. It's only polite to say hello.

"How are you?" I ask tentatively, pausing in the doorway and feeling my shoulders subconsciously hunch in, as if trying to minimize my space.

He jumps, startled. "I didn't see you there."

"Everything okay?"

"Fine. Just . . . thinking," he says, shaking his head as if to clear the cobwebs. "Do you need anything?"

"I don't *need* anything," I say, trying to keep the edge out of my voice. "I just wanted to stop by to tell you something." I pause, and he looks at me expectantly, leaning back in his chair. He's wearing a black suit with a vibrant orange tie. It's an unexpected combination, I think approvingly. Maybe he's finally getting some age-appropriate fashion sense. "I'm the new beauty consultant for Face Group's latest brand."

He doesn't say anything, sitting up straight in his chair and then, as if instinctively, fiddling with his tie. "Right. I saw something in the *Post* about that recently. It's great news. Congratulations."

"Thanks." I don't know what I was expecting from him. A bear hug? A sloppy make-out? Another confession of all-consuming love? Whatever his feelings for me might have been before, it's obvious that these past several months of no contact have completely squashed them. So much for my latent hope that things would, somehow, work out.

"So." He leans forward and cocks his head to one side inquisitively, his voice slightly more uplifted. "Does this mean you'll be leaving *Womanly World*?"

"No, this does not mean I'll be leaving *Womanly World*," I snap. "I'm only a consultant. I'll still be here full-time."

James looks taken aback by my tone and I wonder if we've had another miscommunication. "Oh. Okay. Fantastic."

I smile at him tightly and am about to turn to leave when

I remember that Larissa is throwing an impromptu party to-night. "You know, nothing big," she'd said over the phone earlier today. "Just maybe, like, two hundred people at the Hotel Gansevoort. Eight o'clock? I'll have Julie throw some-thing together." It only now occurs to me that the fact Larissa brought Julie to Face with her means that Julie has finally won Larissa's seal of approval. Good girl. She deserves it.

"By the way," I say. "Larissa is throwing a small party at the Gansevoort tonight to celebrate everything. It's at eight. If you're not too busy, you could stop by. If you want."

To my surprise, he doesn't decline the offer. "Eight? I think I can make that. Thanks for the invite."

"Sure. See you tonight."

By 8:30, the party is in full swing, most people seemingly desperate for something to celebrate in the dead of winter. As is par for the course in early February, New York is still an icy, slushy hell.

Despite the lack of planning time, Julie has managed to turn the Gansevoort into a lush, tropical paradise, with palm trees and tiki torches. In the corner away from the entrance, behind the pool, two buff, bare-chested Hawaiian men clad only in palm-frond skirts are manning a makeshift barbecue pit with roasted pig and steak.

Joss, Nick, and I arrive together, but Nick immediately des-erts us, citing too many hot editors ("untapped chicks" are his exact words) to hang out with us. Within seconds, Joss spots Janelle Morrison and starts groaning. "She's here with the CEO of Artillery. I'd better go schmooze. God forbid one of Janelle's employees enjoys themselves at a beauty function."

"Go," I say, shooing her away. "We'll reconvene later and dissect everybody's fake behavior." I wish Emily were here, but now that her stylist skills are out, she's been inundated with calls at all hours of the day and night from Gabrielle's socialite and Hollywood friends and had to rush over to an actress's apartment tonight for a fitting. *Elle*'s doing a small piece on her in a few months as the new Rachel Zoe, a true sign that she's the next big thing.

Julie rushes by, wearing an earpiece with a microphone attached, barking commands. "No! I told you. Red cocktails! Larissa specifically said they have to be red! Please do not make me come into the kitchen and do it myself!"

I put a hand on her arm and Julie squeals when she sees me, giving me a bear hug. "Jules, this is amazing. I have no idea how you put this together so quickly."

"*Eh.*" She waves a hand dismissively. "You remember what it's like working for Larissa, don't you? After a year, you learn to move mountains and work miracles, all for the sake of concealer and the ego of a crazy lady." She puts her hand over her mouth, looking shocked and giggling at her own audacity. "I said that too loud."

"Larissa's busy over there, anyway." I point to the glassed-in area by the elevators, where Larissa and a tall Indian man are flirting fast and furiously.

"She moves through men so quickly it makes my head spin. How does she keep up? I can't even remember their names!"

I shake my head in disbelief. "If I had one-one thousandth of the luck she does with hot guys, I'd be satisfied. She should set up a dating service, don't you think?"

"No," Julie says firmly. "She'd make everybody pay to join and then would date all the men herself." We giggle. "So, look at you! You look amazing!"

"Me?" I look down at my outfit. I'm going for a high-low fashion mix tonight: a silver Dolce and Gabbana dress Emily's mom sent her, paired with a white Gap jacket and strappy black Manolos sent from Bradenberg PR two years ago as part of a mailing to top editors.

She laughs. "Yes, you! You look different. Relaxed."

"I *am* relaxed," I admit. "Or as relaxed as you can be when you're diving headfirst into something you're completely not qualified for! But I feel happy. And what about you? You seem one hundred percent better than when I last saw you. You were stressed, terrified of Larissa, running around like a chicken with your head cut off—"

"Nothing's changed! But Larissa and I have settled into a groove. At least I know she likes me now, so it makes it easier to deal with her mood swings. It's so much easier being on the other side. You know how it is in the industry—there are only a few good positions, and all the editors are breaking their necks trying to get promoted above everybody else. But on the business side, it's basically limitless."

"Next stop, VP of Face Group, *huh?*" I say, and wink.

"In about a million years, but I'm trying." She suddenly gasps and puts her hand to her ear. "Absolutely not! You heard what she said. She'll kill you!" Julie turns back to me. "Bella, I'm sorry, but there's a crisis at the door. Delilah just showed up and is trying to crash."

"No!"

"Yes. She's the new you. After Larissa fired her, nobody will touch her." Julie's eyes widen as she realizes what she said.

I wave my hand in the air dismissively. "It's fine. I know what you meant."

"Now you're golden," she says with relief. "I just meant, like before."

"Exactly."

"No! No no no! I'll be right there," she barks into her mouthpiece. "I'm sorry, Bel."

"Go," I say, shooing her off as she dashes for the elevator.

A waitress in a bikini walks by and I grab a cocktail from her tray, sipping it as I survey the floor. Julie has installed heating lamps all around the pool and by the balconies, so the freezing night air barely registers. The Gansevoort opened several years ago in the Meatpacking District and is still one of the hottest hotels in New York, with neon lights outside on Hudson Street that fade from blue to green to pink, stylishly minimal rooms, and, of course, the rooftop pool, where tonight's party is. The Manhattan skyline surrounds us like a cocoon, twinkling lights framing the guests as they mill around in groups of three and four, gossiping on lounge chairs and at tropically decorated tables.

Six months ago, if somebody threw a party with my name attached, I don't think a single beauty editor would have come (save, maybe, Larissa—assuming there was free booze). Now, with the success of *Womanly World,* my positive Page Six name check and Larissa's public endorsement, I'm a hot commodity again. Every high-profile editor is here, as well as several Face Group executives, and most of the industry assistants, who can never pass up an exclusive party with complimentary cocktails.

Heidi's talking animatedly with her assistant and two other midlevel editors who I've met but can't place. She sees me look in her direction and gasps, "Bella! Come over here!"

I walk over cautiously. Even though after my *scandale* Heidi was always relatively friendly to me—at least to my face, which is all that counts, no?—I'm still wary. "Hey, Heidi. How are you? Thanks for coming."

"You look fantastic!" she squeals as the girls she's with murmur in agreement. "I love the dress. Congratulations on the new gig. I'm so happy for you!" She smiles widely at me. I get the sense she's being sincere.

"Thanks," I say shyly. "I'm excited. I'm still pinching myself. It's going to be a lot of work, of course, but I can't wait to get started."

Mandy walks up and joins the conversation, greeting me with a kiss on each cheek and standing on my left, so that she and Heidi are flanking me. "Congrats! So, when do you start?" In my three-inch heels, I feel like a giant next to Mandy, who's about five feet and can't weigh more than ninety-five pounds soaking wet. She's rocking the Mary-Kate Olsen boho look from a few years back—a tatty turquoise cardigan over a belted black tank, black corduroy miniskirt, and shredded black leggings—which is, apparently, so out that it's in again. I wonder if she brought a coat—or does she actually traipse around New York dressed like that? Contrasted with her pale, luminous skin, khol-rimmed eyes and artfully disheveled pixie haircut, it's a perfect example of the "I just walked out the door without even trying" look that actually takes forever to achieve correctly.

"Immediately. Since the job is on a consultancy basis, I don't have to tie up any loose ends at *Womanly World*. I can just dive right in, although I'm sure it'll take me several weeks to get into the groove of juggling both."

"You've had a year, haven't you?" says Mandy. "From *Enchanté* to *Womanly World* to Face. Crazy! Are you excited to work with Larissa again?" She plunges her fingers into her spiky brown hair and shakes them back and forth to give it more volume, gold bangles on her wrist flashing.

"She's a little high-strung, obviously, but we get along well, and I think she's going to create some phenomenal things with Face. So, yes!"

"You have got to be the luckiest girl in beauty. I mean, you totally dive-bomb with *Enchanté,* but then you get a job, like, immediately, and just a few months later you're handpicked to create a new line for the biggest company in the industry. How does that even happen? Are you sleeping with Satan?" She laughs giddily. "I think we need a glass of champagne to celebrate! *Um* . . . hi! Excuse me?" she calls to a shirtless waiter. "Can we get some champagne?"

The waiter nods and rushes inside, pecs glistening. He returns in seconds. "Here you go, ladies," he says in a deep, mellifluous voice, smiling at Heidi.

"Thanks," Heidi coos, tossing her long chestnut hair and giving him a big smile. "You're a lifesaver. We were *so* thirsty."

"My pleasure," he purrs.

As soon as he walks away, Heidi turns back to us. "God, how *delicious* is he? We were flirting by the bar earlier. I've decided. He doesn't know it yet, but I'm going home with him tonight."

"Heidi!" I'm surprised. I always thought of Heidi as the cool, refined type—a junior Grace, only slightly friendlier.

"What? A girl has her needs. And he's gorgeous." She lowers her voice. "Between the three of us—" I suddenly realize that the assistants and midlevel editors have slinked away to allow me to gab with Heidi and Mandy "—I haven't gotten laid in six months. It's terrible."

"No!" gasps Mandy. "How do you stand it? Six months? You're practically a virgin again!"

"I know," Heidi says gravely. "It's dire. I don't think the hot, shirtless waiter has any choice."

Grace sidles over. "What are you girls talking about," she declares tonelessly.

"Can I tell her?" Mandy asks.

Heidi shrugs. I notice that, as soon as Grace is around, her entire aura shifts, as if she's invisibly aged five years. "Sure."

"Heidi hasn't gotten any action in *six months*. Can you believe it?"

"Oh my God. I would die," Grace says in a bored tone, looking around the room and running her fingers languidly through her long white-blonde hair. "This crowd . . . Larissa called everybody this afternoon to tell them, and now the entire industry is here. Huge turnout. You must be excited, Bella." Grace fixes her steely eyes on me.

"*Uh,* yeah . . . I am." Despite her I-couldn't-care-less tone, the fact that Grace has walked over to talk with us means she's decided we're worthy of conversation. The two of us haven't had a pleasant exchange since before the Paris press trip. Grace doesn't seem to remember our mild hostilities, however.

"Congrats. Really amazing. Can you believe the nerve of Delilah, trying to get in after everything that happened between her and Larissa," she says contemptuously, switching gears in midsentence. "She can't even get a freelancing gig now. Balls of steel. I always knew there was something off about her. Larissa was stupid to hire her." She shrugs and yawns, flashing a perfectly manicured hand as she covers her mouth. "Live and learn. Now you're back with her, and it's like nothing ever happened. I'm going to go now. Thanks." Grace leans in to give me a kiss on each cheek, her face cold against mine. "Ciao, ladies." She walks over to say good-bye to Larissa, who's now holding court inside with six men surrounding her.

"Grace is *so* strange," Mandy whispers as soon as she's out of earshot.

Heidi nods, raising an eyebrow. "But she's powerful, so . . . ."

"I know," Mandy sighs. "But, *ugh.* What a pill."

It's as if I've been inducted into an exclusive girls' club. Now that I'm "cool" again, they're opening up around me and spilling secrets like we're all BFF.

"Hi, Bella!" a young girl I've never met before says giddily, walking by and waving excitedly. "Congratulations!"

"Thanks!" I smile, wondering who she is.

"Liv Boswell," Heidi whispers in my ear. "Natalia Castellano's assistant at *Physically Fit.*"

"Thanks, Liv!" I repeat. She lights up when I say her name and scurries over to her group of friends. I make a vow: I'm not going to let my surge of popularity go to my head. It's surely temporary. The way the beauty winds blow, tomorrow I could be a pariah again.

Sam walks in the door and I wave at her. She walks over and gives me a hug. "Girl of the hour! I'm proud of you." As Sam dishes on her new role as *Enchanté* beauty director, I notice that Heidi and Mandy have faded into the background, carrying on a conversation of their own. I'm relieved—I'd rather talk with Sam, who I know couldn't care less about what magazine I'm at or my coolness quotient.

The DJ puts on a popular dance song and half the girls in the room start bouncing on their tiptoes, sloshing their drinks around as they dance and sing along. Sam and I chat, looking around amusedly. Suddenly, Heidi and Mandy reappear, standing on either side of me like on-duty bodyguards. I feel a tap on my shoulder and turn around. It's Maddie, the reporter who wrote the incendiary *Post* article that got me fired.

"Hey," she says, smiling at me. "Cool party."

My jaw drops.

She puts her hands up. "Before you have me thrown out, I want to explain what happened. Does the name Toph O'Leary ring any bells?"

"Yes," I say, confused.

"What about Delilah Windsor?"

"Yes . . ." I can only begin to guess where this is going.

"Toph was one of our music and entertainment editors. He was fired a few weeks ago for trying to tamper with quotes in a piece that had already been submitted and approved—*your* Page Six item. I did some snooping, and—" she pauses dramatically "Toph is dating Delilah Windsor. Your nemesis, no?"

Mandy and Heidi look back and forth between the two of us eagerly, as if poised for a fight. "Do you want us to call security?" Mandy whispers.

"No, it's okay," I say, turning back to Maddie, preoccupied with her story. "*Uh,* nemesis is a strong word . . ."

Mandy looks at Heidi, her eyes wide.

"Well, you can guess what happened," Maddie says. "Toph claims Delilah convinced him to do it. Apparently, she got him to hack into the computers and find my notes after our interview. He reedited the story right before it went to print."

"What snakes!" I shriek. "They're unbelievable! That should be illegal!"

"Well, it is, but they can't punish somebody that doesn't work there. All they could do was fire Toph. I never liked him, anyway," she says darkly.

"This is . . . words fail me."

"Did she just tell her what I think she told her?" Mandy hisses at Heidi.

"She told her Delilah is dating her ex and together they planted that article about her last year," Heidi says in a low voice out of the corner of her mouth.

"At least Delilah got hers," Mandy says, "after getting fired for stealing the jewelry."

"Sorry, what?" Maddie asks. "Delilah Windsor was fired from *Enchanté* for stealing jewelry?"

Mandy looks surprised. "What?"

"You just told her—" she points at Heidi "—that Delilah was fired for stealing jewelry."

"You could hear me?"

Maddie laughs. "You were talking right in front of us!"

"Oh," Mandy frowns. "Right. Yeah, she was fired."

"Very interesting," Maddie says, raising an eyebrow impishly. "Very interesting, indeed." She turns back to me. "I hope you can forgive me. I meant what I said when I called you after the story ran. I really *didn't* write half of it. But . . . maybe . . . all's well that ends well?" She gestures around at the party, which is now bursting at the seams with beauty editors, fashion editors, lad maggers, newspaper writers, and a smattering of Z-list celebrities.

I laugh giddily, feeling a rush of goodwill. "It seems so."

"I felt so guilty about what happened, even though I *knew* it wasn't my fault. As soon as I heard whispers about you being up for the Face job, I made sure there was a nice little item about it in Page Six."

"You were behind the Page Six item?" I ask incredulously.

"Of course! I do wield *some* influence, you know. Never underestimate the power of the *New York Post*," she says, and winks.

"Excuse me? Attention, everybody!" Larissa's voice booms around the room. She's standing at the head of the pool, speaking into a microphone, flanked by sexy waiters. Her black dress is dangerously low cut and held together on the sides by what looks like huge diamond brooches—à la Elizabeth Hurley's famous safety-pinned Versace dress at the *Four Weddings and a Funeral* premiere—showing off her fabulously toned body. Her long black hair sparkles in the moonlight, and the four-inch silver stilettos she's wearing, showing off a fire-engine red pedicure, put her at well over six feet. She looks every inch the goddess.

"Thanks for coming tonight! I'll keep this short, because I know you're all *dying* to get back to the party. Do I throw a good one, or what?" Everybody laughs at Larissa's lack of modesty. "So, obviously, we're not just here to fete me, but also my fabulous number-two and beauty soulmate, Bella Hunter." All eyes turn toward me, and I smile and wave awkwardly. "Bella has been there for me through ups and downs, through high and low, through thick and thin—I mean metaphorically speaking, of course, since we all know I would never let myself go and become *literally* thick." I have to physically restrain myself from groaning and putting my

head in my hands. Editors everywhere are laughing, however, no doubt bewitched by Larissa's insane sense of humor.
"Poor Bella was banished from the top of the beauty heap
earlier in the year for some silly little comments she made,
but, honestly, who even *remembers* that now? Bella went over
to *Womanly World,* and helped completely turn the magazine
around, increasing their ad revenue by a zillion percent and
turning her beauty column into the most popular feature
in the magazine. She's got the Midas touch! And, she understands the common woman—not that I'm saying *you're*
common, Bel—" she winks at me "—which is going to come
in handy with our little project, because I, alas, don't have a
clue what they're looking for." Everybody laughs again. "I
offer this toast in Bella's honor: To new beginnings! The sky's
the limit! To Face!"

"To Face!" everybody repeats in unison, raising their glasses
and then downing them. I sip my champagne happily.

"Can I say something?" I look back across the pool, recog-
nizing the male voice, and see, disbelievingly, that it's James.
He's either just arrived, or he's been hiding from me all night.
Larissa has handed him the microphone, smiling impishly
and shrugging at me as if to say, "What was I supposed to
do?"

He clutches the microphone nervously, clearing his throat.
"I'm not great at speeches, but . . . I'll do my best. I'm James
Michaels, publisher of *Womanly World.* When Bella started,
I had no idea what a talented addition she'd be. I knew she
came from *Enchanté,* so I had preconceived notions about her
talent and work ethic—and, besides, all I could notice was
how beautiful she was."

"Oh my God," Mandy mutters. "He is sexually harassing
you *right now*, in front of everybody."

"Shut up," Heidi shoots back. "This is getting
interesting."

"As I got to know her, I realized that she's more than a pretty face. She's kind, she threw herself into projects, even when she had no clue what she was doing . . . which was often—" My cheeks redden as everybody twitters "—and she toiled on her column, writing and rewriting, until she got it just right. She doesn't think like everybody else, but she's incredibly aware of things, which is, I think, proof that she's the perfect consultant for the new Face line. She sticks with things . . . and people . . . that others might deem hopeless." He looks at me. We're on opposite sides of the pool, but his eyes are boring into mine and I feel like we're only inches apart. "She . . ." He clears his throat again. "Bella's helped me realize things about myself. She'll never cut me a break. It's annoying." The corner of his mouth turns up in a wry smile. I stare back at him across the pool, my heart pounding. I realize that, even with months of almost no contact, I'm desperately in love with this man. It's hopeless. "At the risk of sounding . . ." He takes a breath and shrugs, pressing on, ". . . she makes me want to take risks. So, this seems as good a place as any to announce that I'm stepping down as publisher of *Womanly World*."

"What?" I gasp. The room explodes in a cacophony of buzz as everybody reacts to James's huge announcement.

"This party is *crazy*!" Mandy squeals.

He hands the microphone to Larissa, who is grinning from ear to ear and looking at James with interest, and walks across the pool to me. I can't move—I'm rooted to the ground. When he's standing in front of me, mere inches away, I can smell his cologne—my favorite, Givenchy Pi—and my knees nearly buckle.

The room is silent as everybody watches us, but I can't hear anybody; I can't see anything. It's as if James and I are alone together.

He looks down at me, his eyes searching my face. "I can't

get more open. Do you . . . how do you feel? What do you think? Is there a chance?" He touches my face gently with his thumb, then slides his hand to my neck, pulling me closer.

My eyes water as I look up at him. I'm so dizzy with happiness and desire that I feel I could literally melt into his hand, collapse in his arms, and then dissolve into a puddle at his feet. "I . . ." My voice catches in my throat. I can't get any words out.

He looks terrified. "You're . . . I . . ."

His skin crackles beneath my fingers as I touch his neck, as if there's an electric charge. I give him a tiny smile, our eyes locked. "Don't be stupid."

I feel his heart pounding as he gathers me in his arms and kisses me, our lips touching tentatively, then less softly, and then hungrily. I wrap my arms around him tightly, tasting him, melting into him. I could die. Right now, at this moment, I could die of happiness.

The room explodes into cheers and wolf whistles as we clutch each other. "Get a room!" I hear a woman cry, the voice sounding suspiciously like Larissa's.

We break apart, still holding each other, grinning as we look into each other's eyes, our noses almost touching. "I meant what I said. I think I love you."

"I think I love you more."

"Is it a contest?" I giggle and kiss him again, snuggling contentedly in his arms as people start drifting away from us, politely averting their eyes and starting up conversations.

"We need to leave," he murmurs. "Immediately."

"But, wait. What about your job? What are you going to do? You can't leave *Womanly World* for me."

"It's done. I can't take back a public announcement. I wasn't happy there—it's time to do what I want."

"Which is?" I kiss him softly on the cheek, tasting the sweetness of his skin. I can't believe he's mine.

"Focus on my band. Or maybe work as a Chippendale's dancer. I'm kidding!" He laughs when he sees the wide-eyed expression on my face. "We'll figure it out. I can't think about that right now. I need to get you home as quickly as possible."

For once, I don't protest.

We dash hand in hand to the elevator, picking up pink Face Group gift bags from a headphone-wearing flunkie and walking by Maddie, who winks. "Have fun! This is *so* going on Page Six tomorrow."

As the doors close, I see Mandy turn to Heidi, who's trying to flag down the sexy waiter, and demand, "Have we found out what's in the gift bags? If it's Barneys store credit, this is the best . . . party . . . *ever*."

Epilogue

"Did you see this?" demands Nick, bursting through the front door carrying a copy of the *New York Post*. James and I are lying at opposite ends of the couch watching an Eddie Izzard DVD with our legs entwined while Emily sits cross-legged on the floor, blond hair tied in a messy bun held together with a pencil, scribbling on a notepad as she occasionally mutters to herself, "Lanvin . . . no, Burberry . . . Peter Som . . . maybe Thakoon . . ." Joss stopped by earlier in the evening before meeting Gary at Penn Station to spend the weekend in Long Island with her parents.

"Seen what?" I ask.

"This!" he thrusts the paper in front of my face breathlessly.

Industry Darling

The latest hot ticket to get snatched up by the **Face Group** as they begin creating their much-buzzed-about new line is **Nick Darling**, renowned makeup artist to such celebrities as **Jessica Cartier**, **Jennifer Lopez**, and **Scarlett Johansson**. Darling will answer to **Larissa Lincoln**, who famously eloped last week with steel billionaire **Gene Milland** in an intimate ceremony in Aspen, and has reportedly signed a staggering seven-figure five-year contract. An industry source claims, "Nick Darling is the hottest makeup artist in the business; every actress wants to work with him. It's a huge coup for Face." Darling's good friend, girl-about-town and **Womanly World** beauty editor **Bella Hunter**, will work closely with him as consultant on the line.

"Nick, congratulations! That's great!" I say, attemping to maintain a tone of surprise in my voice.

He folds his arms and regards me with a steely gaze. "That's how you're going to play it?"

"Play what?" I ask innocently. James starts chuckling next to me, but quickly wipes the smile from his face and turns back to the TV as Nick shoots him a warning look—one I know isn't serious, since Nick has repeatedly voiced his approval of James to the group.

"I see how it goes. If we're now in the habit of passing crucial information to the *New York Post before* telling our best friends . . . two can play that game."

"*Ooh,* that sounds fun!" Emily pipes up. "Can I join in?" She mimes typing an e-mail. "Dear *New York Post.* My friend Nick Darling, the latest Face Group acquisition, was recently dumped—again—by his girlfriend Arabelle, because she caught him in bed with one of her friends mere days after he'd sworn off his old womanizing ways—"

"Never mind," he mutters, rolling up the paper as his cheeks turn pink. "Forget it."

"You're welcome," I say, and wink at him.

He plops on the love seat and a guilty grin slowly spreads across his face. "I was sick of Arabelle, anyway—she started being *nice* to me. No challenge."

James sighs, shaking his head in mock sadness. "A nice girlfriend? I can't imagine what that's like."

"Do you *want* me to ban you from my bed, Mr. I'm Gonna Be a Rock Star?" I say.

As we start wrestling on the couch, Emily watches us, giggling, and glances over at Nick, who leans back on the sofa, talking to the ceiling dreamily. "Seven figures, huh? Just think of all the chicks I'll be able to get."

Emily shakes her head ruefully. "Some things never change."

Acknowledgments

Thanks to Dorian Karchmar, Carrie Feron, Tessa Woodward, Emily Fink, Nicole Chismar, Sharyn Rosenblum, Pamela Spengler-Jaffe, Wendy Ho, Adam Schear, and everybody at William Morris and HarperCollins. Your support, guidance, hard work, and brilliant ideas were invaluable.

Special thanks to Raaknee Mirchandani for giving me the courage to begin, and to McFly and Red Bull for giving me the stamina to finish.

To my family and friends (you know who you are!) thank you, and I love you.

A+

AUTHOR
INSIGHTS,
EXTRAS, &
MORE...

FROM

**NADINE
HAOBSH**

AND

AVON A

Here are a few of my favorite blog posts from my beauty website. Check out www.jolienyc.com for more!

"The Beauty Hierarchy"

In a very particular order, here's how people rate on the beauty food chain (from what's your name again? to très diva):

Assistant: Despite having likely graduated from an Ivy League college, not to be trusted with anything other than fetching coffee, opening beauty products, or telephoning junior PR people for prices. Salary roughly equivalent to a janitor in Iowa.

Associate: Either granted a byline for small, micro-edited pieces that could have been easily thrown together by an eight-year-old, or writes the entire beauty section with credit going to the director. Salary roughly equivalent to a janitor in New York.

Editor: Free weekly blowouts or pedicures. Spends four days per month working like a dog, twenty-seven days per month attending lunches and parties. Salary approximately twice that of an associate, but receives at least $10,000 in swag per year.

Beauty Director: Arrives in the office at 10 a.m. Leaves at 6. Spends two days per month researching, three days per month writing, one day per month at sales calls, fifteen hours per month at events, one-third of life delegating to associate. Loves her assistant. Has hundreds of dollars in gifted credit at Barneys. Thrilled to have (just barely) broken the six-figure barrier.

Beauty Director at Condé Nast: Arrives in the office at 11 a.m. Leaves at 5. Conducts three hour lunches twice-weekly at DB, once-weekly at Koi, twice-monthly at Per Se. Commands 150K+ for 20 hours per week of actual work.

Beauty Director of Vogue: Too busy for you. More powerful than God. Money is for the little people.

"Yes, I Actually Get Paid for This"

So, I got back from my spa weekend in Arizona last night. It was as predictably phenomenal as three days of spa treatments, palatial suites, and gourmet food can be. On day two, while lying on a private patio getting a moonlight massage in breezy 85 degree weather, I thought, "I can't believe this is my job." And that's the crazy thing about beauty: you get to do the most amazing things, and it's called "work." Everybody knows what a weird, parallel universe fashion is, but nobody delves into the beauty side of things that much. I find that really strange. Beauty is even more decadent than fashion, since beauty companies have so much more money to throw around on press trips, free products, and gratuitous gifts. I took a trip six months ago (again to Arizona) and the company flew us there via private jet. My boss (and sometimes even I, only a mid-level editor) regularly gets Marc Jacobs wallets and coats, plane ticket vouchers, iPods, overnight stays at the Mandarin Oriental, year-long gym memberships, and—of course—all the free highlights and haircuts your poor dyed, straightened and styled hair can stand. It's almost embarrassing. Of course, the entry pay is crap. When my parents found out how much I made at my first job (good ol' Condé Nast!), they questioned the legality of paying somebody that little. (Nope, not slave labor, just your standard editorial assistant position.) Then again, I managed to double my salary in a year-and-a-half, which is the benefit to hopping around from magazine to magazine. It's an incestuous little world, because everybody has either worked with, press-tripped with, or interviewed with everybody else. We see each other about six times a week, at various lunches, appointments and events put together by the PR companies, which means our industry is basically akin to a sorority. With even better hair.

"Pink Is the New Black"

Today, in a fit of whimsy, it struck me: everything I own is pink. I have a pink Marc Jacobs wallet, three pink purses, three pairs of pink shoes, a pink dress, two pink skirts, a pink Lacoste shirt, endless pink tank tops, a pink iPod . . . you get the point. Why is this at all noteworthy? Because nearly every single one of these things was given to me. (Dude, I don't buy pink.) In fact, I actually hate pink. But I love getting free things, and I long ago abandoned any pretense of being too cool to wear gifted swag. This is probably because gifted stuff=I don't have to go shopping=a happy Jolie. The real problem with having all of this stuff you received as gifts is that everybody else has it, too. Try holding on to your pride when you walk into an event to find seven other girls sporting the exact same purse. Most beauty editors adhere to an unbreakable rule: do not wear or carry to an event anything you have been gifted. (Sage advice, but easier said than done, since half the time I end up forgetting it was a gift.) My only salvation: a Very Expensive Bag that I bought years ago as a "Happy Graduation to Me" present. I pull it out on event days, wear it with pride, and silently smirk at the other poor girls who accidentally brought the gift bag. I hope that doesn't make me an asshole.

"Rules for PR People to Live By"

If you are a public relations person, might I be so kind as to offer one or two words of advice? It'll make everybody happier.

1. Please don't ask permission to send press kits. Just send them.

2. Please don't call and ask to speak with "Shirley" when my name is "Jolie" and I have been the only person at this extention for three years. Shirley hasn't worked here since 2002. Pick up a masthead. They're fairly current.

3. Please don't leave a message asking me to call back to let you know that, yes, I did receive the press release that you randomly sent. If it's really that important to you to verify that I received an unrequested piece of paper, call me back until you reach me.

4. Please tell your bosses to make you stop calling "just to check in." I know you've gotta do it (and I know you'd rather not—I feel your pain!) . . . but it's still kind of annoying.

5. Please don't call and read something verbatim off a piece of paper. Maybe you're an intern, maybe you're very nervous over the phone, maybe you really are a robot, but at least try to make it sound unrehearsed. Phew! That wasn't so hard, was it?

"Bare Obsession"

I just took a peek at Sephora's website, and lo and behold, the home page is devoted entirely to mineral makeup! As you probably know—mostly because *I will not shut up about it*—I've been using Bare Escentuals Bare Minerals foundation for years, and consider myself something of an expert on the matter. Not all mineral foundations are created equal, however. Over the years, I've tried this brand and that brand and blah . . . blah . . . blah. I don't like any of them, for various combinations of the following reasons: the powders aren't as finely milled; the coverage is inferior; the packaging looks like it was made from recycled diapers, etc. I'm always amazed when women corner me and ask, with a slight edge to their voice, "But, have you tried (insert mineral makeup here that is not Bare Minerals)??? It's so much better!" Alas, my friends, I've tried them all . . . and the only one I can get on board with is Bare Minerals—people are obsessed with it because it works.

"The Beauty Editor Conundrum"

As a beauty editor, in addition to the aforementioned blowouts and manicures and pedicures (for research, of course), you also get boatloads of products thrown at you. To the uninitiated, magic little bags arriving at your office every day stuffed with conditioner and moisturizer and lip gloss might seem like the coolest thing in the world. But after only a few months, it gets really, really old. (I promise.) I still love getting to try the newest beauty products before anybody else, but once you've sampled literally everything on the market, you can't help but play favorites. And slowly but surely, you resent having to put aside your beloved-and-oh-so-efficacious creams to test the new blah, or the new whatever, or the new I don't really care. Okay, sure, I'll forgo the Phytodefrisant for a morning to see if this new anti-frizz gel works as well. Nope? Not as good? Tomorrow, back to my Phyto. (Or—let's be real—in four days. You don't think I actually wash my hair every day, do you?) But when it comes to moisturizers and serums and cleansers, that's when I dig my heels in. The whole idea of a skincare regimen is to get your skin into a therapeutic routine, and give the products enough time to really start working. But how can you give a routine a fighting chance when you have fifteen other serums and tonics and potions lined up on your bathroom sink, begging, "Pick me! Try me! Write about me!"? You could just stick to the same old routine, of course, forgoing research in the name of a pretty complexion. You could spend every day of every year using a different product, until your skin is raw and confused—but you're, like, a total expert. Or you could perform the insane science project (a little of the old favorite, a little of the new, a little more of the new) that is my daily skincare experience, applying layer after layer of various product in a mad desire to try them all until your poor skin is beaten into submission—yet still glowing! It's a tough job, but somebody's got to do it.

Turn the page for an exciting peek at my other book:
   Beauty Confidential: The No Preaching, No Lies, Advice-You'll-Actually-Use Guide to Looking Your Best

For five years, I worked as a beauty editor in New York City, swinging my way from magazine to magazine and quickly working my way up the masthead. I was on track to becoming a beauty director—one of the younger ones in the industry, if things kept course. Then I started writing a blog called "Jolie in NYC." And then all hell broke loose.

My blog was a poor-man's version of the popular gossip sites that were sprouting like kudzu, with regurgitated celebrity news that I posted and added my own hi-*larious* two cents on. I even enjoyed a brief side foray into the public service sector, cobbling together a side blog called "Nick and Jessica Breakup Watch," which included proof of their imminent demise. (Hey, I *was* right in the end.) After taking a particularly lavish press trip to Arizona, however, I briefly tabled the celebrity content and wrote instead about our journey, marveling at how beauty editors were treated to such perks as private jets, designer handbags, and massages. The blog was anonymous (mistake one) and included commentary on my industry and the often tenuous dynamics between editors and publicists (mistake two). I started getting coverage in blogs like Gawker, Jossip, and Mediabistro, was swiftly outed by the *New York Post*, and had a plum offer at *Seventeen* magazine rescinded . . . the day after I left my position at *Ladies' Home Journal*. (Worst . . . day . . . of . . . my . . . life.)

Except, in retrospect, it wasn't. I learned that flexibility and hard work are not mutually exclusive and decided on a whim to go for broke, trying to make a career out of this craaazy blogging thing. (Cue violins.) Every second I could, I posted, noting favorite products, great tips gleaned from industry experts, celebrity beauty trends, and, most importantly, answering beauty questions from readers. In the flurry of Q&A's, I realized that there's a serious lack of *honesty* in today's beauty information: we're sick of being lectured, talked down to, advertised at, and just generally misled.

The questions are endless. When every dermatologist in

América is touting an astronomically pricey skin-care line, does that mean you're ruining your complexion if you only have money for the drugstore stuff? Why do all the magazines champion that product you spent two hundred dollars on, when it did absolutely *nothing* for you? Why does it feel like you read the same beauty article every single month, in every single magazine? Isn't it a strange coincidence that the product you're reading about on page 53 is advertised on page 55? And why is it so hard to grasp that the label "combination skin" helps nobody? (Fine, you're dry here, you're oily there, but all of the "right" products either make you flake or break out!)

I set out to create a beauty book for *you*—the girl who loves makeup, hair, perfume, and skin care, but wants to find what works for her without blindly following trends or swallowing corporate-placement rubbish. There are millions of beauty books on the shelves by experts, crammed with step-by-step instructions on how to painstakingly create the look that will make you appear as if you've just stepped from the pages of your favorite magazine. While that's fabulous, if you have time to read a complicated manual the size of a World War Two textbook and then spend hours aping the looks inside . . . most of us don't! We want fast, accurate, and *real*, and we want it from somebody who's been there in the beauty trenches with us. Let's be honest: I'm not a makeup artist, I'm not a hairstylist, and I've singed my hair, poked out my eyes, and turned myself orange more times than I'd like to count! But I *have* been surrounded by beauty information 24/7 for several years, and armed with enough knowledge to make over an entire village of frizzy-haired, oily t-zoned, crying-out-in-need-of-highlights women, I hereby pass it all along to you.

Thanks for reading, and stay beautiful!

One

Getting Started

What beauty editors know that you don't

Imagine a life where highlights and haircuts with the world's top experts are free, where there is an endless supply of Crème de la Mer, where you leave work at 2 P.M. to get a massage or pedicure and your boss cheerfully tells you to have fun. (Are you still with me?) Now, imagine you get *paid* to live this life. Welcome to the world of a beauty editor.

Each month, magazines bring you advice on which eye shadow shades are hot, what the most flattering haircut is for your face shape, and which self-tanners work for pale skin. But have you ever wondered how beauty editors know all this? (For me, it's because I was born knowing everything there is to know about beauty. *Obviously.*) In reality, it's because beauty experts have free products and procedures hurled at them. It may not seem fair—why do they get endless supplies of Chanel lip gloss, and all you get at work is an endless supply of paperclips?—but expertise is the name of the game. Without batting an eyelash, a beauty editor can tell you definitively what the best cleanser is, how to get away with not washing your hair for four days, what on earth a peptide is, why the jasmine in perfumes is picked at night, and the difference between alpha and beta hydroxy acid. The advice you see in magazines each month is just a fraction of the actual knowledge they possess.

I'm here to share it with you.

I wasn't always beauty-savvy. A childhood spent climbing avocado trees and shunning Barbies in favor of books does not necessarily a future beauty editor make. But in college, while pursuing a career as a writer, I found myself at a magazine as a beauty intern. The first time I walked into the magical thing known as a beauty closet, I almost fainted. Much like that episode of *Sex and the City* where Carrie goes to *Vogue* and has a heart attack over the fabulosity of the fashion closet, I was shocked to see that the room (Yes! An entire room!) was stuffed to the brim with every product known to man. Better yet, it was ours for the sampling. After all, how are you going to be a beauty expert if you don't try all the products?

There are thousands of beauty products in this world (Hundreds of thousands! Millions!), and your average girl can't be expected to try them all. So, we tireless beauty editors do the work for you, dutifully slapping on face cream, testing hair straighteners, and staring intently at nearly identical shades of lip gloss, trying to figure out which is better for olive complexions and which for fairer skin tones.

See? And you thought it was all fun and games. Beauty is *very serious*.

Actually, I'm kidding. Most people take beauty way too seriously, and it simply doesn't need to be that way. Beauty should be fun! It should make you feel better about yourself and accentuate what you've been blessed with (and gracefully and discreetly hide what you're less than pleased with). All that nonsense about "redheads can't wear red lipstick" and "don't match your manicure to your pedicure" and "young women shouldn't wear foundation" and "never play up your eyes and lips at the same time" is just that—nonsense. It's all about finding what works for *you*. If you're in your teens or twenties and your skin is slightly blotchy and tinted moisturizer simply doesn't give you enough coverage, I say wear foundation until the cows come home! The trick is simply finding the *right* foundation that doesn't make you feel like you have on a mask.

It's not rocket science, people. Sure, beauty is serious in that it's terribly important for your self-esteem. Like it or not, we do live in an image-conscious society, and why not put your best face forward? But, after all, at the end of the day, it *is* only makeup. Lighten up, don't be afraid to experiment and make mistakes, and have fun with it!

And when your friends ask you how you know all about night-blooming jasmine and peptides, well, you can just smile and say that you were born a beauty genius.

First Things First

Beauty editors are very stern about certain things. Now, I don't necessarily live my life according to all of the Stepford-ish maxims, but rather take them as loose guidelines. After all, there are exceptions to *every* rule . . .

The Beauty Editor Commandments

1. Never wash your hair two days in a row.
2. Always wear SPF 30 sunscreen, come rain or shine, winter or summer.
3. Wash your face every night before bed . . . even when drunk . . . even when tired.
4. French manicures are not an option.
5. Everybody looks better with a hint of bronzer or self-tanner.
6. Avoid frowning—just like your mom said, your face will stick that way.
7. Don't smoke—it causes wrinkles, sallow, uneven skin, and yellow teeth. (Oh, yeah, and that whole cancer thing, too.)
8. Introduce acids into your daily routine—glycolic, salicylic, retinoic, whatever. Your skin will thank you.
9. Antioxidants are your best friend. Eat them, drink them, wear them, love them.
10. Smile. When you carry yourself beautiful, you <u>are</u> beautiful.

"MUST" LIST: The Products in Every Beauty Editor's Cabinet

Some beauty editors are drugstore gals, others love department store goodies, still more are verifiable snobs, only using products that cost more than the GDP of a small country.

Whatever each gal's preferences, however, a few products exist that are just *so* effective, you're guaranteed to find them in every single beauty editor's cabinet.

NARS blush in Orgasm: A peachy-rose, universally beloved, makes-every-woman-look-sexy-no-matter-what-her-complexion, no-other-product-can-even-come-close, rock-star blush. The name pretty much says it all—it gives you the kind of subtle, naughty flush that only comes from . . . well . . . you know.

Terax Original Crema: Is there a better intensive conditioner in the world? If so, I have yet to find it. Crema works miracles on dry, overprocessed hair, turning it from straw into silk. Bonus points because it's Italian and has an innate glamour quotient. (Maybe it shouldn't matter, but, c'mon—it *so* does.)

Essie Mademoiselle and OPI I'm Not Really a Waitress nail polish: With these two nail polish shades in your kit, you're pretty much set for life. Mademoiselle is the ideal pale pink—not too white, not too rose—that goes everywhere and immediately makes nails look Rich Bitch chic; I'm Not Really a Waitress fulfills the elusive, eternal quest for the perfect red.

Mario Badescu Drying Potion: When it's Thursday night, you have the biggest date of your life on Friday, and a zit the size of Mount Vesuvius has suddenly erupted, look no further than this tiny bottle of Pepto Bismol–pink pimple destroyer. Within one evening, the blemish will be considerably reduced; if you're lucky enough to have two nights to spare, it'll be nearly gone. (And three nights? Zit? What zit?)

Shu Uemura Eyelash Curler: Okay, so it kind of looks like a mechanical torture device. Don't let that scare you. Use before applying mascara and your eyelashes will be twice as defined, as if by magic. It's the best thing this side of false lashes.

Bumble and bumle Does It All Styling Spray: Whether your hair is curly or straight, frizzy or limp, thick or thin, this styling and setting spray lives up to its name. It doubles as a medium-hold hairspray, keeping tresses in place without any gross, beauty-pageant–like stiffness, but easily brushes out and works fabulously with heat-styling tools.

Cetaphil Face Wash: Dermatologists swear by it for a reason—it's gentle enough for even the most sensitive, dry, or trouble-prone skin. When the mere thought of washing your face is enough to make your skin inflamed, this is your product. Beloved whether you're sixteen or sixty.

Kiehl's Lip Balm #1: Combats chapped lips like nobody's business, lasts for hours, and comes in both a pot and a tube version. Plus, it's unisex and scent-free, so the man in your life won't whine that you taste like a mango-pomegranate-kiwi (and then will probably steal it for himself).

Lancôme Definicils: While other mascaras might get more press, this remains the gold standard, lengthening, defining, and just generally tricking-out even the wimpiest lashes. Lancôme pumps tons of research into their mascaras—which are the best in the business—and this superstar is their bestseller.

Phytodefrisant: Plagued by frizz? Look no further than this plant-based miracle balm, which helps relax curls and waves, keeping locks sleek no matter *what* the humidity levels.

Lancôme Flash Bronzer Instant Colour Self-Tanning Leg Gel: The beauty editor favorite, as championed by industry legend (and, self-disclosure, my former boss) Jean Godfrey-June, who famously uses it everywhere, not just on legs. It gives "have you been at the beach?" color with a hint of shimmer, and looks natural—not orange—even in the dead of winter.

Yves Saint Laurent Touche Éclat Radiant Touch: Tired eyes? Suspicious shadows? Gone. YSL's cultiest product has light-reflecting particles to deflect attention from any unwanted spots or shadows while somehow—mysteriously, magically—brightening the entire face. Try it once, and you'll be hooked.